PRAISE FOR SULARI GENTILL

The Woman in the Library

"A sharply drawn fictional hall of mirrors sure to tantalize."

—*Kirkus Reviews*

"A page-turner from beginning to end. A riddle, wrapped in a mystery, inside an enigma. As Gentill's characters grow, the desire to know more about each ensnares us, and the only way out is to read to the end."

—*New York Journal of Books*

"A wonderfully nimble play on the relationships between writer and reader, and writer and muse…tackling complex literary issues with both wit and panache."

—*Criminal Element*

★ "A smart, engaging novel that blurs genre lines. It's an inventive and unique approach, elevated by Gentill's masterful plotting, that will delight suspense fans looking for something bold and new."

—*BookPage*, Starred Review

"Investigations are launched, fingers are pointed, potentially dangerous liaisons unfold, and I was turning those pages like there was cake at the finish line."

—*Seattle Times*, Must-Read Books for Summer 2022

★ "A complex, riveting story within a story. An innovative literary mystery."

—*Library Journal*, Starred Review

After She Wrote Him
(A standalone previously published as *Crossing the Lines*)
2018 Winner of the Ned Kelly Award, Best Crime Fiction

"A pure delight, a swift yet psychologically complex read, cleverly conceived and brilliantly executed."
—Dean Koontz, *New York Times* bestselling author

"A tour de force! A brilliant blend of mystery, gut-wrenching psychological suspense, and literary storytelling. The novel stands as a shining (and refreshing) example of metafiction at its best—witty and wry, stylish, and a joy to read."
—Jeffery Deaver, *New York Times* bestselling author

"A delightful, cerebral novel featuring a crime writer who grows dangerously enamored with her main character. As the interplay between creator and created reaches Russian-nesting-doll complexity, it forced us to question the nature of fiction itself."
—Gregg Hurwitz, *New York Times* bestselling author

"This is an elegant exploration of the creative process, as well as a strong defense of the crime-fiction genre, as Gentill illustrates the crossing of lines between imagination and reality."
—*Booklist*

"In this intriguing and unusual tale, a stunning departure from Gentill's period mysteries, the question is not whodunit but who's real and who's a figment of someone's vivid imagination."
—*Kirkus Reviews*

"Fans of postmodern fiction will enjoy this departure from Gentill's 1930s series. It's an exploration, as one character puts it, of 'an author's relationship with her protagonist, an examination of the tenuous line between belief and reality, imagination and self, and what happens when that line is crossed.'"

—*Publishers Weekly*

"Literary or pop fiction lovers will enjoy."

—*Library Journal*

Where There's a Will
The Tenth Rowland Sinclair WWII Mystery

"Rowland's leisurely tenth case colorfully recreates the flavor of serial mysteries of Hollywood's golden age."

—*Kirkus Reviews*

★ "Witty, rip-roaring. This is historical mystery fiction at its finest."

—*Publishers Weekly*, Starred Review

Shanghai Secrets
The Ninth Rowland Sinclair WWII Mystery

"A frothy retro cocktail with a whodunit chaser."

—*Kirkus Reviews*

"Eccentric but authentic characters bolster a cracking good plot. Gentill captures in telling detail a political, moral, and cultural milieu."

—*Publishers Weekly*

★ "As series-launching novels go, this one is especially successful: the plot effectively plays Sinclair's aristocratic bearing and involvement in the arts against the Depression setting, fraught with radical politics, both of which he becomes involves in as he turns sleuth. And Sinclair himself is a delight: winning us over completely and making us feel as though he's an old friend."

—*Booklist*, Starred Review

★ "While the vintage Down Under settings might make this debut…comparable to Kerry Fisher's Melbourne-based Phryne Fisher 1920s mysteries, Gentill works in historical events that add verisimilitude to her story. VERDICT: Thanks to Poisoned Pen Press for bringing another award-winning Australian crime writer to U.S. shores. Her witty hero will delight traditional mystery buffs."

—*Library Journal*, Starred Review

"It is rare to find such an assured debut. The novel deserves to be both read and remembered as an insight into the Australia that was; its conflicting ideologies, aims, and desires; the hallmarks of a country still maturing."

—*Australian Book Review*

"Fans of Kerry Greenwood's Phryne Fisher series, rejoice: here comes another Depression-era Australian sleuth! Along the way there is plenty of solid discussion of politics and social status, with enough context to both draw in those new to the era and keep those more well-versed in their history interested."

—Historical Novel Society

Also by Sulari Gentill

The Mystery Writer

A Novel

Writer

SULARI GENTILL

Poisoned Pen
PRESS

Published by Poisoned Pen Press, an imprint of Sourcebooks
P.O. Box 4410, Naperville, Illinois 60567-4410
(630) 961-3900
sourcebooks.com

Library of Congress Cataloging-in-Publication Data

Names: Gentill, Sulari, author.
Title: The mystery writer : a novel / Sulari Gentill.
Description: Naperville, Illinois : Poisoned Pen Press, 2024.
Identifiers: LCCN 2023028422 (print) | LCCN 2023028423
(ebook) | (trade paperback) | (hardcover) | (ebook)
Subjects: LCSH: Authors--Fiction. | LCGFT: Novels.
Classification: LCC PR9619.4.G46 M97 2024 (print) | LCC PR9619.4.G46
(ebook) | DDC 823/.92--dc23/eng/20230622
LC record available at https://lccn.loc.gov/2023028422
LC ebook record available at https://lccn.loc.gov/2023028423

Printed and bound in the United States of America.
MA 10 9 8 7 6 5 4 3 2 1

PROLOGUE

He awoke early on the day he died, lying unmoving for a time under the weight of frustration, the inertia of despair.

The grief was crushing. The realisation that he'd lost it all. Over something that should have been nothing.

He sat up. The bookcase was blurred, and though he tried to pull himself together, it remained so. Slowly, stiffly, he rose from the couch on which he'd spent the night and grabbed a book from the middle shelf. His first novel, once everything—the culmination of dreams, an admission ticket to it all. Until she'd torn it down.

He ran his fingertips over the glossy jacket—the letters of his name were slightly raised. He'd never see that again, never feel it. "Hit the road, Jack, don't you come back…" The tune was harsh on his lips, self-mocking and bitter. "No more…no more…no more…"

A suit had been laid out for him—shirt, shoes, even boxers. Every last thing had been considered, every outcome anticipated, every decision already made.

There was nothing left to do but die.

CHAPTER 1

Caleb cursed in both outrage and triumph. He knew it! There had been something about that congressman's eyes when he'd addressed the rally—a flatness. Like he wasn't really there. Like he was dead. It made sense. Caleb felt physically slammed by the realisation. He'd seen it. It was proof. This was big.

He stared at the screen, rereading, his pulse accelerating with every word. He pounded the table with his fist. "Yes!"

The Shield was growing, strengthening. More and more people were waking up, becoming aware. But Caleb had been there from the beginning—since Primus posted his first panicked cry for help. He'd seen it, known instinctively that there was something to it. God, whoever Primus was, he had guts, he was a patriot.

Caleb got up from the computer. His mom needed to see this.

He hesitated then.

Was it necessary to have this fight now? His mom was looking in the wrong directions—south toward the Mexican border and north to the Canadians. But in preparing for invasion, she was probably doing what needed to be done for insurrection. His brothers, too—well most of them—each with his own idea of how the end would come and ready to fight. They would become part of The Shield when it was required, even if they were not expecting this.

Caleb fell back onto his bed and placed his arms behind his head. If they knew, they would take over. It would be Caleb do this, Caleb do that…like he wasn't the one who'd known from the beginning. They would forget that.

Perhaps it would be better to wait. That way, when it started he'd be the one behind the wheel; they'd have to listen to him. He imagined his mom's surprise and then her admiration as her youngest led them all into battle. His brothers would realize he'd grown up. Well, all except one, he supposed, but even he would have to come round eventually, turn to his little brother for help.

So for now he would keep his mouth shut. Wait and learn what he could.

Caleb blew on his fist, his eyes bright. This would be epic.

———

Theodosia Benton stood on her big brother Gus's doorstep, pausing to enjoy the relief of a long journey's end. But the breath she let out was snatched back as bedlam exploded onto the porch in the form of a massive hellhound of some sort. Though not, as a rule, frightened of dogs, Theo was unsure of her welcome, and tired, and still a little overwhelmed by the enormity of what she had done, and so she disintegrated a little, pounding on the door in tears and panic as the dog tried to raise the dead. A few neighbors poked their heads out to investigate what was apparently a murder in progress.

Gus Benton had been entertaining. After a few moments of scrabbling for clothes, he opened the door.

"Theo? What the hell…?" He stared at her.

Theo tried to make herself heard, but it was futile. The dog was relentless, determined to alert the entire block that there was someone on the threshold. She placed her hands over her ears, cringing away from the din.

Gus broke off to calm his dog, and eventually he managed to persuade it to stop barking. The comparative silence that followed provided an opportunity to explain, but now everything Theo had practiced on the flights and bus trips that had brought her from Sydney to Lawrence in the Sunflower State of Kansas, was lost to her. She stuttered apologies for not having told him she was coming.

"Come on." Gus grabbed her bags and motioned her to follow him inside, where he introduced Pam, the young lady wearing his shirt and little else. Pam didn't stay long. A distressed girl with luggage, even if she was just a sister, was probably less than romantic.

When they were alone, Gus asked again. "What are you doing here, Theo? Do Mum and Dad know? What the hell is going on?"

And so, she told him what she'd done.

"What do you mean you left uni?" he asked. "You've only got another couple of years to graduation. Surely it can't be that bad?"

"It is."

"But you always wanted to be an attorney."

Theo smiled faintly. "Solicitor," she said. He'd become such an American. "Gus, I was eighteen when I enrolled in law school. I'm not sure I even knew what a lawyer really was. I just wanted to be like you, to do what you were doing so that you'd…" She shook her head.

Gus exhaled. "Okay, I get it. But there are lots of people in Australia who aren't lawyers. What are you doing here?"

"I…I thought…" She told him about the creative writing classes she'd taken, the story she wanted to write. The words stumbled out, a confession: her increasing disinterest in the law, the ever-growing sense of panic and loneliness, and the feeling that she just couldn't face another day, another lecture, until all she could do was run. Then Theo made herself stop talking, knowing the frantic explanations, the pleading justifications made her sound quite mad, and she needed Gus to believe that she was at least sane. She bit her lip to stop herself from filling the silence with words.

For a moment he said nothing, simply looking at her as if he were trying to decide if she was really herself. And then he groaned. "Bloody hell, Theo. You could have just said this on the phone, and I would have picked you up at Fort Worth."

"You would have told me to stay…to get my degree."

"I'm your big brother. I have to say that… But I still would have met you at the airport when you ignored me." He told her she could choose from the two unused bedrooms, though he recommended the one farthest from the bathroom, as the pipes had a tendency to make noises in the night.

At first, Theo wasn't sure he'd heard her correctly. "I left," she said slowly. "I told the dean I wouldn't be coming back. I'm not going to be a lawyer, Gus. I've half a degree, which qualifies me for just about nothing…but I can't—"

"You said." He yawned. "Are you hungry? I'm starving…"

"But the trust—"

Gus shrugged. The university education of Gus and Theo Benton was financed through a complicated trust set up by their late grandfather—who had been quite an eminent member of the American Bar. When his only daughter had eloped with a penniless Australian musician, Robert Maclean had cut her off from his life and his fortune, but he had hoped through the trust to retrieve his grandchildren, to lure them back into his world.

"I'll speak to the trustees, if you like," he offered, unperturbed. "Work out a stay of execution for the rest of the year."

"I'm never going back! He's dead now—he won't care!"

Gus smiled. "If anything could make the old bastard come back…" Their grandfather had chosen futures for them, and even from beyond the grave had managed to dictate their lives, through the terms of his trust. Gus had taken the path of least resistance, but he'd clearly not had the courage of his little sister. Still, he'd come out an attorney, and so he tried to preserve an out clause for Theo. "How about we hold off telling the trustees until we absolutely have to? There's nothing to be gained by giving them extra notice. I'll just tell them you're taking the rest of the year off to help me with a case and gain some invaluable industry experience."

"They won't believe that!"

"Making people believe is what I do," Gus replied, looking at his cell phone. "We could get takeout… What do you feel like?"

Despite herself, Theo smiled.

"You have until Christmas to write your novel," he continued. "Then at least you can tell them you're not quitting law school to be a bum…though that might be quite satisfying." Gus pulled out his wallet and handed her a debit card to his account in case she needed money. "The password is *vegemite*."

Theo took the card, too overcome with gratitude and relief to thank him. She wiped her sleeve across her eyes, but her resolve to hold herself together crumbled. The dog, whose name was apparently Horse, licked her face.

Gus handed her a box of tissues and ordered pizza.

"Why...you...so nice?" Theo spluttered finally and somewhat ineloquently for someone who wanted to write. There were more than six years between her and Gus, and they had not lived in the same house or country for more than a decade. He'd left when she was ten years old. She'd grown up in his shadow, admired and resented him in equal measure, missed him, hated him, and loved him... But she wasn't really sure she knew him the way you normally knew family. How could she? "You're not just humoring me, are you, Gus? Because you want me to stop wailing? I know it doesn't seem that way, but I'm not having a breakdown. I promise I—"

Gus laughed. "Yeah, I'm just buying time till the doctor gets here to sedate you..." He waited till she lifted her eyes to his. "Look, Theo, you don't have to be so well adjusted all the time. You're allowed to react to what happened."

"I'm not—"

"I know. But you are allowed, and it wouldn't be a big deal. Okay?"

Theo nodded. She had turned to Gus instinctively, as she had when she was a child. But now she remembered that the instinct had never proved false. And she breathed out. "I'm sorry. It's just that we were supposed to be lawyers... I didn't think you'd understand why I suddenly thought I could be a novelist."

He shrugged. "I wanted to be a professional surfer."

The matter was thus settled. Theo took the room farthest from the bathroom, as recommended.

The old house that Gus had bought a couple of streets away

from what used to be Crane, Hayes and Purcell, and which was now Crane, Hayes and Benton, was badly in need of renovation. It had probably never been a grand house, but in its current state of decline, it was definitely the worst house on the best street… or at least the best street that Gus could afford. Gus's financial reserves had apparently been so drastically depleted by the cost of buying out Gerard Purcell that anything more than plumbing and electricity was deemed nonessential. Even so, he'd adamantly refused to take any money from his sister.

"You came here to write a novel, not to work in a sandwich shop so you can pay rent," he'd said firmly. "As long as you make it absolutely clear to any woman who comes by that you are my sister, we'll be square."

They talked about what to tell their parents and decided that until Theo's decision was irreversible, saying nothing was best. As much as Paul and Beth Benton spurned such things as convention, job security, and wealth, they had been somewhat relieved that their choices were not going to be imposed upon their offspring, that they could reject the capitalist system without depriving their children. Theo feared that telling them would mean they'd want her to come home to meditate and reconnect with something or other, perhaps pick up a tambourine and join her father's act.

As the elder Bentons had originally migrated to Tasmania to join an effort to save the island's forests from development, they had, over the years, been arrested several times trying to do just that. Consequently, criminal records kept them out of the United States, and their aversion to modern technology made contact sporadic and difficult, hasty, fragmented exchanges over bad lines. As a result, avoiding any discussion of the fact that Theo's presence in Lawrence was not a coincidental short visit, was easier that one might think, and the escape of Theodosia Benton was made with barely a ripple.

In the days that followed, Theo cleaned the house, removing years of grime, attacking mold and fixing what she could, as she told herself she was earning her keep. She sanded and repainted, washed and cooked until Gus, somewhat unceremoniously, threw her out.

"Get out."

"What?"

He finished knotting his tie. "I want you to find somewhere else you can write."

Theo stared at him, shocked. "But you said I could—"

"You need to have somewhere to go in the morning, Theo. As much as I appreciate this manic cleaning handyman phase you're going through, you need to find somewhere to write where you won't be distracted by this moldering pile."

"Oh." Theo's heart steadied. "But I can still live here?"

Gus looked at her as if she were an idiot. "Meet me at the office at six—we'll go for a drink." He grabbed his briefcase and sunglasses. "A bar!" he added suddenly. "Always thought a bar would be a great place to write a novel. You should check out a few."

And so, Theo had gone in search of an office, and she'd found Benders.

CHAPTER 2

Caleb paced the room. It was unbearable to know what was happening and not be able to help directly.

If only he could find out who Primus was—perhaps there would something he could do…people he could watch…or research. He could hack most things, and he wasn't afraid to stand up and be counted. But, of course, Primus's identity had to remain secret. Caleb had no doubt the sick psychos behind the Frankenstein Project would kill the man who was telling the world what they were up to, if they knew who he was. Jesus, this was wild.

Caleb sat back down before the computer screen and read the comments on the post—words of support and outrage, corroborative accounts, related reports—a growing movement that would one day save the world against the depravity and evil that Primus called the Minotaur. They were getting ready.

Caleb was compiling a consolidated list of all the corporates Primus mentioned from time to time. Every couple of posts, there was an organization that had not been named before, to add. CrusaderCat15 had created a database of missing persons, particularly children, and was cross-referencing last sightings against the property holdings of the corporates in that area. MoonSoldier1 was doing some work on linking the Frankenstein Project to particular political elites, the powerful men and women behind the Minotaur. There were others going through every post, decoding, looking for hidden messages. They were all working together, sharing what they discovered, and keeping an eye on one another, just in case. Caleb assumed the Minotaur would be looking for anybody helping Primus.

LABYRINTH 32

Experiments on the dead continue. The Frankenstein Project has yielded results and those behind it have been rewarded with gold and power. To date only the dead have been defiled for this purpose, but yesterday it was proposed that living subjects might further improve results. Watch yourselves, and the children. The representatives are complicit. People will start to disappear. The snatchers have been trained by the military in a secret location somewhere in the desert. Perhaps I, too, will be snatched, carved up, and remade. It is for more than myself I fear. I am the only person able to navigate the maze who is willing to breach the secrecy protocols that protect this corporate depravity. The people have a right to know. The sacrifices have a right to fight. Beware the icons: Disney, Coca-Cola, CNN. They are friends of the Minotaur. Prepare. Soon we will rise to lay siege to the Labyrinth. More later.

We Know What We Know.
   Primus

⌐⌐

Benders Bar in downtown Lawrence generally came to life when the hard drinkers arrived at about five in the afternoon. Until then it was quiet, untroubled by the presence of those who lingered far longer than the odd coffee entitled. The fact that Benders even opened before 11 a.m. was unusual, and the result of a dispute between the Bradley sisters, who owned it, one of whom called it a café, while other insisted it was a bar. Consequently, the hours and nature of the business had been divided, though over the years the line between café and bar had become blurred. The extended hours did however make it perfect for those who required an informal office from which they did not need to decamp by midafternoon. As far as writers' refuges went, it was very acceptable, if not ideal.

Initially, Theo assumed that the café and bar had been named in honor of simple alcoholic excess, but a plaque just inside the door identified a much more sinister inspiration. Apparently, the Bloody Benders had been a family of serial killers who, in the late 1800s, murdered travelers who stopped at their inn for a meal or drink. It seemed a strangely passive-aggressive choice for the name of a café-bar, but there was a perverse humor about it that reminded Theo of home. And as much as she had chosen this path, memories of home were not always unwelcome.

The establishment's decor played shamelessly on the dubious notoriety of its namesakes. Dim lighting, macabre memorabilia, and Victorian flourishes—it evoked conspiracy in a less-than-subtle theme-park sort of way. Nooks and booths allowed privacy, even secrecy. A hammer dipped in red paint, a similarly embellished cut-throat razor, and a collection of old arsenic bottles, completed the picture of a murderer's den.

Within a week Theo had staked an almost inalienable claim

on the corner booth. Each day she arrived by nine, ordered coffee, unpacked her laptop, her notes, and the dog-eared Jack Chase novel *Airborne*, which was her muse, of sorts. It had been signed by the author: "For Theo, May the words come quickly and in the right order. In writerly solidarity, Jack."

Theo had never actually met Jack Chase, though as a teenager she'd read everything he'd ever written and seen all the movies that had been made from his books. Years ago, Gus had stumbled into a book signing in New York, a day or two after her birthday, which he had until then forgotten. He'd waited in line to ask the author to sign a book for his little sister, who had just turned fourteen. Why Chase had dedicated the book as he had was something of a mystery... Gus liked to claim that he'd said his sister "had a face like a prizefighter," which Chase had misheard as "prize-winning writer," but Theo was almost certain he'd made that up. At fourteen the inscription had seemed funny; now Theo thought it prophetic. Perhaps it was simply that she'd read it so many times that she'd come to believe it. Whatever the reason, the book had become her charm.

Soon Theo came to know Laura, the extensively pierced server, who would ask her to say random words so she could hear them in "Australian"; Chic, who liked to listen to true crime podcasts in between and sometimes while she brought customers their coffee; and a couple of the barflies who would come in early to avoid the university crowd. There were others, too, who sat at the tables rather than the bar.

One man occupied the table by the window most days, when she came in to write. She hadn't known he was Dan Murdoch, of course, not at first. He was just another café refugee seeking solace in caffeine and anonymity. In the beginning, they paid little attention to each other. After a week or two, he'd raise his eyes and nod or smile in some acknowledgment of recurrent encounter. He was older but not old, handsome in a quiet sort of way, with a beard cut close to the planes of his face. The hair at his temples had begun to lighten with gray. He generally wore jeans with an open-collared shirt and a leather jacket; his glasses were modern but conservative. Still, he might have been a serial killer, for all she knew. She'd returned his smile briefly and retreated to her own corner to write. At some point, a quiet familiarity set in. The nods became "Good morning."

On more than one occasion he was joined by a woman in a suit—beautifully tailored, discreetly expensive. She was so startlingly attractive that she didn't seem to belong to the real world. Theo tried not to watch them, obviously at least, and yet she knew that he seemed chastised and contrite in the woman's presence, and sometimes frustrated. Perhaps he was her errant lover, or she his parole officer. But the woman was not there often. Mostly he sat alone drinking coffee and glued to his phone or his tablet. Occasionally, she caught him looking her way, but he'd never hold her gaze long enough to invite anything more than a fleeting smile.

It wasn't until Theo dropped *Airborne* as she hefted her laptop and notes into Benders one day, that they had their first conversation. He retrieved the book and carried it to her table. He glanced at the cover as if it amused him. Theo felt vaguely defensive. But he didn't ask about the book.

"What are you working on?"

She stuttered, embarrassed. "A novel," she said in the end, cringing at the sound of it. Who did she think she was, calling what she was doing a novel? Surely, he'd laugh.

He didn't.

"Do you want your coffee here, or at your usual table, Dan?" Chic, the waitress, held up a tray with single cup.

He'd glanced at Theo. "Please," she replied a little uncertainly. He was probably not a serial killer.

"Here," he told Chic. "And the usual for...?"

"Theo. Theo Benton."

He introduced himself then, and she recognized that she was speaking to Dan Murdoch—the novelist, whose name was acclaimed enough to appear on his books in a bigger type than the title. Now she was mortified. She'd just told Dan Murdoch that she was writing a novel. She could feel the color in her face. "I'm not a real writer," she said quickly.

He smiled. "I must say it's been a while since I ordered coffee for a figment of my imagination."

"No...I mean...I meant..."

He laughed. "I know. I guess I'm not a real writer anymore either."

"But you're—"

"Becoming a writer is one thing; staying one is entirely another beast."

"Oh..." Theo wasn't sure she understood, but Dan did not seem inclined to explain.

Instead, he put her out of her misery by asking about her work. Specific questions about genre and theme, how long she'd been working on the project. Theo's shyness receded gradually as she spoke about the historical mystery she was writing, set in the twenties in Canberra, a city that was still under construction. She told him that she had once been at law school in the Australian bush capital, which she found had a strange soul for a city—the ancient lands of the Ngunnawal people buried beneath the modern façade of a planned metropolis—and how that had planted a seed that would not leave her be.

He seemed interested—really interested—as opposed to polite or amused or merely kind, and Theo found a new pleasure in talking of the ideas which had been crowding her thoughts. She had previously only spoken of her work to Gus, and even then, with restraint, conscious of boring him with the imaginings that consumed her at the moment. But Dan gave her permission to effuse; indeed, he drew out the depth of her obsession with the story she was fashioning from scraps of history and the wanderings of her mind. And the morning passed unnoticed as they talked.

He'd asked her about *Airborne* as they stepped out to buy sandwiches for lunch. "They made it into a film, didn't they?"

"I was fourteen when I read it," Theo said, a little worried that he would think her literary taste immature.

He flinched. "I was a lot older than that, I'm afraid. What did you think?"

Theo hesitated, a little surprised that the book interested him and wondering if he meant the work or the man. Jack Chase's career had fallen to scandal—allegations of sexual misconduct that had seen him become a pariah, dropped by agents and publishers, destocked by bookstores. She wasn't aware of what Chase had done, exactly—she couldn't even remember if it had been criminal or simply unsavory, and she wasn't sure if it should have changed her mind about the book she had loved when she was fourteen. She opened the volume to the title page and showed him the inscription, and she told him how she came to have it.

"So you keep it for your brother's sake?" he asked, reading the inscription.

"Not entirely." She took a deep breath and made her stand.

She was not a coward. "Jack Chase was an extraordinary writer. His work was nuanced, his world-building complex and layered. His heroines always made me feel powerful and strong…like no one could ever hurt me, and when I was fourteen, that meant a great deal. Whatever else he did, he wrote beautiful books."

Dan had said nothing.

"…And, yes, it was a present from Gus…and an omen, I think. It's my good luck charm."

"Well, I hope that it works better for you than it did for him. It was his last book."

She gasped. "Did you know him?"

He laughed. "No. Not at all. My first book was published just as the scandal broke, so I remember it." He told her then of the roller coaster of first publication, the anxiety, the waiting, the incredible euphoria of first seeing your book on the shelf or reviewed by the *New York Times*.

Theo drew every word into her heart.

She'd returned home that evening full of enthusiasm and hope. She didn't have a key to the kingdom yet, but she'd made a friend who did. It made her feel like this dream of hers could be real.

Theo didn't see Dan Murdoch for several days after that, and the earth met her hard. She wondered if perhaps he'd found another place to have coffee and avoid the wannabe writer who now knew who he was. He must have been afraid she'd bother him, ask him to read her manuscript. For nearly a week, she went to Benders and sat alone, silently humiliated by the judgment she imputed to his absence. And then he was back, with a laptop and new gleam to his eye. He'd thanked her for inspiring him to write again, for shaking him out of a block.

"Were you blocked?" Writing was still so new to Theo, the

creative rush so strong that the thought of not being able to find words, of not wanting to look, seemed unimaginable.

"Well, maybe not blocked," he said. "But bored. I've been writing the same kind of books for a while, found myself distracted by other things—you reminded me what it was like to step into the wilderness and explore."

"The wilderness?" She laughed. "We're sitting in a coffee shop!"

"Yes…" He lowered his voice. "But the coffee's not great."

They'd talked often after that, discussing plots and characters, coffee, and Kansas. She stopped thinking about serial killers altogether. In time, their conversations became so extended and regular that it was easier to work at the same table, companions in the necessary isolation of their work.

Theo stopped in at the Raven Bookstore, bought all the Dan Murdochs she could find on their shelves and ordered the rest. There was a total of six, and each night she stayed up to read as much as she could—something which Gus found amusing.

"You should make friends who don't give you homework assignments, Theo."

"Shut up, I'm reading."

"Seriously…I know a bloke. Doesn't find book reports the least bit attractive…though you may have to do something with your hair…"

"Gus! Leave me alone."

"All right, but if you don't get a passing grade, let me know, and I'll give Mac a call."

Theo ignored him. She liked Dan Murdoch's books—they were dark and exciting, and every now and then there was a sentence or a passage that was so beautiful that she could languish in it. She felt like she was getting to know him as much through his work as his company. Though increasingly she preferred his company. On those days she arrived at Benders early, Theo found herself watching for him, and on those infrequent days he didn't come, she missed him.

Occasionally, there was an unexpected influx of patrons to Benders—students celebrating some varsity win or an office party. On those days, Dan and Theo would give up their table and find another refuge, where they were often welcomed by that establishment's unofficial writers in residence. In the Bourgeois Pig, on Ninth Street, Meg was writing her memoirs; in Aimee's Coffeeshop, Larry was working on his third novel; and an entire writers' group met regularly a few blocks away at Alchemy on Mass Street. While Theo cherished the camaraderie of this network of refugees, she was happiest at Benders, where it was just her and Dan, and the words seemed to come more easily.

Dan appeared to fall effortlessly, even enthusiastically, into the role of mentor. He was generous with his experience and, over the months that followed, progressively more candid. He told Theo stories about writings gone wrong and explained his own techniques. Occasionally, he would take her on what he called a "field trip" to show her a building or a statue or even a tree that he thought might help her add a sense of place to her work. In this way he showed her Lawrence, adding his own potted history and observations to the details he brought to her notice. Through the longer days of summer, their walks extended for hours, along the Burroughs Trail, or crossing the bridge to North Lawrence along the levee in what became something of a peripatetic tutorial.

When she was struggling with a scene set beside the

Murrumbidgee River in the Molonglo Valley near Canberra, Dan took her to the banks of the Kaw.

"My story's set in Australia." Theo pointed out the obvious.

"It doesn't matter where the water is. It's the details, how the light hits the surface of the water, the smell of it, the sound of the water birds that give your writing place. It makes no difference if the place is real or one you made up… In the end it's only got to exist in the reader's imagination."

Despite the great many hours in conversations during which Theo felt she was laying her soul bare and confiding her greatest hopes and fears for her writing, Dan Murdoch was, about his current work in progress, evasive. Theo observed him typing, of course, but he offered very few and only the vaguest details. She did not question him, though she did hope that he would eventually confide in her as she did in him. She hinted occasionally, to no avail. While Dan seemed infinitely interested in what and how she was writing, he remained reluctant to speak about his own work. In time, Theo came to accept that he did not need or want her feedback. The realization was made without her feeling offended or hurt. He was after all a renowned author—there probably wasn't a great deal of insight a newly minted, aspirant writer could offer him.

Consequently, Theo was startled when he turned his laptop around to show her the sites on the web that he was trawling for ideas, the conspiracy theorists he followed as a form of research.

"You can't be serious," she said reading, unsure whether to laugh or be terrified. "This is ridiculous."

"But you're reading it."

"Frankenstein? And zombies… They must be crazy—"

"Maybe, but it's a less absurd than lizard people." He laughed softly. "You wouldn't believe how many people believe that the Clintons, the Bushes, even your Queen Elizabeth are shape-shifting lizards." He tapped the screen. "The folks who come up with this stuff know how to write a story." He smiled as she scrolled down to read more. "They build worlds that have just enough basis in reality to be plausible—okay, maybe not plausible but internally consistent. It's like one of those write-your-own-adventure stories."

"And you get ideas from this?" Theo asked skeptically.

"Ideas...inspiration...motivations, even characters..." He directed her to the comments and discussion forums. "You can check the success of a conspiracy narrative by the reactions here... It's like a focus group."

"But you can't just take someone else's theory...that's plagiarism."

Dan laughed. "These people believe the government is stealing dead bodies to make new people... I'm not sure the intellectual property in their paranoia will be their primary concern."

Theo glanced at a posted pledge to shoot the body-snatchers. "I don't know that I'd be making any assumptions about what these people might think is important."

"I don't take the actual theories," he assured her. "I just use them to understand what makes a narrative work." He pointed out a couple of posts that had incited mockery or been ignored. "See...some don't fly. I'm interested in what it is about the theories that do take off that makes people committed to them. It doesn't seem to have anything to do with logic or plausibility."

Theo nodded, still reading. It was weird, but he was right. "What does *WKWWK* mean?" she asked. The acronym appeared at the end of several posts.

Dan grinned. "We Know What We Know."

"From *Hamilton*?"

He nodded. "It binds those who follow Primus and subscribe to the Minotaur theory. The few who recognize it as a *Hamilton* quote assume that Lin-Manuel Miranda is one of them, possibly the Founding Fathers too."

"But that doesn't make any sense. Why would—"

"There's a pattern, a formula to the theories that take off." Dan scrolled through several threads discussing the elements of each almost scientifically. "They all contain an element of familiarity—something that allows people to say, 'I've seen that'— an explanation with an element of novelty or a twist, and—this is important—an antagonist or system that is motivated to keep the explanation secret, that needs to be overcome. What does that sound like?"

"A novel," Theo admitted.

"This stays between you and me, mind. I don't need people knowing." He grinned. "Consider it a trade secret."

"Of course, I'll take it to my grave… We can only hope my body isn't dug up by a minotaur."

By the fall, Theo had become more confident with her craft, and their conversations were closer to even, and robust: between colleagues rather than teacher and student. When Dan returned parts of her manuscript with suggestions and corrections, she was always deeply grateful but was now more willing to defend her own ideas and decisions.

"I don't want to describe him," she said, when he advised her to give her protagonist more physical definition. "It doesn't matter what he looks like."

"Of course, it does. People react to your physical appearance.

What he looks like tells you a lot about the characters interacting with him. Are they acting out of revulsion because he's hideous, or lust because he's attractive? Are they superficial or ageist or even racist?"

"But that's all a matter of perspective." Theo replied. "What we're repulsed by or attracted to is often about our own stories, our own prejudices. Making your protagonist a blank canvas allows you reflect that; it allows the readers to find themselves in your characters and perhaps to recognize their own biases."

He sighed as he often did when he thought she was being what he called "high art." "Readers aren't interested in reflections, Theo. They want to know whether your hero has a big nose or not, whether he smiles with his bottom teeth showing and might be a lizard."

Theo snorted. "Are you still reading those?"

"Gotta do the research, sweetheart. It's what makes me a professional!"

"Well, if the size of his nose or his underbite has an impact on the story, I'll let them know!" Theo closed the screen of her laptop, so she could see his face unimpeded.

He laughed. "Tell me, Theodosia, what does a young woman like you find attractive these days? It's abs, isn't it? Every woman nowadays wants a man with abs."

Theo studied him, noting the glimmer in his eye. Whatever she said, he would tease her about it later. She shrugged. "I don't know if there is anything in particular. People are more than the sum of their physical parts. And I'm not particularly fussed about abs."

Dan shook his head. "Nobly said, but I don't believe a word of it." He patted his stomach. "Before you ask—two hundred sit-ups a day."

Sometime in the months in which they'd been meeting, her friendship with Dan Murdoch became something slightly more. Theo was sure it wasn't anything as extreme or absurd as love. More a flutter of feeling that she couldn't describe—an admiration, a deepening warmth—one-sided and embarrassing. It would pass, even out, and they would have one of those legendary writerly friendships like Lawrence and Mansfield or Tolkien and Lewis. Still, there was a strange longing when he smiled at her. Theo expected Dan felt a little sorry for her, perhaps nostalgic for the time when he'd been an aspirant writer unburdened by the weight of fame. It was that. It had to be that. And so, she was caught by surprise when it all changed.

CHAPTER 3

Has a stray dog ever followed you home? Did you take pity on it? Feed it? Bring it inside to play with your kids or sleep by your bed? Interesting, right— how easily we'll trust a creature who might have been trained to do us harm, to attack on some unknown command? A sound maybe, that people can't hear but dogs can...and until then they wait, beloved and trusted. Thousands of them across the U.S., placed in particular homes, bypassing security checks with a wag and a lick. Where did your family pet come from? Did fate place him in your home or was it something else? Do you trust Fido with your life? Is that your mistake?

Thousands of attacks reported in the last year—men and women mauled by their own pets. Are these just random tragedies or is there some design to these assassinations?

Frodo 14

    WKWWK

My sister was bit by her dog. Near took off her arm. He was a stray, I think.

Diane from Phoenix

That's BS. My dog's a stray and he would never bite me.
   Space Monkey 2497

I'll bite you. Message me.
   Kansas Karen

———

The day had started badly. Theo and Gus fought over breakfast…
over the milk, to be more specific. It was a petty squabble of the
kind they'd had as children, and that had more to do with the fact
that one of Gus's cases was going badly than what ratio of fat and
calcium suited muesli. On the way to Benders, Theo mailed the
last of the forms and letters that officially and forever gave up her
place at the Australian National University. She was unprepared
for how untethered that act made her feel, how stateless. And for
a while, she was panicked by the finality of it.

And so, when she reached Benders, she was distracted and
uncertain of everything.

The beautiful woman was back, and she and Dan were clois-
tered together in a booth. Dan looked up briefly, smiled, and then
reverted his attention to his companion before Theo had time to
smile in return. Nothing in his manner invited her to join them,
and so she took a seat at another booth and tried not to feel slighted.

For a while Theo typed and deleted and glowered at the screen,
consciously refusing to look in the direction of Dan Murdoch
and his confidant. But she was aware when they rose and walked
together toward the door. Theo forced herself not to look up until
Dan came back into Benders and slid into her booth.

"Hello," he said.

She smiled quickly, brightly. "Would you like a coffee? Or have you already had one with…?"

He regarded her curiously. "Ronnie? We didn't have coffee. She's my agent."

Theo's eyes widened. "That was an agent."

Dan smiled. "Yes, a real live agent."

"I've never…"

"I'll introduce you next time."

"Really?"

He laughed now. "Theo, I said *agent*, not *rock star*."

"Were you talking about your new novel?"

"Not exactly. Ronnie was just checking in…making sure I'm doing as I'm told."

"As you're told?"

He shrugged. "I'm just kidding. The new manuscript is not ready for her to see yet. She was checking to see I hadn't got stuck."

"It must be wonderful to have that kind of backup."

"Uh-huh."

"How did you find her?" Theo asked. "Your agent?" It was more than an idle curiosity. Her own manuscript would be ready soon.

"Day Delos came to me."

"Day Delos? You're with Day Delos and Associates?" Theo didn't even try to hide that it impressed her. "Why they're—"

Dan sighed. "I need to get out of here for a while. You want to come?" He reached across and closed her laptop, and then his.

"But—"

"Hurry up."

Theo hesitated, but unable to find a good reason to refuse, slipped her laptop into her satchel and left with him.

"Where are we going?" she skipped to keep up with his long stride.

"Field trip... A location I'm writing." He grimaced. "I could make it all up, but this place has become something of a pop culture icon, so I thought I'd go gather some details to keep the kids happy."

Theo laughed. "What kind of details?"

"Epitaphs."

"What? Where are we going?" Theo pulled her coat tighter, reminded that summer had long since slipped away.

Dan put his arm around her, and despite the weight of it on her shoulders, Theo felt lighter. Inexplicably thrilled. "First we're going to my house—it's not far—to pick up the car...and then we're going to drive out to Stull." He bent down and lowered his voice into her ear. "It has a rather famous cemetery. Supposedly houses the gates to Hell."

"You're writing a horror story?" Theo asked.

"I like to think of it as a thriller with paranormal elements—"

"And your conspiracy theorists are helping with this?"

He smiled. "In many ways."

For the next couple of blocks, they talked about the films and television productions that had exploited the relatively recent urban legends surrounding Stull, arguing about the relative merits of the various plots and whether a thriller with paranormal elements was just a fancy way of saying horror story.

They reached the leafy street on which Dan Murdoch lived and the Craftsman house with pale yellow walls and a bright blue door that Dan declared was his. The garden was extensively and elaborately planted with box hedges clipped into Celtic knots and decorative spheres and what appeared to be a line of giant ducks.

"I didn't realize you were a gardener," Theo said uncertainly. She'd always associated gardening with the retired. Particularly topiary, not to mention topiary ducks. She wondered, for the first time, how old Dan Murdoch was. He was handsome, but his were not boyish good looks and the lines at the corners of his eyes were deep whenever he smiled. His hair was thick and short but graying at the temples and extensively through his beard. Could he be of ornamental-hedge-clipping age? He noticed her staring.

"All right...you got me. I have a guy come twice a week. I have no idea what he does, but this is the result."

"Why ducks?"

Dan squinted at the hedges. "Honestly, I thought they were Jayhawks...assumed he was a fan...but now that you mention it, they do look more like ducks." He invited her to come in while he grabbed his camera, unlocking the blue door and holding it open for her.

She stepped into a long hallway. The covers of Dan Murdoch's books were framed and hung along an elegantly papered wall.

"That was the decorator's idea," he murmured, as she studied each one.

"It was a good one." Theo gazed closely at each cover. She'd seen Dan's covers before, but enlarged, the details of the artwork jumped from the frames.

"A bit self-indulgent, but I haven't got round to taking them down." He folded his arms. "You'll have your own covers soon."

Theo inhaled. She didn't look at him lest her eyes give her away. She had spent hours imagining cover drafts. She'd even drawn up her own ideas...not that anyone would care what she thought, even if they were publishing her work. Dan had already warned her that covers were the publisher's prerogative alone. Still, it was exciting enough that Dan thought she would have her own covers. She wanted to believe him.

"Would you like to see the concept sketches for these?" Dan asked, still watching her. "The publisher let me have them. Some of the covers they rejected were quite interesting."

Theo nodded, aware of his eyes, a change in the way he looked at her, and suddenly shy.

He took her into the living room and found a folder of pages in the bookcase that surrounded the fireplace. He spread the contents of the folder out on the coffee table, challenging her to guess why each had been rejected, while he opened a bottle of wine.

"Is it because nobody in the book died this way?" she asked, holding up a drawing that showed a woman plummeting down the stairs with a sinister figure at the head.

Dan poured wine into two glasses. "Actually, it was because this guy"—he pointed to the artist's rendering of the villain—"looked exactly like the president of the day. The publisher was sure we'd be arrested or sued or both."

Theo saw it now—the finger-pointing postures, the distinctive coiffure. It was an uncanny likeness. "Surely you couldn't have been arrested!"

"Presidents are powerful, and publishers can be a little paranoid."

"Really?"

"Oh, yes, the only people more paranoid than publishers are agents...but you'll learn that."

"I hope so."

He laughed as he sat down and lifted his glass. "You are a very talented writer, Miss Benton."

Theo hesitated, unsure whether she should raise her glass too.

Would that seem smug? Would not raising it be impolite? Maybe she should just drink.

"Your writing is exuberant, as is it should be in someone your age," Dan continued, "but it has the kind of deep insight it usually takes decades to achieve. You are what they call an old soul—an old soul who can write." Theo didn't know why she left the arm-chair to sit beside him on the couch. Perhaps it was because he believed in her, in her writing, or perhaps it was the wine, but suddenly she wanted to be close to him. Even so, she was surprised when he kissed her. Surprised and astounded and elated.

He pulled back a little, his eyes locked on hers. "Is this okay?"

She nodded; any reservations she may have had were defeated completely by the fact that he had asked. He kissed her again, more urgently than before, and she responded. Again, she felt untethered, but this time it was gloriously so.

"We might go to Stull another day," he murmured moving his lips to her throat and following it down to the hollow at its base.

Theo laughed, giddy. Her senses seemed heightened. She felt his touch on more than just her skin. She could smell his cologne, hear his heart...or was that hers?

Dan released the first buttons on her shirt. Theo watched, fascinated as his hand slipped under the fabric and cupped her breast, the pressure of his thumb against her nipple. For a moment she froze. "Still okay?" he asked.

"Yes." She pushed away the past, made her body relax. She wanted this. It was time.

The remainder of the buttons then, other clothes, until they were skin against skin, heart against heart.

Theo was entranced by just how beautiful he was. Perhaps she'd always thought so.

Dan moved slowly. Theo was nervous and at times scared for no other reason than she was scared. He took his time, overcoming her self-consciousness, exploring her body gently, telling her she was beautiful and desirable. At some point Theo stopped thinking about what she was doing, and gave herself over to the moment, to his touch. And then she took pleasure in his pleasure, amazed and delighted that she could make a man like Dan Murdoch feel this. Afterwards he wrapped her in the blanket that had been folded over the arm of the couch, and they lay together and talked. About nothing in particular—Theo told him about the orphaned joeys and wombats her mother rescued back home, and Horse, who was afraid of the dark; he told her about Rocket, the Saint Bernard he'd once owned, who ate three pairs of his socks in one sitting.

"What happened?" she asked amazed at his ability to make even this small story a saga of suspense.

"Very expensive surgery. When they removed the socks, they found my watch."

Theo's eyes darted to the watch he was wearing, unsure if he was kidding. She noticed the time. "I should head home… It'll be dark soon."

He pulled back the blanket and kissed her breast, beginning it all again. "Stay a while longer. I'll drive you home."

～～

When eventually Theo got home, she was too euphoric to sleep. She was light, unshackled from what had happened before—she was completely free of it now, and there was only today and what could be. She spent the night with her manuscript. It was very nearly finished. In fact she had probably been dithering because as she neared the end, she didn't want it to end, she didn't want to not be writing, to finish with the lives that had occupied so much of her own. And because she was scared it wouldn't be good enough, that she wouldn't be good enough. But now she wanted to move forward, to begin the next phase, and to dream about other things. And so that night, still flushed with the memory of Dan Murdoch's body against hers, she wrote. Theo typed "THE END" and pressed print at about seven in the morning, and then she showered, dressed more carefully than usual, and set out for Benders.

The door swung open at precisely nine, and Dan walked in. He smiled hello and signaled Chic to bring his usual before placing his laptop on the table. Fleetingly, he placed his hand over Theo's, a subtle acknowledgment of the previous day. "You've finished," he said before she could utter a word.

Theo nodded, beaming.

"Well, this calls for a celebration," he said softly. He called Laura over and asked for the establishment's best champagne. "Theo's finished her book," he said when Laura's pierced brows rose.

The server squealed, delighted. "Wow! For a moment I thought...but wow! Just wow! Champagne coming up."

Dan tapped the stack of paper sitting pristinely before her. "Is this it?"

Theo pushed the manuscript towards him. "Yes."

He turned the stack around and read the title. "*Underneath*. May I read it?"

"Yes, of course." She took a deep breath, feeding courage with oxygen. "If you thought it was okay...if you liked it...I was going to ask..." She paused a few moments as the champagne was delivered to the booth and poured into flutes and congratulations offered by Laura and Chic and the regulars. Finally, Theo inhaled again and tried to gather the momentum that had been lost. He was already reading the first page. "If you like it, Dan, will you take it to your agent…Ronnie…? Would you introduce me?"

He did not look up. "You don't want to sign with my agents, Theo. They wouldn't be right for you."

"Of course they would. Day Delos and Associates are the best literary agents in the country and you said—"

"I'm afraid you're not the kind of writer they're interested in."

"Please." The word was out before Theo even realized she was going to say it, and then it was too late to take it back.

"It's not that I don't want to, Theo. I just know what they look for in a writer and I'm afraid you'd be wasting your time."

"But if you were to take it…to recommend it…" She stopped. What was she doing?

Dan looked up, and Theo thought she might die of embarrassment. What made her beg like that? "No…you're right. It's probably awful."

His eyes softened. "I'm sure it's not. I know the first page at least is brilliant." He swigged back the champagne in his flute and topped it off again. "Let me read it, Theo. Then we'll talk about what you should do next."

She nodded, unwilling to open her mouth again. Had she tried to impose on their relationship? Had she come across as desperate? Of course she had. She was. When she'd become so, she wasn't sure. In the beginning it had been enough to write, but now it seemed so important, so necessary to be published. And she was torn about how superficial that sounded.

Somehow Theo had come to love the story she had written…

like a child, which in a way it was. She'd given it life. And now she wanted other people love it too. And yet she wasn't sure if she was entitled to want that. Was it arrogant? Was it absurd?

She was aware that she especially wanted Dan Murdoch to like her story, to sponsor her into that secret club of actual writers. To invite her home and introduce her to his agents. But he'd already said no.

CHAPTER 4

What's going on at Stull? I saw lights there at midnight. I've heard rumors that it was a Hellmouth but thought they were just stories. But those lights were weird.

   Flagman

They were headlights dickhead.

   Southern Son

LABYRINTH 32

Stull cemetery has been chosen for the first rising. Read the headstones— they will tell you when. I have been locked out of the labyrinth for now—but I will find my way back. There will be a book. It will be published by an ordinary publisher, with an ordinary jacket as if it were an ordinary story... but this story, my friends, will be what we have been waiting for. A flag, a guide, a manifesto of those who will not be sacrificed. I will tell you more when I can but take heart that our proclamation is being drafted. And when it is the greatest best- seller this country has ever seen, they will know that we are not to be taken lightly. Be strong, lay down provisions and always watch over the children. More later.

WKWWK
   Primus

Yes! We know what we know!
   Southern Son

I have read the headstones. They are clear: 15 December.
   Patriot Warrior

———

Gus dropped the pizza boxes on the kitchen table and headed for the shower. In an attempt to balance pain and compensation, he'd devised a jogging route that took him past Papa Keno's.

"Shall I put these in the oven to keep warm?" Theo called after him as she heard the water come on.

"Nah...I can shower in five."

Theo took plates and cutlery from the cupboard and set two places. Gus emerged with a towel around his waist, shaking the water from his dark hair like a wet dog.

"Gus!"

"What's with the plates and silverware?" he asked, taking a slice from each box and sandwiching them, cheese sides together.

"Call it a nervous tic." Theo put a slice on her plate and stared at it.

"What's wrong?" Gus began on his third slice. "It's not that I expect you to keep up, but this is embarrassing."

Theo shrugged. "I'm not really hungry."

He studied her thoughtfully. "Is there some bloke I should be punching out?"

"No!" Theo pulled the crust off her slice of pizza. "Why would you punch anyone out?"

"For breaking my little sister's heart."

"Don't be an idiot," she said quickly. "No one's broken my heart."

Gus dropped a second slice onto her plate. "Is it that bloke you meet at Benders?"

Theo picked at a circle of pepperoni. "In a way, I guess…"

"I'd better get dressed and go have a word with the bastard—" He scowled. "Do you want me to make him marry you?"

Theo laughed now. "You really are an idiot."

He smiled, though a hint of real concern lingered in his eyes. "You've got to be careful falling for an American, Theo. They're not as direct as Aussie blokes."

"It really isn't that."

"So tell me then?"

Theo groaned. She told him then, partly because he clearly didn't intend to stop poking until she had, because she didn't want him to jump to conclusions, and because she felt some compulsion to confess the hubris, the madness that made her ask Dan Murdoch to take her manuscript to his agents. "I made a complete and utter fool of myself, Gus."

"You asked him for help—how is that making a fool of yourself?"

"I don't know. I just feel like I did." She liberated another piece of pepperoni and proceeded to tear it into smaller pieces. "Who did I think I was, asking Dan Murdoch to take my manuscript to his agents?…He must think I have tickets on myself…"

"Bollocks!"

"I saw that look in his eyes, Gus. That oh-God-how-do-I-get-out-of-this look."

"I know it well."

"I imposed too much."

"On what?"

"Our friendship. Maybe he thinks I planned this all along, that I—"

"Now you're being absurd." Gus filled the kettle and set it on the stove. At some point, he couldn't remember when, Gus had fallen into the habit of drinking tea with pizza. In public he drank beer like everyone else, but this was his kitchen with only his sister to bear witness. "There are plenty of other reasons he may be reluctant to take your book to his agents." He sat down again while he waited for the water to boil. "For one thing, maybe he's about to drop his agents, or they him."

"You don't understand Gus—he wouldn't leave Day Delos and Associates. They are the best agency in the country…probably the world. Being represented by them virtually guarantees your career. Leaving would be like—"

"—throwing away an ANU law degree?"

She stopped.

Gus poured her a cup of tea. "Either way, Theo, this bloke and his agency aren't your only option. You can send your manuscript out to other agents."

"Yes…"

Gus squinted at her. "But you wanted him to like it?"

"Yes."

"Are you in love with Murdoch?"

Theo shook her head, but hesitantly.

"But you're on the way?"

Theo was a little startled, but she answered truthfully. "Maybe… I'm not sure. I still don't know how to read Americans, Gus."

He smiled. "You'll get used to them. It just takes a few years." He bit into another slice of pizza as he considered the wisdom he was obviously about to impart. "They're generous—possibly the most generous people in the world—but they're also a bit paranoid. That's why they have guns…or maybe it's because they have guns. It may be that Murdoch wants to help you find an agent, but he's concerned that your manuscript is a bit too good. That introducing you to his agents might relegate him to second favorite child."

Theo's brow arched. "I think perhaps you should be the novelist."

He laughed. "Wouldn't the ancients love that?"

Theo sighed as she thought about their parents. "I'm going to have to tell them soon."

Gus raised a finger. "I was thinking about that. Perhaps you should send them your manuscript."

"Why?"

"I think it might help them see why you want to write, why you should write." He pointed at her. "I listen sometimes when you read aloud. I think even the ancients would agree it would be a crime to bury your talent in the law."

Theo said nothing, was able to say nothing, caught off balance by such a surge of love for her brother at that moment. Late of an evening, she would read aloud what she'd written that day, listening for rhythm and pace, testing the sound of the spoken words against the voices in her imagination. Gus was often in the living room reviewing files and drafting advice. He'd never said a word about the noise, so she'd had no idea he'd listened.

"Good grief, you're not going to cry again, are you?" Gus said, handing her the paper napkins that had come with the pizza. "I thought Americans were emotional!"

"Shut up." Theo ignored the napkins and used the heel of her hand instead.

Gus picked up yet another slice of pizza. "Look, Theo, I'm not going to get all big-brother on you about this bloke Murdoch, but just promise me you'll be careful. I probably should—"

"You shouldn't anything, Gus. I'm an adult."

"I probably should tell you he's too old for you, but at least he and the ancients will have a lot in common."

"He's not that old!"

"You said he was old."

"I said he was older."

"Do you know how old he is?"

"No."

"Do you know much about him, Theo?"

"Of course, I do. He's famous, for one thing." Theo frowned, aware suddenly that though she knew Dan Murdoch, she didn't know that much about him. They had talked often and for hours, but about writing. For her, newly enamored with the craft, that had been everything. She had neither noticed nor cared that the conversations had not included revelations or anecdotes about his life. And then yesterday they'd spent the afternoon making love, and he'd mentioned a dog who ate his watch, and it seemed that he was beginning to let her farther in. But thinking about it now, they had never talked of family or friends. He'd never said much about his past, had never asked about hers. Maybe he thought her too young to have a past. Maybe he thought her too young, period.

"Would you like to meet him?" she asked quietly. Somehow, she'd never introduced Dan Murdoch to her brother. She wasn't entirely sure why. Gus worked long days at the firm, and she and Dan parted ways every afternoon to write on their own; whenever Dan had dropped her home, he'd stayed in the car…and perhaps she had not wanted to share her time with him.

Gus shrugged. "Sure."

"I'll invite him to come to dinner next Saturday."

Theo set out for Benders the next morning determined to carry on cheerfully, to demonstrate that there were no hard feelings on her part. She would ask Dan to join her and Gus for dinner on Saturday, and she would cook something she could pass off as an Australian delicacy if it didn't come out quite right. She would never bring up her manuscript again, and the whole embarrassing episode would be put behind them. He would not need to feel guilty about his reluctance, and she would not need to feel humiliated by it. Today she would draft letters to the list of agents she had compiled the night before. Some part of her was invigorated by the thought of doing it on her own. She'd not known Dan Murdoch when she'd dropped out of law school and caught a flight to the U.S. with two suitcases and her research notes. Then, she'd believed enough in an idea about the spirit of a city to gamble her entire future on it. She'd been consumed by the thought of saying something important about the lives that belonged to the land upon which a city was raised, about how what was buried formed the foundation of new buildings in the sun. It was both terrifying and wonderful to need that level of belief again, to return to it.

She arrived before Dan and got straight to work trying to write the perfect three-hundred-word synopsis for *Underneath*. The process of condensing the essence of her novel into so short a summary was torturous.

It was midday before she thought to check the time, to note that Dan had not yet arrived. Fleetingly, she wondered if he was avoiding her, before she told herself not to be ridiculous. Dan sometimes went to the gym in the morning. She ordered a coffee and returned to work. But as the afternoon passed Theo became more and more aware of the fact that he was not there. By the day's end, she had begun to wonder if she would ever see him in Benders again. Had what she asked been so outrageous, such an imposition that he would shun her forever? And after they'd been lovers... At some point she stopped being mortified by the thought and began to get angry.

It wasn't such an unreasonable thing to ask a friend, and she had not pressed when he seemed reluctant.

Theo checked her watch. It was nearly seven. She packed up her laptop and notes before rummaging in her bag for her phone. Hoisting the bag onto her shoulder, she left Benders as she dialed. There was no answer..

She tapped the phone against her chin as she walked. Dan always answered his phone. It didn't seem to ring often, but he never declined a call...something about his agent requiring that he be always contactable should some media opportunity arise. She glanced at her watch again. Dan lived just a couple of blocks away. Perhaps it would not be too weird or clingy to swing by on her way home.

She winced as she remembered what Gus had been doing when she'd arrived unannounced. Of course Dan wouldn't be...

would he? The thought was painful. She was surprised by how acutely. By this time, she was only a block from his house.

She straightened her shoulders. She'd drop by. It was a normal thing for a friend to do. She could always not knock if it looked like he had a visitor.

Dan's house came into view. Theo felt her heart sink. There was a car in the driveway. A black Cadillac. Of course there was. She was an idiot.

She stepped back behind one of the taller topiaries as the front door opened. A man walked out briskly and climbed into the car. Tall, dressed in a business suit and overcoat. He pulled out quietly with the headlights off. Theo watched the vehicle turn and disappear. She was ridiculously relieved and determined now to invite Dan Murdoch to dinner.

She was smiling when she knocked. "Dan! Dan, it's Theo." A large ginger cat jumped onto the doorstep and rubbed itself against her calves.

The blue door moved. That did not alarm Theo particularly. It was an old door that probably needed to be locked with a key. She peered round it into the hallway and called out again. "Dan?"

The cat ran past her and down the hallway.

"Damn!" Theo hesitated. Dan didn't appear to be home, and she had no wish to break and enter, but she couldn't just leave the cat. She wasn't sure if it belonged to Dan, and she knew full well the damage a cat could do if it chose to. What if it…? No. She'd just go in, get the cat, and leave.

The house was dark and silent. Not knowing where the switches were, Theo used the wall to guide herself down the hall. Her footsteps fell lightly on the floorboards. She counted off the framed book covers as her hands made contact with the frames. If her memory was correct, the room at the very end of the hallway was the kitchen. Perhaps it was Dan's cat after all, seeking out its supper bowl.

She felt inside the doorway for a light switch, taking just a single step into the room before she slipped on something wet and sticky and crashed to the floor. As she got onto her knees, Theo cursed the cat who had no doubt spilled something. Her eyes were starting to adjust a little. She could make out the leg of the kitchen table, the shape of the cat lapping at whatever it had spilled. And then, as she turned, the outstretched form of a man. Dan. He was lying with his legs beneath the table. Even without light, Theo could see the whites of his eyes, staring and fixed. And she knew suddenly that she'd slipped in his blood.

CHAPTER 5

I am in trouble, and I may already be gone. Watch for the book. It will speak to you of what lies Underneath. Study it. Press a copy into the hands of everyone you love. Buy copies to hide away so that the story may not be taken from you.

WKWWK

Primus

Theo suppressed the instinct for flight and reached instead for his neck to check for a pulse, but her fingers fell upon a throat that had been slashed so deeply that she could feel severed tendon, slippery lumps of cartilage and muscle. His body was still warm, but she knew he was dead.

She pulled back gagging, pressing herself into the corner of the kitchen, and for a time all she could do was stay there, shaking. And then her phone rang.

"Theo, how do you feel about Chinese food—"

"Gus...help me."

"Theo, what's wrong?"

"Oh, Gus—" Theo struggled to get her mouth to form words when all she wanted to do was scream. In the end she managed to tell Gus where she was, what she'd found. The extra light from her phone allowed her to make out Dan's face, his eyes staring, frozen.

"Theo, get out of that house."

"I have to call the police."

"Theo, listen to me. Whoever did this might still be there."

"The police..."

"I'll call them. You get out of that house! I'm on my way."

Theo pulled herself up against the wall. In doing so her hand passed over the light switch and she flicked it, closing her eyes against what she knew she would see. She counted to three before she opened them. A large pool of blood haloed Dan, smeared where she had slipped. Theo did not let her eyes linger near his throat. Grief started to seep into the shock. As did the past. Theo staggered under the combined weight of anguish and terror and shame. She turned to go, to run.

A plaintive meow cut the fog. The cat she'd followed in had climbed onto Dan's body. She couldn't leave it, she couldn't leave Dan like that, with some stray trying to eat him. And so she attempted to grab it. But the cat leapt out of her lunge and into the sink. She went after it, but by that time it had escaped through the open window.

Theo grabbed the sink gasping. She felt hot and dizzy, and for a moment she was afraid she might faint. She turned on the faucet and splashed her face, struggled against the urge to be sick. Her phone rang. Gus.

"Theo, are you okay?"

"Yes, where are you?"

"Just pulling up—I can't see you."

"I'm still inside."

Gus swore. "Don't touch anything, Theo; the police are on their way."

Theo stepped back from the sink.

The door opened down the hallway, and Theo started.

"It's just me," Gus entered the kitchen. "My God, Theo, what are you doing?" He blanched as he looked at Dan's body, the pool of blood, streaked where Theo had fallen, her bloody handprints on the wall, a blood-splattered garbage bag discarded near the door. Gus held out his hand. "Theo, come with me."

"Shouldn't we wait for the police?" she asked, shivering now.

"We'll wait outside," he said. Gus looked over his shoulder. The police would enter the house, guns drawn. He wanted his sister safely outside when that happened, just in case. "Come on, Theo."

Theo stepped around the kitchen table and took his hand. Hers was shaking. Gus moved between her and the body and, placing his arm about her shoulders, gently guided her back to the front door. He sat her down on the small porch and held her as they waited.

The first squad car arrived quietly, without lights or siren. Gus spoke to the uniformed policemen, who instructed them to wait outside while they secured the scene. They entered the house as Gus expected, with their weapons drawn. One of the officers emerged shortly thereafter and radioed for assistance. The cars that arrived after that did not do so quietly. The house became webbed in police tape as men in forensic overalls dusted, and sprayed, and swept. Theo watched mutely. Gus had wrapped her in his own jacket. He was worried that she might be in shock. Even now, he was trying to convince the detectives to let him take her home.

But they insisted upon taking her statement first. They did so in the back of a police van because Theo did not want to go back into the house.

She gave the young policeman her name and address and told him how she came to find Dan Murdoch's body.

"And what's your relationship to the deceased, ma'am?"

"We were friends." Theo wiped the edge of her eye with the heel of her hand.

"So you had a spare key?"

"No. The door was open."

"And you followed a cat in?"

Theo looked up sharply as she caught the note of skepticism in the policeman's voice. "I don't have a key," she said again. "We weren't..."

"Have you found the cat?" Gus interrupted.

The officer ignored him. "Can I ask why you washed your hands, ma'am?"

Theo looked down at her hands. The cuffs of her sleeves were wet and pink where the stain of blood had run. "I didn't... I just splashed water onto my face... I didn't think..."

"Officer, can't this wait?" Gus said again. "I'd like to take my sister to see a doctor."

The policeman studied Theo. "I'm sorry, ma'am, were you hurt?"

"No, I wasn't..."

"For pity's sake, man, the poor girl's in shock." Gus was frustrated now. "She's just had the bejeezus scared out of her!"

"Would you care to wait outside, sir?"

Gus refused, declaring himself Theodosia Benton's lawyer as well as her brother.

Theo thought he was overreacting, overprotective, but she was glad he was there, that he refused to go.

The officer called in an officer in plain clothes—a Detective Mendes, who seemed to recognize Gus. He looked over the notes of the interview and instructed them to make sure they'd be available the following morning for further questions. "I'll send an officer with you to take your clothes."

"Our clothes?"

"You know the routine, Benton. You were both on the scene—there may well be evidence on your clothing."

"Yeah, all right, fine," Gus murmured grudgingly.

The police officer that Mendes sent home with them was female. Theo undressed in her bedroom, systematically handing each item of clothing over as she took it off. The constable was discreet and considerate. Theo felt vaguely violated nonetheless.

"Just to be clear, I'll need that suit back," Gus reminded the officer, pulling a T-shirt over his head as his suit and shirt were sealed into a large brown envelope. "Contrary to popular myth, men cannot get away with wearing the same suit every day."

Theo curled up into Gus's old couch, listening as her brother joked with the policewoman. Gus was a natural flirt—he got away with it because he was cute and funny and maybe because he had an Australian accent. Whatever the reason, Officer Reaves gave him her number before she left.

Gus brought Theo a cup of hot chocolate that smelled like it had been laced liberally with brandy. He took the other end of the couch and said nothing for a while. Then finally. "Are you all right, Theo?"

She cried for a while then, grieving for the first friend she'd made in Lawrence, the man who'd become her lover barely two days before, weeping at the horror of it, the loss of it. For the memories elicited by the blood. Gus let her cry, held her at times, and ordered Chinese food. In his experience sorrow made you hungry. He was a lawyer. He'd met enough people on the worst day of their lives to know that.

Eventually Theo's tears seemed expended. Gus handed her a takeout carton of moo shu pork and a fork. Theo had never mastered chopsticks. She was surprised by how good the food smelled—it didn't seem right to be thinking of something like food right then.

Gus watched her carefully, "I'm sorry about your bloke, Theo."

"He wasn't *my* bloke, Gus—not really."

"I'm sorry anyway."

She avoided the risk of tears anew by filling her mouth with a forkful of food and chewing diligently.

"Do you want to tell me exactly what happened?"

"You were there when I told the police."

"I want you to tell me. You might remember something you didn't think of then...something you left out..."

"Why would I leave anything out?"

"Just trust me. What were you doing there in the first place?"

"Dan wasn't answering his phone... I wanted to invite him to dinner so you could meet him."

Gus smiled slightly and nodded encouragingly. "How did you know where he lived?"

"We dropped by there a couple of days ago to pick up his camera. Dan invited me in to see the original sketches of his covers.

Gus flinched. "Slightly less clichéd than etchings, I suppose."

Theo shook her head. "It wasn't like that."

"And while you were there, did he...? Did anything...?"

Theo swallowed. "Yes."

"Oh, sweetheart..." Gus hugged her. "I'm so sorry."

Theo fought resurging tears. "It was the first time..."

He held her tighter. "You're going to have to tell the police, Theo. They'll find out anyway."

She nodded. "I know. I just wasn't ready to think about it tonight."

Gus kissed the top of her head. "So, you walked up to this bloke's door and..."

"There was a man. He came out of the house just before I arrived..." Theo paled. "Oh, my God...it was him. He killed Dan..."

"Calm down, Theo." Gus grabbed her hand and held it till the agitation passed. "Who was this man?"

"I don't know... He walked out just as I got there. I forgot... how could I have forgotten?"

Gus's hand pressed tighter on hers. "You're probably still in shock. Did he see you?"

Theo shook her head. "I don't think so."

Gus relaxed just slightly. "Would you recognize him?"

"I don't know. I only caught a glimpse his face. He got straight into his car and drove away."

"What kind of car?"

"It was big...and black...a Cadillac I think."

Gus nodded. "Right...so what did you do then?"

Theo told him about the unlocked door, and the cat, and then what she'd found after she'd slipped in the kitchen. Gus stared silently at her for a moment. "Don't ever do anything like that again."

"Like what?"

"Like walking into a strange house alone, with no idea who's in there. This isn't Hobart, Theo. People here have guns, and if you wander into their house, a lot of them would be quite happy to shoot you."

"It wasn't a strange house…it was Dan's house."

"He wasn't expecting you. Americans respond to surprises by shooting."

Theo smiled. She wasn't sure if Gus was trying to cheer her up with his ridiculous warnings. "Clearly, Dan wasn't like that… He might still be alive if he had been."

Gus pondered that. "Maybe he was killed by someone who didn't surprise him."

"What do you mean?"

"Just that maybe he knew this guy in the black Caddie."

Theo swallowed. She felt cold suddenly, reminded again that the man she'd seen leaving Dan's house was probably his killer. Not just probably…definitely. She had been standing right there, just feet away when the man who slit Dan Murdoch's throat had walked out.

Gus looked at her. "Sorry. You don't want to talk about this."

Theo shook her head. She didn't.

"The police will ask you about this again tomorrow," he warned gently.

"I haven't any idea who that man was, Gus." Theo rubbed her face. "To be truthful, I'm not even sure I'd recognize him again."

"Try telling me what he looked like," Gus suggested. "You may remember more than you think."

Theo closed her eyes, trying to conjure the man she'd seen. But the image wouldn't hold. "He was ordinary, I think," she said frustrated. "If he'd had a big nose, or a scar, or a moustache, I would have had something to notice, to lock onto. But everything was ordinary. I'm so useless!"

Gus shrugged. "Not entirely useless. The police can rule out men with big noses, scars, or facial hair. That narrows it down a little."

Theo shuddered. "Gus...what if he saw me after all?"

Gus's eyes darkened. "Sweetheart, if he'd seen you, he probably would have followed you into the house and killed you too—"

"Don't!"

"I'm not trying to scare you, Theo." Gus sighed. "Whoever killed your friend Dan knew what he was doing. He knew when Dan was home; he got into the house, cut his throat, and walked out as if nothing had happened... Oh, God, Theo, I'm sorry I didn't mean to—"

Theo wiped her eyes fiercely.

"I'm sorry." Gus put down his takeout. "I'm an idiot. I was just trying to analyze the facts... I'll shut up now. I promise." He took the half-eaten container of moo shu pork out of her hand. "Go to bed."

"Sleep won't change anything Gus."

"No, but it might help you deal with tomorrow."

CHAPTER 6

Where is Primus?

Frodo 14

Has anyone heard from Primus?

WKWWK

Patriot Warrior

Give the guy a break! It hasn't been that long!

Space Monkey 2497

Fuck! Maybe they've got him. He said this would happen. What the Hell do we do now?

Frodo 14

Has anyone noticed that FLOTUS does not age? It's worse than you think. I've seen pictures from the Civil War and she's in them. How do you think she does that? Is it connected to the Frankenstein Project? Is this what Primus was about to tell us, when he disappeared?

WKWWK

Patriot Warrior

How do we know he's disappeared when we have no idea who the fuck he was!

Space Monkey 2497

That's the definition of disappear you moron.

WKWWK

Frodo 14

No, it isn't. You have to appear before you can disappear!

Space Monkey 2497

Theo woke to the gritty-eyed feeling of too little sleep. After she suffered a couple of screaming nightmares, Gus had made room for her in his bed. But even safely beside Gus, she'd lain awake for most of the night, weeping silently so as not to wake him. The darkness brought back that moment when she first realized that she'd slipped in Dan's blood, the clawing wetness of his severed throat under her hand, the stillness of him, the smell of blood… and that cat. God, the cat! Crouched on Dan's body like some malevolent sprite, a yellow-eyed portent of doom. In her dreams Dan ravished her, then bled out as they were kissing; Gus held the knife and skinned the cat, and she was trapped in blood and fear and guilt. And now in the light of day, without the cloak of darkness, it was worse.

She could hear Gus in the kitchen, talking on the phone as the kettle boiled.

The floorboards were cold underfoot, and so she went back to her own room to find socks before she joined him downstairs. Gus was making pancakes, while explaining that he wouldn't be in the office until that afternoon. "Sorry, David, no potential clients… unless they find the bloke who did it. He'll need a defense attorney, I suppose." He grimaced as he spied Theo in the doorway.

She smiled to let him know it was all right. Gus hadn't known Dan Murdoch. She couldn't expect him to grieve. She was pretty sure he was joking, that he wouldn't consider defending Dan's murderer.

Hanging up, Gus pocketed his phone and flipped two pancakes onto a plate.

"Hungry?" he asked, dropping it onto the table before her.

Theo wasn't, but he had made her pancakes, so she nodded.

"I could only take the morning off." Gus set down his own plate and handed a pancake to Horse. "Will you be okay on your own this afternoon?"

"Yes, of course."

He spread butter over his pancake and reached for the maple syrup. "What do you plan to do…after we drop into the station, I mean?"

Theo shrugged. "I'll work, I guess."

"You're going back to—"

"I think I should."

"Why?"

"They'll be wondering where we are…Dan and me. I should tell them."

"This isn't that big a town, Theo; they'll have heard."

"They should hear it from me."

Gus started to say something and then stopped, thinking better of his objection. "I'll meet you there if you like…walk you home."

Theo shook her head. "You can't go in late and leave early."

He smiled. "I'm a partner."

Theo laughed. It sounded strange, felt strange to laugh. Still, she would not countenance asking anything more of her brother's time, his life. She didn't want to become that relative…the one who imposed, who always needed looking after. Gus had already cheerfully done more for her than anyone had a right to expect. But she could see that he was worried.

"I'll take Horse with me," she said as the hound rested its large head on her arm and looked hopefully at her pancakes. "He'll protect me—won't you, Horsey?"

Gus groaned. "Please don't call him that—it makes you both sound ridiculous."

Regardless, Horse seemed amenable to the plan, and so it was decided. Once Horse had finished the pancakes, Theo and Gus made their way to the Lawrence Police Department as promised. They gave their statements again. Theo answered questions about her relationship with Daniel Murdoch, and her memories felt desecrated by the harsh factual detail demanded, the knowing looks that passed between the officers. They asked her about Dan Murdoch's friends and relatives. She directed them to Benders… Perhaps someone there knew more… As for kin, he had never spoken of any. They asked about her last conversation with Dan, persisting until she had given them an almost verbatim account.

"So you felt angry that he refused to help you?"

"No…just embarrassed."

"Why?"

"Asking for help is difficult, I guess."

"Especially when it's refused."

Theo said nothing. It was true. She'd been humiliated.

"And after you'd slept with him."

"That wasn't why I—" Theo choked.

"So you were in love with Mr. Murdoch?"

"Yes." Theo stopped trying to deny it. It was a just a fledging love, but however new and fragile and impulsive, it had been love.

Detective Mendes leaned back, tipping his chair onto two legs. "So you went to his house to confront him about his refusal to help you…?" he prompted casually.

Theo looked up sharply. "Of course not."

The detective glanced at the file before him. "Our records indicate you found Mr. Murdoch's body."

"Yes, I did…I just meant that I didn't go to confront him."

"What were you doing there?"

"I…I wanted to invite Dan to dinner."

Mendes snorted derisively.

Gus spoke up. "Look, George, *I* asked Theo to invite Murdoch to dinner. I wanted to meet the bloke."

"Why?"

"He was spending a lot of time with my little sister. I wanted to make sure he wasn't a creep."

The detective's brow rose.

Theo told him about the man she'd seen leave Dan Murdoch's house just before she'd found his body. Mendes called in a police artist, and they spent the next hour coming up with the portrait of an entirely average man with no scars, moustache, or big nose. She could describe the car but couldn't even recall seeing a license plate. Mendes was clearly frustrated with her as a witness. "If I didn't know better, Miss Benton, I'd suspect you didn't want to help us find your friend's killer."

Gus intervened. "Fair go, George. Theo didn't know he was anything other than a visitor when she saw him... She had no reason to pay any attention to him or memorize the license plate number."

Detective Mendes called Gus aside then. They argued quietly so that all that Theo and the other officers could hear were strident murmurs. In the end, Mendes came back to the table and told Theo she could go, but that they would be in touch. He advised her not to speak to the press.

"Of course not," Theo said, startled. It had never occurred to her to speak to the press.

As they walked back to Gus's truck, she asked him about Mendes.

"I've worked with him on a couple of cases. He's not a bad bloke, Theo. Just diligent. And a bit of a jerk to witnesses, by the looks of today's interview."

"I wish I could have been more useful." Theo frowned. Why couldn't she remember the man's face more clearly? She couldn't even picture him now.

"Some people are not good at faces."

"But I'm supposed to be a writer. I describe characters all the time...but now, when it's important, I can't..."

He put his arm around her shoulders. "Don't try. It may come back to you if you don't force it."

Gus took Theo back to the house and helped her find a leash for Horse. "Are they going to let you into Benders with him?" Gus asked.

"There are tables outside, remember? People bring their dogs all the time."

"Let me show you something." Gus called Horse to his side. "Danger!"

The hound placed itself in front of Gus, lowered his massive head, and snarled threateningly. Theo stepped back, alarmed. Gus grinned. "It's okay, Horse. Relax."

Immediately the snarl was replaced by what Theo had always fancied was a smile. The dog ambled over and licked her.

"Horse used to belong to a client." Gus knelt to scratch his dog's flabby jowls. "Poor old mutt wouldn't know how to bite anyone, but she trained him to look as though he might."

"Oh. Why did she give him to you?"

"I suppose she didn't really give him to me. I'm just looking after him for a while."

"How long is a while?"

Gus shrugged. "Twelve to fourteen."

Theo clipped the leash to Horse's collar. "You'd better go to work."

Gus checked his watch. "Yes, I should." He grabbed his briefcase and then turned back. "Promise me you'll head home before it gets late—Horse is afraid of the dark."

Theo smiled. "You have my word." She shoved her brother fondly. "Thank you, Gus. For everything. I'm not sure what I would have done without you."

He shoved her back. "You would have been all right."

"You're a liar."

"That's pronounced *lawyer*." Gus opened the door. "Call me if you need anything." He met her eye. "Anything. If you start to feel—"

"I'm okay, Gus." She straightened to show him that she was. "I'm a grown-up now, remember?"

He nodded. "You are. I'm sorry if I still treat you like a kid sometimes, but after—"

"I know. Go—you'll be late...or later."

When he'd finally gone, Theo slipped her laptop and notebook into a satchel out of habit more than anything else. It was unlikely she would write anything today. She looped Horse's leash through her arm and locked up. It was something of a relief to be alone, to be able to think about what had happened.

She began walking toward Benders. Horse was well trained. He walked happily beside her without straining the tether, which was lucky, as Theo was pretty sure she would be unable to hold back an animal his size if he decided to chase.

She tried to think calmly about the night before. The man who'd walked out of Dan's house without a backward glance. She'd watched him drive down the street. If he'd glanced into his rearview mirror, he might have caught a glimpse of her. Theo shuddered.

She wondered what Dan had gotten himself into. He didn't write the kind of controversial books that made readers want to kill you...she didn't think. It was sometimes hard to tell what would upset people. His books were literary thrillers, fast-paced and exciting, but written with a visceral sense of place and a sharp insight into the human condition. His victims were rarely minorities or women and never children, and there were no political undertones to his writing.

He'd not spoken to her of siblings, so she'd assumed he didn't have any. And she realized he had not spoken of family at all—no passing mention of his childhood or school days in all the time they had talked. Perhaps there was someone from his past who had done this, someone he had once wronged, who after years of repressing a murderous rage had been triggered by an unrelated incident to find and murder Dan Murdoch. She stopped, startled and a little appalled that she was already starting to storify Dan's death. Dan, who she had been starting to love. What was wrong with her? It was positively ghoulish.

There were quite a few people at Benders when she and Horse arrived. It was unusual at this time. When she was close enough to hear snippets of conversation, she understood why. Dan's death had reached the media, and those who knew him had come to Benders in search of information. For a moment, Theo considered turning around, leaving. Indeed, she might have done so if Laura had not called her name. The server was dressed as usual in unbroken black. But today her eyes were rimmed red as she embraced Theo.

"So you've heard?" Laura asked, wiping her face with the bell sleeve of her blouse. "Oh, Theo, it's just too awful. Here in Lawrence! How could this happen to Dan?"

Theo nodded silently. Clearly, Laura did not know that she had found Dan's body.

Laura clasped Theo's face in her hands. "Come on, let's sit down. Would you like a cup of tea...or perhaps something stronger? Everything's on the house today."

Theo secured Horse outside and gave him the bone-shaped biscuit treat she had in her bag, before allowing Laura to bustle her inside. The other members of staff who had known Dan were there, though they were not on shift. They each hugged her like family. It seemed this was an impromptu wake.

Laura grabbed Theo's hand and introduced her to the woman who sat a little apart from the others, in the booth in which Theo had first seen her with Dan Murdoch months before.

"This is Veronica Cole," Laura said. "She wanted to meet you especially. Veronica is…was poor Dan's agent."

"Professionally," Veronica qualified. "Aside from that, beyond that, Dan and I were the best of friends. He wanted me to meet you just a couple of days ago, but I had to get to another meeting. I can't tell you how sorry I am that I rushed off. If I'd known…"

Theo was still not accustomed enough to the spectrum of American accents to pick the agent's origins, but she recognized a privileged education in her voice. "I'm very sorry for your loss, Ms. Cole."

"Ronnie, please. My sympathies in return. Dan spoke often of you."

"He did?"

"Of course. He thought you were very talented. In fact, he sent me your manuscript…but we can talk about that later. This is not the time."

"He sent my book to Day Delos and Associates?" Theo asked, bewildered. Dan had refused her request.

"Yes. I'm sorry—it was gauche of me to mention business at a time like this. I came here hoping to meet you, and maybe find out more about what happened." She stopped, closed her eyes, inhaled and exhaled slowly, and began again. "I'm afraid the police would only tell me that Dan had been the victim of violence… that he'd died in his own home."

"The papers don't say much more." Jock, a dedicated barfly who wore his long gray hair in a ponytail and generally occupied a stool quite close to their table, held up the *Journal-World*,

Lawrence's local paper. "Sounds like a burglary." He shook his head. "In that neighborhood—hard to believe."

Theo wondered whether she should tell them what she knew, what she'd seen. A part of her desperately wanted to do so, to unburden herself from knowing somehow, and the other part could not bring herself to talk about it. The decision was made for her by a sudden swell of tears, and Laura's arms were around her again. "Oh, honey, let it out. Crying's the best medicine for a broken heart."

If Theo had wished to protest that her heart—though sore— was not actually broken, she was not given the opportunity, as she was plied with tea and sympathy and platitudes.

Theo pulled herself together, embarrassed. "I'm sorry, it's just been a bit of a shock."

They all murmured in agreement.

"Benders is gonna be strange without Dan," Jock said. "He's been coming here for years. Gave the place a bit of class to have a writer-in-residence—like the old days, when Burroughs used to hang here."

"He never really spoke to anyone before you," Laura said. "Used to be quite standoffish." She smiled knowingly. "That first day he sat with you, I knew it was the beginning of something—

"We weren't—"

Jock interrupted. "If it was or it wasn't, it ain't our business." He cast a warning glance at Laura.

"I just meant that at least Dan was happy these past months," Laura said putting her arm around Theo and scowling at Jock. "And I think that was down to you, Theo."

Veronica Cole stood to leave. She handed Theo a card. "Let's have lunch. There are a few things I'd like to discuss, if you're available."

Theo looked down at the embossed business card. *Day Delos and Associates Management: Literary Agents.* She remembered her last conversation with Dan. Oh, God…this was fraudulent, indecent. "Dan and I really weren't… I mean, he didn't think—"

"Call me. We'll arrange a time, and I'll book a table somewhere quiet. I'm sure Danny would have wanted us to get to know one another."

CHAPTER 7

Caleb studied the biography of the writer. The photograph that accompanied it was arty, posed with the subject half turned away from the camera. You could only really tell that the guy had a beard and that he was old. Not ancient but old. He clicked through to the news reports of the murder. It fit. Dan Murdoch was killed on the day Primus made his last post. And he'd spoken about Stull—it made sense that Primus lived in Lawrence...or had lived in Lawrence. Murdoch was a writer...perhaps he'd discovered the Frankenstein Project while researching a book. A famous author would probably be able to get access to all sorts of things.

Caleb sat back, amazed and excited. He'd found him. He'd found Primus. Fucking awesome!

Now to break the news.

Theo lingered at Benders throughout the afternoon, with the people who had known Dan, who had known her and Dan. Most of them hadn't known that he was a famous writer. They believed he, like Theo, was working on his first novel. She felt strangely proud, telling them of his books, the Edgar nominations, the best-sellers. Dan had been unassuming and private. She wanted him to be given his due. Already, she missed him.

Larry, the novelist from Aimee's, and two members of the writing group that met at Alchemy also came to Benders. They delivered their commiserations to Theo, who accepted them with not a small degree of guilt. She and Dan had been lovers for a day; they had not talked of the future; there were no promises. She had no real right to be treated like a grieving widow. And yet everybody seemed determined to afford her that status, to prioritize her feelings over theirs. Perhaps her reluctance to accept the assumption that she bore the greater portion of grief was an attempt to keep that grief at bay.

She left at four, telling Laura that she had to get Horse back before dark. "You take care, Theo," Laura said. "And you speak to that Veronica Cole about your book. Perhaps she was Dan's parting gift to you."

Theo smiled. "I don't know if I'll come in tomorrow... But I'll see you soon."

Outside the air was brisk. The leash remained slack in Theo's hand as Horse allowed her to set the pace. She walked out thinking of Dan, of the day they'd made love, and the day he'd died. That was the only way she could explain what she did next. Why she walked back to the yellow house with the blue door.

The property was cordoned off with police tape. Two officers drank coffee in a cruiser parked on the street outside. Theo stood on the other side of the road. She was aware of her heart beating, the pulse pounding in her ears. She tried to take herself back to the evening before, to remember every detail of what she'd seen outside and inside Dan's house.

Theo wasn't the only person watching the house. A number of people stood in clusters behind the police tape—ordinary people, in jogging gear, business suits, a woman in yoga pants with a couple of kids. They took photographs and selfies, clutched at their throats for the camera. Some carried coffee or snacks. Almost every car that passed the address slowed as it rolled past until the police moved them on. Dan Murdoch's home had, it seemed, become a tourist attraction.

A thickset man with blond dreadlocks decided that she need a tour guide. "Some dude got killed in there," he said. "It's a gen-u-wine crime scene."

"I see."

"Sorry, you probably already guessed that, seeing as the place is wrapped in that tape." He shook his head. "They must go through miles of that stuff every year."

Theo nodded vaguely, hoping that he'd stop talking and move away.

"If you ask me, it was a drug thing."

Theo turned sharply. "Why do you say that?"

"Look at the garden. You'd have to be high to do that to a hedge. Check out the fuckin' ducks!"

Despite herself, Theo smiled. She wondered if the police had spoken to Dan's gardener. She remembered Dan had said he came twice a week. Perhaps he'd worked the day Dan had died. Perhaps he'd seen the man in the black car on some other occasion while he tortured Dan's hedges into embarrassing shapes.

She excused herself before her new acquaintance settled too

far into conversation. He asked if he could walk her somewhere. She declined politely and turned to move away.

"You sure?" He grabbed her arm. "Ain't you scared? People are being murdered, for chrissake…"

Theo recoiled. "Don't touch me."

He held up his hands. They were dirty, like he'd just rubbed them in soil. "Just being friendly—lookin' out for you."

"Is this man bothering you, Miss?" One of the officers who'd been sitting in the cruiser had spotted the exchange and crossed the road to investigate.

Theo moved to stand beside the policewoman.

The man backed off. "I didn't mean nothin'—just being friendly."

The policewoman waited until he'd gone before she moved to return to the property. Theo thanked her.

"You're welcome. But I'd be careful… Crime scenes attract some pretty strange types."

"Yes, of course." Theo faltered. Was she one of those strange types? Why had she come here, why did she feel compelled to return to the worst moment of her life? Theo couldn't even recall making the decision to walk this way; she just had.

The temperature had cooled further in the last half hour, so Theo walked briskly, partly to compensate for the fact that her jacket was light and partly because now she wanted to be as far away as possible from Dan's house and the rubberneckers who surrounded it.

It wasn't till she was a couple of blocks from home that Theo thought she heard footsteps behind her. Over her shoulder, the street was deserted. Then she saw him, across the road. The man who'd accosted her outside Dan's house was leaning against a fence, just watching her silently. She tried not to give any sign that she recognized him, and picked up her pace, keeping Horse on a short leash. The hound seemed to sense something was wrong. Horse's head lost its relaxed loll, and his ears sprang up.

The man was crossing the road now, his stride noticeably long and purposeful. Theo suppressed an impulse to run. He was just behind her now. She stopped and turned. He ran toward her.

"Horse, danger!" Theo said urgently. "Danger!"

The hound moved between Theo and the oncomer, lowered his head, and growled.

The man stopped sharply. "It's me. From the crime scene."

"Why are you following me?"

"I wanted to see you got home safely, make sure you didn't get snatched or nothin'," he said keeping his eyes on Horse. "I'm old-fashioned, I guess."

"As you can see, I have Horse to see me home," Theo said, trying to keep her voice calm. It was beginning to get dark, and for some reason, the street seemed deserted—no children playing or people walking dogs. "Thank you, but I don't need anyone else."

"All right…or good-on-ya, as you Aussies say." He smiled. "I'll see you around… You too, Horse…" He didn't move, just stood there smiling.

Theo thought about running. But she didn't want to turn her back on him, and she couldn't walk away without doing so. In the end she pulled on Horse's leash. The hound stood his ground, snarled and snapped, as if at any minute he might break away and tear the man into more digestible bits.

"I don't know what's got into him," she said, "but you may have to walk away so that Horse will let us do likewise. I don't think he's going to calm down until you're out of sight."

For a moment the man just looked at her, still smiling, and she thought he was going to refuse, but then he nodded, waved, and turned. Theo and Horse watched him go, waited till he could no longer see them before they resumed the walk home. And then they ran.

Theo took Horse into the house with her, locked and bolted the door before checking the back door and every window. Some of the window catches were rickety, unlikely to hold under pressure. She drew the curtains. God, how she wanted to call Gus, ask him to come home, but she wouldn't. She could handle this.

Theo knelt to hug Horse. "Thank you, Horsey. Thank you for being fearsome. You, old mate, are a fabulous actor." She filled his food and water bowls, and for a while she watched him eat. "You have to guard the house now, just in case. You can do that, can't you?"

Horse rolled onto his back, his hind legs spread, as he looked at her pleadingly. She rubbed his stomach and his eyes rolled back with pleasure as he made happy grunting sounds. Theo smiled. "Yes, you're a fearsome beast, you are."

It was nearly completely dark, and now that the exertion of sprinting home was wearing off, Theo felt cold. She wasn't sure how to start the central heating. She found the thermostat on the wall in the kitchen and flipped the switch to "on." Nothing happened, but she wasn't sure if the system just needed time to heat up to a comfortable temperature. It, like everything in Gus's old house, might have seen better days.

Theo decided to take a shower to warm her up a little. She hoped that by the time she finished, the furnace would have kicked on.

She took a deep breath and retrieved from the kitchen drawer the one big knife Gus owned. She set it on the soap dish when she turned on the water. Even armed, she showered quickly with the shower curtain open so that she could see the door. At one point the knife slipped, narrowly missing her foot as it fell into the tub. She placed it on the vanity, blanching as she thought of how badly that could have come out and how embarrassing it would be to explain. She washed the conditioner out of her hair with one eye still on the door, and towel dried in seconds.

The mirror was completely fogged, possibly as a result of the open curtain, and the floor was wet and slippery. Theo pulled on her bathrobe, calling Horse to her side as soon as she stepped out. "I know, Horsey, I'm being idiotic…but just hang with me for a while." She ducked up to her room to change into pajamas and slippers and a couple of sweaters because the house was still arctic, and then fetched a mop to rectify the bathroom. Through all of this, Horse followed her happily.

Theo checked the thermostat again. It was definitely on, but there was no heat or movement of air from any of the vents.

Opening the drawer to return the knife, she changed her mind, and slipped it into the pocket of her sweater. Theo wasn't sure what to do. It was marginally warmer upstairs, but if anyone was going to break into the house, they'd do so on the ground floor…probably through the living room window, which had the dodgiest catch. She decided then, running upstairs to grab a blanket from her bed. She moved the sofa in the living room so that curled up on it she would be facing the window. She placed the knife and phone on the coffee table, both within easy and rapid reach, and opened her laptop. Theo knew she wouldn't be able to write, but she could edit. Maybe she wouldn't be able to do that either, but it was comforting to have the laptop open, the screen between her and the world.

She pulled up her manuscript and stared at the opening page. The detective's accusations that she'd intended to confront Dan Murdoch about his refusal to help, soured her reading. It wasn't true of course, but *Underneath* had come between them. Perhaps it was spoiled now.

Theo closed the file, and in the black screen she could see her reflection. God, she looked a wreck. She shut the screen, wanting to crawl under the blanket and hide, but she had to watch the window, and sometime in the next day or two, she would need to have lunch with Dan's agent. That Dan had sent Veronica Cole her manuscript confused her. Had she misunderstood him? Had their last meeting been marred simply because she was oversensitive about her work? The thought hurt, and Theo turned her mind away, and somehow it fell upon the man who tried to follow her home. And she looked to check that the knife was still in easy reach.

CHAPTER 8

Primus is dead! His name was Dan Murdoch. He lived right here, in Lawrence Kansas, where he worked to unearth the truth about what's been going on in Corporate America. And he died for that. Murdoch was murdered in his own kitchen last week. Nobody has heard from Primus since.

    WKWWK

    Wayward Son

It's only been a week. Let's not get hysterical.

    Space Monkey 2347

Come on, man. He posted every day for months and then suddenly he stops. Do the math!

    WKWWK

    Frodo 14

What did they do with Murdoch's body?

    WKWWK

    Patriot Warrior

It wasn't particularly late when Gus got home, but the house by then was frigid. And quiet. He could see all the lights were on, though the curtains were drawn. That was odd. Theo was a little paranoid about his power bill. There was no sign of Horse in the backyard.

Gus frowned, uneasy. He let himself in. "Theo...? Theo! What the hell?"

His sister met him in the hallway with Horse and armed with a kitchen knife. The dog bowled him over.

"Oh...it's you." Theo lowered her weapon, so immensely glad to see him that she could understand Horse's blind joy.

"Why is it so cold in here?" Gus asked once he'd calmed Horse down.

"The thermostat...I turned it on but—"

"The pilot light's probably gone out. I'll go down and relight it." Gus handed her a bag. "Dinner," he said. "I'll just get the heat going before it begins to snow in here. And then you can tell me what's going on."

Theo nodded. Shivering, she took the bag to the kitchen while Gus went down to the basement. Returning the knife to the cutlery drawer, she took out plates for the burgers and fries Gus had brought home, wishing she'd thought to make dinner but glad he'd decided to bring it home.

A bang from the basement was loud and sudden, and jolted her back to panic. She screamed. "Gus!" She ran to the stairs. "Gus, are you all right? Gus!"

He looked up. "Of course, I'm all right. I just had to give the furnace a bit of the thump to get it going." He squinted at her. "What's made you so jumpy?...Oh, God, don't start crying. What the hell's going on?"

Theo told him then about the crime scene and the man with dreadlocks who'd tried to follow her home and the fact that she couldn't really lock the living room window...not properly. Gus said nothing for a while. He climbed out of the basement and shut the door. "Come on, I'm starving."

"Why'd you go back to Murdoch's house, Theo?" he asked when they were back in the kitchen.

Food warmed Theo a little and made her feel steadier.

"I don't know. I just did. I don't remember deciding to."

"This bloke who spoke to you, what precisely did he look like and what exactly did he say?"

"Blond dreadlocks under a bandana. He was wearing a flannel shirt and jeans. There was a cobweb tattoo on his neck. He smelled like fuel and cigarettes."

Gus's brow rose. "Bloody risky combination."

Theo recounted their conversations, both outside Dan Murdoch's house and when she'd confronted him on the street.

Gus smiled as she explained how she convinced the man to leave. "Good thinking. Hopefully you've kept the bastard from working out where you live."

"Hopefully."

"What I can't work out is how he knew you were Australian," Gus added scowling. "It's an unusual nationality to guess out of the blue...and, generally speaking, the world doesn't realize that Australians come in all colors."

Theo's brow furrowed. Gus was right. She had taken after their father and was much darker than her brother. People had, in the past, asked her if she was Egyptian, Greek, even Peruvian, but no stranger had guessed Australian before. "The accent, I suppose," she offered half-heartedly.

"Most Yanks can't tell the difference between an Australian and a British accent…and your accent is pretty weak." He clearly disapproved of the last. "If it was me, yeah, someone would be able to guess, but you?" He screwed up his face. "I don't know."

Theo said nothing. It was true. Her accent was at best faint, though Gus's was still quite marked, despite all the years he'd spent in the States. Perhaps he'd stubbornly held on to home through it. "Perhaps he has an ear for inflection," she said, unsettled further.

"Are you sure you haven't seen him before?" Gus pressed.

"Did I mention the blond dreadlocks and tattoo? I think I might have remembered."

Gus shoved the last of his burger into his mouth and stepped into the living room. Theo followed and watched as he fiddled with the window, testing the catch. "Grab my toolbox, will you, Theo? It's under the kitchen sink."

"You have a toolbox?" Theo had never known her brother to be particularly handy. She found the box and took it to him.

He set it on the coffee table, loosened his tie, and opened it. Inside, a hammer lay in a nest of business cards. Rolling up his sleeves, Gus rummaged through the cards till he found the one he wanted. He rang the twenty-four-hour locksmith and arranged for him to fit locks on all windows the next day.

"Just to be on the safe side," he said as he closed the toolbox, satisfied. "I think I deserve a beer."

Theo cleaned up the takeaway boxes and wrappers as Gus looked in the refrigerator. It was amazing how much more secure a warm house felt. And, of course, Gus was home now…though she didn't know what use he'd be if the house were broken into… Possibly he had the card of someone who could help.

She sat down with a coffee while he sipped a Copperhead Pale Ale, and she asked him about his work.

Gus was surprised. Considering the events of the last couple of days, his work seemed if not trivial, a little uninteresting. "You haven't decided you want to go back to the law, have you, mate?"

"God, no! I'm just not sure I could take thinking about Dan right now."

"Because you loved him?"

"Because I miss him. I miss talking about writing and books. It breaks my heart that those conversations are over forever."

Gus swigged his beer. "I've read books. You could talk to me."

Theo smiled.

"No, really. Don't let the beer fool you. I like wine and cheese too." He sat up and rested his chin on the crook of his thumb and forefinger in a rather good facsimile of the kind of author portraits that graced the back jackets of novels. "I'm ready; bring it on."

Theo was laughing now. God, she loved Gus. "You're an idiot."

He relaxed. "Really. Tell me. You've finished your book?"

She nodded. "I've finished the first draft."

"So now you get a publisher and become famous?"

"Now I polish and *try* to get an agent." Theo told him about Veronica Cole, whom she'd met that morning.

"She wants to have lunch with you?"

"Yes…but I'm not sure I will."

"Why the hell not?"

"It feels a bit indecent, Gus… Dan refused to introduce her, to show her the manuscript, remember. I only met Veronica Cole because Dan was murdered. It feels like I'm taking advantage of his death."

Gus sipped, contemplating her words. "Well, he couldn't have meant what he said, because he's obviously given her your manuscript. In fact, he must have given it to her straight away."

Theo signed. "I know."

"Then what's the problem?"

"I don't understand how he could go from being so reluctant to sending the manuscript directly to his agent. It doesn't make sense."

"Could it be he wasn't reluctant? That he just didn't want to get your hopes up?"

Theo stopped. There had been something protective about Dan's refusal. Perhaps that's all it was. Perhaps she could allow herself to believe that. There was a funny release in her chest, like her heart had been clenched all this time. "Maybe I will meet with her."

Gus nodded approvingly. "I have some news for you." He placed his empty beer bottle on the table. "I spoke to the trustees today. They want to know when you are going to recommence your studies."

Theo swallowed. It was time to pay the piper. "I'm not."

"Are you sure?"

Theo nodded. "I don't want to go back." She looked up at him as a thought occurred. Her voice became hesitant. "Do you want me to go?"

"No. I've got kinda used to you." He sat back. "The trustees, in their wisdom, have made an offer to settle your interest in the trust. If you relinquish any further claims, they will pay you one hundred and twenty thousand dollars…U.S. of course."

Theo gasped. "What?"

"Don't looked so shocked. How much do you think law school costs…not to mention your accommodation and living costs in Canberra, plus the option under the trust to do postgrad study?

In fact, I think they may be lowballing you—I could probably get them up to one fifty at least."

Theo was still too stunned to say anything. She'd only wanted to walk away.

"So, should I?" Gus prompted.

"Should you what?"

"Arrange a settlement?"

"Yes, of course. Take it. Run!" She exhaled. "You'll be able to fix this place up."

"This is your money, Theo."

"I know. I want you to have it."

He shook his head. "That's sweet of you, mate, but I got my share out of the old man's trust. This is yours."

"But—"

"You might need it someday," he said firmly. "I'll make arrangements to have it transferred into your account."

Theo swallowed. It felt weird to suddenly have this kind of money. "Can I at least pay for the locksmith?"

Gus sighed. "Okay, but that's it. I'll have you know that urban squalor has become a very popular decorating choice."

CHAPTER 9

I went to Dan Murdoch's house in Lawrence today. Just to see if there was anything to see. It's a nice place but pretty ordinary for a hotshot author. I thought it would be bigger, flashier. See photo.

> *WKWWK*
> *Wayward Son*

Me too. The hedges are weird. Do you think they mean anything? Was he trying to leave us a message?

> *WKWWK*
> *Patriot Warrior*

The hedge is clearly a cry for help.

> *Space Monkey 2347*

He's trying to warn us. They're Jayhawks. He's telling us that the Jayhawks are part of Minotaur.

> *WKWWK*
> *Loyal Boy*

Or he could be telling us that the Jayhawks are in danger from Minotaur.
Think about it.

   Frodo 14

———

Veronica Cole had booked a table at a restaurant called Story in Prairie Village, which was nearly an hour's drive from Lawrence. It seemed a long way to go for lunch, but perhaps the agent had chosen the venue for its name. It was more probably a coincidence, but Theo was secretly delighted. Perhaps in time she would be able to say she was signed by Day Delos and Associates at a place called Story.

Gus approved of the choice. "It's time you started exploring beyond Lawrence, mate." He tossed her the keys to his truck. "I'll get Jac to give me a lift to work."

Jacqui had replaced Lauren, who had replaced Pam. Theo had become accustomed to occasionally meeting Gus's latest passion at breakfast. They were invariably lovely and ate breakfast wearing one of Gus's work shirts. Theo wasn't sure if that was just because they hadn't brought anything to sleep in or because her brother had some sort of preference for women in his business shirts. She tried not to think too much about it, and simply made extra toast without blinking.

On that morning, Jacqui had helped her choose an outfit for the meeting with Veronica Cole, insisting that Theo shouldn't look too businesslike. "Artists should have a quirky flair, don't you think, Gus?"

Gus had grunted something unintelligible from the shaving mirror, and Jacqui had swapped Theo's black suit jacket for a sage velvet one, attached one of Gus's cuff links to the lapel, and added a woolen scarf. "There, that's better."

Theo had to admit that it was. It looked more like her, and less like a frightened lawyer at least. She'd been trying to appear more professional, but she'd got the profession wrong, she supposed. The thought that she might never have to dress like an aspiring lawyer again made her absurdly happy.

Theo left early, in case she got lost or had a flat or was caught in traffic. But none of those things happened, and so she stopped the car in the village shopping center and wandered over to look at the concrete and stone sculpture across the road, to keep herself from dwelling on Dan and undoing Jacqui's efforts by dissolving into tears. Viewing the statue of the pioneer family from every possible angle and sitting for a while on the fountain's edge used up about ten minutes, and so she walked around Prairie Village, looking into shop windows, to avoid arriving at the restaurant early. She didn't want to sit on her own waiting for Veronica Cole. A tiny part of her still worried that the agent would never arrive, that this would not happen. She remained uneasy about being given an opportunity out of tragedy. Though this might have been Dan's last gift, it seemed indecent to want it, to be excited about it.

And yet she was.

An audience with an agent from Day Delos and Associates was...well, significant. A sign that you might belong, that you had enough talent to be entitled to dream of a writer's life. How was it possible to be excited and devastated at the same time?

In her satchel Theo had an updated version of her manuscript. She'd worked on it all of the previous day and half the night, becoming progressively more mortified by the draft she'd given Dan Murdoch, the draft he'd passed to Veronica. The typos! How had she not seen them before?

Gus had laughed at her panic and lectured her about a great

Australian tradition he called "Good enough," which he suggested she embrace.

Veronica was already seated when Theo finally walked into the restaurant. She waved and smiled as the waiter directed Theo to the table.

"Have you been waiting long?" Theo asked, nervous now that she was late.

"Not at all!" Veronica said, shaking Theo's hand. "I came a little early to make sure there was a familiar face when you arrived."

The waiter bought menus and a bottle of sparkling water to the table.

Theo sipped. Her mouth felt dry.

Veronica looked at her and laughed. "I'm going to put you out of your misery: I really like what I've read of *Underneath*."

"Oh." Theo squeaked into the pause, almost overcome with both excitement and uncertainty.

"At this stage, we'd like to ask you for exclusivity—Day Delos and Associates policy, I'm afraid—until we've decided finally if we can offer you representation."

"Of course. I haven't submitted the manuscript to anyone else."

"Excellent. Day Delos does have a slightly more stringent definition of exclusivity than most agents, however. I know you showed your manuscript to Dan, but has anyone else seen it? Anyone at all?"

"No. Just Dan." Theo wondered if she should mention that Gus had heard her read a few passages aloud. She decided against it—surely that wouldn't count.

"We require that any manuscripts we take on are entirely between the writer and us until we take it to our preferred publisher. A great deal of our success is because we can guarantee that only the publishers we select will see the manuscript we are pitching, that it is a privilege to be offered a manuscript from one of our authors. It creates a buzz from the outset and almost ensures that the resultant book goes immediately to the top of the *New York Times* bestseller list."

Theo nodded.

"Of course, it means our authors must be very disciplined. In this day of social media, we do not want any hint of your novel, its plot, its style, or substance getting out before it is time."

"I understand."

"To that end, we ask that you refrain from posting on social media until we've made a decision, and if we do offer you representation, we will expect you to close all your personal accounts. Day Delos and Associates will, of course, create and maintain accounts for you on all the major platforms."

"I only have one account...so that I can keep in touch with my parents..."

"That one too," Veronica said firmly. "We aspire to make all our writers big business, Theo, and big business attracts hackers and extortionists. The only way to fight it is if we maintain control of all public interfaces." She smiled. "We also find that taking that burden from our writers frees them up to write."

"Yes, of course."

"We have the very best people, who will maintain social media in your voice and speaking on subjects designed to create and enhance a following of you as a person, which will, of course, feed into your readership."

Theo pulled back a little. "Someone will speak for me?"

"In your voice," Veronica said. "This is an era in which writers are, as public figures, expected to have positions on current events.

An unwise position could be very detrimental to your career and the brand we build for you. Day Delos relieves you of the stress of representation by employing professionals to maintain an appropriate public profile and engage with the public for you."

"But isn't that…wrong? I mean…if it's not really me…"

Veronica laughed. "Wrong? I don't know. It's standard practice." She studied Theo for a moment. "If we can attach Theodosia Benton to an appropriate issue that has already caught public attention, so that you come to represent that issue, then the millions of people who are invested in that issue will see you as one of them, and they will buy your book."

Theo wasn't sure what to say. She'd never really participated in social media—perhaps that's how it worked—but she instinctively balked at the thought of handing over her voice, even if she didn't use it.

Veronica reached over and patted her hand. "I'm sorry. It must be confronting to have me open with terms and conditions. I just wanted to get it out of the way so we could relax and have lunch. I'm sure once you've had time to think about it, you'll see it all makes sense."

They ordered then. Theo followed Veronica's lead, as the agent seemed to know the menu. Perhaps she'd been here with Dan. Theo asked shyly.

"Yes, Dan loved it here." Veronica sighed. "He thought the fact that the place is called Story was lucky or something. I am going to miss him… He was a unique, infuriating talent and a beautiful man."

Theo felt her throat tightening. She blinked to hold back the sadness that welled suddenly.

There was a sympathetic softness in Veronica's eyes. She took a purse-pack of tissues from her bag and handed them to Theo. "I do know how you feel, Theo. I'm barely holding it together myself."

Fleetingly, Theo wondered if Veronica's relationship with Dan Murdoch was more than professional. A prick of jealousy… or guilt. If anything, Theo was the other woman. Thoughts entwined with loss.

"Dan was my first writer at Day Delos and Associates." Veronica seemed to hear the questions Theo left unsaid. "We became very dear friends. He stayed with Lucas—my husband— and me, whenever he was in New York."

Theo tried not to breathe out too obviously.

Food arrived, and for a few moments they talked about their respective meals. Veronica asked about how Theo and Dan had met. Theo recounted how he'd returned the book she'd dropped, the conversation they'd struck up from there.

Veronica laughed. "How like Dan! He was always such a gentleman. Not all writers are that considerate." As evidence, she told Theo of an unnamed writer who insisted she drive him personally to appointments with publishers and pick up coffee on the way. "Of course he only drinks scalding hot, half-strength, soy milk, decaf caramel macchiatos," she said rolling her eyes. "The Frankenstein of coffee, and I have to find it in New York traffic!"

Theo laughed. They talked some more of Dan.

"You must forgive me if I'm being nosy," Veronica said eventually. "But you and Dan were more than friends, weren't you?"

Theo felt her cheeks warm. "Yes."

Veronica smiled, delighted. "Well, I'm glad for him. It's harder for you, of course, but at least he knew that kind of happiness." She sighed. "And considering what happened, I'm pleased he decided to ignore the conduct clause."

"The conduct clause?"

"In his contract. It's a part of every Day Delos contract. Before a client begins a relationship, the person in question must be vetted by the agency."

"What?" Theo did not even try to suppress her shock.

"It sounds draconian, I know, but it's part of the service, in a way."

"The service? I'm not sure I understand."

"Day Delos and Associates is a holistic agency. We manage our clients' careers, not just their books, and careers can be destroyed by an unwise assignation. So when a client wishes to form an association, he or she sends the particulars to the agency. The agency then runs general checks…criminal history, public platforms—nothing particularly intrusive."

Theo wasn't quite sure what to say.

"Day Delos's greatest asset is the reputations and careers of our writers. Naturally, we wish to protect them, and without exception our writers are very grateful. You'll find it's standard practice among the better agencies."

"Really," Theo replied. "It seems extreme. Writers are entitled to private lives, surely."

Veronica shrugged. "That was the case once…but not anymore. The public now requires the creators of art to be beyond reproach. Any sort of ethical indiscretion will destroy not only the artist but all those associated with his or her work. Think, Theo, about all the writers you know of whose careers have been rendered to dust by, say, an allegation of sexual misconduct."

Theo thought of *Airborne*, the book that, in a way, had introduced her and Dan. "Like Jack Chase?"

Veronica looked uncomfortable, though she responded

candidly. "Yes, exactly like Jack Chase. His publisher nearly went to the wall when everything came out. Other writers in his stable were boycotted by association. The fallout was huge. Publishers know that when they take on a Day Delos writer, they are not investing in an asset that is going to be unsellable because of some awkward revelation down the track."

"But Dan didn't tell you about me?"

"Not directly." Veronica smiled. "Not that we would have had any objection to you...though we may have had to do a little PR about the age difference. Honestly, Theo, it's just a precaution... like a prenuptial. We otherwise have no interest in the activities of consenting adults."

Theo exhaled. "I just can't believe that it's a consideration."

"Dan's last book sold over a million copies worldwide." Veronica maneuvered salad onto her fork. "That's before the film and television rights, the audiobook, and merchandising rights, not to mention the translation rights. If, for example, you had been underage, or a criminal of some sort, or even simply married, Dan's brand would have been compromised. It's not just *his* income that would have been affected."

Theo swallowed, digesting more than food. It made perfect sense when Veronica explained it, and yet the thought made her uneasy.

"Are you no longer interested in signing with Day Delos and Associates?" Veronica laughed.

"No...it's not that at all," Theo said startled. Was she talking her way out of representation? "I was just surprised."

"Everybody is until they've been in the industry for a time." Veronica signaled the waiter. "Let's order something really decadent and fattening for dessert, shall we? After the last week, we both deserve it."

Theo nodded, relieved that she had not offended the agent. They ordered chocolate torte with cherry ice cream and strawberry mousse with pistachio pound cake and coffee. Veronica asked about Australia, and Theo spoke of her nomadic Tasmanian childhood following her father's act to country pubs and small music festivals—funny stories of adolescent mortification.

"It sounds ideal." Veronica sighed. "The perfect childhood."

Theo faltered, the phrase scraping against the echo of a memory buried. "It wasn't always," she said quietly. "There were times that were unbearable." The words were out before she could pull them back.

Veronica looked at her curiously.

Theo tried to undo what she had said. She forced a laugh. "It wouldn't be adolescence if it wasn't unbearable occasionally." And she explained how she went from that existence to boarding school on the mainland, then law school in Canberra, and finally to Lawrence.

Veronica confessed that she too had once dreamed of writing but, after years of working on the great American novel, concluded that she had not the talent to do it naturally, nor the persistence to write regardless.

"Working with writers, championing them, was my calling—it just took me a while to realize."

Inevitably, the conversation drifted back to Dan, and without quite knowing why, Theo found herself talking to the agent about how she'd found Dan's body, seeing the killer leave, the blood, even the cat.

"Oh, you poor darling…how awful! You must have been terrified. I'm so sorry you had to see that."

"You've known Dan longer than I have. Who would want to do that, to kill him?"

Veronica frowned. She lowered her voice. "When his first book came out, Dan had some trouble with fans—a few readers took things too far. He wasn't the first thriller writer to have to deal with this, but the individuals involved in his case were quite scary…a history of mental instability and violence." She shook her head. "It's why he moved to Lawrence, though officially he lives in New York. We made sure that we didn't publish images of him unless absolutely necessary, and that any that were published were disguised by shadow—we made a motif of it: the mysterious Dan Murdoch. We thought that would be enough."

"My God, do the police know about this?"

"We've spoken to them. Given them all the information we could."

"So, Dan was in hiding?"

"Not so much in hiding as keeping a low profile."

"But why would a fan want to kill him?" There was a strained note to Theo's voice that even she could hear.

"Some readers fixate on the writer, imagine a personal relationship of some sort. That person may have felt betrayed by Dan because he moved, or because of his friendship with you, or even because he wore a blue sweater and not a red one. It's not rational."

Theo felt cold as the implication of Veronica's words settled. Dan was probably being watched, observed, stalked. All those times she was with him—at Benders, around Lawrence, and then at his house—someone may have been watching. Perhaps they were still watching. Instinctively, she glanced around the restaurant. It was about half full…businesspeople in suits, an older couple, and one or two people eating alone.

"Hey," Veronica said gently, "you mustn't let this get to you. Dan's death may be something completely unrelated to his writing and his readers. Long ago he was fond of the track. Perhaps he went back to gambling. The police will find the bastard who did this soon and lock him up."

Theo nodded. She asked Veronica about Dan's funeral, his family…to whom she should send her condolences.

The agent sighed. "The body won't be released for a while, but when that happens, Day Delos and Associates will arrange the funeral. I'll make sure you're informed in plenty of time to be there."

"Day Delos and Associates is seeing to the funeral?"

"Dan was quite alone in the world. No family to speak of at all."

Theo closed her eyes. She wasn't sure why that idea made her want to weep. She was struck in hindsight by the loneliness of Dan Murdoch. If only she'd recognized it then, she might have been able to ease it somehow.

"What did Dan tell you about himself?" Veronica asked.

"Almost nothing," Theo admitted, embarrassed. "We talked about writing mostly."

"Perhaps he was telling you more than you appreciated at the time. What exactly did he tell you about his writing?"

"Oh, he didn't say much about his manuscript… It was about ghosts, I think." Theo smiled wistfully as she thought about the long conversations she and Dan would have about process and inspiration. She forgot Veronica was there for a few moments.

"Theo?" Veronica prompted, and Theo realized the pause had been marked. She offered a memory in apology.

"Dan was following conspiracy sites…for inspiration, or research, I guess. He had some mad notion that conspiracy theories were written by people who understood the structure of the novel."

Veronica swallowed; her brow raised into an elegant arch. "He said that?"

"More or less." Theo laughed. "He was particularly interested in something called the Frankenstein Project, which was run by a minotaur…or something like that anyway. It was absurd. But I expect he's turned it into a brilliant manuscript."

"So you've read his manuscript?" Veronica's eyes narrowed.

"No," Theo replied hastily. "I don't know how close he was to finishing it…or if he would have shared it with me when he did finish."

"I'm sure he would have," Veronica said softly. She laughed. "Clearly, you were more important to him than Day Delos or its expectations."

Theo wasn't sure what to say. She wasn't sure if she was being complimented or accused.

Veronica may have seen her confusion. "I'm glad," she said. "Very glad that he had you. Technically, showing you the manuscript would have been in breach of his contract, but really, considering what's happened, it's immaterial. So please don't think—"

"I wish he had shown it to me," Theo said, "but he didn't." She regarded the agent, puzzled. "Don't you have it?" she asked. "His manuscript, I mean. Wasn't it among—?"

"The police haven't been able to locate his laptop, and it seems Dan didn't do anything remotely as sensible as backing up to Day Delos's server or even the cloud." Veronica sighed. "We're his agents, Theo. The only thing we can do for Dan now is to protect his last work, make sure it ends up in the right hands, with publishers who'll truly honor his memory and his talent."

Theo nodded. She was not so naïve as to believe there was no financial motive in Day Delos's interest in Dan's manuscript, but she thought Veronica, at least, was sincere.

The agent moved the conversation gently to Theo's writing, her ambitions, and where she wanted her work to go in terms of style and genre. Theo knew it was an attempt to take her mind off murder and tragedy, but she was glad of it, and relieved that her work, thinking of it, talking of it, was still able to take her away.

"Would you be open to commissioned writing?" Veronica asked. "Sometimes we come across opportunities for our clients to ghost-write a book or write in response to a particular need in the market."

"Oh." Theo had never thought about writing anything but her own novels, but she didn't want to come across as difficult or precious, and so she tried to sound enthusiastic. "Of course. I don't know how to ghostwrite, but I'd be open to trying."

Veronica nodded, pleased. "Excellent."

They lingered over coffee in this way, and Theo was intrigued by the acuity of Veronica's insight into structure and plot. Even her general suggestions were something of an epiphany. They talked about the technical craft of writing, as well as the mysterious art, and Theo felt safe and understood when she spoke of the solace and the ecstasy of sculpting life with words. Eventually, Veronica called for the check and they walked out of Story together.

Theo thanked the agent effusively, and with sincerity.

"Thank *you*," Veronica said. "It was truly lovely to talk about Dan with someone who cared about him too. We'll be in touch. In the meantime, you will remember what I said about exclusivity, won't you? No one must see your manuscript before we've had chance to decide. Day Delos and Associates is very strict about that."

Theo nodded. "I understand. Aside from Dan, you are the only people who'll see it."

Veronica kissed the air an inch or so from Theo's cheek. "Until it's a bestseller, of course."

CHAPTER 10

Theo stepped lightly as she walked out to Gus's old Ford pickup. She wasn't exactly excited, but there was the first stirring of a kind of hopeful anticipation, cautiously checked by a fear of disappointment, but surging, nonetheless. Day Delos and Associates Management and Veronica Cole gave her a connection with Dan, and it was strangely comforting. It wasn't until she had climbed in and started the engine that she noticed the white Prius across the street. The car itself wasn't extraordinary—it was a popular car— but there was something about the man sitting behind the wheel and talking on the phone. He was bald, wearing small spectacles, a black turtleneck, and a bomber jacket. And he was familiar. A writer, perhaps…someone she'd met at Aimee's or one of the other coffee shops. But she couldn't quite place him. She contemplated at least waving hello…but since he didn't appear to have seen her, she decided it was best to just go and keep awkwardness to a minimum.

She pulled out and began the trek home. She exhaled as she

settled into the drive. The meeting was done, and as far as she could tell, it hadn't been a disaster. And it was three thirty. Surely a long lunch was a good sign. Who'd waste that much time if they weren't seriously considering a potential client?

Veronica's revelation that Dan had been entirely alone played on Theo's mind. She wondered why... Had there been some horrendous accident that had wiped out Dan's family, or had he been an orphan brought up in the system; was he the only child of only children who had now passed away? How could someone have no one at all? No one but his agent to bury him. How lonely Dan Murdoch must have been... She decided she would make dinner for Gus when she got home...a roast like their father would cook on Sundays—when they were living in a house—with gravy and potatoes and peas and biscuits. Their father had never made biscuits, of course, but they were in America now, so she'd add them to her Australian roast. And however weird and embarrassing it was, however much he would mock her for it, she'd tell her brother how much she loved him, how grateful she was for everything he'd done to protect her.

To that end, she stopped at the Dillons Food Store on Eighteenth Street to pick up what she'd need, adding the ingredients for a pavlova to her basket. It was when she was loading the last of her purchases into the back seat of Gus's pickup that she noticed the Prius and its driver again. This time he was parked directly behind her, and close enough for her to see the edges of the cobweb tattoo on his neck. Theo cursed as she dropped the eggs. Leaving the oozing carton where it was, she climbed up behind the wheel. She stopped, trying to calm down before she turned on the engine. She could see the Prius in her rearview mirror.

The driver was watching her, car idling, waiting for her next move. She picked up her phone and opened the door pointing the camera at the Prius. A sharp moment as their eyes met and the Prius plowed into the back of the pickup. Half out of the car, the impact was enough to throw Theo from the truck and onto the roadway. Someone screamed as the sage velvet jacket was shredded against the asphalt.

People rushed out of the store. Kind hands and voices. Shouts for someone to call an ambulance and then in protest as the Prius reversed out and screeched away.

When Gus arrived, Theo was trying to convince the paramedics that she did not need to go to the hospital. There was an ambulance parked in front of his truck and a police car in front of that. Theo was sitting in the back of the ambulance—her jacket ripped, the side of her face and hands grazed. An intrigued crowd had gathered to watch.

"I'd know if there was something broken. I'm just a bit bruised."

Gus pushed his way through the crowd. "Theo, are you all right? What the hell happened?"

Theo reached out and embraced him, holding on tightly. "I want to go home," she whispered into his ear.

A policeman asked for his name.

"Gus Benton. I'm her brother. Can you tell me what happened?"

"Your sister was involved in a hit-and-run, sir." The officer read from his notebook. "A white Prius ran into the rear of a stationary Ford pickup driven by Miss Benton. Miss Benton believes it followed her from Prairie Village, and that the man driving it approached her near her home two days ago. The door of the pickup was open, and Miss Benton was consequently flung out by the impact. The Prius then sped away."

"Did someone get the license plate?"

"Miss Benton says she took a photo of the vehicle shortly before the incident, but her phone has not yet been found."

"It was in my hand when I fell," Theo said vaguely. "I must have dropped it."

"Is she okay?" Gus directed the question at the paramedics. "She seems a bit odd."

The man shrugged. The female officer nodded. "Probably just a bit of shock."

"Gus, I'm fine," Theo insisted. "I just want to go home."

"Can I take her home?" Gus asked. "I can take her to the hospital myself if it's necessary."

The male paramedic threw his arms in the air in a way that shouted be-it-on-your-own-head. The woman said, "Oh, sure. Just keep an eye on her, won't you, buddy?"

Gus promised he would. He called over a man who until then had stood back. "Theo, this is Mac Etheridge—he works with me."

Theo stared at the man who stopped beside her brother and smiled awkwardly. Dressed in a tweed jacket, he looked more like a young academic than a lawyer. "You brought someone..." she said confused.

"He's not my date," Gus replied. "I needed a ride—you took my truck, remember."

"Oh...yes." Theo flinched.

"What's wrong?" Gus took her hand alarmed.

"I'm fine. I was just thinking about your truck. Is there much damage?"

"There's a new dent in the fender, but otherwise the old girl's fine." Gus shook his head. "What kind of moron uses a Prius to ram anything? I'm surprised he managed to drive away." He helped Theo stand. "Careful...are you all right? Mac will drive you home—it'll be more comfortable than the truck. I'll follow."

Theo thanked the paramedics and allowed her brother and Etheridge to guide her gently into the passenger seat of a black Mercedes Benz S-Class Coupe. She settled into the soft leather upholstery, and Etheridge showed her the button to control the seat warmer. It was indeed comfortable.

"Gus, there are groceries in the back of the truck," Theo murmured grabbing his sleeve. "I was going to cook a roast...and a pavlova."

"Good grief! Why?"

"I wanted to say... I just thought I would."

Gus smiled. "I can manage the roast, I think. But we may have to leave the pav for a couple of days."

He patted the roof of the Mercedes and signaled Etheridge to drive on.

As they pulled out on the road, Theo apologized for disrupting his day and Gus's. Etheridge laughed. "You gave us both an excuse to leave a very dull meeting."

"Are you one of Gus's partners?" Theo asked shyly.

"No, I'm not a lawyer, I'm afraid."

"Oh...Gus called you a colleague."

"I work for Gus sometimes when he needs information, or people checked out or found."

"You're a private investigator?"

"More a researcher."

Etheridge parked the Mercedes on the street in front of Gus's house, leaving the driveway clear for the pickup. He sat in the car and chatted with Theo. She told him what exactly had happened.

"He rammed you on purpose?" Mac asked, clearly appalled.

"Yes. He followed me from Prairie Village. I saw him outside the restaurant."

"He was following you? Why?"

Theo found herself telling him. Slowly, hesitantly at first, then in a kind of headlong confessional rush. She was aware she was doing so, but not sure why. He was, after all, almost a complete stranger and yet she was confiding in him about the most horrifying, terrifying moments of her life. For the most part, he listened with only the occasional nod. She told him about the man she'd seen leave Dan's house, what she'd found in there, and the man with blond dreadlocks who had tried to follow her home the next day.

"Have you told the police about this clown?" he asked in the end. "The hair mightn't be real, but that cobweb tattoo sounds like an identifying mark."

Theo nodded. "But until today he was just a weirdo who was trying to…well, I'm not sure what he was trying to do. He didn't ram his car into mine until today."

Gus arrived, pulling into the driveway. He climbed out and inspected the back of his battered pickup as Theo opened the door of the Mercedes. Mac Etheridge slid out from behind the wheel and ran around the car to help Theo out. It might have been quaintly gallant or because the seats were so low that a hand was welcome.

"Sorry I took so long," Gus said. "The back bumper fell off at Ninth and Vermont—had to stop to pick it up." He pulled a face. "It was a little embarrassing, to tell the truth." He handed Mac a large bag of groceries and took the other two himself. "Why don't you stay for dinner, Mac?" He looked pointedly at the bags. "Looks like we have plenty of food."

———

Theo could hear Gus and Mac in the kitchen when she stepped out of the shower. Wiping the condensation from the mirror, she inspected the gravel rash and bruising on the right side of her body and face and glanced regrettably at the sorry remnants of her sage velvet jacket. She put on a dress because it was loose and soft against the damaged parts of her, and went downstairs.

Gus refused to let her help with the cooking and banished her to the couch. "I'll be right. If I remember correctly, we just add salt and throw everything in the oven for a couple of hours." He handed Etheridge a beer and tossed Theo a bottle of Tylenol. "You better take a couple of these," he said filling a glass from the tap.

Theo didn't fight him. She was suddenly tired and sore. Taking the Tylenol, she retired to the couch with Horse to keep her company. She tried not to think about what Gus was doing to the beautiful cut of meat she'd chosen. Mac Etheridge brought her a mug of tea.

"How's it going in there?" she whispered.

He smiled. "Touch and go… He's making the batter now."

"For roast beef?"

"Probably best not to ask."

"What's he doing with the potatoes?"

Mac sighed. "I think he's cross-examining them. Don't worry. I'm sure they'll break eventually."

Theo groaned.

"I'd better go back and…help." Mac glanced somewhat furtively toward the kitchen.

"Come and get me if there's a fire."

Theo wasn't really sure for how long she'd been asleep. She'd dreamt of Dan and Veronica, and Gus and, inevitably, blood. She woke to the sound of men's voices—Mac and Gus discussing what had happened. And another voice—Jacqui's. It was dark; someone had placed a blanket over her. Theo was ravenous and the air was so deliciously fragrant that it made her more so.

"Gus?"

"You're awake. Good—we're starving." Gus stood over her now, his brow furrowing. "Are you okay to get up?"

"Yes, I'm perfectly well." She took his hand and pulled herself out of the couch.

The kitchen table had been set, rather finely.

"That's Mac," Gus said rolling his eyes. "Worked in a restaurant during college and can't seem to shake the training."

Mac ignored him and pulled out a chair for Theo.

Jacqui embraced her. "How are you feeling, you poor thing?" she asked, flinching as she regarded the grazes on the side of Theo's face.

"I'm…hungry."

"Good!" Gus opened the oven and proudly pulled out a roast duck with all the trimmings. "Ta-da!"

Theo stared.

"Don't you like duck? What's wrong with you—duck's delicious!"

"No…I love duck… I just thought I'd bought beef."

"You must have banged your head in the accident," Gus replied solemnly. "Let's eat."

Theo glanced at Mac unsurely. He shrugged. "It's amazing what you can do with salt and an oven."

The conversation that evening was mostly about Dan Murdoch's murder and what had happened since. Once again Theo went over the incident in the parking lot. Gus's eyes darkened. "Don't worry, Theo; Mac will find the bastard."

"Mac?"

"That's what he does…he finds people."

Jacqui laughed. "Missing heirs, bail jumpers, defaulting debtors—there's no one he can't find. Mac's our very own private eye."

"I'm a researcher," Mac said firmly.

"He's been shot," Gus offered by way of qualification.

"By accident," Mac added wearily. "My mom shot me by accident."

"Your mother?" Theo was aghast.

Gus shook his head. "Tough family."

Jacqui was laughing now.

"My uncle was showing her his new .45, and she didn't realize it was still loaded," Mac explained in protest. "She shot me in the leg by accident."

"She alleges," Gus persisted.

"How old were you?" Theo clasped her hand over her mouth as she waited for him to answer.

"Twelve."

"Your poor mother!" Theo shook her head. "She must have been devastated,"

"More embarrassed than devastated, I think. I was on crutches for weeks. She told everyone I'd had an accident on my bike." He smiled wickedly. "I made out like a bandit selling her my silence."

"Mac is by nature entrepreneurial," Gus informed her. "It's the American dream."

Mac raised his glass. He took a sip before he continued more seriously. "You should speak to the police about the fact that the guy who rammed you followed you home the other day, just in case he turns up again. I'll see what I can dig up."

Gus frowned. "If you even think you might have seen him again, Theo, you call me straight away. I'll tell Jenny to put you through regardless of what I'm doing."

"You have to go to New York the day after tomorrow," Jacqui reminded him.

"I can cancel—"

"Don't be absurd!" Theo said alarmed. "I'm not five years old!"

"You might have been killed today…"

"I'll be careful, Gus. I'm just going to stay home and write anyway."

"What if he's worked out where you live?"

"The locksmith came today and fixed all the windows…and I have Horse."

Horse raised his head at the mention of his name and then rolled onto his back.

Gus studied his sister, looking for any sign of false bravado. Theo met his gaze fiercely, silently reminding him that she'd grown up, that she was no longer a terrified little girl. Still, he seemed torn.

"Mac and I will both be in town," Jacqui said placing her hand on Gus's. "If Spiderman shows up, or Theo has any concerns at all, she can call us. You've got to go to New York, Gus. You can't let old Crane go by himself…he'll go too far."

The conversation diverged into tales of John Crane's ability to offend almost anyone, but clients especially. It was an unusual talent for the partner of a law firm.

"Many clients believe that a rude lawyer is somehow better,"

Gus explained. "I expect they think the rest of us are too polite to defend them properly."

"But we always send someone with the grumpy old jerk," Jacqui added. "Just to make sure he doesn't get the entire firm fired. Gus is very good at making it sound like John Crane is joking."

Gus nodded. "It's why they asked me to be a partner."

Theo smiled. "Well, you have to go, then."

CHAPTER 11

Theo tried her best to disguise the abrasions on her face, but there
was only so much she could do. She wanted to keep Gus's concern
to a minimum, and she knew the bruises were a stark and visible
reminder of what had happened. It was not that she was entirely
blasé about the danger, but that she was aware of how hard her
brother had worked for this partnership, how much he had risked
buying into it, and how much he loved living in Lawrence. He'd
thrown in a career at a slick New York firm to buy out Gerard
Purcell, against whom he'd appeared in court once or twice. What
Purcell had said to convince Gus to buy his share in a small Kansan
firm, Theo had no idea. She wished that she could talk her brother
into taking the money he'd negotiated out of the trust for her. But
Gus would have none of it.

He'd taken her into the police station before work the day
before. Detective Mendes had seemed irritated by the fact that
they had not come in immediately, muttering about the inepti-
tude of the officer on the scene. He intimated that Gus at least

should have known better. Gus became noticeably curt with the detective. Theo intervened to send her brother to work while she waited for the police sketch artist, and then worked with her to come up with an image of Spiderman. When she was finished, Mendes had driven her home himself. He'd asked her about her writing, and though Theo knew that this was an unofficial extension of her interrogation, she also had nothing to hide. Except that Veronica Cole had asked her not to say anything about her manuscript. And so Theo was vague about her work, redirecting his questions about the story and finally mumbling some joke about spoilers that, even to her, sounded coy.

Veronica probably hadn't meant disclosures to the police, but Theo didn't want to risk it. The attentions of Day Delos and Associates seemed too miraculous, so fragile that any pressure might cause it to disintegrate and disappear.

Gus had stopped in at lunchtime and then come home early to check on her, despite her protests that she was fine. They'd gone back to the parking lot outside the grocery store to look again for her cell phone, before stopping downtown to buy her a new one when the search proved fruitless. That evening they'd eaten on the couch while Gus worked and Theo read. Horse had barked ferociously at one point, but investigation revealed nothing. Horse had been known to overreact to cats. They'd brought him inside and all seemed well with the world again.

Gus was leaving for the airport straight after breakfast. He'd be back the next evening. And Horse would be only too pleased to sleep indoors. With an uneventful day intervening, they were all a lot less uneasy.

Theo made scrambled eggs while Gus ran around the house looking for files and briefs and socks. She added the leftover duck, which she assumed Gus had ordered in, when he did whatever he did to the beef she'd bought. She asked him about it as she served the eggs on toast.

"Ex-client who's a chef at On the Hill. Jac called in and picked it up."

"What happened to the beef?"

"Horse. It turns out he likes his meat very well done."

Gus ate his eggs while shaving in the kitchen. He delivered garbled instructions about being careful as he brushed his teeth. Theo gathered his files for him and searched the living room for his phone. John Crane's car had pulled up and was sounding its horn when Gus raced out with his tie stuffed in his pocket and his arms full of files. "Oh…Mac may come round to borrow a thing."

"A thing?"

"Yes…a tennis racquet. He wants to borrow my tennis racquet."

"A tennis racquet? Why?"

"He wants to play tennis, I suppose…something about the country club… Gotta go."

"Where is your tennis racquet?"

"In one of the cupboards. Lock the door."

Theo shook her head as she closed the door after him. "Fly safe." Mac could have easily picked up the tennis racquet at dinner the night before last. She had no doubt that Gus had asked the poor man to check that she was all right.

She cleaned up after breakfast and fed Horse before letting him out into the backyard. Now that she'd promised to stay home, the thought of going out was enticing. She laughed at the predictable contrariness of it, with no intention of giving in to the impulse.

Theo had decided to begin a new novel that day. A ghost story.

The idea had set seed when she and Dan had discussed the Stull Cemetery. Perhaps that's why she loved thinking about it. It was a little like talking to Dan again. On the kitchen table she set out and taped several pages of clean paper end to end, and upon the blank pages, she began to plot a general sequence of events—a plot derived from a single flyaway thought that had passed through her mind in that conversation with Dan. A strange thought that came from she knew not where. Were the dead haunted by the living? After Dan had died, the thought had returned in quiet moments when loneliness caught her unawares, and she had started to mull over the possibilities.

It was past midday when the doorbell rang, and Theo was startled out of her immersion. The banner was scrawled with hundreds of notes and arrows and the odd symbol that only she understood. She glanced at it with not a small measure of satisfaction before she went to the door. A squint through the peephole revealed Mac Etheridge on the doorstep, and she remembered the tennis racquet. She opened the door and invited him in. "I'm afraid I haven't found Gus's tennis racquet yet... Would you like a cup of tea...or a beer? Gus drinks something called Copperhead."

"In that case, I'll have tea." Mac glanced at the kitchen table. "Is that a manifesto of some sort?"

"Not entirely. It's the notes for my next novel."

"May I look?"

"If you'd like," Theo said a little shyly. "It probably won't make much sense."

"Would you explain it to me?"

Theo hesitated.

Mac apologized. "Sorry...being nosy is a something of a professional habit, I'm afraid."

"Oh no, I didn't mean… It's a ghost story."

"For real…a horror then?"

"Not exactly." Theo explained the concept.

Mac folded his arms, listening intently. "So why are the dead afraid of the living?"

Theo thought about that. "For the same reason that we're afraid of ghosts…because seeing them might mean we are about to join them. Perhaps the dead are afraid to live as much as we are afraid to die."

Mac was nodding before she'd finished speaking. "That's brilliant."

Theo stopped. "Really?…Thank you."

Over tea they talked some more about the new book. Theo was surprised by how much she enjoyed talking about her work at this stage, when it was all just possibilities, and how much conversation helped the nebulous uncertain ideas coagulate into a storyline. Mac wasn't a writer. He could not, unlike Dan, offer her advice on technique or voice, but he was interested, and right now that was enough.

"I better see if I can find that tennis racquet," Theo said eventually.

"Oh, yes…that's why I'm here."

She rummaged through various cupboards before she found an old wooden racquet in a box under the stairs.

"I'm not really sure what you could do with this." Theo said as she handed it to Mac.

His brow rose. "An antique fair, perhaps."

"Gus said you had a game at the country club."

"The country club?" He laughed, though he did not elaborate on why the idea was so absurd.

"I'm sorry Gus dragged you out here to check on me," Theo sighed. "As you can see, I'm fine—there was no need to waste your time."

Mac smiled. "It would only have been a waste of time if I actually needed a functional tennis racquet." He glanced at his watch. "I don't have to be back in the office for a couple of hours. I don't suppose you'd care to have lunch in town?"

Theo glanced at the dining table spread with her notes and then the window, which was lit with the cold muted light of winter sun. She suspected she would be feeling restless and claustrophobic by that evening if she didn't step out for a little a while at least. And she was more than a little intrigued about what Mac Etheridge did for a living. "I'd love to."

———

Johnny's Tavern was in North Lawrence—it reminded Theo of an Australian pub. They removed outer layers of scarves and coats and ordered burgers and mozzarella sticks.

Theo asked Mac about his work…what exactly he meant by research.

"Mostly it's sitting in front of a screen, going through records, searching databases, government files, social media, that sort of thing. Everybody leaves a trail of sorts. Nowadays it tends to be electronic."

"But not always?"

Mac shrugged. "Gossip, rumor, and what people saw are still handy."

"So the man who rammed me with his Prius…have you found out anything about him?"

"I'm afraid Spiderman's body art is not all that original or unique. There are a couple of gangs who favor cobweb tattoos… or it could have been done in prison. It's a shame the blond dreadlocks weren't real. That at least would have been more distinctive."

Theo helped herself to a mozzarella stick. "You know, to be honest, I'm inclined to believe Spiderman was just your garden variety pest. I probably panicked him when I took that photograph." She pulled apart the battered morsel, stretching the elastic cheese till it finally broke apart. "I don't think we'll ever see him again."

"Rear-ending your outfit was a rather extreme reaction," Mac said frowning. "That worries me…but you could be right."

Theo changed the subject. She didn't really want to think about Spiderman, or murder. "Are you from Lawrence, Mac?"

"I was born in Great Falls, Montana. My family moved here after the accident. My mother thought everybody back home would always think of her as the woman who shot her son."

"Was she right?"

"You betcha." The corners of his eyes crinkled when he smiled. "Mom was president of the church auxiliary. It was the most exciting thing that had happened in Great Falls for a while."

"It must have been awful."

"For her, certainly. I became a kind of schoolyard folk hero in Great Falls once I decided that the fame was worth more than what Mom was paying me to say I'd had a bike accident. By the time the story had been round town a couple of times, Mom had hunted me down, put a gun to my head, stabbed me with a hunting knife for good measure, and then gone after my brother." Mac chuckled, clearly enjoying the memory. "We packed up and moved to Lawrence to escape the scandal."

"And did you? Escape it, I mean."

"Pretty much. New town, new school—Mom had by then persuaded me not be as forthcoming about the incident."

Theo stared at him for a moment, trying to work out what parts of the story were fictions or exaggeration. She saw nothing that told her, and in the end she laughed, deciding that it didn't matter.

He asked about her parents, hers and Gus's. She answered, guiltily aware that they still had no idea she'd left law school, let alone the events of the past couple of weeks.

"So they were hippies?" Mac said clearly amused.

"The Tasmanian term is *ferals*," Theo corrected. "And the verb you're looking for is *are*." She told him about the various communes of her childhood, the unorthodox, carefree, wild life that was replaced by boarding school when she was in her teens.

"That must have been a shock."

"I was a rebellious teenager. When your parents are ferals, you rebel by becoming quiet and conventional and wanting to be a lawyer."

"Gus too?"

"Possibly." Habit prevented Theo from revealing that Gus had been sent to live with their American grandfather to ensure he didn't come to the attention of the Tasmanian police. Habit, loyalty, guilt, and shame. "Gus was always Gus... Apparently he wanted to be a professional surfer."

"For real?"

"Yes...I'm not even sure he can swim."

Mac signaled for the bill. "All the more reason to stay on the board, I suppose."

Theo nodded. It gave her an idea.

They stepped out into the first drifting flutters of snow. Theo raised her face to the sky, delighted. She'd arrived in the States the previous February, so this was barely her second winter, and she had not stopped being surprised by snow. The past days had been cold, but she'd been too preoccupied of late to even look forward to the promise of the season. "Oh, my God! Look!"

Mac laughed. "We'd better get you home before the roads get crazy."

Traffic was already becoming heavier as Kansans tried to get their cars off the roads before the fall became heavy. The snow was beginning to settle on the asphalt. Even so, it was only a couple of minutes before Mac was turning the black Mercedes left onto her street from Ninth. Theo was focused on finding her gloves, and so she did not see why Mac swerved and braked hard. The car lost traction, fishtailing wildly.

CHAPTER 12

Theo screamed, certain they were going to roll over, and for several moments it looked like they might, but then Mac managed to get the vehicle under control. He pulled over and stopped the car immediately. "Are you okay, Theo?"

"Yes. What happened?"

Mac unbuckled his seat belt and opened the driver's side door. "That was Horse!"

"On the road?" Theo released her belt and climbed out of the car. "Oh, God, did you hit him?"

"I don't think so… Don't call for him. He might run across the road again to reach you."

They dodged the traffic to get to the other side of the street and ran up a few houses to where Mac had seen Horse emerge onto the road. Only then did Theo call while Mac kept his eye on the road for cars just in case.

At first there was nothing, and then as Theo's calls became pleas, the hound poked out from behind a hedge. He trotted over, looking almost sheepish. Theo dropped to her knees and hugged him, relieved and perplexed. "What are you doing out here, Horsey?" Gus's backyard was completely secure, and she'd checked that the gate was latched.

The snow was quite heavy now, and wet.

"I'll walk back with Horse," Theo volunteered as the dog rolled in the snow. "You don't want him in your beautiful car."

"Don't be silly… It's freezing and it's only a car." Mac took off his tie and turned it into a makeshift leash. They pulled Horse, whose short-lived freedom had left him rather excited, and pushed him into the small back seat of the Mercedes Coupe. Theo winced as the wet hound shook himself all over the leather upholstery. Mac did not seem to notice.

As they pulled into the driveway, Theo spotted the gate to the backyard. It was wide open.

"That's not right," she said shaking her head. "I know that gate was closed."

"We couldn't have pulled out without seeing that it wasn't," Mac agreed, frowning.

A glance, and the mutual realization that someone had deliberately opened the gate.

They coaxed Horse, who had now made himself comfortable, out of the Mercedes. Theo held on to the dog with the leash fashioned out of Mac's tie as they walked up to the gate.

Mac pointed to the ground. "There's no sign of footprints, so it must have been opened before it started snowing. I'll just go check out the yard."

Theo placed a cautioning hand on his arm. "What if he's still in there?"

Mac looked through the gate. "If he is, he'll be frozen

stiff...and Horse doesn't seem concerned, so it's likely he's long gone."

Anxiously, Theo let him go. As he'd predicted, Mac found nothing. The windows facing the backyard looked into the kitchen and living room. But there were no signs that anyone had tried to break in.

Theo brought Horse into the house with them and found a towel to deal with the wet dog issue. Mac put the kettle on to boil. Theo was quietly glad he made no mention of leaving immediately. She didn't want to overreact, but she was unnerved. Someone had come into the backyard. Had they known there would be no one home to stop them? Was someone monitoring the house? Was it Spiderman?

"When's Gus getting back?" Mac asked.

"Tomorrow."

"Would you mind if I came by tonight?" he asked. "I know it's absurd, and a little hysterical, but I'd just like to make sure..."

"I don't mind," Theo said quickly. She didn't think it was absurd or hysterical, but she wasn't ready to admit she felt uneasy. There might, after all, be some simple and perfectly ordinary reason why the gate was left open.

He made her a cup of tea. "I'm going to leave my car here."

"But it's snowing."

He snorted. "I'm from Montana, remember? This is a mere frost by Montana standards." He took a business card out of his wallet and handed it to her. "My number. I'll walk up a couple of blocks and call someone from the office to come get me. That way it will look like I haven't left." He glanced at the kitchen table. "You'll be able to get on with your plotting, and I'll be back tonight."

"I'm sorry… You must have things to do."

He met her eye. "I am honestly being overcautious, Theo. Some kid might have opened the gate to play with Horse or just to be a nuisance, or the latch might have come loose in the wind."

Theo nodded. "Absolutely, it was probably the wind."

Mac elected to leave via the back door, which was not visible from the road. She opened it for him and thanked him for lunch.

"You'll lock it after me, won't you?"

"Yes, of course."

⌇

Theo returned to the ideas she had spread out on the table. At first, she would look up often, watch the windows, listen, but in time she became consumed by the story, which was being pieced from the fragments of ideas like a jigsaw revealing its greater picture. She was fascinated by the accidental linkages, motifs that seemed to emerge from nowhere.

She wondered what Dan would think of it. He'd have advice on structure and perspective and voice. She was only now beginning to see how lucky she had been to have him these past months. He'd nurtured her as a writer, held her hand, been honest but gentle with his criticisms and lavish with his praise. Theo missed his voice, his conversation, his laughter. She regretted sleeping with him, only because now she missed so much more. If she tried, she could still feel his hands on her body…and his lips on hers. Sadness had lodged like a hard stone somewhere below her heart, and she was a little afraid it would always be there… She couldn't imagine it not being there.

Horse lay on his back at her feet, apparently exhausted by his break for freedom. Theo bent occasionally to rub his belly, grateful that they had found him before anything happened. She shuddered at the thought of having to tell Gus that she had lost his dog.

Sherlock came to mind then in a memory first stirred when Mac had asked about Tasmania, and that had been struggling for her attention ever since. Theo tried to turn away from it because she knew where the memory would end, and she didn't wish to think about it. But it was too late. Already her mind was moving from the cattle dog Gus had given her before he left, to the reason her big brother was sent away. Theo remembered the look on his face when he'd found Jake Curtis with his hands under her dress—disgust, fury, grief. The fight. The knife. The blood. Theo could feel her heart pounding now. She sat down on the floor before she fell, and tried to concentrate on slowing her breathing, and forcing her memory to Sherlock instead. Sherlock, who'd slept in her bed, who protected her, who remained by her side till the day she'd left for boarding school. Who'd jumped up on his arthritic hind legs to lick her face every time she came home, and who, when he eventually died, had left her feeling scared and alone all over again.

She talked to Horse about Sherlock, burying the other memories beneath thoughts of the old dog who had made her feel safe.

The knock at the door took Theo by surprise. For a moment she froze, and then she told herself not to be ridiculous. A glance through the peephole revealed an older man, shirt and jacket in clashing plaids, snow boots, red muffler, and a flat cap. Theo summoned Horse to her side and opened the door.

The visitor removed his hat. "Good afternoon, ma'am. Howsit goin'?"

"Hello. Can I help you Mr.—?"

"Winslow. Burt Winslow. I live a couple of blocks up at number 277."

"What can I do for you, Mr. Winslow?"

"Are you Miss Benton?"

"Yes—I'm Theo Benton…this is Horse." Theo thought it prudent to bring his attention to the dog, just in case. Though, as he knew her name, she expected he was a friend of Gus's.

"Dang! That pup is part pony!" He took a step back to fully appreciate the dog's size. "I have something for you," Winslow reached under his jacket, pulled out a large folded envelope, and handed it to her. "It was delivered to my place… Some folks write their ones funny, you see… Makes 'em look like sevens. I'd opened it before I saw it wasn't for me, I'm afraid. Mrs. Winslow wanted to send it back, but I figured it was worth checking if there was a Miss Benton at number 211—which it seems there is."

Theo looked at the envelope. It was large, but thin, torn open on one end. "There is indeed. Thank you, Mr. Winslow. It was very kind of you to bring it by."

"It's no trouble at all, Miss Benton."

Theo turned the envelope over to read the return name and address. She froze. Dan Murdoch.

"That's a pretty sweet ride you've got." Burt Winslow looked over at the Mercedes parked in the driveway.

"Ride?…Oh, that's Mac's car…" Theo tried to keep her voice from shaking. "When did you say this was delivered, Mr. Winslow?"

"I can't rightly say for sure. Mrs. Winslow and I got back from visiting the kids in Virginia the day before yesterday… There was a pile of mail waiting for us. Not as much as there would have been once, mind you. Folks don't really send letters anymore—a dying art. Anyways, we'd been in Virginia for ten days."

"Oh…"

"I'm sorry…was it urgent?"

Theo forced a smile. "I don't think so."

"Well, I should let you get back to your day."

Theo thanked him for his trouble and his kindness. She invited him in for a hot drink because he'd obviously walked from number 277, and it was snowing, but to her relief he declined.

"Mrs. Winslow will start to fret if I stay out too long in this weather."

Theo waited till he was out of the front gate before she shut the door and reached into the envelope.

It began, for want of a better term, as a love letter. Dan wrote of the day they'd set out to visit the Stull Cemetery and had spent together instead. His words made her blush, and they made her lonely. And then he wrote about *Underneath*, which he'd read in one sitting through the night because he couldn't bring himself to leave it. He told her how much he admired it and how honored he would be to send it to a friend of his who was with the Sandra Djikstra Literary Agency in California.

Theo dabbed at the letter with her shirt, blotting tears and ink. She read it over.

Another knock at the door. She checked quickly. Mac Etheridge, shaking the snow from his hair with a bag in each hand: a bulging plastic one from India Palace and a smaller brown paper bag. Theo opened the door. His smile faded as he saw her face.

"What's happened?" he said, alarmed. "Did he come back?"

Theo shook her head.

"Are you okay, Theo?"

"Yes…come in. You must be frozen…"

"I think our dinner might be… We might have to reheat it."
He followed her into the kitchen and placed the bags on the bench.

"Is there something I can do?" he asked.

"No…I'll just put it all in the microwave."

He leant back against the old pantry cupboard, his arms
folded. "I meant about whatever has upset you. Just say if it's none
of my business."

Theo swallowed. A moment to decide to trust Mac Etheridge,
and she told him about Burt Winslow and the letter he'd delivered.

Mac was a little alarmed that she had opened the door, all
things considered.

"It was an old man on his own…and I had Horse."

"He might have been armed, Theo."

" You're right. I should have been more careful."

"So this letter was written…?"

"It's not dated. But it was after I'd given him my manuscript."
Theo busied herself reheating Indian food. "He was… I found his
body the next day."

Mac found dishes and cutlery.. "How did Murdoch generally get in touch with you?" he asked. "Was he always moved to
penmanship?"

Theo served out generous portions of rice and curry, and they
took the plates to the living room as the kitchen table was buried
in her notes. Horse followed and lay on the rug, regarding them
with eyes that seemed determined to let them know that he was
open to Indian cuisine. "No. I saw him nearly every day…but
if there was anything, he'd phone or text." She looked at Mac
sharply. "Before you say it, he wasn't that old."

"I wasn't going to say it. My grandmother knows how to text."

He smiled. "But it is a little odd that he would choose to write a letter on this occasion."

Theo could feel the color rising in her cheeks. "It was a…the kind of letter you'd write by hand." She picked up the second bag, surprised to hear the contents clinking as she did so.

"I dropped by Cottins and picked up a padlock and chain for the gate," Mac said. "It'll be a bit of a nuisance, but at least you'll be sure that Horse isn't walking the streets."

"Oh…thank you." Theo hadn't planned to let Horse out of her sight until Gus got back, but a padlock would also work. There was something very thoughtfully practical about Mac Etheridge.

They did not talk of the letter as they ate. Instead, Mac told Theo tales of Great Falls, Montana, and a family that seemed prone to public disaster. His brother Caleb's ill-fated attempt to build an ark, which ended in him being mauled by the breeding pair of cats he'd selected to survive the next flood. He made her smile and then laugh.

"So how did you end up a private eye?" she asked.

"Didn't every kid want to be Dick Tracy?"

"In the fifties, maybe."

He laughed. "I work for law firms and corporate entities, doing what really amounts to research. I have a knack with computers; I know how to get into databases and systems. I'm afraid calling me a private eye is somewhat romantic."

"I see." Theo blinked. "You're a hacker."

Mac sighed. "You and Gus seem to share a penchant for the sensational."

"And you seem determined to convince the world that you are some kind of lower-order clerk…which I suppose would be an excellent disguise for a private eye."

He groaned, placing his plate on top of her empty one. "I'll make coffee."

"I can do that." Theo started to get up.

"No, let me. Gus has been teaching me to make Australian coffee. I need the practice. Come on, Horse… Looking at me like a starving waif has worked."

Horse followed him, his tail creating its own breeze. Theo curled up on the couch, listening as Mac moved about the kitchen making coffee. She heard the water running and dishes being washed. She smiled… His mother had trained him well, but then, you probably would mind a woman who'd shot you.

Theo was glad he'd come round. She was no longer as unnerved as she had been that afternoon. In fact, she'd decided the gate had been opened by a precocious neighborhood child, or perhaps Burt Winslow had called earlier with the letter and gone to the backyard to see if there was anyone home. The gate was left unlatched accidentally.

And Dan's letter had refocused her.

By the time Mac returned with coffee, Theo had retrieved the emergency chocolates she kept in a hollowed-out volume on the bookshelf.

He eyed the cache, amused. "Most people hide their valuables."

"These are my valuables." She inhaled courage and held it for a moment before handing him the letter Burt Winslow had delivered. She told him what it was. "Please don't read the other side."

CHAPTER 13

Mac Etheridge did not lower his eyes to the page. "I don't have to read any of it, Theo."

Theo swallowed. "Yes, you do. I want to hire you."

"I beg your pardon?"

"I want to hire you to find out who killed Dan Murdoch."

"It's not really what I—"

"I can afford it," she said quickly. "Whatever your fees are, I can pay them."

Still, he did not look down at the letter. "Theo, the police are—"

"Please, Mac. Dan was...he was my...my friend..." She brushed angrily at the tears that broke through her resolve against them. "He has no one else...no family. I need to do something." The tears were unstoppable now.

Mac hesitated. He placed his hand tentatively on her shoulder clearly unsure of his place. Theo only sobbed harder. In the end he put his arms around her and let her cry. Eventually, she stopped.

"I'm so sorry," she said, embarrassed. She pulled away from

the sodden patch on his shirt, mortified. She had never thought of herself as weepy, and yet now she seemed so easily reduced to tears...and she felt reduced, though Mac was unwaveringly kind and courteous. "I'm not sure why I'm so—would you read the letter, please?" She stood up. "I'll go find you one of Gus's shirts..."

Mac let her go.

Theo gave him a couple of minutes to read, glad too for a moment to gather herself, and returned with a business shirt and a T-shirt. Gus had placed the page down on the coffee table. Theo didn't know why she was certain that he had not read the first part of the letter in her absence, but she was. "I wasn't sure which you'd prefer," she said, holding up the garments.

He smiled. "Since I've lost my tie anyway, I'll take the T-shirt."

Mac changed while she returned the rejected shirt to Gus's closet.

"What's a Hilltop Hood?" he asked as he pulled the T-shirt over his head. "Is it an Australian term?"

"It's an Australian band." Theo responded from the other room. "Though I think Gus was over here when he first became a fan. I sent him that T-shirt."

Theo returned to the living room and sat down again. "Did you...?" she asked looking at the letter.

"Yes." He watched her nervously fold his soiled shirt.

"Did it tell you anything?"

Mac shrugged. "The writer has excellent penmanship, but the cursive is old-fashioned. I'd guess it belongs to someone over fifty years of age who possibly attended a Catholic elementary school."

"Dan might have been that old," Theo said quietly. "I have no idea where he went to school."

"The agent you met, the day Spiderman drove into you—" Mac asked.

"Veronica Cole."

"Yes—she's from this agency, Sandra Djikstra, I presume."

Theo shook her head. "No. She's from Day Delos and Associates. They represented Dan."

"Then how exactly did she get your manuscript?"

Theo frowned. Mac was right. "I suppose he changed his mind and sent it to Day Delos instead."

"Seems odd, though."

"To be fair, I had asked him to send it to Day Delos. It's just that he refused...then."

"Do you still have the envelope this came in?"

"Yes." Theo retrieved the torn envelope from the shelf on which she'd left it when she first opened Dan's letter.

Mac looked at it carefully. "It's a large envelope for a letter," he observed.

"Perhaps it's the only envelope Dan had."

"These last lines: *I am so deeply honored that you have trusted your manuscript to me. I know how hard it is to allow your thoughts, your dreams and secrets, to be viewed by strangers. I want to return that trust.* What did he mean by returning your trust?"

"I suppose he meant sending my manuscript to Sandra Djikstra or Day Delos."

Mac's brows furrowed. He turned the envelope over in his hand slowly.

"What if it wasn't? Could there have once been something else in this envelope? This fella, Winslow, had already opened it, right?"

Theo nodded, a little shocked. It had never occurred to her

that the envelope had contained something else...but it was possible. And she remembered what Veronica had said about Dan's missing manuscript. But why would he have sent her a hard copy when he could just have emailed the digital file?

Mac pointed out that the envelope bore several postage stamps, but no postmark.

"So what does that mean?" Theo asked, confused.

"Well, first, there's an excess of postage on the envelope... much more than would be required for just one letter...which corroborates the notion that there was something else in the envelope when Murdoch stuck the stamps on it."

"I see." Theo did see now, and she was impressed that Mac saw it from the outset.

"As for the missing postmark," he continued, "it could be a number of things. The post office might just have missed marking it, which does happen, but it's very unusual. It's more likely that it was not delivered via the postal service." Mac tapped the envelope on the coffee table as he contemplated. "He might have delivered it himself, but why would he apply postage stamps if he was going to do that...and why wouldn't he just come in and talk to you if he was going to walk out here?"

"Gus," Theo offered.

"That's true. He might not have been ready to meet your protective older brother...but it wasn't delivered here, remember. It was delivered to 277. Was Murdoch likely to have made that mistake?"

Theo shook her head. "I don't think so. He dropped me home after...a couple of days before. He'd been here before."

"So it's more likely he gave the letter to someone to post, and that person decided to hand-deliver it instead."

"Maybe…does it matter?" Theo was more than a little fascinated with the systematic logical manner in which Mac Etheridge's mind worked.

"Possibly not." Mac's eyes narrowed like he was homing in on some unseen thing. "Dan Murdoch wrote this letter, gave it to someone to post, then changed his mind, and sent your manuscript to Day Delos and Associates a few hours before he died."

"It's possible."

Mac conceded that. "Yes, of course it is. I wonder what made him change his mind, though."

"And why didn't he tell me that he had?" Theo said quietly. Surely Dan had known how much his support had meant to her.

Mac paused. "Perhaps he intended to surprise you or something equally stupid… Men in love can be idiotic."

Theo looked up. "I don't think he was in love with me."

"I don't see why he wouldn't be."

Theo thought about it. "No. Even if he was in—even if he was, Dan wasn't some giddy teenager. When I asked him to introduce me to Day Delos, he was adamant that he would not, that they were not the right agents for me." Haltingly, she told Mac how she had begged Dan Murdoch to take her manuscript to Day Delos and Associates, how he would not be moved on the subject. "Something must have happened for him to change his mind."

Mac shrugged. "And maybe that something is related to why he was killed."

"So, you'll take the case?" Theo cringed inwardly as the words left her mouth. When did her life become a pulp fiction?

"I'll talk to Gus about it."

"Gus?" Theo ignited. "What on earth for? I don't need Gus's permission to—"

"Of course, you don't, but I'm afraid I do," Mac said calmly into her indignation. "Not only is Crane, Hayes and Benton a client, Theo, but Gus is my friend."

"But—"

"I will help, Theo, but you can't actually hire me. And I have to let Gus know in case it gets awkward."

For a moment Theo said nothing. "Yes," she said in the end, embarrassed by her own prickliness. "I'm sorry—kid sister syndrome. I should speak to Gus, too. I owe him at least that."

They talked about Theo's reverse ghost story then, sharing the stash of chocolates while they discussed the possibilities. Mac recounted tales of apparitions in Great Falls, most of which were more funny than haunting, and Colonel Eldridge, whose spirit apparently resided not only in the hotel he'd built in Lawrence but the ones that replaced it. She told him about Min Min lights and George Grover, the brutal flagellator, reportedly killed by his convict charges, who appeared from time to time around the Richmond Bridge.

Gus called at about ten. He sounded tired.

"Difficult clients with more money than ethics," he said when she asked. "We only got back to the hotel five minutes ago. Everything okay at home?"

"Yes, fine." Theo decided not to bother him with the details of Horse's escape. That could wait.

"Mac there?" he asked.

"How did you know that?"

"You sound even less Aussie when there are Yanks in earshot. When it's just me, you sound vaguely like a girl from Tassie should."

"Oh." Theo hadn't been aware of any change in her inflection.

He laughed. "Put Mac on, will you?"

She handed her phone to Mac, who jotted a few notes as he spoke to Gus. She could hear only Mac's side of the conversation. "Now?... Can it wait till morning?...All right—leave it with me...*mate*."

Theo smiled. Gus used the word *mate* to invoke some kind of blokey Australian law that rendered the request that accompanied it unrefusable. "What does he want you to do?" she asked when Mac had hung up.

"He needs me to track down some information tonight. Apparently, the client is busting his chops." He frowned. "It should only take an hour or so."

She smiled. "I'll be fine, Mac. I don't know how Horse got out, but I suspect it was just one of those things." She ruffled the hound's ears. "The ratbag probably talked some kid into setting him free. You really don't have to babysit me."

He hesitated.

"Go. And for pity's sake, take your car while you can still get it out of the driveway without a shovel!"

He laughed. "Yes, ma'am!" He pulled on his jacket and draped his scarf around the back of his neck. "If there's anything, you have my number."

Theo got back to the plot on the kitchen table. But she couldn't concentrate, her mind instead on what might have been in the envelope. Perhaps Dan had taken it out himself before sealing the envelope...but if he hadn't, then Burt Winslow must have taken it. It didn't make any sense. If Winslow was a mail thief, why deliver anything to her at all? She would never have known. God, she'd invited him into the house.

She picked up the letter and read it again. Mac was right. The last line did sound like something more than just assistance finding an agent, but what could Dan possibly have wanted to send her?

Horse got up from under the table and walked to the back door and whined.

"Do you need to go out, Horsey?" Theo placed the letter back on the bookshelf under her old copy of *Airborne* and opened the back door. Horse ran out barking furiously. It was snowing lightly, and the hound's paws left imprints in the fresh powder.

The footprints caught her eye immediately. From the gate to the window, to the back door, and then out again. The gate had once more been left open.

Theo called Horse back, running out to the gate in socks to shut it before the dog got out again. There was a figure across the road, walking briskly. The red plaid was distinct against the snowfall. Theo slammed the gate shut and dropped the latch into place before running for the back door. Her wet socks slipped on the floorboards, but she didn't pause to notice. She banged around the kitchen until she found where she'd left second bag that Mac had brought with him and pulled out a heavy-gauge chain and padlock. She went back out immediately and chained the gate shut, clicking the padlock into place with a force that was both angry and panicked.

Many men wore plaid lumberjack jackets in Lawrence, but she was sure it was Burt Winslow across the road. Shivering now, she called Horse into the house, locked the back door, and removed her sodden socks. She couldn't feel her feet, and the shivering became quite violent. Theo picked up the phone and called the police.

CHAPTER 14

Where is Primus's book... the word he promised us? Did whoever killed him
take it?"

Frodo 14

What would it be worth?

ThinBlue

You buying or selling?

Wayward Son

I might know someone who's selling. What's it worth?

ThinBlue

Fuck off! You don't have shit!

Patriot Warrior

We can raise money. But we'd need proof.

   WKWWK

   Wayward Son

———

Caleb waited for a reply. Was ThinBlue a cop? That might be how he got hold of the manuscript. A cop may have taken it from the crime scene. Or maybe he was some scammer. The site had all sorts of people join lately, newcomers to the way of the Shield. But if he was actually some light-fingered cop, then he could well have Dan Murdoch's manuscript, and if that was the case, Caleb was determined to acquire it, buy it if he had to. Of course, he didn't have that kind of cash himself, but he knew people who would give it to him. He was one of Primus's lieutenants… Well, he was sure he would have been if Primus had selected lieutenants. This was his responsibility.

Caleb returned to the screen and began typing—he had found Primus, identified him as Dan Murdoch. He would find ThinBlue as well.

———

The Lawrence Police Department was, it seemed, particularly busy that evening. It was always the case when it snowed, and people appeared to forget how to drive. An officer took down her details. Theo told him what she'd seen. He asked her if she was reporting a crime of any sort. Theo stuttered. He sighed. "We'll alert any units in your area to keep an eye out, ma'am, but it could be that this Mr. Winslow found more of your mail that had been mistakenly delivered to him and was trying to return it."

"Wouldn't he have come to the front door then?"

"Perhaps he got no reply and thought he'd try the back instead. He really hasn't done anything aside from leaving a gate open, ma'am."

Theo put down the phone, irritated. But the officer was right, mortifyingly so. She couldn't even be sure that the man she saw was Winslow, and footprints would have been long obscured in the current snowfall.

She still couldn't feel her feet properly. She checked that both doors and the windows were locked and then went upstairs to take a shower. The hot water brought the circulation back to her feet. She got into her warmest flannel pajamas and two pairs of socks before padding downstairs again to make cocoa. She warmed milk on the stove and checked the doors and windows once more. Confirming for herself that they were secure, she finally began to feel warm again, or less cold at least.

She turned off the stovetop and poured the hot milk over generous scoops of cocoa powder, and returned to her notes on the kitchen table. She sipped as she contemplated: her protagonist would need to be dead for the narrative to work, and to explore the idea, she would need to build the world of the dead somehow. She thought about Dan then, or perhaps she'd never stopped thinking about him. Theo was self-aware enough to wonder if this conceit was a way to think about Dan's death from the safety of story, to allow herself to dream about him, to miss him.

It was only when she heard the knock that she realized that she had been listening for it. Mac's voice. "Theo, it's me."

She tried not to run to the door, and when she did, she told herself that it was because she didn't want him waiting in the cold.

"I'm sorry I took so long," he said, shaking the snow off his hair before he stepped inside. It seemed to be blizzarding. He looked at her, smiling faintly at the dachshund-patterned pajamas. "Did I wake you?"

She shook her head. "I got wet and so…" She told him about the footprints, the plaid-jacketed figure across the road, the pad-lock, and the police.

He didn't dismiss her alarm, opening the front door again to check the street.

"You think he might still be there?" Theo asked anxiously.

"Probably not—it's pretty cold, but he approached the house once I'd left. Maybe he was watching the house… You said he was elderly?"

"Not rocking-chair-and-blanket elderly, but definitely retired." She went through their conversation in her mind. "He has kids in Virginia. Grown-up, I presume." She made a fresh batch of cocoa. "This doesn't make sense. He refused when I invited him in—"

Mac rolled up his sleeves and began washing the pot and the mug she'd left in the sink. "You invited him in?"

"I thought he'd walked from number 277 just to return my mail… A cup of tea seemed the least I could do."

Mac rubbed the shadow on his jaw. "You know, Theo, it could be that whomever is coming into the backyard is not related to Winslow at all. It could be you've got a garden variety Peeping Tom on your hands. Who lives next door?"

"On the left—Mrs. Milson. She's about one hundred and sixty years old. Used to work for the Red Cross. On the right, a bunch of students, I think. They haven't been there long, and I can't be certain which of them actually live there. Gus told me to knock on their door if I'm ever in desperate need of beer."

Mac nodded. "I'll see what I can find out. In the meantime, I might just call on number 277 tomorrow morning."

"I'll come with you?"

He shook his head. "I was just going to make up some plausible excuse... He'd recognize you."

"He'd recognize your car," Theo replied. "I'll tell him that I wondered if something might have fallen out of the envelope... that I came by in case it was with his other mail."

Mac sipped the cocoa she'd handed him. "That's very private eye of you."

It was still early when Mac Etheridge arrived the next morning, but Theo had never been prone to sleeping in, even when the night had been late. It had stopped snowing, though Lawrence was under a glistening six-inch blanket.

Theo pulled on her boots and gloves. As number 277 was just a couple of blocks away, Mac had suggested they walk Horse the distance, and make calling in seem more like a thought on passing. The idea of a walk on a morning after snow delighted her, regardless of its purpose.

Mac held Horse's leash. The hound was more than a little excited by the snowfall, and so the line was taut as he strained against it. People had just begun to shovel their driveways.

"You have two cars?" Theo asked noticing that the Mercedes had been replaced by a Buick Enclave.

"This one's a little better in the snow... Are you going to wear that?" Mac directed his eyes at the Australian stockman's hat Theo held in her hand.

She laughed. "Gosh, no! We keep this for snowmen." She hung it on the peg by the door, over an old scarf and a pair of mismatched gloves. "We like our snowmen to be distinctly Australian."

"You're going to build a snowman now?"

"Don't be absurd! I'm a grown woman. I'll wait till we get back."

The scream was so unexpected amidst talk of snowmen, it took Theo a second to register what it was. Mac turned immediately. Across the road, a girl was screaming hysterically. Mac handed the end of the Horse's leash to Theo and started to run toward her. Theo shoved Horse into the house and told him to stay before she shut the door and followed Mac.

By the time they reached the teenager, her parents and a couple of neighbors had come out. She was still screaming—pointing and screaming. A short distance from where she stood now, beside a discarded snow shovel, was a lump in the snow. Her shovel had, it seemed, removed enough coverage to reveal a face. Mr. Turner tried to calm his daughter, though he was a little hysterical himself. Mrs. Turner called the police. Mac stood over the body.

Theo stepped closer to stand beside him. She gasped. The corpse's eyes were open, faded blue, his mouth open, surprised. Against the snow a glimpse of plaid.

"Theo, is that—?"

"Yes. That's Burt Winslow."

———

Forensics finished with Burt Winslow, and he was removed from the Turners' driveway in an ambulance. The task of finding out how he came to be there commenced.

It did occur to Theo that she had given an absurd number of witness statements in the last week. She told the officer who took it that she thought the deceased was Burt Winslow, who she had met for the first time the previous day, that he lived at number 277, and returned some mail that had been delivered to him accidentally. She mentioned the open gate and that she thought she'd seen someone in a plaid jacket standing across the road at about half past ten in the evening but it had been too dark and too snowy to say for sure if it was Winslow.

"How did he die, officer?" she ventured.

The policeman shrugged. "We have to treat it as suspicious, but it could have been a heart attack. The coroner will determine the exact cause of death." He took her details. "We'll be in touch if there's anything else."

Mac put his arm around her as they walked back across the road. "Are you all right?"

"Yes." Theo felt a bit weird, but it was not like finding Dan's body. Guilt pricked. "Maybe I should have checked when I saw him across the road. If he had a heart attack, I might have been able to—"

"He was standing when you saw him," Mac reminded her. "And you called the police, Theo. Whatever happened to Mr. Winslow, it wasn't your doing."

Theo unlocked the door. Horse looked up resentfully. It had been rather a long time to expect a dog to stay. Theo dropped to her knees and hugged him. "I'm so sorry, Horsey. I didn't realize we'd be so long."

Mac glanced at his watch. "Do you want to take him for a walk now?"

"Don't you have to get to work?"

"I've already missed most of my morning meetings. Another half hour won't make a difference."

"I'm so sorry, Mac."

"Don't worry about it—Bernie will have handled the meetings."

"Bernie?"

"Bernadette. My assistant…or maybe I'm hers. It's hard to tell. I've already called her to say I won't be in till after lunch, so we might as well walk Horse."

Theo pulled her gloves back on. She felt strangely agitated. Horse was, if truth be told, reasonably indifferent to walks, but perhaps it would be good for her.

They headed out, crossing the road to the other side once they got past the crime scene tape and remaining police cars.

"Where are we going?" Theo asked, recognizing that Mac had a destination in mind.

"Number 277."

"What?"

"I thought I'd check exactly how far it is…while we're out walking anyway."

"Isn't that a bit ghoulish?" Theo stared at him. "The man's just died."

"We're not going to knock on the door. Just get an idea of what he might have passed to get to your place."

"You're not convinced he died of a simple heart attack, are you?"

"No, I'm not."

"Why?"

He hesitated. "I saw blood in the snow—when they put him into the ambulance."

Theo swallowed. "Are you sure?"

"Yes." He stopped, glancing down at her sheepishly. "I'm sorry, Theo. I should have told you that this was a walk with a purpose. Checking stories is a professional habit, I'm afraid."

Theo smiled. "Because you're a private eye?"

He rolled his eyes. "Shall we turn back?"

"We're nearly there…what are you looking for, exactly?"

They started walking again. Though he spoke to Theo, Mac's eyes were focused on the street, scanning. "Nothing in particular. Anything that might indicate that he was or wasn't the kindly old neighbor that he purported to be...aside from the fact that he was peering into your house in a snowstorm. I think that's it." Mac pointed to a house across the road, a Tudor-style home with a large birdbath in the front yard.

"There doesn't seem to be anyone home," Theo said.

"I presume his wife is identifying the body."

Theo flinched. "Yes, of course."

They crossed the road. A small fluffy dog came tearing out of the house next door, snarling and snapping. Mac pulled Horse back, though the hound seemed more amused than provoked by the diminutive challenger. A woman ran out flapping and shouting, "Puddin', Puddin', come back!"

Theo picked up the runaway dog and returned it to its anxious owner.

The flustered woman thanked them profusely, raining kisses upon Puddin'. "We lost his sister—God rest her poor little soul—to a truck just two months ago." She looked sadly at the dog in her arms. "I think Puddin' still goes looking for her...but I couldn't lose another fur baby."

Theo offered her condolences. "Have you lived next to the Winslows long?" she asked.

"Winslows? I think you must have the wrong address, dear. The Ngyens live at 277. She's a doctor; he works with computers, I believe." She looked at them suspiciously. "You're not with one of those churches that go door to door are you? Because if you are—"

"Not at all," Theo said quickly. "I live a little farther up... I must have misheard the number."

"To my knowledge there aren't any Winslows on this block, dear."

"Thank you. I'll have to check the address."

"So...that was interesting," Mac said once they'd taken their leave of Puddin' and his owner and started heading back.

"You knew, didn't you?" Theo accused.

"I suspected that there was more, or possibly less, to Burt Winslow from number 277. It's hardly Holmesian-level deduction."

"I told the police he lived at number 277... We should call them."

"I assume they will have worked it out by now... They dispatch someone to inform next of kin pretty quickly."

"Oh." Theo rolled what she'd just learned over in her mind. The man who called himself Burt Winslow did not live at number 277. The letter could not have been delivered there accidentally; in fact, considering that the stamps on the envelope had not been cancelled, it had probably never been posted. So how did he get it? Did Dan give it to him to post...or did he take it? If he took it, why did he bring it to her in the end...? Was it a change of heart or guilt? And if he was just trying to salve his conscience, why did he need to hand-deliver the letter and linger afterwards? And then a thought occurred: could Burt Winslow have been the man she'd seen leave Dan Murdoch's house? She shivered, suddenly feeling the cold.

CHAPTER 15

I called Dan Murdoch's publishers and asked when they'll be publishing his latest manuscript—said I was a fan. They wouldn't tell me anything.

WKWWK

Wayward Son

What about the guy who said he had the manuscript?

The Watcher

He hasn't posted since. He didn't have shit!

Wayward Son

When he and Theo arrived at the house, Mac Etheridge was reading a text from his assistant that advised that the police wished to talk to him, and he was therefore not completely surprised to see Detective Mendes and two uniformed policemen waiting. Both he and Theodosia Benton were politely asked to come into the station to answer questions.

Theo met Mendes's eye. "Certainly, Detective. We were just coming in to call the police."

"We'll put Horse inside, and I'll drive us both in," Mac said calmly.

"We have room for Miss Benton in the squad car," Mendes insisted.

Theo glanced at Mac. "It's all right," she mouthed. It was probably standard procedure. She handed Mac the keys to the house. "Maybe ring Gus...his flight should have gotten in by now."

Mac nodded. "I'll be right behind you."

Theo was aware that some of her neighbors were watching her get into the police car. She could see faces in the windows on either side. It was a couple of minutes to the station, where she was ushered into an interview room and invited to sit on one of the hard chairs positioned around a laminate table.

She volunteered what she knew about Burt Winslow before they asked.

"Where is this letter now, Miss Benton?"

"At home."

"We'll organize a search warrant—"

"You don't have to do that. I'll give it to you."

"You reside with your brother, don't you?"

"Yes."

"In that case, a warrant might the best course...to avoid any confusion."

Theo shrugged. "Okay."

They asked specific questions then. At what time had Cormac Etheridge left her house that evening? *Cormac...* Theo was aware of feeling mildly surprised. It hadn't occurred to her that Mac was a nickname. "About half past ten, I think." What time had he returned? What time had she seen the footprints in the snow, locked the gate, seen the man in plaid across the road? When had Cormac Etheridge left the second time? How long had she known Cormac Etheridge? Had she ever seen the man calling himself Burt Winslow before that day? Could she remember Dan Murdoch mentioning Burt Winslow at any point? Did Cormac Etheridge know Dan Murdoch?

Theo answered as best she could. She wasn't certain about the exact times, and the questions were asked in such quick succession and so repeatedly that she became confused.

"What is your relationship with Cormac Etheridge?"

"He's a friend of my brother's."

"But your brother is not home."

"I think Gus asked him to check up on me."

"And why exactly do you need to be checked up on?"

"I don't." She turned to Mendes. The detective knew Gus; surely this wouldn't surprise him. "My brother is occasionally overprotective, and considering the events of the last couple of weeks, he wanted to make sure I was all right, I guess."

Mendes's face revealed nothing. "And he sent Mr. Etheridge to do that?"

"I think *sent* is too strong a word."

The door to the interview room was opened sharply. Gus Benton walked in. He was visibly furious. He sat down beside Theo. "I understand my sister has been here for three hours."

"Miss Benton has come in voluntarily to assist with our inquiries."

"Excellent. I assume that in the past three hours you have made all the inquiries with which you require assistance. I'm taking Theo home."

Mendes put up his hands. "Of course. But you should know that we're currently searching your home under warrant."

Theo noted that Gus had the ability to swear with a look. He directed that look at Mendes.

Mendes loosened his tie a little.

Gus stood. "Come on, Theo, we'd better head back and make sure someone explained this bloody warrant to Horse."

Gus put his arm around his sister as they walked out of the station. "Are you all right, mate?"

She embraced him. "I'm glad you're back, Gus."

"We have a bit to talk about."

Theo turned back toward the station. "Mac…"

"Mac's fine—he called me as soon as he got out."

"Is he still here?"

"No, he left when I arrived…said he'd come by tonight."

Theo nodded.

Gus frowned. "You look knackered… Let's grab a pizza and head home."

———

The police were just leaving when they arrived. They served Gus their warrant on the way out and stopped to say goodbye to Horse, who wagged happily at his new friends until he noticed Gus.

Gus shook his head as he rubbed the hound's belly. "You're a bloody hopeless guard dog, Horse. I might as well have a cat."

Theo looked around, horrified by the mess. Everything had been pulled out and placed in piles around the room. "I told them about the letter, I said I'd give it to them—they didn't have to… Oh, Gus, I'm so sorry."

Gus rubbed his jaw. "Not your fault, Theo. Anyway, this is how it always looked before you moved in."

Theo walked into the kitchen, hoping, but she was greeted

with a similar mess, and worse. "They've taken my notes," she said.

"What notes?"

"For my new novel."

Gus cursed quietly at nothing in particular as they put some of what had been the contents of the fridge back in the fridge. He filled the kettle. "Come on, let's find somewhere to eat this pizza, and you can tell me what's been happening."

It took them a couple of minutes to return the pile of books on the couch to the bookshelves so that they could sit down. "Start from the beginning… Don't leave anything out." Gus sandwiched two wedges of pizza, cheese side in.

So Theo told him: lunch with Mac, Horse's escape, the open gate, Burt Winslow, the letter, his body, and the Ngyens of number 277. Gus asked about the police interview. Theo told him what she could remember.

Gus handed her a slice of pizza. "Eat. Clearly they're treating Winslow's death as suspicious. Did they tell you anything about how he died, and when exactly?"

Theo shook her head.

Gus glanced at this watch. "Worry not, Mac will have found out by now."

"They took him in for questioning too."

"They always do that. The police have been trying to pin something on Mac for years."

"Mac? Why?"

Gus's lips pulled to one side as he thought about it. "It's to do with his family more than anything else, I suspect."

"His family?"

"Yes, the Etheridges make the Bentons look utterly mundane."

Theo bit into her pizza, interested, but not wanting to appear too much so.

"They're preppers, you know," Gus said.

"What?"

"Doomsday preppers. On the crazy end of the scale. His folks, his brothers, his uncles and aunts…all preparing for the apocalypse, or various apocalypses. The Etheridges will outlast the cockroaches. Between them, they have more guns than the Kansas PD."

"Mac too?" Theo's eyes were wide.

"No, not Mac." Gus made another pizza sandwich. "He's a regular bloke. I reckon he must have been adopted, or maybe it was being shot by his mother that did it."

"Have you met her?" Theo found herself morbidly intrigued by the woman.

"Yes…they have an end-of-the-world fortress out past Lone Star…one hundred acres or so. She's formidable."

"What do you mean?"

"Well…when she shot Mac, for example, she had his brothers hold him down, gave him a Bible to bite on, and took out the bullet herself before she called 911."

"Oh, my God!" Theo pulled back unconsciously. "He said that?"

"He was very drunk when he told me," Gus said. "He knows his family's mad, but they're his family. And I suppose doomsday is not such an absurd concept after the pandemic." He stopped and then shook his head. "Nope, even in a postpandemic world, they're mad. But Mac's fairly protective of them. In fact, he's quite fond of them in an only-sane-child-of-lunatics way."

"So how did Mac end up…?"

"The same way we avoided being ferals shaking tambourines and selling crystals in the pubs of Tasmania, I guess." Gus shrugged.

"He's one of the best freelance investigators in the business, which is why the police have always suspected that he's some kind of evil mastermind with a private army to do his bidding."

"And he's not, right?"

Gus looked at her, sternly. "What do you think, Theo?"

Theo smiled. "Of course he's not."

She might have asked more, if Mac Etheridge had not arrived.

The men shook hands warmly. "I was gone for one day," Gus grumbled.

Mac laughed. "Well, you know how to pick your exits." He handed Theo a box. "To replenish your secret stash."

"What stash?" Gus demanded.

"Hardly be a secret if I told you." Theo opened the box of handmade chocolates. "I'll replenish tomorrow...tonight we need chocolate."

"That's probably true," Gus conceded. "It looks like this man calling himself Burt Winslow was murdered."

Theo inhaled sharply. "How?"

"He was shot. They expect there was a silencer of some sort involved because nobody heard the shot. They haven't found the murder weapon. The snow made determining the time of death quite easy. Between quarter to and quarter past eleven." Mac turned to Theo. "As we worked out this morning, he does not live at number 277, and the police know nothing else about him."

Gus groaned. "Well, why are they turning this place over? They couldn't possibly suspect Theo—she's never even touched a gun, let alone one with a silencer."

"It's the letter," Mac said grimly. "They suspect that Burt Winslow was trying to blackmail Theo, or that his murder and Dan Murdoch's are somehow linked."

"Of course they're linked," Theo said angrily. "Just not by me!"

"Judging by their line of questioning, they are considering some ludicrous scenario in which I supplied Theo with a gun and then took it away again. They're searching my house now."

"So what did this letter say?" Gus asked grabbing three exquisitely made chocolates from the box.

Mac said nothing. Theo recounted everything she could remember from the second page. Then she explained what she and Mac had already discussed about the fact that despite professing to send her manuscript to a friend at the Sandra Djikstra Literary Agency, Dan Murdoch had sent it to Veronica Cole at Day Delos and Associates instead.

"That's a little weird, don't you think, Theo?"

"Maybe." She curled into a corner of the couch. "I don't know."

Gus's brow rose. "Perhaps he made a copy of the manuscript and sent it on to both."

"It should be fairly easy to find out if this agency in California has Theo's manuscript," Mac said.

"It'll be under Theo*dosia* Benton," Theo said thinking for no particular reason, of the fact that his name was Cormac.

He smiled. "I'll remember."

Gus reached out to scratch Horse behind the ear. "I'll have a security system installed tomorrow, since this turncoat has proved he's anybody's for a pat."

Mac nodded. "I think that might be a good idea." He looked at Theo, noting the suppressed panic in her eyes. "Mendes is looking at two murders in the space of a week," he said. "He's clutching at any straw right now. As the police learn more, they'll work out that they're barking up the wrong tree."

Theo looked up. "I meant what I said—I want to hire you."

"Hang on," Gus said. "You want to what?"

"I want to retain Mac to find out who killed Dan. I have that money you got out of the trustees—"

"That's what you want to do with that money?"

"Yes," Theo replied firmly. "I need to know, Gus."

Mac shook his head. "You don't need to retain me, Theo. I'll find out what I can, off the books."

"I can't ask you to do that."

"Why not? Isn't it what you people call *mates rates*?"

"If you were a plumber."

Mac stood. "I'm curious now, anyway. Even if you were to tell me to mind my own business, I'd probably nose around of my own accord."

"I suppose private eyes can't help themselves," Theo said innocently.

Gus grinned.

Mac sighed. Clearly, he didn't have a chance against both of them. He surveyed the mess. "At the moment, you need a maid service more than an investigation agency. Come on—I'll help you clean up."

CHAPTER 16

Theo felt vaguely unfaithful working at Aimee's Café, but the thought of writing alone in Benders was not yet bearable. She'd entered the establishment tentatively. After all, Aimee's already had writers. Perhaps the incursion of one more would upset the creative balance, particularly at this time of year when it was too cold to work at the tables in the muralled courtyard out the back.

She didn't have her laptop with her that day—because the police had confiscated that too—just a large notebook into which she was trying to recapture the notes that had been seized. Gus had promised to do what he could to have them returned quickly, but until then she was starting from scratch.

Larry looked up from his laptop and smiled a welcome before returning to his screen. Theo relaxed a little, the acknowledgment like a grant of refugee status. She ordered coffee and a breakfast burrito.

She began the task of trying to remember the details that had come to her in a burst of spontaneous inspiration, ideas of the moment that were a struggle to recollect and recreate, particularly when competing with thoughts of what had happened since.

Mac had recommended a security system, which they'd had installed the day after Burt Winslow's body had been discovered. She and Gus had fought over who would pay for the system until she threatened to move out if he didn't allow her to do so. Theo was excruciatingly aware that she had brought this trouble into his life, however inadvertently. Once before, Gus had paid dearly for trying to defend her, and it seemed it was happening again. She knew having his sister questioned in connection to two murders was awkward for Gus's practice. Lawrence was not large enough that the murders would not be the subject of general conversation, and as much as Gus was trying to protect her, Theo knew that unless the killer was found quickly, there would be rumors that could embarrass him professionally.

Theo had overheard Gus arguing with his partners on the phone. Clearly, they believed the potential scandal would impact business. It tortured her that this was hurting Gus.

Mac Etheridge was helping them clean up more than the house. She wasn't quite sure of the nature of his relationship with Crane, Hayes and Benton, but he seemed to have influence with Gus's elderly partners. And so Theo had all the more reason to be grateful to him. And she was.

Mac had also kept his word about looking into Dan Murdoch's death. He'd started by looking into his life, though he had not found a great deal apart from sanitized social media posts that read like they'd been drafted by publicists. Theo was not surprised. Dan had been a very private man. His public biographies said nothing about where he'd been born, or raised, where he'd attended school...or why he'd been alone. Mac had questioned

Theo about everything she could remember, casual comments about the past that might give him some clue as to where to look.

She'd remembered the story Dan had told when they'd lain together in his living room. She hadn't looked at Mac as she recounted it, somehow afraid he would see the context in which it had been told. "Dan had a dog once. A Saint Bernard called Rocket who ate three pairs of socks and a watch that had to be surgically removed."

"That might actually help." Mac hadn't taken any notes. Theo noticed that he never made notes.

She was becoming increasingly intrigued by Mac Etheridge. He was so polite, almost genteel, and yet he seemed to have a ludicrously incongruous past. The Australian in her was shocked, the storyteller fascinated. He took teasing about his mother shooting him in good humor, but surely it couldn't have been funny at the time. Secretly, guiltily, she wanted to meet Mrs. Etheridge.

Mac had also ascertained that no one at the Sandra Djikstra Literary Agency knew Dan Murdoch, though they had heard of him, and they had not received Theodosia Benton's manuscript. The revelation disturbed Theo. Had Dan been lying when he wrote he was sending the manuscript to a friend at Sandra Djikstra's? The thought hurt; it undermined her memories of him. She pushed the notion away. Dan had died less than twenty-four hours after she'd given him her manuscript. That he'd read it before he'd died was amazing. Expecting him to find the time to send it on as well was ridiculous.

So it was with her mind and her heart full of all these things that she was trying to recapture the details of the plot she'd written at the kitchen table. It was like grabbing for a life preserver while being tossed in a dark sea. Theo was doing her best not to panic, but death seemed to be clustering around her for some reason she could not fathom.

She worked through the morning. Larry dropped by her table at midday to ask how she was doing. They drank coffee, talked about his novel and the weather and, eventually, Dan.

"You know," Larry admitted. "I had no idea he was *that* Dan Murdoch until he died. I've known him for three years, and I didn't connect it. He was such a regular guy."

Theo nodded. She hadn't ever thought Dan was regular. She'd always been a little in awe of him, but she had begun to realize that it was only with her that he'd ever spoken of being *the* Dan Murdoch. Was it just humility? Dan had never lorded his success over her, but then he didn't need to. Theo had afforded him that deference from the first. It had been so easy to fall in love with a man in whose presence she felt honored to be, who seemed to be giving her something by just being who he was.

In the lonely early hours since his death, Theo had begun to analyze her feelings with an eye that was made critical by grief and fear. Had she been drawn to Dan Murdoch because he embodied the success she wanted for herself? Had she loved him for reasons that were ambitious? It horrified her to think of it, filled her with a loathing of herself that was only surpassed by how much she missed him.

Once Larry had returned to his own table, a woman approached her. She was about Theo's age, blond and very pretty. Her hair was cut short, nearly shaved on one side, and her clothes had an air of edgy chic. Theo had noticed her speaking to Larry earlier, silently admired her style. She introduced herself as Mary Cowell. "Jock from Benders mentioned that you knew Dan Murdoch... I'm an old friend from New York. I came as soon as I heard. I was hoping I could buy you a coffee and talk to you about him."

Theo stuttered. "Yes…of course. My condolences for your loss."

"And mine for yours. You knew Dan well?" Mary sat down.

"Yes."

"Can you tell me what happened?"

Theo swallowed. "He died…he was murdered."

Mary closed her eyes for a second. She took a deep breath. "I had heard, but I was hoping it wasn't true." She shook her head. "Oh, my God. Fuck! Do they know who?"

"No. They haven't arrested anyone."

"Dammit. Was he in any kind of trouble?"

"I don't believe so. He didn't seem worried about anything."

"Where…where did he—"

"At home…in his kitchen."

"How do you know? Were you there?"

"Yes—well, no…" Theo dropped her notebook. She slid out her chair to retrieve it from under the table. Her hand was shaking.

"I'm so sorry," Mary said. 'I didn't mean to upset you. I'm just trying to understand what happened."

"I'm not sure what happened," Theo lowered her voice. "I found Dan's body, but I hadn't seen him that day. It's why I went to his house."

"Were you and Dan…you know?"

Theo was startled. "We wrote together… I mean in the same place…not the same book." She paused wondering if she was speaking to an old flame of Dan Murdoch's. Theo's first thought was that Mary was too young…but then she caught herself. Mary Cowell was probably older than she. "How did you know Dan? Did you work with him?"

"Not the way you did. Jesus! You poor thing! I can only imagine what it was like to find him like that."

Theo tried not to allow her mind's eye to conjure images. "It was horrible," she whispered. "There was so much blood."

Mary reached across the table and took her hand. "I know we've only just met, but if you want to talk?"

Theo pulled herself together. "I'm fine—really."

Mary released her hand. "Dan and I moved in the same circles back in New York. He used to make me laugh. Was it a robbery, do you think?"

"I beg your pardon?"

"Did the killer take anything? Oh, my God, they weren't after a manuscript or something, were they?'

"I don't know… I don't think so."

"Because that would be a story—*Writer Killed for Manuscript!*"

"I don't think—"

"There was another man killed in Lawrence the other day, wasn't there?" Mary clutched the large silver cross that hung on a leather cord around her neck. "Did he and Dan have anything in common? Do the police believe we're dealing with a serial killer?"

"I don't know," Theo said flustered.

"But you were there…when the second body was found?"

The question was like cold water. "How did you know that?" Theo demanded.

"Someone must have mentioned it. What exactly was your relationship to the second victim?"

"Who did you say you were?" Theo moved her chair out.

The woman placed her business card on the table and pushed it towards Theo. "Mary Cowell. The *Kansas City Star*."

Theo left the card where it was. She'd been talking to a journalist. "I have to go," she said, standing.

Mary stood too. "Can I walk you somewhere?"

"No."

"You don't look well. Why don't you sit for a minute?" Mary sounded concerned. But then she had sounded like she was upset by Dan's death too.

Theo left Aimee's via the back exit, cutting behind a barbershop and Papa Keno's pizza place toward Eleventh Street. By the time she reached the Japanese Friendship Gardens on Mass Street, the instinct to get as far away from Mary Cowell as possible had calmed. She stopped. What had she done? Mendes had warned her not to speak with reporters under any circumstances. Dammit. She'd have to warn him. Theo began walking home, her eyes open for any sign of Mary Cowell or Spiderman. She jumped now when a friendly passerby said hello. How could Lawrence, to which she'd fled for refuge, have become so menacing?

She reached home, trying to remember the code for the new security system. The snow had just melted, and Theo could feel its lingering chill in the air, but she stopped and sat on the porch steps in what was almost an act of defiance. This was ridiculous. This was the same place that it had been a few weeks ago, when their windows had no locks and she'd walked everywhere exploring quieter places without a second thought, when everyone seemed nearly too friendly, and the neighbors would come out to say 'howsit goin?' when they saw her. The neighbors had been almost invisible since Burt Winslow had been found and a police car had taken Theo Benton away for questioning.

Theo sat where she was for a while, watching the street quietly. The houses here were not quite as grand as those in Dan's immediate neighborhood, but they were beautiful and they seemed, to her, more like homes. They had verandas like Australian houses, though they were more ornate, with detailed woodwork and brackets, some with circular ends that looked a little like attached gazebos. The blocks were large and bare in comparison to gardens back home. Australians were happy to clean out gutters incessantly, so they could have trees close to the house, and were less in love with lawn. There were a couple of properties like Gus's—in need of renovation—and others that had been restored to the glory of another age. The Turners across the road had been the focus of reporters for the period immediately after Burt Winslow had been found. So much so that the Turners themselves had fled to a hotel. The media had watched the empty house for a day after that, before, one by one, they'd given up, and now the street seemed normal again. Like nothing out of the ordinary had happened.

A car pulled up in front of the house. Theo didn't react at all at first. All four doors swung open at once, and four people got out. The two in the back carried a camera and microphone. Mary Cowell was one of the two who stepped out of the front.

Theo stood immediately and fumbled for her keys. Another car pulled up as she unlocked the door. She was inside and punching numbers into the security system before the third arrived. A knock. Mary Cowell's voice. "Miss Benton. Miss Benton…we just have a couple of questions."

"You're trespassing," Theo said, not sure if it was strictly true. "Please leave."

She ran through the house to the back door, admitting Horse before locking it again. The hound followed her up the stairs into her bedroom. From the window she could see the news crews and reporters setting up. She stared dumbstruck until someone noticed her face in the window and directed the cameras in that direction. She pulled away and drew the curtains, panicking now. Theo grabbed her phone and started to dial Gus's number, stopping midway through the sequence. Gus had already lost so much time because of her—she couldn't call him out of work again. But she had to do something. She needed to warn him, and she needed help. How could she have been in Lawrence for nine months and made so few friends?

Steeling herself, she pulled up Mac Etheridge's number and dialed.

"Theo, hello. How are you?"

"I've done something really stupid, Mac."

"Are you all right? Where are you?"

Theo told him about Mary Cowell and the media crowd now in front of the house. "I don't know what to do," she said, her voice breaking.

"Stay put. Don't go near the windows. I'll be there in a few minutes—I'll come to the back door."

"Gus—"

"I'll let him know he should work late till we give him the all-clear. Don't worry, Theo."

It was only after she'd hung up that Theo wondered how Mac would get to the back door. The backyard was fenced and gated. He could scale the gate, she supposed, but surely that would attract the attention of the reporters out front. God, they might follow suit.

She headed back downstairs, determined not to be cowering in the bedroom when he arrived. She filled the kettle, set it on the stove, and fed Horse, trying not to count the passing minutes. When she couldn't stand not knowing any longer, Theo opened the drawing room curtain a crack and saw that the reporters had not given up.

She knelt to put her arms around Horse. "Oh, Horsey, what have I done?"

Mac knocked on the back door as promised. Theo opened it immediately, the relief plain on her face. He came in and locked the door behind him. His suit was a little scuffed, his shoes muddy.

Theo fought a ridiculous impulse to hug him. "How did you get to the back door without anyone noticing?"

"I climbed a few fences and cut through a couple of your neighbors' yards." He smiled. "I'm not sure I wasn't noticed… I thought I heard someone scream."

"This is such a mess, Mac."

"Sit down and tell me exactly what happened."

And so, Theo explained her conversation with Mary Cowell. "I thought she was a friend of Dan's—she said she was a friend of Dan's…and seemed so genuinely gutted by his death that I didn't even think she could be a reporter."

"Of course, you didn't; why would you?" He accepted the mug of tea she'd made him. "How did she know to find you at Aimee's—don't you usually write at Benders?"

Theo frowned. "I don't know. She said Jock mentioned I knew Dan—he's one of the regulars at Benders. But I have no idea why she was speaking to Jock or how he knew I'd be at Aimee's. Did you speak to Gus?"

"He's thinking about renting out advertising space since there are cameras pointed at the house."

Theo flinched. "Are Mr. Hayes and Mr. Crane very upset?"

"Yes, but they'll get over it. Your brother is a very good attorney, Theo, not to mention a partner. They can't fire him."

"But this isn't good for Gus or the firm."

"No." Mac spoke gently. "But it isn't your fault. You didn't ask for any of this."

Theo blinked furiously, undone for a moment.

"Gus wanted me to make sure you were all right. It was all I could do to stop him coming with me. Believe me, Theo, he does not hold you responsible for this in any way."

Theo wiped her eyes with her sleeve. He handed her a handkerchief.

"What am I going to do about them?" she asked glancing toward the front door.

"Snow is forecast for tonight. It should clear them."

"But they'll come back?"

"The police don't seem to have any other suspects, so probably."

Theo stared at him. "I'm a suspect?"

He took her hand and said calmly, "Only because they haven't got anyone else at this stage." He waited until her breathing slowed a little. "Don't be frightened, Theo. We're going to sort this out."

CHAPTER 17

Who is Theodosia Benton? Why is she a person of interest in the murder of Dan Murdoch?

Whistler

She must belong to the Labyrinth. The bitch killed Primus!

WKWWK

Flagman

Why hasn't she been arrested? Someone needs to lock her up!

Loyal Boy

It began to snow heavily at about eight o'clock. Gus retuned home at nine. He looked tired.

"Looks like they've gone," he said, removing snow-dusted layers while greeting Horse and shaking Mac's hand. He put his arm around Theo. "Are you all right, Wombat?"

Theo nodded. He'd not called her Wombat since they were children. Since she'd decided she was too old for the nickname their father had given her. She smiled tightly. The idea of hiding in a burrow underground was very appealing at that moment.

"I'm sorry, Gus. I didn't know that she—"

He interrupted her apology. "Of course, you didn't. It was only a matter of time before the press got interested, Theo. We were both at the crime scene." He grimaced. "We'd better talk to the ancients tonight in case the Australian press picks up the story."

"Do you want a grilled cheese?" Mac asked, returning to the kitchen where he and Theo had been trying to make dinner.

"Yeah, sure." Gus grabbed a Copperhead from the fridge and sat down at the kitchen table. "We need to convene a bit of a war cabinet, I reckon."

Mac nodded. "The ladies and gentlemen of the free press will be back unless the police arrest the real killer tonight."

"So they believe the same person killed Dan and Mr. Winslow?" Theo placed a pile of grilled sandwiches in the center of the table.

Gus shrugged. "I'm afraid my old friend Detective Mendes is no longer sharing insights with me."

"Mary Cowell's story will be in the papers by morning, I presume." Mac sat down and poured Tabasco sauce over the toasted sandwich on his plate before biting into it. "Things will probably get a lot worse then."

"Can't we call the police?" Theo poured herself a glass of milk. "Surely it's trespassing, or public nuisance...or something."

"I don't like our chances getting help from the police, Theo," Gus replied. "Chances are they leaked this to the press in the first place."

"But why?" Theo said aghast. "Why would they do that?"

Mac glanced at Gus before he spoke. "Generally, it's to put pressure on a suspect, to try and force them into a mistake."

"Oh, God, they really think I killed Dan..."

"I don't think they've found any other suspects," Mac replied. "But we will."

"Have you had any luck tracking down Spiderman?" Gus asked.

"Not a lot." Mac frowned. "I'm beginning to wonder if the cobweb tattoo is a misdirection."

"What do you mean?"

"Tattoos are only an identifying mark if they're permanent." He took a pen from the inside pocket of his jacket and drew and cobweb on the back of his hand. "Say I attack you and you see that I have a tattoo on my hand. You focus on that rather than my face. The police also focus on that, looking for suspects with a cobweb tattoo. And I simply wash my hands."

"But I would never have known that the man who ran into me was the man with the blond dreadlocks if it hadn't been for the tattoo," Theo protested.

"But what if they weren't the same man?" Mac said.

"You don't think the incidents were related?" Theo was confused now.

"No, no. I think they were." Mac tried to explain. "But because of this tattoo, we think the same man was involved. So all the identifying features you noticed in the first man—the blond dreadlocks, the color of his eyes, his height, and so on are compromised by your description of the second. So the police are left with the impression that either the man is a master of disguise who accidently failed to cover his most identifying feature, or..."—he paused—"that Theodosia Benton is an unreliable witness."

Gus groaned. "Bloody hell! A halfway decent attorney will make her look like she's either mad or a liar."

Theo looked at them both in dismay. Mac was right—the only reason she'd thought Spiderman was one man was the tattoo. And perhaps her mind had merged what she saw to fit with that.

"On the other hand," Mac continued, smiling encouragingly at Theo, "it does tell us that whatever's going on, it's not the work of a single random killer. This is much more coordinated."

"You need to concentrate on looking into Murdoch," Gus said, taking another grilled cheese from the platter between them. "Organizations don't kill people on impulse or indiscriminately. There's a reason…gambling debts, organized crime, espionage of some sort."

Mac nodded. "I'll talk to his publisher tomorrow…assuming they don't just pass me on to his agents, perhaps I can get something out of them."

"Wouldn't the police have already talked to them?" Theo asked.

Gus grinned. "Yes, but Mac's going to do his private eye thing."

Mac ignored him but Theo was intrigued. "What are you going to do?"

"I'm going to get them to let their guard down a bit."

"Exactly how?"

Mac rummaged in his jacket and found his wallet. From it he extracted a business card which he handed to Theo. *Hamilton Pendleton-Smythe of Lionsgate Films.*

"Who is Hamilton Pendleton-Smythe?"

"The chaps call me Ham." Mac Etheridge's inflection became English—Oxford. "Lionsgate feels that Mr. Murdoch's last novel will translate very nicely to the big screen, and considering the interest generated by his tragic passing, such a project might be rather timely."

"Isn't this illegal?"

"I'm only after information, not money." He glanced at Gus. "And I have a good lawyer."

"Who knows nothing about what you're planning," Gus added pointedly.

Mac laughed. "It's okay, Theo. If I do my job properly, they won't catch on, even if they never hear from me again. Producers are notoriously fickle and easily distracted."

"Why would they talk to you?"

"Because nothing sells books like talk of the movie, and since Dan Murdoch won't be writing any more books, I expect they'll be keen to make as much money as they can from the books they have."

Theo gave in. Mac seemed far too relaxed to be contemplating anything particularly dangerous or illegal. Perhaps this sort of minor subterfuge was perfectly ordinary in the world of private eyes.

"So in the meantime, I just don't leave the house," she said despondently.

Mac wrinkled his nose. "Afraid so…unless you want to leave now while there're no reporters about."

Theo smiled. "If I had anywhere to go… No, I think I'd better just sit out the siege."

It snowed quite heavily overnight. Even so, the reporters were back by seven. Theo closed the curtain unhappily. Gus had wanted to leave before the media scrum returned, but he'd only just gotten out of the shower. Now he'd have to run the gauntlet of microphones and cameras just to get to his car.

She stood outside his bedroom door and broke the news. Gus sighed. "I'd better wear the green tie then. It'll bring out my eyes for the cameras."

Theo snorted. "Idiot." She shook her head. "Would you like breakfast?"

"I don't think I'll have time, mate."

"A sandwich?"

"Sure. I keep vegemite in the back of the cupboard where it won't scare our American friends."

Theo laughed, running down to the kitchen to make him a sandwich. Vegemite was an acquired taste which had to be applied sparingly over a thick layer of butter. Americans tended to apply it too thickly and expect it to be sweet, with the result that they reacted quite badly to what many Australians considered their national dish.

Gus came down the stairs with a green tie in his pocket. He grabbed a cup of coffee and the sandwich, half of which he gave to Horse. "I should go."

"Gus, wait… What if I step outside and distract them so you can slip out?"

He sat her down. "Look, Theo, I face reporters every time I leave the court. I've become quite good at it, if I do say so myself, not to mention photogenic—you mustn't worry."

Theo groaned. "I am sorry, Gus. Everything's gone to hell for you since I arrived."

He took her hand. "Come on, mate. I've had clients go through this—it passes. You've just got to try not to panic." He ruffled her hair as he used to when she was ten and hated it. "They're just reporters."

"They've got us trapped in the house."

"I'm going to work, so mostly just you." He winked as he slung the green tie around his neck and proceeded to knot it. "Actually, as much as the reporters are a nuisance, at least I know nothing will happen to you with them standing guard on the lawn."

"Happen to me?"

"The same facts that make the police suspect you of being involved in two murders make me concerned for your safety." He sat down opposite her for a moment. "You seem to have got caught in the gravitational pull of whatever trouble Dan Murdoch was in."

Theo swallowed, trying in vain to dislodge the lump in her throat. "You would have liked him, Gus. If you'd met him, you would have liked him."

Gus smiled. But Theo could see the skepticism in his eyes, a fleeting flash of something like anger when she mentioned Dan Murdoch's name. "Well, I'm afraid that's a moot point now, mate," he said. "I'm sure Murdoch was a terrific bloke, but he was clearly involved in something unsavory."

"We don't know that. He might have been dragged into something the same way I have…just by being in the wrong place at the wrong time."

Gus conceded, or at least he didn't argue. "Mendes says he'll have a squad car drive by periodically. I'll pick up dinner before I come home."

"Don't be silly… I'm stuck here all day, I might as well cook."

He looked at her warily. "What are you going to cook?"

"I don't know… I'll see what we have."

"I suppose we can always have something delivered if things go wrong—I'd better go." He pulled on an overcoat, opened the door, and then shut it immediately. "Damn!"

"What's wrong?" Theo asked, alarmed.

"The bloody snowplows have piled up the snow on the curbside. I'm going to have shovel if I'm going get out." He grimaced. "Bugger!"

"I could help—"

"I can just imagine how the papers would caption a photograph of you with a shovel. You stay inside; I'll deal with it."

Theo watched through the curtains as Gus retrieved a shovel from outside the back door and then walked out into the waiting gathering, as if doing a media stop from your front porch was the most natural thing in the world. She couldn't quite hear what he was saying. The reporters laughed, so she assumed he'd made a joke. Gus handed the shovel to one of them, a young man, who proceeded to shovel the curb while he answered questions. Once the driveway was clear, Gus headed calmly for his truck. The reporters followed him; some even waved as he reversed out.

Theo smiled. Gus had somehow persuaded a reporter to shovel the driveway—her brother was brilliant, and completely mad. The crowd on the lawn seemed less threatening now—just people doing their jobs. Perhaps she could just ignore them... like Horse, who seemed entirely indifferent to the strangers who were camped outside the house. Gus was right—aside from his growling trick, which was clearly just acting, Horse was a hopeless guard dog. But it was nice to have his company.

Theo spent the morning tidying up. The kitchen was spotless aside from what she'd used to make Gus's vegemite sandwich. Mac had washed the dishes before leaving the night before. She noticed he was quite fastidious about washing up. Just the dishes, though...it did not seem to be a generalized compulsion. Perhaps it was something to do with not leaving a trail of DNA behind him. Theo shook her head, laughing at herself. She was becoming absurd. He was probably just neat.

It was when she'd finished vacuuming that Theo noticed the noise outside.

Curious, she moved the curtain aside an inch. She paled.

There seemed to be hundreds of people in front of the house. Not reporters. Many carried pickets. Some of the slogans proclaimed love for Dan Murdoch; others called for justice; still others bore images of his book jackets. Theo opened the curtain a little farther, incredulous. Where did all these people come from? The rally seemed to stretch down the street, but it was focused on number 211. Reporters were talking to the protesters.

Theo stepped back from the window, stunned by what was outside it and terrified now. And then the window exploded in. Glass shattered in all directions. Theo screamed. A pop from outside and the protesters began to scream and run. Theo dropped to the ground. Horse barked at the window. She called him back desperately. She heard sirens. She saw blood a few moments before she realized that it was hers.

CHAPTER 18

Gus ignored Mendes and walked straight into the hospital room. The doctor was just finishing suturing Theo's arm and gluing the cut on her brow. Gus waited until he was done before he embraced his sister. She clung to him for longer than usual, but she was still the first to let go.

"Horse—" she began. It was muddled, but she could remember him growling at anyone who tried to come near her, and at Animal Control.

"Mac has gone to spring Horse," Gus said, looking critically at the smaller cuts on her face and arms.

"That was the glass," she said. "Someone threw a brick through the window before the gunshot."

Gus rubbed his face, and then he swore.

Theo nodded in agreement. This was insane.

Detective Mendes walked in. "How are you feeling, Theo?"

"What the hell happened?" Gus demanded.

Mendes paused as if considering whether or not to tell them.

And then said, "It seems Mr. Murdoch's fans decided to protest outside your house. We've arrested the young woman who threw the brick, but she denies having anything to do with the gunshot.

"But someone must have seen the shooter pull his gun."

Mendes shrugged. "If they did, they're not saying."

"So some lunatic is targeting writers in Lawrence," Gus said angrily.

"Someone killed Dan Murdoch," Mendes replied carefully. "Burt Winslow was not a writer."

"Theo—"

"Seems to have been the victim of an overzealous protest over the murder of Dan Murdoch."

"Don't be ridiculous, George!" Gus stood between Theo and Mendes. "Someone tried to kill Theo."

"Someone shot at your house, Gus—it wasn't a sniper attack. Judging by the crowds, Mr. Murdoch's readership is the devoted kind."

"But to try and shoot someone—" Theo stopped as she remembered what Veronica Cole had told her about Dan Murdoch's fans, the reason they had tried to keep his image and his location out of the public domain.

"Anyway," Mendes continued, "there remains the possibility that the shot was intended as a warning for you, Gus, rather than your sister. Lawyers are not always popular."

"Why would my clients suddenly start shooting up my house?"

"I'm just pointing out the possibility."

"What are you going to do about protecting Theo?" Gus demanded.

"We have no real reason to expect a repeat of this incident, but you both might need to stay in a hotel for a while. At least until forensics finishes with your house. We can arrange for you to collect what you need in terms of clothing and toiletries."

"That's it?" Gus was furious. "Someone tried to kill my sister and all you can suggest is that we go to hotel! George, for God's sake—"

"No that isn't all I can suggest." Mendes bit back. He reached inside his jacket and pulled out a folded newspaper, which he tossed onto Theo's bed. "I also recommend your sister stops giving interviews!" He turned on his heel then and walked out.

Theo tried to open the paper, but her hands were trembling too much. Gus took it from her. Mary Cowell's article. A feature on the death of beloved novelist Dan Murdoch. The accompanying picture however was not of Murdoch but of Theo, taken while she was at Aimee's and without her knowledge. The article talked about the brutal slaying of Dan Murdoch and his "friend" Burt Winslow in the university town of Lawrence, Kansas. It presented Theo Benton as the connection between both deaths.

"I'll sue the buggery out of her and the fuckin' paper!" Gus was apoplectic.

The room seemed to close in on Theo. She began to shiver, her breathing became shallow, and Gus forgot about his threats of legal action.

"Theo, are you okay?" He called for help.

It arrived promptly. "Delayed shock," the doctor said as the nurse checked Theo's vitals. "I'm afraid I'll have to ask you to leave, sir."

———

Theo felt a little embarrassed when Gus and Mac were allowed to come in. The doctor had put her on a saline drip and various monitors. She felt a bit of a fraud. "I'm fine," she said before Gus could utter a word. "Really."

"You scared the hell out of me," Gus said.

"I'm sorry," she said. "I overreacted."

"Actually, I don't think you did, mate…but try not to do it again."

Theo looked at Mac. "Did you find Horse?"

"He's at my house. The housekeeper is keeping an eye on him."

"Is he okay?"

"I had a vet check him over. He's fine." Mac pulled up a chair beside the bed.

Gus sat on the end of it. "We're going to have to figure out what we're going to do."

"Can we go home?"

Gus shook his head. "They want to keep you overnight, just in case. But, Theo, it's too dangerous to go back to my place."

"A hotel?"

"I'm not sure that would be any safer. Regardless of what George Mendes thinks, I doubt very much that some overexcited book fan shot at the house."

Mac agreed. "Why don't you come and stay at my place for the moment? It'll be more secure than a hotel."

Theo began to protest the imposition, but Mac waved it away. "Let's call it settled then. Can you tell us exactly what you remember, Theo?"

Theo recounted what had happened. "I didn't really notice the protestors arriving. They were suddenly just there. I walked away from the window, and then it seemed to explode."

"That would have been the brick," Gus said.

"I heard a pop and the crowd started screaming."

"A pop?"

"Yes… It wasn't what I expected a gunshot to sound like."

Mac looked at Gus. "A silencer perhaps," he said.

"Was there just one shot?"

"There might have been more, but by then everybody was screaming, and Horse was barking." She shrugged. "I might have been screaming a bit too."

"Naturally," Mac said distractedly. "I know people get caught up in their favorite books, but this protest, if that's what it was, seems a bit extreme. Readers are not generally violent…sports fans, yes, but readers?"

Theo told them about what Veronica Cole had said: why Dan Murdoch had moved to Lawrence, why he stayed off social media, and why there were no publicity photos of him.

Mac Etheridge listened carefully. "I might have to read a couple of his books." He loosened his tie. "It could explain why his publishers could give me so little on him."

"Did they tell you anything useful at all?"

"That his latest manuscript was submitted to his agents the day he died. That they hadn't seen it yet, but rumor was that it was a work of genius, and they would be happy to put me on the list of producers who'd asked to read an advance copy."

"Dan had finished?" Theo asked surprised and a little hurt. "He didn't say a word."

"Is that odd?" Mac asked.

"I don't know. Dan was reading my manuscript. I just thought he might have mentioned…"

Gus's eyes darkened. He started to say something but held back.

Theo watched her brother's face. She was not entirely oblivious to her brother's reserve on the subject of Dan Murdoch. There were times she doubted Dan too, and perhaps when she was trying to convince Gus of his bona fides, it was because she was trying to convince herself.

"Go home, both of you," she said.

"I'm not leaving you here alone with someone trying to kill you, Theo."

"Don't be melodramatic, Gus. I'm perfectly safe here."

"Probably—but I think I'll stay anyway."

She smiled. "You're being absurd. You have to work tomorrow, and Horse will think we've abandoned him."

Mac tossed him a set of keys. "You go. I'll stay."

"For God's sake!" Theo groaned. "You're both being idiotic."

Mac pulled Gus aside. They argued in whispers. And when they turned around again, Gus had agreed to go. He kissed Theo's forehead. "I'll see you tomorrow."

Not willing to risk him changing his mind and remaining stubbornly by her bedside, Theo did not ask him what had changed his mind. But she asked Mac as soon Gus had left.

He shrugged. "I just assured him I'd make sure nothing happened to you."

"How did you assure him?"

"I've been trained to protect people."

"By whom?"

He laughed now. "My mother mostly." Mac pulled his chair closer to the bed. "Gus has a few things to sort out at the firm tomorrow."

"Because of me?"

"I wouldn't worry about it, Theo. Gus can look after himself. He's not going to let two old men push him out of his own firm."

"Could they do that?"

"Not without one helluva fight. But he does need to prepare for the partners' meeting tomorrow."

Theo nodded. The thought that Gus could lose everything was horrifying.

Mac pulled out his phone. "With all due respect to hospital food, I'm going to get something delivered. Do you have any preferences?"

"They can't deliver here!"

"I know people," he said. "Don could get takeout into prison for the right price."

CHAPTER 19

The car that picked them up from the hospital was from a private service. Discreet, professional, anonymous. They left early and somehow avoided the reporters and picketers outside the hospital. Even so, the route they took to Mac's house was circuitous.

If Theo had thought about it, she knew that Mac was wealthy. Gus had said so at some point, and Mac did drive a Mercedes sports car when he wasn't trying not to be noticed. But she hadn't expected the house. It was the kind of building that made you gasp. An American Gilded Age mansion that had lost none of the glory of its heyday. Theo craned her neck to gaze up at the round tower capped by a domed roof. The property was surrounded by a high wrought-iron fence and gate, its traditional red and sage paintwork striking against the surrounding snow.

"Gus says he packed a bag for you when he collected his own things."

Theo grimaced. She could just imagine what Gus would pack for her.

Mac smiled. "We can try to sneak by later if it turns out to be a bag full of evening gowns and socks."

They alighted in the driveway and walked up a brick path—which someone had shoveled—to the grand portico. Theo almost expected to find a line of servants waiting to greet them at the bottom of the stairs, but Mac opened his own door and let her in. Inside, the house was as breathtaking, but Theo's attention was diverted by Horse, who was clearly pleased to see her. She knelt to avoid being knocked over and hugged the exuberant hound with the arm that wasn't injured.

Once Horse had been calmed, Mac led the way up the wooden staircase and showed her to a bedroom. The bag Gus had packed was sitting on a chair. Like the rest of the house, the bedroom was beautiful, the warm wood of the craftsman style featured but not deified. Theo assumed there had been a professional decorator involved in picking the furniture and paint—except for the painting on the far wall. A violent abstract. It was hard to look at.

Mac might have noticed the slight widening of her eyes. "Dang, sorry. I forgot that was still in here." He took it off the wall. "A gift from my mother—she's a big fan of William Burroughs. I keep it up here so I don't have to look at it."

"That's a Burroughs?" Theo had of course heard of the Beat Generation icon who had spent the last decades of his life in Lawrence. She'd read a couple of his novels and seen the odd painting. "Your mother likes William Burroughs?"

"Yes, she's particularly fond of the gunshot paintings," he said referring to Burroughs's technique of creating art by shooting at cans of spray paint.

Theo looked sharply at him. Was he joking? "But after…"

"She shot me?" He smiled. "My mom's made of sterner stuff than that. It'll take a bit more than an accidental shooting to turn her off the inherent artistry of guns." He held up the Burroughs. "Actually, this isn't one of the gunshot paintings, but it is a hard thing to fall asleep looking at…so I'll find a dark, lockable cupboard for it."

"You don't have to do that," Theo said a little half-heartedly. The agonized faces in the painting unnerved her.

Mac laughed. "Believe me, I'd get rid of it entirely if my mom didn't look for it every time she visits. She occasionally stays in this room when she's in town."

"I'm not putting her out—"

"She never comes to town in the winter," he assured her. "Or anytime that she can avoid it, really. She thinks Lawrence is something of a left-wing Sodom and Gomorrah. Come on, I'll show you around the rest of the house before I go to work."

He took her on a tour of the mansion, which included a cavernous room with a stage at one end. "The guy who owned this place before me was a musician. He and his friends would jam in here—I'm afraid I haven't decided what exactly to do with it."

"Roller-skating, perhaps," Theo said taking in the size of the room. She'd always imagined private eyes sleeping in their dingy offices on the wrong side of town and living paycheck to paycheck. Clearly not.

He chuckled. "It's handy for parties… There're always a few closet musicians in the crowd and they're drawn to stages."

The tower Theo had seen from outside turned out to be a library, with a series of mezzanines connected by a wide spiral staircase. Horse, it seemed, was frightened of the staircase and so settled to wait for their return at its foot. The uppermost mezzanine was furnished with armchairs and ottomans and a view that stretched in all directions.

"Could I write up here?"

"Sure…but it's a long trek down to the bathroom or to get a drink."

"It'd be worth it."

Mac showed her how to operate the security system, made her breakfast in the magnificent chef's kitchen, and showed her where he kept the chocolate before he left. "I've given the housekeeper a few days off, so no one should know you're here," he said, grabbing his keys. "Make yourself at home… If there's anything, call me, or press the panic button on the security panel."

Once he'd left, Theo went upstairs to shower, and to change out of the clothes she'd been wearing when she was admitted to the hospital. The sleeve of her shirt was quite stained with blood and probably beyond salvation. Gus had made some interesting choices in packing a bag for her. She couldn't help but wonder why he thought she'd need a swimsuit and shorts in the middle of a Kansas winter, but he had managed to throw in a pair of jeans, an old ANU sweatshirt, and her notebook. There were no socks in the bag, so she went into the next room to steal a pair of his.

Gus had managed in one night to turn the adjoining room into a comfortable mess. The contents of his own bag were draped over chairs, and there were stacks of files on the bedside table and more on the bed. She picked up a couple of neckties from the ground. Poor Gus. She knew he was under pressure and that what was happening was not helping. She found the socks and tidied up before she left, hanging up his jackets and shirts and remaking the bed as best she could without disturbing his papers.

She explored the house on her own now, pausing on the things that caught her interest. Aside from the Burroughs painting, Mac seemed to have quite an interest in art. The collection was eclectic:

paintings, sculpture, items of Americana. The mantle in the living room held family photographs—a group of young men, including Mac, in flannel shirts, holding up fish freshly caught. Another family photo…the stilted studio variety. Mac seemed to have three brothers and a sister. He looked the most comfortable in a suit. The others all had a certain cowboy flair to their attire. Their mother presided undeniably over the image, a broad white smile, large glasses, and a Liberty print blouse. She did look very much like the president of a church auxiliary, but there was something about her gaze that made Theo think that she probably killed her own meat as well. She remembered what Gus had said about his friend's family being survivalists. She wondered what they thought of the urban mansion in which Mac lived.

Mac's father didn't seem to be a part of that family photograph, though he was in others, with Mac mostly. Perhaps Mac's parents had separated. Theo went back to Mrs. Etheridge, intrigued. She wondered what she would have felt in the moment she saw that she'd shot her son… What had possessed her to take the bullet out herself? Theo had never sensed any animosity in Mac towards his mother…more a vaguely embarrassed but affectionate resignation. She supposed she and Gus regarded their own parents in much the same way. Theo wished that Mrs. Etheridge had been an idea and not a real person. She would play out wonderfully as a character, but she was real, and Theo could not accept Mac's hospitality and put his mother in her novel. Surely that would be rude?

She grabbed her notebook and a pen, settled Horse with a biscuit, and climbed the spiral staircase to the top of the round tower, stopping to take in the view. She could see easily into the neighbors' yards and over the tops of smaller houses on other streets.

Lawrence was still heavily blanketed in snow. People were out shoveling driveways and sidewalks. Dan Murdoch's garden with its clipped hedges and flower beds came unsummoned to mind. There probably wasn't any work for his gardener right now... Theo toyed with that thought. Dan Murdoch had employed a gardener who, if she remembered correctly, came two days a week. Had she mentioned that to the police? Had they known to question him? Dan had probably just paid him cash—there might not have been any record. The poor man would have just turned up to find his employer dead and the house a crime scene.

Theo thought about where she might find the gardener's name. The hedges had been quite established, so he could conceivably have been trimming them for years. Perhaps he'd been recommended by Dan's decorator, whoever that was. It occurred to her then that Veronica Cole might know.

She could make a call and then, if Veronica knew, pass on the name to Mendes. Theo remembered suddenly that she hadn't yet informed Veronica that she had a new phone and number. She cursed. How could she have forgotten something so important? For all she knew, Veronica might have been trying to contact her.

She ran down the spiral staircase, and then up the wooden one to her bedroom. Horse opened his eyes as she passed, and then closed them again, obviously deciding that she would return shortly and it wasn't necessary for him to move. Theo checked the room. Yes! Gus had remembered to bring her satchel. She forgave him for the shorts and swimsuit and rummaged through until she found Veronica's card.

The phone was answered immediately by a receptionist, who, after inquiring after her name, put her through to the agent.

"Theo! Hello!"

Theo babbled about the change in phone and number.

Veronica laughed. "If we needed to get hold of you, we wouldn't let a little thing like an incorrect number stop us! I'm afraid I have no news for you yet, Theo, but I'm sure a decision will be made soon."

"Yes, of course, thank you." Theo was embarrassed to be seen as nagging. "Actually, I was hoping to speak to you about something else entirely."

"Anything."

"Dan employed a gardener, a man to clip his hedges and plant flowers—that sort of thing. I don't suppose you remember his name?"

"A gardener? Are you sure?

"Yes. I thought he might have seen or noticed something that could help locate Dan's murderer."

A pause. "Well, listen to you, Nancy Drew!"

"I just thought it might…help the police… I'm not sure they know…" Theo stuttered. She suddenly felt ridiculous.

"Yes, I can understand why you'd want to do that. Unfortunately, I can't help you. I didn't know Dan employed a gardener—I just thought he had a green thumb."

"Oh…"

"Actually, we should talk. Are you free for breakfast tomorrow?"

"Yes, of course. What time?"

"How about I pick you up? Eight-ish?"

"Sure." Theo hesitated for a moment, then gave the agent Mac's address, explaining vaguely the reason for the relocation, and telling herself that she didn't need to hide from Veronica.

"Oh, yes, I did read about that. I'll see you tomorrow—in the meantime, I'll look through my emails from Dan. Maybe he mentioned this gardener…and you'll have something worth taking to the police."

Theo returned to the tower and her notebook quietly excited. With all the craziness going on, she had thought little of *Underneath*—there had been no time for dreams of publication. Perhaps the last few days were payment to the universe for the karmic debt that that much happiness would incur.

She allowed herself to fantasize briefly about covers and launch parties, even reviews in the *New York Times* before she drifted back into her ghost story via a memory of sitting cross-legged on the floor of some house in Hobart, listening to the sermon of a visiting monk. Her parents had been Buddhists from time to time, and when they were, she and Gus had been dragged to makeshift suburban temples. To her recollection, Buddhists considered nirvana the point at which one was enlightened enough not to be reincarnated, when one had no more to learn and was therefore no longer condemned to the suffering brought about by life. Perhaps she could use that to understand the fear her ghosts had of the living… Perhaps they considered life a regression to suffering and lack of understanding. In the end she fell asleep as she often had during those sermons.

Theo was aware of someone else being in the room before she opened her eyes, though she couldn't recall any sound or movement that alerted her to the fact.

"Don't fuckin' move." The voice was low and male, and entirely unfamiliar. He was a blur behind the muzzle of a gun, and Theo could not refocus her gaze to see him. She couldn't seem to breathe properly.

CHAPTER 20

"Caleb!" The blur with the gun called down the stairs. "Call Mac and tell him we found someone in his house."

A second man ran up the spiral staircase, arriving out of breath and wheezing. "Mom says there's someone staying in her room, Sam. Could be she didn't break in."

Theo began to come out of the mute terror of waking to a gun. And in its place outrage. "I'd hardly break in to have a nap, would I, you fool! Put that bloody gun down and call Mac."

Caleb hooted. "Dang, she sounds like a Brit." He squinted at her. "Who woulda thought...? Mom ain't gonna be happy."

The one called Sam lowered the gun and pulled out his phone. "Mac? It's Sam." He announced that he and Caleb had apprehended an intruder. A pause and he pulled the phone away from his ear, grimacing. "Yeah, all right. Keep your shirt on... Yeah, okay."

Sam thrust the phone at Theo.

Mac was brief. "Theo, I apologize. These are my brothers,

Sam and Caleb. I'm on my way… Hopefully I'll arrive before the dowager queen comes up the stairs."

Theo gave the phone back to Sam. Caleb watched her, grinning.

"Where's Mom?" Sam asked.

"She was doing something about that fuckin' dog."

Instantly, Theo was on her feet. "Horse! What have you done to Horse?"

"I have fed him." The woman who appeared at the top of the stairs was small and slight. An older version of the matriarch who had presided over the family portraits below. She fixed sharp blue eyes on Theo. "I don't believe we've had the pleasure."

Theo swallowed, wrong-footed. "I…I'm Theodosia Benton." It felt idiotic to introduce herself to people who a couple of minutes ago had held her at gunpoint. "How…how did you get in?"

"Dear girl, I have a key. Cormac didn't mention he'd put a… someone in my room."

Theo began to apologize. She wasn't sure what she was apologizing for, but Nancy Etheridge made her feel like she should.

"It's not your fault, Theodosia—my, that is a mouthful! Cormac should have let me know… Good heavens, one of us might have shot you!"

"What are you doing here?" Theo said almost to herself.

"I should be asking you that, don't you think?"

"Yes, of course. I'm sorry… I didn't mean…"

"Jesus!" Caleb squinted at her. "You're that girl in the papers."

"Yes," Theo said. There seemed no point in denying it.

"So…you and Mac…" Sam smirked.

Theo glared at him. What was the gun-toting idiot suggesting?

For a time, nobody said anything. They all just stared at one another. And then a call from downstairs. Mac's voice. Theo took a breath. Thank God!

Nancy Etheridge began down the stairs. "Shall we go ask Cormac to explain?" She motioned and her sons fell into step behind her.

Theo stayed where she was. Maybe it would be better to give Mac a chance to explain her presence. But her initial shock was being eroded by curiosity now, and she did wonder what Mac would tell his family. And so, she padded quietly down the staircase.

Nobody noticed her at first, too involved in argument. Mac didn't shout, but it was clear he was furious. "This is my house, you moron."

"Which I was defending," Sam growled in return. "You should be thanking me! For chrissake, this place could be taken in seconds."

Caleb leaned against the wall, his arms folded. He seemed amused. "She speaks funny."

"She's Australian," Mac said his eyes still on Sam.

"She doesn't look Australian. She's—"

"My guest. You don't pull a gun in my house. You certainly don't pull it on one of my guests."

"One?" Nancy Etheridge interrupted. "There are more?"

Sam cheered his approval. "Go, Mac!"

"Grow up." Mac shot him a withering glance, which had no effect at all.

"Who are these people?" Nancy demanded. "And why have you taken them in?"

"You've met Gus," Mac said tightly. "Theo is his sister."

"Really?" Caleb again. "They don't look alike. Are you sure, or is that just what she told you?"

"Well, what are they doing here?" Nancy interrupted as Mac turned on Caleb.

"That's really none of your business, Mom. They're my guests. What the hell are you doing here?"

Nancy straightened to her full height, which couldn't have been much more than five feet, and yet, she did not seem small. "Language, Cormac. I did not raise you to be foul-mouthed and disrespectful, regardless of the company you're keeping."

"What do you expect from the Left!" Sam added fuel to the fire.

Mac tipped his head back and sighed. "Would you all just go? Mom, that key was for emergencies...not for you to bring the rednecks out for an excursion!"

"Don't call your brothers names, Cormac. This might have all been avoided if you'd let me know you'd put someone in my room. I'd like to know what else you'd expected your brother to do when he discovered your home had been invaded!"

Theo smiled faintly as Mac expressed his frustration. He seemed to sense her presence then, and looked up to the stairs.

"Theo, hello. Allow me to introduce my mother and brothers."

What followed was to Theo a little surreal. It was a perfectly normal introduction, with polite inquiries as to how she and Mac knew one another. Sam wouldn't stop grinning, and Mac seemed a little tortured, but otherwise it was utterly conventional aside from the fact that she now knew the family with whom she was becoming acquainted were all armed.

Of course, this was America, where people had a constitutional right to be armed. But it was, for an Australian, unsettling.

Sam apologized for holding her at gunpoint. "For all I knew, you'd already buried Mac in the backyard," he said by way of excuse. "But I wouldn't have shot you," he assured her.

Mac shook his head. "Idiot."

Nancy raised a reproving finger at Mac. "Don't start."

"What are you doing in town, Mom? More to the point, what are you doing *here*?"

"We came to pick up some supplies. They're being delivered here." She smiled. "And of course, we thought we'd visit with you awhile."

"Interesting that you arrived while I was at work then."

"Don't be petulant, son. We intended to call you once we got here."

Theo looked at Mac, unsure what to do next.

"Would you like something to eat?" Nancy asked. "I brought pie—apple and blueberry."

"That sounds lovely," Theo said in an attempt to ease the awkwardness. If eating pie was what it took…

Nancy smiled triumphantly at Mac. "See, darling, there's no reason to be in a temper. Shall we use the kitchen?"

And so Theo sat at the antique oak table in Mac's kitchen and ate Nancy's apple and blueberry pie with the Etheridges. It was as much like a family meal as any other. Nancy dished out wedges of pie with whipped cream, Mac took care of drinks and extracted cheese and crackers out of the refrigerator. The familial bickering became almost friendly. For this, Theo was particularly glad, unable to forget entirely that at least one of Mac's brothers had a gun. The knowledge was always there. She wondered if she'd ever get used to it.

They hadn't finished eating when a truck pulled up to the house. Mac's brothers went outside to transfer its cargo into their pickups.

"What's in the sacks?" Theo whispered as she and Mac watched the proceedings through the window. Sam and Caleb were heaving large canvas sacks from one vehicle to another, frozen breath a visible flag of their exertions.

"Cement."

"That's a lot of cement."

"They're extending the bunkers on the Ponderosa, I believe."

"Why didn't they have it delivered there?"

"They don't want anyone to know what they're doing, so they have it delivered to me, and transfer it themselves." Mac sighed. "I'd better help them. The sooner they finish, the sooner they can all leave." He removed his jacket.

"It's freezing outside," she reminded him as he hung the jacket on the back of a chair.

"I'll warm up soon enough," he said ruefully. "Will you be all right if I...?"

Theo waved off the query. "Go help them. I'm sure your mother won't shoot me..." She paused. "Will she?"

He laughed. "Just don't talk politics, and you should be fairly safe."

Theo lingered by the window. She could hear Nancy in the kitchen. Clearing up after pie perhaps. She should help...or at least offer to do so. Theo breathed deeply. No politics.

When she walked back into the kitchen she found Nancy emptying all the kitchen cupboards. "Just thought I'd wipe them out while I was here," she said from inside a cupboard. "That woman who cleans for Cormac is slapdash at best. Lord! Nothing is in its rightful place... Who on earth stores the teacups with the dinner plates?"

"Can I do anything to help?" Theo asked.

"Sure, sweetie. Perhaps if you were to wash up the lunch dishes. I cannot bear dishes in the sink!"

Theo opened the dishwasher door and proceeded to stack it.

"Tell me, dear, why are you and your brother living with Cormac?"

"Gus's house is…undergoing repairs."

"Oh…what happened to it?"

Theo swallowed. Nancy Etheridge was pretending to be engrossed in cleaning the back of one of the lower cupboards. Only her protruding bottom half was still visible. From that angle Theo could clearly see the holster on the erstwhile church auxiliary president's hip. It was a strange way to have a conversation. "Gus's house is pretty old. There were all sorts of things that needed doing."

"So you're not in hiding?"

For a moment Theo wasn't sure what to say… Actually, it was much longer than a moment. She was still not sure how to respond when she finally asked, "Did Mac say I was in hiding?"

"Cormac, bless him, doesn't tell me anything…which is why I have to ask." Nancy climbed out of the cupboard so she could face Theo. "It's his job I suppose…uncovering secrets, keeping some, exposing others. Strange way to make a living, if you ask me."

"You don't approve of his job?" Theo grabbed the opportunity to divert the conversation.

"I'm afraid Cormac doesn't much care about my approval." Tiny lines of irritation appeared on the bridge of her nose. "It's not really a necessary job, is it?"

"Necessary? I'm not sure what you—"

"Well, it's like this: Samuel is a mechanic—can fix any engine—and Caleb is a builder by trade. Their eldest brother,

Ezekiel, is a physician. We'll be able to use them. The world will need them."

"But they won't need Mac?" Theo asked, confused.

"He doesn't really do anything of use, does he? Nothing that will feed or shelter or defend his family." Nancy sighed. "Cormac makes a lot of money, but there'll come a time when money won't mean anything."

"It won't?"

"Of course not! We'll be too busy finding food and water and defending our homes—"

"Right, the pickups are loaded." Mac walked into the kitchen. His tie was in his pocket and his sleeves rolled to the elbow. He was smiling, relaxed. "Sam says he's ready to go."

Nancy dismissed the notion with a flick of her hand. "We can't leave before dark in broad view of anybody watching."

"Of course—it's much less suspicious to have a convoy of pickups leave my house in the middle of the night."

"Don't be ridiculous, darling; we won't leave together." Nancy rinsed out the sponge she'd been using. "In the meantime, I'll sort out these cupboards. How on earth to do you find anything at all?"

"Mom—"

Caleb lugged in a large box of produce and a substantial joint of meat. "Where do you want this?"

"Just put it on the table," Nancy directed. "I'll need to sort out this kitchen before I start cooking."

"Cooking?" Mac asked. "Why are you—"

"Ezekiel will be here soon."

"Why is Zeke coming here?"

"Ezekiel is your brother, Cormac. I would have hoped he'd be welcome in your house."

"He is—of course he is." Mac's voice was even. "I just want to know why the entire clan is descending on me today."

"I just thought it was time we sat down to a family dinner…and since it's almost impossible to get you out to the farm these days…"

"Mom, Theo is—"

"Delighted to meet you," Theo interrupted. She turned to Mac, trying to let him know she understood. Her mother, too, was unstoppable. "Gus and I could go out to dinner, so you could all—"

Mac shook his head. "You've just gotten out of the hospital—"

"Hospital!" Nancy removed her rubber gloves. "Oh, honey, what are you doing washing dishes? Cormac, what could you be thinking? Sit down, sweetie, sit down!" She bossed and bustled Theo to a chair. "I'm going to put on a pot of my chicken dumpling soup, and then you can tell me all about it."

CHAPTER 21

Let's go to Lawrence! For Primus. Let's show the Minotaur that we know.

    WKWWK

    Loyal Son

I'm in! WKWWK

    Patriot Warrior

We'll bring 100 soldiers.

    True Men

—~—

Mac called his mother aside. The argument was conducted in terse, restrained whispers, but it was in earnest. Theo sat at the oak table trying not to look in that direction, trying to pretend that she was completely unaware the exchange was over her. She gathered from the occasional phrase that became audible that Nancy Etheridge had guessed why she was here.

And she'd noticed that the Burroughs that usually hung in her room was missing.

"Just for once, Mom, mind your own business," Mac said quietly. "This has nothing to do with you. Leave the poor girl alone—she's been through enough."

The situation might have escalated if the doorbell had not sounded.

"Zeke is here," Caleb shouted from the front door.

A simply enormous man walked through, shouting greetings to Sam and Caleb. He placed a case of beer on the bench and then threw his thick arm about Mac and rubbed his hair. "How are you, kid? Mom's decided to bring the war cabinet to you, I'm afraid."

Mac introduced Theo.

"Well what d'ya know? Gus the Aussie's sister."

"The poor thing's just got out of hospital, Ezekiel," Nancy said. "Perhaps you could check her over."

"I'm fine." Theo stood and backed away, alarmed. "It was just a cut."

Zeke smiled at her. "Don't worry, Theo. Unlike my mom here, I don't conduct medical procedures by force…not without at least checking you have insurance first."

"By force?" Nancy reared, jumping immediately to his meaning. "That bullet had to come out. I saved Cormac's life."

Zeke and Mac exchanged a glance. Clearly, the necessity of the bullet extraction was something they had discussed before. But all Zeke said was, "Lucky Mac." He took two cans of Budweiser from the case, handed one to Mac, and held the other inquiringly towards Theo. She shook her head.

"I could change the dressings on your arm if you like," Zeke offered. "Save you a trip back to the hospital—but only if you like. Though you should let me know before I start drinking."

Theo smiled. Zeke, too, wore a holster, but perhaps she was becoming used to them. She could not help but like him. She was a little surprised when he offered to check her arm—only because she'd thought the gauze bandage invisible beneath her sleeve. "It was only changed this morning," she said. "But thank you."

"In that case," Zeke twisted the cap off his bottle, "Cheese!"

"Cheese?"

"Isn't that what you Aussies say?"

Theo laughed. "I think you'll find that's 'cheers.'"

"That's what I said. Cheese!" He sat down at the table with his beer.

Mac threw him a bag of potato chips and proceeded to finish washing the dishes by hand, while his brother talked with Theo.

Ezekiel Etheridge was an unusual man. He had all the swagger and manner of some kind of television cowboy—he was large and friendly, his features endearingly ugly. That he was a physician was fascinatingly incongruous. She wondered if he wore the gun on his rounds at the hospital. She didn't ask because she was afraid of the answer. He seemed to have more effect stemming their mother's questions than Mac did, asking Nancy pointedly if she was working for the government now. Though it was delivered in jest, the accusation seemed to be so unthinkable to Nancy Etheridge that she was struck into appalled silence.

Mac did not leave Theo alone with his family again.

Nancy cooked such a feast that Theo was convinced another dozen family members would drop in unexpectedly soon. But only Gus arrived. Perhaps Mac had messaged him a heads-up because he took the presence of the Etheridges in his stride.

"Are you okay?" he asked quietly as he tried, somewhat unsuccessfully, to keep Horse from licking his face.

"I'm fine...but I should be asking you that." Theo's brow furrowed with concern. Gus looked exhausted..

"Bugger of a day at work, that's all," he replied, rubbing the loose flaps of Horse's muzzle until the hound's eyes rolled back with pleasure.

Zeke, who it seemed had taken on the role of alcohol distributor, handed Gus a beer. "There you go, buddy, though you look like you could use something stronger."

"This will be just fine." Gus lifted the bottle in salute. "What are you all doing here?"

"Mom decided we had to all go check on poor Mac."

"Why?"

Zeke shrugged. "Who knows? She decided it was time for a family dinner—I came along to keep the peace, is all."

Nancy called them all to dinner. The Etheridges unstrapped their various holsters and placed them on the kitchen bench—within easy reach, but not on their person. Each of them seemed to have a number of weapons. Theo noted that Mac either did not carry or refused to relinquish. She wondered which. They held hands around a table burgeoning with the meal Nancy had cooked, while she thanked God for it. The prayer did not stop there. Nancy Etheridge thanked the Almighty for many things including the "American way," the Constitution, and the flag.

Gus caught Theo's eye and pulled a face while the Etheridges still had their heads bowed. She was glad he was there to confirm that this was bizarre. Not unpleasant but decidedly odd.

Nancy finished by thanking the Lord for Gus and Theo and

asking him to expedite the renovations on their home. "Amen" came as something of a relief.

The meal was a surprisingly sedate affair. Nancy Etheridge insisted on formal manners at the table. One person spoke at time with no breakaway conversations. And so it was difficult to avoid or deflect when Nancy raised the article on the death of Dan Murdoch.

"You know, I've read almost all his books, but I had no idea he lived in Lawrence."

"I think Dan tried to keep a low profile," Theo said.

"Tell me, sweetheart, how did you meet and fall in love?"

Theo choked slightly.

"Mom," Mac said sharply, "that's none of our business."

"Nonsense. It was in the paper—it's hardly private."

"We both used to write in Benders," Theo said, smiling briefly at Mac.

"The bar? I suppose it's nice that some people still meet in bars rather than online. Harvey and I met at church of course. What church do you and Gus attend?"

Mac sighed audibly.

Zeke and Sam chuckled.

"Oh, we tag along with Mac on Sundays," Gus responded, grinning.

Nancy looked up at ceiling and shook her head. "I'll pray for you all."

In a desperate attempt to change the subject, Theo asked Sam and Caleb what exactly they planned to do with cement. A beat of silence, and then Sam spoke with his eyes on his plate.

"What cement?"

"The bags you were moving…" Theo started, confused.

"What are we pretending was in the bags?" Mac asked wearily.

"Feed," Caleb said. "Pig feed."

Theo looked to Gus for help. He mouthed the words, "Don't ask." She didn't, but she did begin to doubt the wisdom of accepting Mac's invitation. He was terrific, but his family was as mad as cut snakes.

It was about nine o'clock when they finished eating. The Etheridges strapped on their holsters as Mac made coffee.

Gus excused himself. "I have a few briefs to go through this evening, so I might say good night."

"I'll go up with you," Theo said quickly. "I'm a bit tired."

Nancy agreed wholeheartedly. "Of course, sweetie. If you don't mind me saying, you do look a wreck!"

Gus placed his arm around his sister, vaguely amused but slightly protective nonetheless. "You just need some sleep... Mac, you don't mind if we—"

Mac shook his head. "For God's sake, save yourselves."

⌒〜

Theo sat cross-legged in the armchair in Gus's room with Horse's large head resting in her lap. Gus flicked through some briefs while she told him the circumstances in which she'd first met Sam and Caleb.

"They did what?" Gus swore. "I'm beginning to think we might have been better off in a hotel."

Theo had had that same thought herself, but she felt the need to defend Mac. "He had no idea they were going to turn up, Gus."

"He should change the locks."

Theo laughed. "They're his family. We're in no position to throw stones on that score."

Gus looked at her over the top of the file he was perusing. "How are you, really?"

"I'm not sure. A little numb, maybe—like this isn't happening to me."

He sighed. "I'm sorry it is happening to you. If I could talk Mendes into being reasonable, I'd send you back to the ancients. At least nobody will shoot at you there."

"I may, however, shoot myself," Theo muttered. "Mum and Dad were living in a tent somewhere near Cradle Mountain when I spoke to them last."

Gus grinned. "I see your point." He rubbed his face wearily. "I'm not sure what we're going to do, mate. Apparently, there are busloads of Murdoch's fans pouring into Lawrence on some kind of pilgrimage, and with that fuckin' news article...I just don't know..."

Theo looked up, startled. The tension was clear in Gus's voice. Her calm, unflappable brother was worried, and that, on its own, frightened her more than overbearing detectives and grieving readers with guns. "Gus..."

"I'm not going to lie to you, Theo; things don't look good. Mendes is being a complete dick." He put aside his brief and beckoned her over to him.

Theo moved Horse's head gently from her knee and climbed onto the bed beside Gus.

He placed arm around her shoulders. "Do you want to tell me what happened in Canberra? The university has records of complaint against you, for assault."

"What?"

"A lecturer of some sort. Hugh Carrington? He claims you threatened to kill him."

Theo closed her eyes. "That bastard!"

Gus's arm tightened around her shoulders. "Theo?"

"He tutored me in Torts... I thought we were friends." Theo's voice was shaking already. She forced it. "We started meeting for coffee. We talked about school, and books... He'd tell funny stories about the other lecturers...and then one day I met him at his office and he...he tried to..." Theo couldn't get the words out.

Gus didn't press her. He waited until she was ready.

"There was some kind of award on his desk. I hit him with that. He grabbed me before I could unlock the door, but I kneed him, and bit, and scratched...and then I ran."

"Did you tell anyone, Theo?"

"I didn't have any friends, Gus. Other than Hugh. And I wasn't sure... When I looked back, I wondered if I gave him the impression that I—I just wanted to forget about it."

"Why didn't you tell me?" Gus's voice was tight, livid.

The answer Theo knew, because she had thought about telling him, debated telling him. "I was scared that you'd think it was something about me... After what happened with Jake, I thought you'd think it was me, that I was inviting this somehow—"

He hugged her fiercely. "Dammit, Theo—"

"I'm sorry. I don't know what I was thinking... I just knew you'd be angry—"

He tensed. "What were you afraid I'd do?"

"Nothing!" she said desperately. "I just didn't want you think that was the reason I was leaving, the reason I didn't want to be a lawyer." She turned to look at his face. "It really wasn't, Gus. Never having to see Hugh again was just a collateral benefit."

Gus exhaled slowly. He tried unsuccessfully to keep the fury from his voice. "I presume this fuckwit lodged a complaint against you with the university just in case you decided to lodge one against him. You left, and it was not pursued...but it's on record."

Theo nodded. She understood the implications. He had complained and she hadn't... Of course he had—he was professor of law; he knew how it worked.

"When he finds out about this, Mendes will want to question you," Gus said. "Just tell him what you told me. And don't worry, I'll be there." He paused. "Your thing with Murdoch...he didn't try to—"

"I wanted to be with Dan. He was nothing like Hugh."

"He was an older man," Gus reminded her. "Mendes could well suggest his advances, too, were unwelcome, and you reacted in the same way you did with Carrington, but that this time you killed him."

"That's absurd."

"I know, but I want you to be ready."

"What's happening, Gus?" Theo dropped her face into her hands. "It feels like everything is going wrong, and there's nothing I do that helps. I can't find my way out."

"Darkest before the dawn...I hope. All of this is circumstantial at best." He kissed her forehead. "Just hang in there, Theo, we'll get through this. I have it on good authority that you're represented by a legal genius."

A tap at the door. Mac's voice. "Gus, it's me."

"Come in."

Mac opened the door. He didn't seem surprised to see Theo. His eyes were sympathetic. "You told her then?"

Gus nodded. "Mac found the record of complaint this morning," he explained for Theo's benefit. "He figured the police wouldn't be too far behind, so he called me just before he came back here to rescue you from the Kelly gang."

Mac seemed to understand or guess the reference to Australia's most famous bushranger and his family. He apologized for his own. "They're gone." He shook his head. "Quarter hour intervals and in different directions in case Homeland Security is watching."

Theo glanced at Gus. He nodded. Mac needed to know, and she needed to become accustomed to recounting what had happened, however difficult or mortifying the words were. Theo did not look at him when she explained why she had a record of assault.

"Right." Mac's tone was gentle. "I'll see if there are any other complaints involving or by Carrington. This could be a pattern, and if we can establish that, then the probative value of Carrington's complaint against you is minimized."

"How long do you think it will be before the police find out?" Theo asked tentatively.

"They might already know by now," Mac admitted. "They will probably want to speak to you about it soon."

"Oh." Theo tried to imagine telling Mendes about Hugh Carrington. Telling Gus, whom she loved, and Mac, whom she trusted, left her feeling flayed, exposed in a way that made her want to curl into herself away from the world. All this time she had refused to think about what had happened.

"It may have been my fault," she said.

"How could it possibly be your fault?" Mac asked.

Theo swallowed and compelled herself to say it, to face it. "There were times when I wondered if he thought...if he wanted..." She took a breath. "There were times when he made me uncomfortable, but I ignored it, told myself that I'd misunderstood, that it was an accident. I may have given him the impression—"

"Aw, mate." Gus's arm was still around her shoulders, and he pulled her closer. "Men don't have nuclear codes. They can always stop, always turn themselves off...even if you were giving him a bloody lap dance!"

Mac flinched when he mentioned lap dancing, but he agreed. "He grabbed you when you were trying to leave, Theo. He couldn't have been under any misapprehension then."

"Yes, as far as I'm concerned, you were within your rights to kill him to get away," Gus growled. "I may yet."

Theo smiled slightly. At that moment she felt completely safe for the first time since Dan Murdoch had been killed. She knew that she was clutching at threads, that it was an illusion, arising from the fact that she was protected and defended, and by her brother, loved. That was not the same thing as being safe, but for the moment she felt it.

CHAPTER 22

Caleb kept his eyes on the road as he went over what had just happened. Fuck! Theodosia Benton was living in his brother's house. What did Mac think he was doing? Of course, Mac wouldn't know. As much as he thought he knew everything, he wouldn't know this.

Caleb scowled as he thought about the young woman his brother was harboring. She wasn't very big. He couldn't see how she had killed Primus...not unless she'd had a gun. Which was unlikely given the way she looked at their weapons when they disarmed for dinner. Like they were rattlesnakes or something. And she was Gus's sister... They'd all known Gus for a while... He didn't *know*, but Caleb was sure he wasn't complicit either. Theodosia Benton, on the other hand, had been there when Primus died...she had to be involved somehow. Caleb thought about turning his truck around, confronting her with what he knew and warning his brother. Of course, Mac wouldn't believe him. Caleb shook his head. He wasn't sure when Mac had gone wrong. Their mother spent a lot of time praying he would see the light. But Mac was obstinate—it would probably take more than divine intervention.

Still, they were brothers. He'd have to do something or Mac might end up like Primus.

———

It was half past seven when Theo remembered that she had agreed to meet Veronica Cole for breakfast. All thought of the appointment had been dislodged by guns and Etheridges and memories, and so she showered and dressed in a panic and hurtled downstairs with just minutes to spare. Gus was flicking through a file as he talked to Mac.

"He came back to talk about musicals and tell me to lock my door," Mac said, rummaging in the cupboards.

"Don't you usually?"

"Not to the house, to my bedroom. In case you or Theo tried to murder me in the night, I suppose." Mac placed a box of cereal on the counter.

"So what did you do?"

"Told him I would—it was too late to listen to his latest fantasy. It was the easiest way to get him to go home."

"As much as I want in on this conversation, I have to go!" Theo told them about the appointment as Gus poured her a cup of coffee.

"We're supposed to be in hiding, Theo," Gus said. "That doesn't work if you send out change of address cards."

"Veronica's my agent...at least I hope she will be. I can't mess this up..."

"Fair enough...but no one else, okay?"

"I promise."

Mac opened a drawer in the kitchen and took out a mobile phone, which he handed her. "Leave yours here and take this one."

"Why?"

"Because this one has its GPS tracker turned on, but only Gus and I know you have this phone. It means we'll be able to find you, but no one else will."

"Oh." Theo took the phone. "This is a bit James Bond, isn't it?"

Mac smiled. "More helicopter parent than Bond, but let's be on the safe side."

"Why do you have a spare spy phone?"

"It's a perfectly ordinary phone with a few functions enabled," Mac replied. "My brothers keep a few burners here for reasons that are too embarrassing to explain, but in this instance it's handy."

"Burners?"

"Phones that can be used and thrown away without a trace of the owner…generally favored by criminals and paranoid lunatics."

Theo laughed as she slid the phone into her pocket. "Okay. Thank you." She turned back as a thought occurred. "What if someone calls? What if the police—"

"They'll call your attorney," Gus said. "In fact, I'd prefer they go through me. But Theo"—he met her eyes earnestly—"be careful. I know this agency means a lot to you, but make this breakfast meeting short and try not to go anywhere public."

"How about I suggest we get drive-through and sit in the car to eat it?"

"Perfect."

"I was kidding."

"Do it anyway."

A black Porsche pulled into the driveway, and the video monitor showed Veronica Cole behind the wheel.

Gus stood. "I should probably walk you out."

"Why?"

"To throw myself in the way of bullets."

"Don't be an idiot."

Gus glanced at the screen. "Not to put too fine a point on it… but she's hot."

"Married."

"Oh." He sat back down and returned to his brief. "Good luck, then."

Theo wished the men a hurried farewell. Before she left, Mac gave her the code to his security system, which he had changed that morning in light of the previous day's invasion.

Veronica Cole was waiting in the car.

It had snowed again the previous night. Someone had already shoveled the driveway. Veronica Cole waved from the Porsche, and Theo climbed into the passenger seat, trying valiantly to do so elegantly despite the low profile of the car. Veronica laughed.

"You have to free-fall into the seat," she advised. "There's no other way."

Theo landed in the leather upholstery with a thump and then opened her eyes. It had worked.

Veronica laughed. "That little heart-starter came as a standard feature."

"Where are we going?" Theo asked as the agent pulled her car out of the driveway.

"I thought we could grab breakfast in my hotel suite. We can be assured of privacy there…unless that makes you uncomfortable."

"No…not at all." Theo was relieved she didn't have to explain her current need to keep a low profile. The venue would satisfy Gus and Mac.

Breakfast was already set up in Veronica's elegant room at the Oread. A small table had been draped with crisp white linen and laden with fruit, croissants, eggs, pancakes, and almost anything else one could dream of eating for breakfast. The room was fortunately large enough for a second table, at which they sat with plates gathered from the first. This was clearly not a standard service.

Initially they talked of *Underneath*. Veronica had no official news, but she could say the manuscript was "causing a stir" at Day Delos. "Of course, there is more than the quality of the manuscript at play when we consider a writer."

Theo recalled what Veronica had told her at their last meeting about the impact of the writer's reputation. She felt sick. Had the article in the *Star* stolen her chance? She stuttered an explanation. "I thought Mary Cowell was an old friend of Dan's. I didn't know she was a reporter."

"Oh, Theo, I know." Veronica steadied her. "But I won't lie to you. The partners are concerned that you may always be associated with the death of Dan Murdoch, even if the real killer is apprehended."

Theo nodded, not trusting herself to speak and hating Mary Cowell at that moment.

"You mustn't fret," Veronica said calmly. "As I said, your manuscript is exceptional, but I did want to talk to you about our conversation on the phone."

"Yes," Theo said, though she was not sure what the agent meant.

"You asked me about Dan's gardener," Veronica prompted.

"Yes, I thought the police might not have known about him. That he might be able to tell them something about Dan."

"That's very proactive of you, Theo."

"It's the least I can do for Dan…"

Veronica smiled. "I can understand why you feel that way—it's natural, of course. But has it occurred to you that your interest in the case might be read another way?"

Theo stopped, startled, bewildered. "What other way?"

"It may be assumed that your interest is indicative of a guilty mind."

"But I didn't—"

"I know that, Theo." Veronica cut short her horrified protest. "It's just the association that's a concern. It may not be the best idea to take such an active interest in the investigation while you're still a subject of it. Certainly, Day Delos and Associates would be happier if you were to put as much distance between yourself and Dan as possible."

"But Dan was…"

"Dan was a successful writer, and he wanted that for you, for your work. He, more than anyone, would understand, I promise you."

Theo's words were lost, her thoughts confused. The idea of distancing herself from Dan seemed so callous, so treacherous.

"I understand Dan's death is having an impact on your brother's practice," Veronica said quietly.

"Gus?"

"Yes, I believe his firm has lost a lot of clients."

"But this has nothing to do with Gus. He's never even met Dan."

"It's ironic, but true, that criminals want their lawyers to be beyond any kind of reproach." Veronica sighed. "And I'm afraid Gus's partners are the conservative sort."

"How do you know?" Theo asked. She did not doubt the veracity of what Veronica said, but she did wonder how she knew so much about Gus's firm.

"Day Delos has a lot of contacts in Lawrence...and we keep our ears to the ground." Veronica poured Theo a cup of coffee. "Crane, Hayes and Benton is the least of our concerns, I'm afraid. I don't suppose you recall me telling you about the fans Dan was forced to flee?"

"Yes, I remember."

"I am concerned that with news of Dan's death, they'll make their way to Lawrence." She looked Theo in the eye. "It is really important, for your sake and the sake of those around you, that you do try to distance yourself from Dan Murdoch."

Theo stared. "Shouldn't we tell the police about these people?"

"Day Delos has already handed over all the information we have." Veronica put down her fork and dabbed the corner of her mouth with a linen napkin without disturbing her lipstick. "You mustn't panic, Theo; we have no intention of allowing anything happen to a talent like you. But you must do your part...if not for your own sake, for your brother's—"

"Are you saying Gus is in danger from these people?" Theo tried valiantly to sound calm, but she could hear the fear in her own voice.

"Oh no...Theo, no. I was talking about the impact on his firm, his professional reputation. Your brother is fierce in his defense of you—so fierce that his better judgment is occasionally compromised."

"Do you know Gus?" Theo wasn't sure why she asked this—it was a sudden feeling.

"I have met him professionally, a year or two ago," Veronica said smiling. "He won't remember me—it was a straightforward contract negotiation. I have heard the odd word of him recently from mutual acquaintances." The agent studied her. "Of course,

I'm not telling you anything you don't know. I presume you're well aware of the pressure Gus is under as a result of all this."

Theo felt sick. She hadn't been aware...not really, not enough.

"All I'm suggesting," Veronica said gently, "is that you don't try to become too involved in the investigation." She stood and fetched a sheaf of papers from the writing desk. "I do have something else on which you might want to spend some time instead." She handed the paperwork to Theo. "Should we offer you representation, there are few things we'll need—a number of biographies of different lengths for media of various sorts. We find it works best if our clients write us a bit of a life story, which we will then edit and piece together to get a targeted bio tailored for the audience in question."

"Oh...okay." Theo took the papers, embarrassed. Veronica was obviously giving her busywork to keep her occupied...like a child who was getting into scrapes.

"There are also usual questions about social security numbers, bank accounts, passports etc."

"But Gus... Maybe I should—"

"You're not going to be able to get him to stop being your big brother. I'm afraid the best way to keep him out of trouble is to stay out of it yourself."

Theo closed her eyes. She felt ashamed. She'd been so pre-occupied with what she owed Dan that she hadn't even thought about what she owed Gus. She wouldn't let his life be destroyed again because he tried to look after her.

"Theo... Oh, I'm sorry. I didn't mean to upset you."

"You didn't—it isn't you I'm upset with. I should have insulated Gus from this somehow."

Veronica sighed. "Easier said than done." She exhaled. "Look,

I'm breaking all sorts of rules telling you this, but I'm almost sure Day Delos is going to offer you representation. If it were up to just me, it would be done already."

"Really?" Despite herself, Theo's eyes brightened.

"I think so. There's just couple of checks we still need to make."

"What checks?"

"We need to be certain you really want to be writer."

"I do…of course I do."

Veronica smiled. "I'm sure the partners will decide that you do too. Once you're a client, we'll help sort this mess out."

"Gus—"

"Even Gus. We have a lot of resources and excellent connections."

Theo nodded. She did not doubt it.

⌐⌐

Veronica dropped Theo back at Mac's and waited while she punched in the correct security code and let herself in. She waved goodbye in the video surveillance.

Theo let Horse in and spent several minutes accepting the hound's feelings on her return. Indeed, she sat on the floor and enjoyed the simplicity of the dog's joy, the boisterous panting that seemed to say, "You're back—thank God you're back—where'd you go?"

"I was at a very important meeting, Horsey, old mate," Theo said, pulling back as he licked her face. Her life seemed to have become so complicated.

She finally calmed Horse and sat at the kitchen table to think. It was all such a jumble, like random extracts from different novels. And then it occurred to her that to sort it out she needed to write it down…like a plot. Perhaps then she would see what was happening, be able to make sense of it.

She used the large notebook in which she had been writing notes for her ghost story. Beginning with everything she knew about Dan Murdoch—which admittedly was not a great deal—Theo timelined it all, starting with a nebulous date several years earlier when he'd moved from New York to Lawrence to avoid deranged fans. She wrote down every detail she could remember of finding Dan's body, and the police interviews that followed, her first encounter with Spiderman, the collision in the parking lot, the open gate, Mac Etheridge and his family, Burt Winslow, and now that bastard Hugh Carrington. The process helped to calm her, gave her an illusion of order in the chaos, and made her realize that she still had no idea what was going on. She tried to see herself through Mendes's eyes: an aspiring writer who fell into a relationship with a successful established author, decades her senior. Perhaps Detective Mendes thought she had set out to seduce Dan Murdoch. Hugh Carrington's complaint gave him reason to believe she attacked older men at random. Or perhaps he thought it was some kind of literary spat—an argument over adjectives. As far as she could tell, Dan had been killed by someone who knew what he was doing, who thought to protect his clothes from the blood, who was calm enough not to walk through the blood. That was hardly what you'd expect from five-and-a-half-foot law school dropout. He'd have to see that…and then he would be able to focus on who really killed Dan Murdoch, all this would fade, and Gus would stop having to pay for being her brother…unless she did something to make Mendes keep looking at her. Like phoning him with what she thought were leads. Veronica was right. She was making things worse.

She wondered just how bad things were at Crane, Hayes and Benton. Gus wouldn't tell her even if she asked.

Theo glanced at her watch. It was just past noon. She found her usual phone where she'd left it on the kitchen bench and dialed Jacqui Steven's number.

CHAPTER 23

Caleb pulled the article up on the screen and read it again. Mac wasn't taking him seriously—he knew that. It was up to Caleb to save him. He cursed...and typed *Mary Cowell* into his search engine.

———

Jacqui waved as Theo's cab pulled up at the diner. It was a small establishment near the Spencer Art Museum, close enough to the university to hear the "Big Tooter," KU's beloved steam whistle, which blew hourly to signal the beginning and end of classes. An official sign bearing a gun in an interdictory circle prohibited firearms within the café. Theo had until recently thought such signs in cafés odd, more political than practical, and then she'd watched the Etheridges disarm before dinner. Now she appreciated the line it drew. Knowing people might be armed was a little like knowing there had been a spider on the wall just a minute ago.

As she pushed open the door, Theo did not miss the makeshift shrine at the nearby bus stop shelter. Candles, flowers, and stuffed toys below a poster advertising one of Dan Murdoch's books.

She and Jacqui grabbed coffee and an order of fries between them and took one of the small booths along the wall. Jacqui's corporate attire might have stood out among the primarily student clientele who, this close to the end of the fall term and finals, were drinking a lot of coffee. But the café was not well heated, so they kept their outer layers on and preserved a kind of great-coated anonymity.

Theo thanked her brother's colleague for agreeing to meet her. "I'm worried about Gus…well, not him specifically…the firm… and him…but because of work, not because of him…"

Jacqui pulled off her mittens and placed a calming hand on Theo's arm. "You're babbling, but I do know what you mean. I take it Gus hasn't told you what's going on."

"No. Gus's life has been subsumed with my problems lately." Theo blew gently on the steaming beverage in her hands. "But I can see how tired and worried he is."

"Have you asked him about it?"

"No," Theo said guiltily. "Not yet—"

"Good. If he hasn't refused to tell you, then how am I supposed to know he wants it kept secret?" Jacqui raised her latte triumphantly. "Loophole identified."

Theo smiled.

"There is a clause in the partnership that allows the founding partners to force Gus out," Jacqui continued. "Phillip Hayes wants to use it; John Crane isn't sure. The firm lost a big client who used the article in the *Star* as an excuse…but Hayes is an idiot and can't see that Bellevue Industries would have left anyway. When a big client jumps, there is often a ripple effect; other clients get nervous." She sighed. "And we do represent a couple of jerks. One of them apparently said something out of line about you yesterday, and Gus kicked the guy out of his office. But he was a jerk."

Theo swallowed. "What can I do?" She raised her eyes to meet Jacqui's. "There must be something I can do."

Jacqui's face softened. "Theo, this isn't your fault."

"I've just lobbed up on Gus's doorstep and blown up his life."

"That's only true if you really have been running round killing people."

"Of course I haven't—"

"Then it's really not your fault, Theo." She pulled a fry from the plate before them. "Gus calls these chips, you know. Refuses to acknowledge they're fries."

"It's not fair," Theo said. She was aware she sounded like a child, that fairness or the lack of it meant little in the wider world.

"Oh, Theo, Gus will work his way through this. Philip Hayes is an asshole. And your brother is an exceptional attorney. He'll be all right."

"But—"

"There is nothing you can do, Theo. Even if you were to get another attorney, people would then wonder why you fired Gus. We just have to ride it out."

Theo nodded, struggling against the creeping onslaught of tears. Tears were not what Gus needed. There had to be something she could do.

Jacqui pushed the plate of fries toward her. "For God's sake, eat some before I end up the size of a barn… For what it's worth, Gus loves having you here. I think being an Australian in America can be lonely sometimes. I know Gus likes America, but he thinks we're all a little mad. He's probably right."

Theo smiled faintly as she recalled the times Gus had lectured her on the peculiarities of the American condition—observations delivered with affection and a kind of amused bewilderment. She helped Jacqui finish the fries, and they talked about the Kansas City Chiefs and Christmas.

It was to be Theo's first Christmas in the U.S. The previous year she'd been home, to spend the holidays with her parents in the middle of an Australian summer. This year, neither she nor Gus would return for the crazy communal barbecue to which her parents invited everybody they had ever met—wishing them all a "Happy Saturnalia" and feeding family, acquaintances, and virtual strangers with equal warmth and generosity and celebration, until they all lay in food comas under the shade trees. A prick of homesickness. She and Gus had explained the current situation with enough vagueness to make it sound more like an administrative difficulty than a murder investigation. They'd both promised to come home for the Winter Solstice, which in Australia took place in June.

"I'd better get back to work," Jacqui said, checking her watch, "or that jerk Hayes will want to sack me too." She saw Theo into a cab first. "I know Gus has got you on some kind of lockdown. He seems to think Dan Murdoch's readership is armed and dangerous."

Theo sighed. "I wish I could say he was wrong. Don't worry, I'm heading straight back." She embraced Jacqui. "Thank you, Jac. Really."

Theo paid the cab driver in cash, not wanting to leave an electronic trail of her movements. She laughed at herself. Perhaps she was becoming as paranoid as the Etheridges. She got out a couple of doors from Mac's house, telling herself it was a precaution. It was probably more to do with the fact that she wanted to walk outside, to enjoy the cold on her face and gaze at the magnificent houses in Mac's neighborhood like it was just another Friday. The sidewalks had been shoveled, but they were treacherous nonetheless. Like many of the sidewalks in Lawrence, they were made of cobbled brick rather than flat cement and prone to unevenness and ice. Theo had always found them charming, and she'd learned to walk carefully.

Some houses were decorated for Christmas. Indeed, Theo had noticed that morning that Mac's door, too, had acquired a wreath and the porch, swagging. She was sure they'd not been there when she arrived. Perhaps his mother, armed to the teeth, had decorated the house before she left in the middle of the night.

Theo smiled. Poor Mac. Still, at least Mrs. Etheridge was not wishing everyone she met a "Happy Saturnalia."

Theo let herself into the house, punching in the appropriate code. She was surprised by how much she breathed out when the door was once again locked and the security system armed. They had never locked the doors when she was a child. Her father used to say that doors should always be about possibilities, and locks were an anathema to that. Of course, they had never owned anything that a thief would regard as a "possibility" either, and more often than not, there was no actual door on the tent, or the caravan, or the pub in which they were living. She eventually learned to lock doors, but this was different; this need to hold out the world was recent. Not irrational or excessive, considering the circumstances, but definitely recent.

Staying with Mac had been a precaution. There was no reason to think anyone cared enough to look for her beyond the fracas at Gus's, which, after all, had been stirred by the article in the

Star and the presence of the media. They would all have moved on by now.

She made a sandwich, gave half to Horse, and returned to the tower to gaze listlessly at her notes as she thought about Gus, and his partners, and the demise of his practice. As much as her brother claimed his passion was surfing, she knew Gus liked being a lawyer, that he was proud of the career he'd built. "Oh, Dan, what have you done to us?" she said into the quiet. But it wasn't Dan's fault. It wasn't fair, but it wasn't Dan's fault.

In the end, Theo gave up trying to write and stared out of the window, watching as one of Mac's neighbors hung lights on his roof. It was only because she was watching, because the street was laid out before her, that she noticed the car that drove past twice, and then a little later came back again and parked across the street. A woman stepped out.

Theo recognized Mary Cowell's sharp haircut immediately. The reporter held up a phone. For a moment Theo thought she was trying to get reception, and then it became clear that she was taking a photo. Of Mac's house.

Theo pulled away from the window. She started down the staircase, furious, intent on going out to confront Mary Cowell, to make her understand what her article had done. By the time she got to the ground floor, she'd calmed enough to stop. Theo took out her own phone. She didn't even think of calling Gus. She would not interrupt his work again—not now, not for this.

Theo hesitated before she dialed Mac's number.

"Etheridge here."

"Mac, hello…it's Theo. I'm so sorry bother you…and I'm perfectly okay, but I thought you should know because it's your house and—"

"Theo, what's happened?" Calm, practical Mac.

She explained. "I think she took photos of your house."

"I'll be there in a few minutes."

"No, Mac, I'm all right. You don't have to—"

"I was about to call it a day anyway. I'll see you soon."

Theo ran back up to the tower where she could see the street clearly without opening a curtain. The car was still there. Mary was sitting behind the wheel talking on the phone. Theo started to panic. What if she was phoning in another story, one that involved Theo Benton's current address? A black Mercedes pulled up behind her, and Mac climbed out. He approached the reporter's car briskly. Theo saw Mary turn sharply and Mac step back and show his hands. She could see his lips moving. Slowly, he moved closer, and then he leaned against the car with his arms folded. Theo watched as he and Mary talked. It began to snow again, and still Mac stood by Mary's car chatting. It seemed an age before he stepped back and watched her drive away.

Theo frowned, unsure of what to make of what she'd seen. She went back downstairs. Mac Etheridge walked in, dusting snow from his hair.

"Do you know her?" Theo blurted. "Do you know Mary Cowell?"

"I just met her then…"

"What were you talking about?"

He looked at her a little surprised.

"You don't talk to strangers for twenty minutes in the snow!"

"Well," he said evenly, "it was probably closer to ten minutes. And for the first five or six I was trying to talk her into putting down the gun."

CHAPTER 24

Theo gaped at Mac Etheridge. "A gun? She had a gun? Why? Was she going to—"

"Mary keeps the gun in the glove box." He pulled out a chair for her. "She got it out when she saw me pull up and get out— clearly the girl has enemies."

"Are you crazy?" Theo demanded, still standing. "You walked toward her! I saw you!"

"The gun wasn't loaded, Theo."

"How could you possibly know that?"

"That particular weapon, the Ruger SR9, has a loaded chamber indicator...it's a safety feature. Because she was sitting in the car and I was standing, I could see the indicator. I expect it's not Mary's gun, or it's a recent acquisition, otherwise she would have known. All that said, I'm not sure what else I could have done."

A little unsettled by his knowledge of guns, Theo stuttered. "You could have run! Any sane person would have run."

He shrugged. "I'm not sure who Mary thought I was, but

she wasn't trying to assassinate anyone. She was trying to protect herself."

"From you?"

"Or whoever else I might have been. She's afraid of someone."

Theo sat in the chair he'd pulled out for her. "What did she say?"

"Initially, she said 'Make my day,' somewhat unconvincingly." He smiled and took the seat beside Theo. "Once I'd persuaded her that I wasn't trying to carjack her, I made her aware that I didn't appreciate her invading my privacy by photographing my home."

"She was holding you at gunpoint and you complained about a photo?"

Mac continued. "She said something about the freedom of the press and asked me if you were living here, and why. I told her that I had no idea who you were."

"Did she believe you?" The hope was weak but it was there... briefly.

Mac shook his head. "I doubt it. Mary Cowell claims she has it on good authority that you are hiding out here."

"What authority?"

"I don't know, Theo." He rubbed the slight shadow on his chin and loosened his tie. "In addition to being a reporter, it seems Mary was a fan of Dan Murdoch...fancies herself as a sword of justice."

"A sword with a gun," Theo murmured.

"I know it's probably not a lot of comfort, but she didn't hold it like anyone who knew what she was doing. She's probably more likely to hurt herself than anyone else. And her intent is to expose you, not to kill you."

"You're right. No comfort at all." Theo sighed. "What do you think she's going to do?"

"Hopefully she won't want to go public and give away her 'lead' too soon," he said.

"Shouldn't we call the police?"

"She hasn't really done anything. She didn't trespass to take the photo, and here she's within her rights to point a gun, especially an unloaded gun, at someone who approaches her car."

Theo groaned. "This just gets worse and worse."

Mac stood and removed his jacket. "Come on, let's make dinner."

Theo could see that he was trying to distract her, and in recognition of the effort, she complied. They surveyed the cupboards for a few minutes, taking of stock of ingredients and looking for inspiration. In the end they decided on lasagna. Theo began on the sauce while Mac made pasta.

"I dated an Italian for a while," Mac replied when she questioned why he felt the need to make lasagna sheets from scratch, when there was a packet of the dried variety in the cupboard. "She insisted on fresh pasta and got me used to it. The packet of dried sheets came in one of the survival boxes my mother leaves here from time to time."

"Survival boxes?"

"To keep me alive while I fight my way through Russians, cyborgs, or zombies back to the family compound. That's why there're so many canned goods in the cupboards—I hate eating things out of cans. They're also some water purification tablets there somewhere…in case the Democrats poison the water supply."

Theo laughed, though she guessed he wasn't kidding. "Do they really believe all that?"

"I'm not entirely sure. Sometimes I think it's just some crazy hobby…like cosplaying or those guys who dress up like medieval knights and try to kill each other. And of course, after the pandemic, having a few extra canned goods is not insane."

"Sometimes?"

"When I'm in a generous mood. Mostly, I know they're crazy."

"Zeke...?"

"Dr. Etheridge?" Mac kneaded his pasta dough quite expertly. "You'd expect him to be more rational, wouldn't you? And he was until the pandemic. After that my mother managed to talk him into lunacy. I'm not sure if that makes him more or less crazy than the rest of the family."

"And why aren't you?" Theo asked.

"Crazy? I'm not sure." He shrugged. "I had to see a psychiatrist after I was shot—it was mandated by Child Services or Mom would never have allowed it. Dr. Henry deprogrammed me, I think... After that, it was kind of like knowing Santa Claus isn't real but going along with the charade for the sake of your folks."

Theo pulled back. "Santa Claus isn't real?"

Mac laughed. "All families have that one kid who everybody thinks must have been adopted, I guess."

Theo would have indeed wondered exactly that if there hadn't been such a strong physical resemblance between Mac and his brothers. She helped him roll out the dough and feed it through the pasta machine. And sometime while they were grating cheese and assembling a lasagna, she talked to him about what Veronica Cole had told her and what Jacqui Steven had confirmed.

Mac dried his hands. "Your agent is well informed."

"She's not my agent...but that's not the point. Gus—"

"—didn't want you to worry about Crane, Hayes and Benton. There's nothing anyone can do about it, Theo. It's not like Gus can hide the firm at a different address."

Theo closed her eyes.. Of course. The reporters would have tracked her to Gus, and Gus to the firm. She could only imagine the havoc it was causing. "Mac, please, I've got to do something…"

He grimaced. "I think you'll be taking the heat off Gus very soon, Theo. When Mary publishes her photos, the reporters, Murdoch's deranged fans, the tourists, they'll all be camped out here."

Theo stared at him. "Oh." He was right. "That's a silver lining, I suppose."

He chuckled. "You could look at it that way." He switched on the oven and slid the product of their efforts into it. "Would you like a glass of wine?"

"Sure." A thought occurred then. "God, Mac, I'm sorry… I didn't think… If I stay here, then your home is going to be the center of this nightmare."

Mac opened a bottle of wine. "Maybe. But it won't be forever, and you're still safer here than in a hotel."

"But you saw what happened at Gus's house—"

"Let's not panic prematurely. As I said, Mary may decide not to show her hand just yet." He handed her a glass of red. "When Gus gets back, we'll eat lasagna and work out what we need to do."

It was quite late when Gus came in. They'd drunk the bottle of wine waiting for him and so Theo was relaxed and, to be honest, somewhat sleepy. Red wine, in fact most alcohol, had that effect on her. She'd never really been drunk because she generally fell asleep long before she was otherwise compromised. It was probably because of that sedative effect that she did not react dramatically when Gus broke the news that the police had finally discovered the assault allegation made by Hugh Carrington.

"They want to speak to you, Theo. We have an appointment tomorrow morning at ten."

"You'll be there."

"Of course."

"Then what could go wrong?"

Over the meal she and Mac told Gus about Mary Cowell and her information.

Gus grimaced. "It was only a matter of time. I've tried to be careful, but it wouldn't be hard to follow me back here. It's probably a wonder that it's taken two days."

"Perhaps we shouldn't be living in the same place," Theo suggested. Surely if they weren't living together, Gus could distance himself a little…maybe that would help.

"I'm not abandoning you, Theo."

"You wouldn't be abandoning me. I'm an adult. I could simply move into a hotel…"

"With the publicity our friend Mary Cowell's given you, I can only imagine the kind of hotel that would be willing to take you—and you'd be on your own, Theo…and I wouldn't be able to get any work done because I'd be worrying about whether someone had cut your throat in the lobby."

"Theo could stay here," Mac suggested cautiously. "You could move back to your place. I could make sure Theo was all right, and Philip Hayes might calm down and call off the dogs."

Gus stared at him. "You know about that?"

For a moment, Theo thought Mac might give her and Jacqui Steven away, but all he said was, "I know everything, Gus. Private eye, remember?"

Gus turned to Theo. "What do you think?"

"It's worth a try, Gus. I don't want you to have lost everything by the time they find whoever really killed Dan."

"And what if they don't?"

Theo took a deep breath. She wasn't consciously aware that she'd been thinking about this, but she must have been because she knew. "As soon as they decide that I didn't kill anybody and allow me to leave, I'll go home…to Tassie. I can still play the tambourine."

Gus cursed. "So you're going to let them run you out of town, out of the country, for God's sake. Bloody hell, Theo!"

"It won't be forever… I have dual citizenship, remember."

"No. I'm not letting you go home with your tail between your legs like—"

Mac interrupted. "Look, guys, I think you may be getting ahead of yourselves. At the moment, with no other suspects, Mendes is not going to let Theo leave anyway."

Gus exhaled. "Which means she could be living here for months as Mendes stuffs around trying to build a case out of nothing."

"Yes…but you going back to your place might take the heat off a bit at the firm and the distance might have other benefits. You could concentrate on being Theo's attorney rather than her big brother. It may make it easier. She's welcome to stay here for as long as she wants."

"And if you wake up tomorrow with a hundred reporters on your front lawn?"

"We'll deal with it. You'll be in the same town, Gus." Mac glanced at his watch and stood. "I'm going out for a couple of hours, so you can talk about it without me here."

"You don't have to—" Theo began.

"You and Gus need to work this out. I'll be back in a while."

And so the Bentons were able to argue freely. And they did. Fiercely. Gus demanded his right to protect his sister. Theo insisted on the same right against him. "You're less able to help me if you lose the firm, Gus. You can't blow everything up just because you think this bloke Hayes is a bastard. We're adults now."

"This is not your fault, Theo."

"No. But it is what it is. Mac's right. You need to go back to your place."

Gus's face softened just a little. "Are you comfortable staying with Mac on your own?"

Theo regarded him, startled. "Don't you trust him?"

Gus smiled. "Yes, I trust him. With my life and my sister, in fact. He's a good bloke. I just wonder if he's starting to think of you as something more than my kid sister."

"I should hope he is!" Theo bit back.

"You know what I mean."

"You don't seriously think that he wants to get rid of you so he can be alone with me?" Theo knew her brother was tired and under pressure, but this was ludicrous.

"Of course I don't. But if we're doing this, I want to be completely sure you feel comfortable. 'Cause, if not—"

"Gus, you idiot, there is nothing romantic between me and Mac. After what happened with Dan, falling in love with anybody ever again is pretty much off the table."

"Well, I wouldn't want that for you, Wombat," Gus said gently. "Maybe just stay away from the senior citizens from now on."

Theo leaned over and punched him in the shoulder. "What happened had nothing to do with Dan's age, Gus."

"A younger bloke might not have had time to make that kind of enemy."

"What kind of enemy?"

"The kind that murders you."

"Gus—"

He put his arm around her. "I'm sorry, mate. I'm tired and cranky and furious that I can't make it go away."

Theo leaned into him. "Go back to your house, Gus, if it'll make Mr. Hayes happier. I'd never forgive myself if you lost the partnership."

"You're not going home."

"We'll talk about that if and when I'm allowed to leave town."

And so, by the time Mac returned, Gus was ready to go. Theo felt a moment of panic when he threw his bag into the cab of his truck and started the engine to let it warm.

"If you change your mind, just call," he whispered as he hugged her goodbye.

"I'll be fine." She didn't hug him too tightly lest he sense her uncertainty. "Don't worry about me...or at least try not to spend all your time worrying about me."

Gus shook Mac's hand. "I owe you, mate."

"I'm fairly sure that someone in my family will need an attorney again, sooner or later."

Gus laughed. "You're on."

He climbed behind the wheel, leaning out to speak to Theo. "I'll pick you up tomorrow and we'll go into the station together."

She waved him off, feeling strangely desolate as his truck disappeared into the street. It was ridiculous. He was only going a few streets away. And she would see him tomorrow before she even had time to miss him. She hoped this would make things easier for him at work.

Despite everything that lingered in her mind, Theodosia Benton slept soundly that night. Perhaps it was the wine. Perhaps she was simply becoming so used to fear and disaster that it no longer had the capacity to keep her awake. There was a labyrinth in her dreams, vast and dark. Gus reached out and grabbed her before she wandered into it, and then she was in Mac Etheridge's arms. Someone began knocking from inside the labyrinth wall.

Theo opened her eyes. The pounding was real. Still in pajamas, she met Mac and the police on the stairs. He was dressed and for a moment she panicked that she had overslept and somehow missed her appointment. But it was still not yet six. Gus has said ten...she was sure he had said ten.

Mac had out his phone. "Theo, you may want to get dressed. Detective Mendes would like us to come into the station to answer some questions."

"Now? Why?"

Mac lowered his voice. "It seems Mary Cowell was killed last night."

CHAPTER 25

A policeman waited outside Theo's bedroom door as she changed. For a couple of minutes, she just sat on the bed trying to gather her thoughts. Mary Cowell was dead. Young, ambitious, brazen Mary Cowell with her ruthless reporting. The article in the *Star* had made Theo's life a nightmare, and she'd hated Mary for it. But dead. She just been here yesterday, holding a gun on Mac... He'd said she seemed frightened.

Theo pulled herself together and got dressed, grabbing jeans and the first top that came to hand. Then she caught a glimpse of herself in the iconic LFK T-shirt and thought better of it. Perhaps it would be read the wrong way. She was an immigrant after all... and Lawrence Fucking Kansas was a local inside joke. Was she entitled to be part of it? She stopped. This was stupid...it was just a T-shirt. She pulled a Jayhawks hoodie over her head, hiding one Lawrence icon with another. Scooping her hair into a ponytail, she opened the door and told the officer she was ready, no doubt reassuring him that she'd not escaped through a window.

There were two police cars outside. She and Mac were invited into separate vehicles.

"Have you called Gus?" Theo whispered.

"Yes," Mac replied grimly. "There's a complication."

"What complication?"

"They want to question him too. They've just picked him up."

Gus was in the station when they arrived. He was furious, accusing Mendes of questioning him simply to deny his sister the presence of counsel. Jacqui Steven arrived, declaring that the interviews could not be held simultaneously as she was representing each of them and would not allow her clients to answer any questions without counsel being present. Mendes was clearly unhappy but it seemed that since Jacqui had invoked their rights, there was little he could do but comply. They spoke to Gus first. Theo and Mac were taken to separate rooms to wait with paper cups of weak coffee. It was two hours before an officer returned for Theo. He handed her a large chocolate chip cookie sealed in plastic.

"From your brother."

Theo smiled, recalling Gus's stories about criminals who would confess to anything once their blood sugar dipped. She was hungry, and the vending machine cookie tasted strangely delicious at nine in the morning. She caught a glimpse of Gus as they took her into the interview room. She waved the cookie at him, her mouth full. He winked.

Theo felt calmer now. Jacqui was already in the interview room. She looked fresh, sharp, though she must have been through this with both Gus and Mac now.

Mendes began by asking Theo where she was the night before. Theo told them. They created a timeline then: when she got back to Mac's house, when Mac returned, when Gus returned, when Mac left, how long he was away, when Gus left, when she went to sleep. Theo was sure about the sequence but not the times, not exactly.

Then Mendes asked when she had last seen Mary Cowell. Theo wasn't sure whether they knew about the reporter's visit, so she answered carefully. "I haven't spoken with her since she approached me at Aimee's—what was it? Five days ago."

"And that was when you last saw her?"

"No. I saw her yesterday." The question was too loaded for them not to be aware, and she was still lawyer enough to know lying was a bad idea. She explained that she'd noticed Mary's car pass the house twice and then seen Mary step out and take photographs of the house on her phone.

They asked her for specifics. "How many photographs?"

"I don't know… It was a phone, not a flash camera. It might have been video or she might have been taking a selfie with the house across the street, for all I know."

"What did she do then?"

"I'm not sure… I got away from the window and rang Mac."

"Cormac Etheridge?"

"Yes."

"Why?"

"It's his house. I was concerned."

"And then what?"

Theo told them that she'd peered through the curtain, that Mary Cowell had been in her car parked across the road talking on the phone. She recounted Mac's arrival and what had occurred thereafter.

"Did you see a gun?" Mendes asked.

"Well, no…I didn't actually see it. I couldn't see Mary below the shoulder."

"So you base your claim that she held a gun on Cormac Etheridge purely on his account?"

Theo tried to think. "I saw him show his hands."

"Show his hands, not raise them."

"It wasn't a holdup. He seemed to be talking her down."

"According to him."

"No, that's what it looked like."

"So you knew, though you could not see it, that she had some kind of weapon?"

A breath. "No. I didn't then. Mac told me about the gun, but in hindsight that fit with what I saw."

"How long did Cormac Etheridge speak with Mary Cowell?"

"About twenty minutes, I guess."

More questions then, about Mary Cowell: how she seemed, did she look frightened by Cormac Etheridge?

"Not particularly."

How did Theo feel about Mary Cowell? Did she resent her for the article in the *Star*?

"I resented the article, was angry about the article. It was sensational and made me the focus of all this and dragged Gus into the whole mess, but I didn't think about Mary personally."

What about Gus Benton? Was he angry with Mary Cowell?

Theo glanced at Jacqui, alarmed by the question. "You couldn't possibly imagine that Gus—"

Mendes repeated the question.

"No. Gus doesn't get angry about much other than skim milk and basketball. As far as I'm aware he's never given Mary Cowell a thought."

They showed her photos then. Mary Cowell was lying on some kind of bench. Her throat had been cut. The blood had pooled around her head and matted her hair. She was wearing an LFK T-shirt that may once have been white, sweatpants, and sneakers. The images battered Theo. Mary was about her age. Like Theo, she'd been looking for a career in words, and it seemed that before she died, Mary had, by grisly inconsequential coincidence, put on the same T-shirt that Theo had grabbed that morning. And that last thing seemed indecent somehow. Dan's body intruded, and grief with it, and suddenly Theo found herself weeping over the death of woman she barely knew and unable to explain why.

Jacqui demanded a break. Mendes poured Theo a glass of water, stopped the recorder, and he and the other officer left the room. Jacqui placed a box of tissues in front of Theo.

"You're doing well, Theo. Those photos are tough when you're not used to it."

"It's the third body I've seen in the last month, Jacqui," Theo said hoarsely. "I'm never going to get used to it. God, I hope I don't get used to it."

"No. You shouldn't." Jacqui took her hand. "You're not under arrest. I can bring this interview to an end."

"No. Let's get it over with. You won't tell Gus I fell apart, will you?"

"That information would be privileged." Jacqui smiled. "You ready?"

"Yes, call them back."

The officers had a new line of questioning. They wanted to know about Hugh Carrington and the complaint of assault he'd made against her.

Theo told them about her relationship with Hugh Carrington

and the manner in which it ended. She could tell it less emotionally now. As before, they spent a great deal of time establishing details. When, where, how many times did she hit Hugh Carrington? Did she want to kill him? Had she told anyone what happened? Why did she leave the Australian National University? Why did she come to Lawrence? Had Dan Murdoch attacked her as she claims Hugh Carrington did?

Theo concentrated on staying focused, answering each question as clearly and precisely as she knew how, but answering only what she had been asked. The detectives seemed to change their line again, asking her about Benders. How often she frequented it. Why she'd stopped. Who she saw there. Where she sat when she was there. Theo answered, though she was confused by the purpose of those questions. Perhaps this was to do with Dan. Eventually Jacqui objected that Mendes was covering the same ground for the fourth time and either fishing or looking to write a restaurant guide. "I'm afraid, George, that unless you have some charge to lay against my client, we're going to have to be on our way."

The detective was clearly irritated, but it seemed he had no charges he was willing to bring at that stage. "This is Lawrence, Miss Benton, not New York, and yet in the last month, there have been three murders, and you seem to be the common factor."

"Yes, I can see that," Theo replied. "But I don't know why, Detective."

"There are many common factors, Detective," Jacqui said curtly.

Mendes's eyes narrowed and, for a moment, Theo thought he might have more questions to ask, or the same ones again. But if he did, he thought better of it. "We'll be in touch, Miss Benton."

Mac and Gus were waiting for them. "There are reporters outside," Gus said quietly. "Someone's tipped them off."

"We're going to go to the Oread, check in, and then leave through the kitchen." Mac had clearly made arrangements. "Sam will pick us up outside the delivery door."

So they made their way through the media pack in the Kansas PD car lot to a police vehicle that took them to the Oread Hotel, a multistory late art deco construction. Mac checked them all in. Security was called to push the members of the press who had followed them, out of the hotel lobby. They entered the Bird Dog Bar ostensibly to have lunch, and then slipped into the kitchen. The chef greeted Gus and Mac like brothers long lost, and took them through to the back door where a catering truck was waiting.

Mac swore. Clearly the catering truck was something of a surprise.

"It's Sam," Gus told Theo as Mac called his brother an idiot.

"Sam drives a catering truck?" Theo asked.

"Occasionally."

"He's a caterer?"

"No, I think he's still a mechanic."

Mac opened the back of the truck shaking his head. "Apparently my brother knows a caterer who lends him the truck, no questions asked, in exchange for maintenance."

Theo wondered how often Sam had had cause to borrow a caterer's truck—but now was probably not the time to ask. They climbed into the back, among crates of bakers' rolls and stacks of white tablecloths.

"Hold tight." Sam Etheridge shut the doors and the hold of the truck became dark as well as cold.

"Where is he taking us?" Theo asked, shivering.

Gus put his arm around her. "Fort Etheridge. It's out of town and...defended." Theo could almost hear the grimace in his voice. "As far as we know, Mary died without revealing your current residence, but the police are searching both Mac's place and mine."

"Searching them for what?"

"Mary Cowell's phone."

"Oh." Theo realized now why the police had been so interested in the comings and goings of Mac and Gus. Perhaps they believed Mary had been killed to keep her from publishing the photographs of Mac Etheridge's house. It was stupid and ludicrous and utterly implausible, but Mendes seemed committed to believing she was somehow related to every crime and misdemeanor committed in Lawrence.

Gus called Crane, Hayes and Benton to ask his secretary to reorganize his calendar and Jacqui's for the day. Clearly their absence was being felt. Gus listened for a while and then said, "Well, tell Philip to—" He stopped and exhaled before finishing. "Tell Mr. Hayes that I shall speak to him when I get back."

He hung up, tight-lipped. Jacqui cursed for them both.

"Has something new come to light about Dan's murder?" Theo asked.

"Not that I'm aware," Mac replied. "Jacqui?"

"Nope—I've not heard anything."

"They were asking me a lot of questions about Benders," Theo confessed. "I thought perhaps—"

"They didn't tell you?"

"Tell me what?"

"Mary Cowell's body was discovered this morning on the back porch of Benders."

CHAPTER 26

Caleb clenched his fists in his hair. He felt sick. She was dead—Jesus! What the fuck had he done? And the cops were looking at Mac for it. He wasn't going to be able to keep this quiet—especially if they were going after Mac. And then it would be out, and his brothers would kill him first.

———

The truck pulled up. Theo blanched as the doors were opened and light flooded in. They were on the side of the road, she didn't know exactly where, but it was outside the built-up areas. Caleb was waiting beside a black Yukon with tinted windows.

"Is all this really necessary?" Mac demanded wearily.

"You asked for our help, brother," Sam reminded him. "We know what we're doing and this old heap might find the roads up to the Ponderosa a challenge."

The Ponderosa. Theo had thought Mac was being sarcastic when he called his family's compound "the Ponderosa."

Perhaps everything she'd been told about the Etheridges was in fact literal.

They transferred into the Yukon, and Caleb took the wheel, taking them off the blacktop for several miles before he turned into an isolated driveway. They passed through three separate locked gates, each equipped with video surveillance. The Ponderosa, when they came upon it, was a sprawling brick construction, architecturally eclectic and set on high ground. It was a confusing building with no defined entrance, makeshift turrets on the roofline, and gun slots beside the windows.

Theo tried not to look too alarmed, too uncomfortable.

Gus looked around. "There're no mantraps we should be aware of are there, Mac?"

Mac shrugged. "Caleb?"

"Just follow me," Caleb said. "Don't wander off."

They fell into line behind Caleb, who led them past a series of doors until he finally opened one. Inside the Ponderosa was something of a surprise, more akin to a genteel villa from another era than a fortress. The furniture was Victorian, the rooms spacious and fastidiously neat. Nancy Etheridge was making food parcels, sealing cans and bags of rice in large plastic bags, and placing them into a wheelbarrow on the veranda. "Caleb, honey, this lot is ready to bury outside the gate," she said as they walked in. She welcomed them then, warmly. "Another murder! It's how it begins, you know. Luckily, we are ready."

"Mac," Caleb interrupted. "I need to talk to you."

"After you bury the donations," Nancy ordered. "You can talk to your brother later."

"We're not staying long, Mom," Mac warned. "We just need to use the library."

"I'll come with you," Caleb jumped. "We can—"

"Not now, Caleb. I need to work some things out with these guys—we can talk later."

"Those packages aren't going to bury themselves." Nancy pointed to the wheelbarrow.

Caleb glared at both of them for a moment before throwing up his arms and stomping toward the wheelbarrow.

Nancy tossed another couple of bags onto the pile in the wheelbarrow. "Not too deep, mind you; they'll have to dig with their hands." Nancy smoothed out her apron. "I'll just see to some refreshments." She walked out of the room, and for a moment they listened in silence to her fading footsteps.

Theo had to ask. "Why are they burying food outside the gate?"

Mac replied wearily. "So that when the apocalypse comes and the unprepared and starving arrive at the gate, the Etheridges will be able to give them food without letting them in. Christian kindness."

Theo tried to offer consolation. "It is very charitable, if you think about it."

"It's best not to think about it." Mac shook it off. "Come on, we'd better talk while Mom's busy making hors d'oeuvres."

"She's not going to make us dig for them, is she?" Gus murmured.

Theo elbowed him sharply, but Mac laughed. "Geez, I hope not."

They sat down in the room Mac called the library. Theo could not help but scan the shelves. Manuals mainly: construction, electronics, mechanics, first aid, even midwifery. The collection was clearly for reference, not pleasure. Vaguely she wondered about a future without stories. It was bleak. However troubled her present, at least it was not without stories.

They shared information about their respective interviews. Jacqui had been present at all three.

"Everything they have is circumstantial. That said, they might have arrested Theo by now if it didn't seem so physically unlikely, though not impossible, that she cut Dan Murdoch's throat or shot Burt Winslow. Which is why they're interested in the two of you as possible accomplices."

Gus exploded. "What the hell has Mendes been smoking?"

Mac reacted more calmly. "He thinks we're some kind of tag-team murder cartel?"

"Detective Mendes didn't exactly share his theories with me, but I suspect he believes that you and Gus are at least accomplices after the fact. However"—Jacqui's tone was confident and absolute—"it is all circumstantial. They haven't got any murder weapons, or witnesses. Nothing we couldn't tear apart, and Mendes knows it."

"So what's his play?" Mac asked.

"I think he's hoping Theo will crack under the pressure and confess."

Theo exhaled. "Well, that's just…lazy."

Mac laughed. "And what now?"

"We carry on," Gus said. "I presume the media will discover Mac's place quite soon."

"Yes, I think you're just going to have to accept the attention of the media until they find out what really happened." Jacqui shook her head. "I don't think you're going to be able to hide. The police might be willing to—"

"We'll hire security," Mac said curtly. "Let's not be beholden to Mendes."

Gus agreed, but he refused to return to Mac's house himself. "I'm going to be pretty much living at the office for the next few weeks anyway." He glanced at Jacqui. "I'm in more danger from Hayes than anyone else."

Theo didn't try to argue with him. Hopefully the media wouldn't bother waiting if Gus was rarely there.

"What are we going to do?" she said.

"I thought we just decided that."

"No…I mean about finding out who really killed Dan, and Burt Winslow, and now Mary Cowell." Theo looked around at each of them. For a moment, Veronica's advice that she not appear too interested in the investigation returned, but she continued regardless. After today her name would probably be too tainted for Day Delos and Associates anyway. "We can't just wait for the police—they're not looking for anyone else, and frankly I'm a little fed up with this nightmare."

"Hear, hear!" Gus applauded against the table. "What do we know already?"

"Mary Cowell's throat was cut in much the same way that Dan Murdoch's was," Mac said. "She died on the back porch of Benders. Her body was placed on a bench and covered with an old blanket. The poor woman who found her mistook her for one of the homeless until she tried to move her on. Apparently they do sleep there sometimes, although the heaters are turned off at two in the morning, and the police believe she came in sometime after that."

"How do we know all that?" Theo asked.

"Mac did some digging around while they were questioning you," Gus replied.

Theo nodded. She should have known. Mac had probably hacked the police database or something. "What was Mary doing at Benders after two in the morning?"

"My guess is that she was meeting someone," Mac replied.

"How would they have gotten in?" Gus asked.

"The back porch of Benders is not all that secure," Theo said. "Laura sometimes leaves the door open when it's cold…in case someone needs somewhere out of the wind to sleep."

"Mary wasn't from Lawrence. She wouldn't have known that," Mac said.

"So whoever she was meeting did." Jacqui wrote herself a note. "We're going to have to look closely at Benders's regulars."

"I can do that," Theo said.

"What?" Gus stared at her. "Theo, you can't—"

"The people at Benders know me; they'll talk to me," Theo said earnestly. "And, unlike the three of you, I don't have a job."

Gus was adamantly against the idea. "Downtown is crawling with Dan Murdoch's deranged fans, who all seem to think you killed him—"

"That's interesting, isn't it?" Mac interrupted.

"Interesting?"

"Yes…why are they so convinced Theo is a murderer?"

"Mary Cowell's article."

"I don't think it was strong enough to rally fans across the nation to form a posse and ride on Lawrence." Mac frowned. He didn't raise specifically the vitriol being levelled at Theodosia Benton on social media. He wasn't sure if Theo was aware of it. "It might be worth finding out how all this rage is being generated."

"Good," Theo said. "You hack Twitter or whatever you're planning. I'll speak to the people at Benders."

"I'll go with her," Mac said as Gus opened his mouth to protest once again. "If there are any problems, I'll call in the cavalry."

"I've got to do something, Gus," Theo said as her brother shook his head. "I can't write with all this going on… I can't have a life; and it's destroying yours. We're in the middle of this because of my relationship with Dan. And people are dying."

"I know, I just don't want you to be one of them."

Mac tried to reassure him. "I won't let her out of my sight, Gus."

"Don't you have a job?" Gus muttered.

Mac smiled. "Not a real one. We private eyes don't really punch clocks."

"I've got to go back to Benders anyway—see that Laura and Chic are okay." Theo met Gus's eye. "They're my friends, Gus. Before Dan was killed, I saw them nearly every day for months. I want to know how they're doing."

Gus sighed. "Just be careful." He rubbed his jaw. "We need background checks on Mary Cowell and Burt Winslow as well as Dan Murdoch."

Mac nodded. "I'll get Bernie started on it."

"I hope you kids are hungry!" Nancy Etheridge wheeled in a serving cart laden with sandwiches and cakes and fried chicken. As preposterous as catering seemed under the circumstances, Theo was starving.

"We'd better get back." Gus put a sandwich in his pocket and grabbed an elaborately iced cupcake. "I have a deposition this afternoon if Philip Hayes hasn't changed the locks."

"Caleb will drive you back," Nancy said.

Jacqui glanced at her phone. "Mendes has already left a message."

"They're probably wondering where we all went," Gus said. "We'd better go before they decide to…"

Mac shook his head.

"…worry." Gus's eyes flicked to Nancy.

Theo wasn't sure what Gus had been about to say, but Mac

clearly didn't want to alarm his mother. An alarmed Nancy would probably be dangerous.

It was decided they would return to Lawrence separately. Caleb would drop Gus and Jacqui at Crane, Hayes and Benton. Mac and Theo would take one of the other pickups a little while later.

As soon as Gus and Jacqui left, Nancy began her interrogation. She directed it at Mac, though she looked at Theo.

"Sorry, Mom, you know I can't talk about work."

"Were you arrested? Just tell me if you were arrested. A mother has a right to know."

"I wasn't arrested."

"Then why are the police—"

"Can't talk about it, Mom."

"Your brothers could—"

"No, they couldn't."

"Is it to do with this serial killer?" Again her eyes were on Theo. "The Lawrence Slayer."

"The what?"

Nancy preened. "That's what I'm calling him…or her."

Mac rolled his eyes. "I can't talk about it, Mom. We'd better go."

"Cormac, darling, if you're in any kind of trouble, family is where you should turn."

"Good to know. Thanks, Mom."

"Nobody could get to you here. Your brothers wouldn't allow them past the gate."

"Are you offering me a siege if I need it?"

"Son, you need to take this seriously."

"We'd better go." Mac stood up. "Let Zeke know he can collect his pickup at my place, or I'll bring it back when I get a chance."

"Cormac, you can't—"

Mac kissed his mother's cheek. "Thanks for the food, Mom."

"You haven't even said hello to your father—he's just watering his flowers."

"Don't disturb him, Mom. I'll see him at the Jayhawks game next week."

Theo thanked Nancy Etheridge for her hospitality.

Nancy folded her arms. "You're welcome, honey, but just what have you got my boy involved in?"

Mac told his mother not to be ridiculous as he took Theo's hand and headed for the door. Nancy followed them all the way out to the pale blue Chevy pickup in the property's multiple bay garage.

Nancy watched as they pulled out and drove toward the first gate. Theo noted that Mac had a master key to all the locks and padlocks. Despite the open squabbling, his family trusted him.

"I'm sorry about that," he said, as they passed through the gates. "We wouldn't have come here if we could think of anywhere else to wait out the police search without being harassed by reporters." Mac rolled his eyes. "The catering truck was Sam's idea—he thinks he's CIA."

"What exactly are they preparing for?" Theo asked as they passed silos fortified with barbed wire.

"My mother is getting ready for a war—civil, or some kind of invasion; Zeke thinks there'll be another worldwide pandemic or several; Sam is convinced that electromagnetic solar pulses will render all forms of technology inoperative leading to a breakdown of the social order; and I think Caleb still believes in zombies. Between them, they've got all the bases covered."

"And your dad?"

"He roots for the Jayhawks."

"And he grows flowers?" Theo said as they caught sight of Mac's father in one of the paddocks. He waved as they passed.

"Not so much flowers as ditch weed."

"Cannabis?" Theo asked, surprised.

"More like hemp. It grows wild—he isn't actually planting it. You can get a better high with dried parsley, but Dad seems to like it."

"But your mother—"

"Has convinced herself he's testing and storing potential natural medicines, because conventional drugs will become unavailable when we are invaded."

Theo tried not to laugh.

Her phone rang. "It's Veronica," she said, checking the number.

"Go ahead and answer it," Mac said, pulling up. "I have to unlock the gate anyway." He opened the door as Theo picked up the call.

"Theo, I have good news!" Veronica was excited. "I'm delighted to be able to offer you representation. We'd like to fly you to New York to sign the contracts."

"New York?" Theo inhaled.

"Yes. Why don't you grab a couple of things and you can fly out with me tonight."

Theo suddenly felt joy crash. She couldn't leave Lawrence. The police would never allow that, but if she told Day Delos and Associates she was a suspect in three murders… "I'm afraid I can't leave tonight."

"Whyever not?"

"I…I need to think about it before I sign anything…talk to Gus."

"Theo, do you know how many writers, some of them already

bestsellers, would give anything to be represented by Day Delos and Associates?"

"I do...and I am so honored, Ronnie. But I need to settle some things first. Please, can I just have a couple of days?"

"This is not... It will be hard to explain to the partners." Veronica's voice was a little sharp. "Are you sure you want to do this, Theo?"

"I'm sorry, Ronnie, I really am. But I just can't sign anything right now."

"Very well, I shall see what I can do. But I really would advise you to make your decision quickly. I'll be in touch, Theo."

Theo listened to the dial tone for a while.

Mac climbed back into the pickup. "Everything okay?"

Theo nodded. Her old dreams seemed trivial at the moment. And as keenly as she felt the disappointment, this was not important right now. She smiled determinedly. "So do you think the police will have finished tossing your place by now?"

"Not according to Detective Mendes. He's going to text me when they're finished."

"He knows where we are?"

"Yes. I didn't want him to think we'd all skipped town. It might have got ugly if he'd sent squad cars to the Ponderosa."

Theo flinched. "I can imagine. What do we do now?"

"Well"—Mac glanced at his watch—"hopefully, the media and Murdoch's acolytes will be watching my place and Gus's, so this might be a good time to grab a coffee downtown."

CHAPTER 27

They killed Mary Cowell. She obviously got too close to the truth. What the fuck is going on in Lawrence?

    Flagman

Just after she spilled the beans on Theodosia Benton.

    WKWWK

    Lostboy

Theodosia Benton might be innocent. She might just have got sucked into this thing. We need to stay focused on finding the Minotaur.

    Wayward Son

What? Have they got to you Wayward Son? Why are you defending the woman who killed Primus?

    WKWWK

    Patriot Warrior

Mass Street was busy. The keepers of the various vigils for Dan Murdoch about the city became tourists when they took a break from the candle-lighting and memorial readings. During these times they contributed to the economy of the downtown cafes, bars, and restaurants, not to mention the Raven, the Dusty Bookshelf, and a handful of other bookstores that had become drop-in centers for grieving readers in need of support.

"What if someone recognizes me from the article?" Theo asked nervously.

"The photo was taken from a distance, and you were looking down," Mac said. "I don't think anyone who doesn't already know you will recognize you. But if you're not comfortable—"

"No." Theo checked her reflection in the rearview mirror. There were shadows beneath her eyes. She hadn't put on any makeup that morning when she'd gotten dressed to go to the station and answer questions. "I'd really like to get out, to be honest."

Mac found a parking spot on New Hampshire, off Ninth.

"Surely, it will still be a crime scene," Theo said as they climbed out of Zeke's Chevy.

"Yes, probably. I'm afraid you might have to wait till it reopens to catch up with your friends." Mac shrugged. "We could grab a coffee from the Pig… They may have some gossip about what went on at Benders."

Theo frowned. "I've got a better idea… I don't suppose you need anything framed?"

The Gilded Edge was a picture framer and gift store that framed and stocked the work of local artists—though nothing of the caliber or notoriety of a Burroughs. It also kept a quite extensive line of candles. The store shared the back alley with Benders.

"Laura works here in the evenings," Theo explained as they walked in. "Maybe—"

"Well, hello, stranger!" The lady in question emerged from between the display shelves with her arms outstretched. "Aren't you a sight for sore eyes!"

Theo embraced her and introduced Mac Etheridge. "Oh, Laura, this so awful. Are you all right?"

"I don't know. It's just terrible. She was so young."

"You found her?"

"Oh, no. That was poor Chic. She thought it was one of the street people at first and then she saw the blood and screamed and screamed. I'm not sure she'll ever be right again." Laura wiped her eyes. "Who would want to hurt little Mary—"

"You knew her?"

"She's been coming to Benders some in the past few days. She was a student here, I think—always typing away on that laptop of hers, when she wasn't talking to Jock." Laura looked at Theo and corrected herself. "I guess she could have been a writer too—"

"She knew Jock?"

"That's right; he'll be so cut up when he finds out."

"He doesn't know?"

"No, I don't think so. Chic found poor Mary first thing, before we opened, and Benders has been closed since." Laura shook her head. "The crime scene people won't be finished for another couple of days they say."

"I wonder how Mary got into the back porch?" Theo asked as casually as she could. "Was the door open?"

"No, it was locked. Locked it myself... It's only when it's snowing that I leave it unlocked...though I won't be doing that again—no, sir!"

"Then Mary broke in?"

"No...it's the darnedest thing. There was no sign of a break-in, and the door was locked this morning."

"Then how did she get in?"

Laura shrugged, her eyes widening. "It's like she walked through the wall."

"Or," Mac said evenly, "whoever killed Mary has a key, opened up, and locked the door again once they were done."

The idea had clearly not occurred to Laura before. She gasped. "Fuck!" she whispered.

Mac intervened as she began to hyperventilate. "Who has a key, Laura?"

"Well, the owner, of course." Laura clasped a hand onto her forehead as she tried to think. "But Joe wouldn't kill anybody... and me, I have a key... Well, I had a key...the police took it. Oh, fuck, fuck, fuck!"

Theo tried to calm her down. "Are they the only keys, Laura?"

"Yes... No!" Her eyes lit up. "There's a key kept behind the bar...on a hook."

"When you locked up," Mac asked, "did you use your key?"

"Yes, of course."

"So you have no idea if the key behind the bar was still there?"

"No..."

"Who would have known about the key behind the bar?" Theo asked gently. Laura was beginning to look quite flushed.

"Oh, almost anybody. Most of the regulars."

Theo held her hands. "Laura, you need to tell the police about this, if you haven't already."

"Oh, no...I don't think I did... I was so upset about Mary..."

"They'll understand that."

Laura pulled herself together. "I'll call them. Tell me, Theo, how are you doing? People have been asking after you."

"What people?" Mac asked sharply.

"Oh, Jock and Chic and that grad student who drinks bourbon at midday and a few strangers. We miss you."

"Strangers?"

"There were some New Yorkers and tourists who claimed they were speaking for Dan after that article came out in the *Star*, but we sent them on their way pretty quickly. We won't have anyone speaking trash about one of our own."

Impulsively Theo hugged Laura.

"You do know that Mary wrote that article, don't you?" Mac asked.

Clearly, Laura hadn't. The revelation shook her. "But she never asked anything about you…just sat in that corner—at your table—and worked on her laptop. Oh, Theo, I'm so sorry—"

"It's not your fault, Laura," Theo tried to console her. "Mary was just doing her job—she's as entitled to drink coffee as I am."

A group of people came into the shop looking for candles. Mac quietly put his arm around Theo and turned her away. "We'd better be going," he said, glancing at the new customers.

Laura nodded. "With all the vigils, we're running out of candles," she whispered. "Look after yourself, Theo. I'll just serve this bunch and then I'll call the police about that key."

Theo and Mac walked out of The Gilded Edge and onto Mass Street. Only then did she breathe out properly. Her mind was swirling with everything Laura had said, but part her of her was also exhilarated by the fact that she hadn't been recognized. Her name had been tainted by Mary's article, but for now at least, she could still be anonymous.

Mac checked the time. Half past six. "How about we go Mayberger's for a drink? The crowd there is unlikely to care about anything but whichever game's on the television. No one will look at you twice in that hoodie, and the police will have had time to make as big a mess as possible before we go back."

"Sure." Theo smiled up at him, enjoying the feeling of being among people without being scared. Things were worse than they'd ever been, but this felt like a glimpse of normal. "Look, Mac, I'm so sorry about what's happening to your house because of me. I wish I could—"

"My house has been searched before, Theo. It's par for the course in this business." He leaned down and admitted quietly, "My place gets tossed every time one of my brothers does something stupid...which is regularly. I'm afraid the police know their way around it quite well."

"Still..."

"I owe Gus Benton a lot, Theo, and I like his little sister. It's no big deal."

Theo faltered, unsure how to respond. But Mac didn't seem to require a response.

"Come on, I could use a beer."

They walked the block down to the sports bar. The snow from a couple of days before had melted, but it was cold and crisp. Some of the shop fronts were decorated for Christmas now, and the buildings decorated with colored lights. All the trees on both sides of Mass Street were strung with white lights. Christmas. Theo shook her head. It would be Christmas soon and all she was thinking about was murder.

"Good grief, why did they bother?" Mac muttered as they passed a shop front displaying an undecorated tree, a couple of poorly wrapped bricks, and a handwritten sign taped to the glass that said "Happy Holidays."

Theo laughed. "It has a certain minimalist charm."

"Nonsense…it says, *I hate Christmas and am only decorating under duress…possibly at gunpoint.*"

After that, they critiqued each storefront and display they passed, giving points for effort and originality. Mac was harsh, pointing out decorations that carried greetings for the wrong year, or that had clearly been recycled from Easter, Halloween, or Thanksgiving displays. "I'm sorry, there is no such thing as the Yuletide Bunny, and while Dickens might have given us the ghosts of Christmas, I really can't buy a festive zombie."

Theo called him unfairly traditional and defended the less conventional displays on principle. By the time they reached Mayberger's they were laughing, and Theo felt a little less devoid of Christmas spirit. And she was holding Mac's hand, though she couldn't remember quite when she'd taken it.

They went in to find a table or a couple of spare stools. A Jayhawks game was in progress so there was already a press of people in the bar. It was a more diverse crowd than the kind that patronized Benders. Graying ponytails and beards, and plaid flannel, the occasional pierced youngster, as well as frat boys and their elaborately dressed dates. The more devoted Jayhawk fans wore stripes. Mayberger's was expansive, designed to accommodate even larger crowds. The bar was long polished wood with "Mayberger's" inlaid in brass on the top. Jayhawks memorabilia, signed play photographs, and a collection of basketballs decorated the wall behind the bar, which also sported a formerly used basketball hoop from Allen Fieldhouse, complete with net. A number of large television screens were fixed to the upper wall and angled so that there was nowhere in the venue where one could not see a screen. They found a gap at the bar and ordered drinks, which the bartender delivered without taking his eyes off the closest screen.

The Jayhawks were winning and so every now and then the bar would erupt into cheers and chants, but otherwise it was relaxed. It reminded Theo of the country pubs back home...the ones that had not given in to the demand for a bistro and poker machines. Mayberger's was a watering hole, frequented by regulars but not hostile to those who wandered in.

She and Mac drank their beers and talked and raised their glasses to the chants of "Rock chalk, Jayhawk, KU!" Theo had no idea what it meant, but it was fun. To Theo it felt like years since she'd had fun.

"Does your father come here to watch the games?" she asked.

"Only if he can't get tickets to the actual game." Mac brought his head close to hers so they could hear each other over the noise of the television and the bar.

"Today?" Theo glanced around the bar for the man she'd seen in the paddock.

Mac looked up at the television. "He's at the Fieldhouse... We might see him if the camera pans to the crowd."

Theo swallowed. They had to return to reality sometime. It might as well be now. "Do you think someone took the key from the bar at Benders?"

"It seems more likely than Laura or the owner doing it. I don't know this Joe guy—he could be an idiot, I suppose. But he would have to be, to kill Mary Cowell and leave the body in the back of his own bar."

Theo agreed. "It had to be one of the regulars...otherwise how would they know about the key?" She shuddered. "I know those people, Mac. To think that any of them could cut a girl's throat—"

"Let's not get ahead of ourselves," Mac cautioned. "The person who killed Mary may not be the person who took the key. One of the regulars may have lent the key to the murderer or to Mary herself. The murderer may have taken the key from Mary's body."

"Oh, God, poor Mary." Theo paused as she thought of the ambitious young journalist. "We have to try and figure out who took that key. I could make a list of the regulars…"

Mac considered that. "You only know the daytime crowd, Theo. There's probably a whole different shift that comes in after five, who you might never have laid eyes on."

Theo's face fell. He was right. Benders was open till midnight. She had no idea who came in or looked after the bar at night.

Mac touched her arm. "But it makes more sense that it would be someone who hung out at Benders when you and Dan, not to mention Mary, did. Make that list, and I'll have Bernie do some background checks."

Theo looked at him. "Thank you, Mac. I know you say you owe Gus, and maybe you do…so do I…but if you hadn't—" Theo was only aware she'd decided to kiss him when her lips were on his. She decided to pull away long before he did.

CHAPTER 28

Theo gasped, mortified, unable to do anything but stare at Mac. He was clearly surprised, and for a moment they were both unsure what to do next. Then Mac kissed her. It was less impulsive and therefore less hurried, and when he pulled away, it seemed they were lost for words once again.

Mac spoke first. "So…"

Theo smiled. In fact, she grinned. Not particularly at him but because she couldn't help it.

He laughed and kissed her again.

A three-pointer incited celebration and cheering while their gazes were still locked. It was when the cheers died suddenly that they looked away from each other. Some of the patrons were still glued to the game; others were looking at their phones. But something had changed.

Theo looked up at the television. The game hadn't finished, but a banner was flashing across the bottom of the screen. Shooting on Mass Street in Lawrence, Kansas.

"There's been a shooting," Theo said grabbing Mac's arm.

Mac looked up. "Where?"

"Nearby, I think."

A banner across the bottom of the screen gave more news… The offices of Crane, Hayes and Benton, where a man has been shot…

Mac was already on the phone. Theo called Gus. The phone rang out. She tried Jacqui.

"Theo?"

"My God, Jac. Are you okay? We saw—"

"It's Gus." Jacqui was crying. "They shot Gus."

Theo's knees buckled. Mac caught her. He took the phone.

"Jac…Jac, calm down… Where? We're on our way." Mac put his arm around Theo and maneuvered her out of the bar amongst the movement of panicked people already leaving.

"He's at the hospital," he whispered into her ear. "He's not dead."

The cry seemed to burst from Theo's lungs like a breath held too long. She buried it in Mac's chest and no one saw.

Outside they tried to get back to their vehicle. Theo bolted. Mac caught up and grabbed her hand. He steadied her. "Come on."

They ran back to where they'd left the Chevy.

"What did she say?" Theo asked desperately as Mac pulled the pickup out. "What exactly did Jacqui say?"

"She said Gus had been shot. That they were taking him to Lawrence Memorial."

"She didn't say he was alive?"

"If they're taking him to the hospital, he's alive."

"Did she say who shot him?"

"No. I assume it was whoever was laying siege to Crane, Hayes and Benton…a disgruntled client, maybe."

"Was anyone else hurt?"

"Jac didn't say."

Theo noticed that he didn't tell her Gus would be all right. Because he didn't know. Mac wasn't about empty reassurances. She felt sick. She wished he'd lie to her.

Mac parked, and they ran in through the main reception. Theo spoke to the receptionist at the counter marked "Information." Her badge read "Patty."

"Excuse me. I'm Theodosia Benton. I was told my brother, Gus Benton, was brought here."

"Just a minute." Patty made a call. "Gus Benton." She put the receiver down and spoke gently. "He's been taken straight to surgery. I've told the doctor you're here."

Theo gasped with horror and relief. He was alive… If they were operating, then he was alive and was not so badly injured that he couldn't remain so.

Patty nodded encouragingly. "If you just go to the waiting room in the surgical ward, someone will come out to see you."

Theo and Mac found the ward and took seats in the waiting room. She kept her eyes on the double doors that led to the operating rooms. Someone would come through there soon…to tell her Gus was all right. As they waited, she kept hold of Mac's hand, aware that her grip was probably too tight but unable to release it. If he was uncomfortable, he gave no sign.

Eventually a woman in scrubs came down. She was not alone. George Mendes walked beside her. Theo noted the detective's presence without undue attention. Of course the police would be involved. Mendes hung back, making a phone call as the doctor moved over to them.

Dr. West explained the situation directly but kindly. Gus had been brought in with two separate gunshot wounds. The first bullet had gone through his shoulder—it was of less concern. The second had entered his pelvis, injuring major vessels and resulting in significant blood loss. He was currently in surgery to remove this second bullet and try to control the bleeding. Gus was young and fit so they were hopeful, but Theo had to understand that he had already lost a great deal of blood.

"What if you can't control the bleeding?" Even as she asked, Theo didn't want to know,

"We're doing everything we possibly can."

Theo shook her head. "Will I be able to see him when he comes out of surgery?"

Dr. West hesitated. "At the moment, things are touch and go…" She glanced back at Mendes, who had now been joined by two uniformed policemen.

Mendes took over. "I'm afraid the police will need to question him first."

"Surely that can wait until—"

"No. I'm afraid it can't."

"Mr. Benton is not going to be speaking to anyone for a while," Dr. West said, settling the matter firmly. "He's been intubated and is likely to remain so for some time after surgery."

"Theo?" Jacqui Steven came into the waiting room. Her suit was stained with blood; there was spatter on her blouse and the cuffs were soaked. "Is he—?"

Theo embraced her. "He's in surgery, Jac…" She glanced back at Mendes and his officers. "The police still want to question him."

"They shot him," Jacqui whispered. "The police shot Gus."

"What?" Theo choked. "The police? No… Why would they—"

Mac turned on Mendes furiously. "What the hell—"

"Mr. Benton was shot while resisting arrest," the detective said flatly.

"Arrest?" Mac stared at Mendes. "Why?"

"He was being charged with the murder of Mary Cowell."

Theo recoiled. "That's impossible. That's idiotic."

Mac took a step toward the officers. "Look, George, you can't be—"

The police officers with the detective moved quickly, seizing and cuffing Mac. He was clearly startled, but he didn't resist. They arrested him under suspicion of being an accessory to murder and read him his rights. Then Theo. She wasn't technically arrested but asked to come in for questioning with the threat that she would be arrested if she refused.

Theo turned to Jacqui, desperate now. "Stay with Gus…please don't leave him alone."

"You need a lawyer—"

"Please, Jac." Tears now, and terror. "What if he wakes up?" She held Jacqui's gaze and left unsaid: "What if he dies?"

Jacqui nodded. "I won't leave him. I'll hold the fort till you get back."

Theo cried in the police SUV. She didn't care that the police saw her, she didn't care what they thought or suspected or bloody imagined. Mac was being transported in another vehicle. She didn't understand. She was taken straight to an interview room, brought a cup of tea, and asked if she would like to see the police doctor.

"No…I just want to go back to the hospital."

In what may have been a tactic or simply an act of kindness, Mendes told her exactly what had happened at Crane, Hayes and Benton.

"A search of Mr. Benton's house produced evidence that ties him to the murder of Mary Cowell."

"What evidence?"

Mendes hesitated. "A key and the murder weapon."

Theo shook her head. "No."

"Given the violent nature of the crime, police officers sent to apprehend him were warned that he may be armed."

"That's insane!"

"Mr. Benton was trying to leave the building when officers arrived. After being told to put his hands up, he reached inside his jacket. That was when the officer shot him."

"Twice."

"Yes, twice."

"What was he reaching for?"

"Mr. Benton was not in possession of a weapon."

"Right." Theo wasn't crying anymore. She was angry.

"Miss Steven and the officers on the scene tried to stop the bleeding until the ambulance got there."

"Was he conscious?"

"I'm told he was. I believe he called for you."

"Great! Meanwhile, I'm here." Theo was shouting now. "Answering questions while my brother tries to hang on to life."

"Unfortunately, Mary Cowell did not have that chance."

"What happened to Mary was terrible, and I am sorry, but Gus had nothing to do with it."

A knock at the door. It was opened almost immediately by a policeman in uniform, past whom strode a man in a sharp pin-striped suit.

"Alexander Wilson of Wilson Freeman. I'll be representing Miss Benton. To which end I am instructing her to say nothing."

He looked at his watch. "You are within your rights to hold her without charge for another twenty hours, by which time her brother may well be dead, and you, good sir, will have a public relations disaster as well as one hell of a civil suit on your hands."

Theo said nothing. Jacqui must have called her a lawyer. If he wanted her to stop talking, she would. If he wanted her to sing the score from *Frozen*, she would. She had to get back to Gus.

She listened silently as Wilson and Mendes threatened each other. Another knock and another officer with a message for the detective. Mendes read the slip, swore, and stormed out.

Alexander Wilson smiled. "I think we can go."

Theo wanted to go straight to the hospital, but Wilson insisted they claim her phone from the desk sergeant before they left.

"What about Mac?" Theo asked as they walked out. "He was brought in too, but I haven't seen him since I came in."

"Let's just worry about getting you out of here to see your brother. We'll deal with Mr. Etheridge later."

A black BMW pulled up in front them and Wilson opened the back door. Theo stepped in.

CHAPTER 29

Gus Benton wasn't sure if he was awake. He knew he was alive because he was in too much pain to be dead. He could sense light outside his eyelids…he just had to open them. Someone had tied him up. He was trussed up like a bloody roast chicken. And yet somehow he knew that struggling against the bonds would really hurt, and so he didn't move. Someone was holding his hand.

Gus opened his eyes.

Theo. Theo was holding his hand. She was crying. Maybe he was dead.

"Gus…I'm so sorry."

He tried to speak.

"Please don't hate me, Gus. I love you."

Fuck. If he wasn't dead, he was clearly dying. He tried to say her name, but he couldn't make a sound. She looked up. God— her eyes: terrified, desperate. What had happened?

She slipped something under his pillow. "I don't think there's any other way, Gus."

Something beeped.

A man's face above his now—speaking to him like he was a toddler, telling him he was in the hospital. More beeping, the man started shouting at him. And he couldn't see Theo anymore.

Mac Etheridge had lost count of the hours, of the days. The terrorism charges had been unexpected. But the endless rotating interrogation was easier to bear than not knowing what was happening outside. Had Gus survived? Had they arrested Theo? He'd asked, of course, but they'd said nothing aside from implying that that information might be exchanged for a confession.

They were using the deliveries of materials to his house as evidence of some sort. Perhaps bombs could be made out of cement? They knew, of course, about the Ponderosa. The authorities had been aware of the mad Etheridges for years. But they also knew that his family was obsessed with surviving an apocalypse, not starting one. He rubbed his face. What if the feds had decided to search the Ponderosa? God, what would his mother do then? It might be the very incursion his mother feared, and the response could be disaster.

He'd been eventually allowed one phone call. He'd called Bernie, asked her to make sure Horse was all right, and to get him a lawyer. She'd told him that his U.S. assets and bank accounts had been frozen, that Gus was in surgery again, that she had no news of Theo, and that Mac's brothers were being questioned.

Mac shook his head as he thought about it. Zeke would be all right, but Sam and Caleb were idiots and likely to get them all executed by accident. He knew the terrorism allegations complicated matters.

"Mac, there's more."

Mac braced himself.

"A man's come forward after seeing Gus's picture in the news. He's spoken to the media. He says that twelve years ago Gus Benton attempted to kill him, that he stabbed him."

"What? Gus would have been a kid."

"Jacob Curtis says he was sixteen. Apparently they all lived in the same commune on the east coast of Tasmania. According to Curtis, Theo was infatuated with him, would follow him around asking questions—that sort of thing. Gus was apparently a very jealous big brother. Curtis was talking to Theo one day and Gus attacked."

"Bernie, I need you to find out everything you can about Curtis."

"Already on it. He's forty-two, a bit of a drifter, but he can verify that he was living in Tasmania twelve years ago…arrived in the States last year. I can't find any Tasmanian hospital admission record but he's lifting his shirt to display his scar whenever there's a camera or a checkbook around. There's no record of a police report into the incident. Curtis claims he was too frightened of retribution to go the police, but he does have an old photo of himself with Theo."

Mac cursed. "The police?"

"Are looking into it, but aside from the photo, there's no evidence and no witnesses. Gus is not in any condition to be questioned."

"What does Theo say?"

"I don't know where she is, Mac."

"What?" Mac had assumed Theo was at Gus's side. Why wasn't she? What could possibly keep her from Gus? Mac cursed, frustrated, worried, and exhausted from keeping his anger in check. He was thinking about Theo more often than he expected. He tried to direct it to the sequence of events that had led to their current situation, the things that didn't make sense, the people who seemed to have an interest. But, more often than not, his contemplation of crimes and suspects and motives was interrupted with a memory of her smile, the way she called that giant mutt "Horsey" to annoy Gus, that kiss...especially that kiss. God, the timing.

Gus Benton was well aware of his sister's absence. Initially it had been through a fog of anesthesia and pain, tubes, and drips, so that he did not have the strength or clarity to focus on it.

The Australian Embassy had contacted Paul and Beth Benton to inform them of Gus's condition, and to have the appropriate authorities question them about the claims of Jacob Curtis, but, having both been arrested at various protests and demonstrations over the years, the couple had been denied entry into America. Gus was secretly glad. He didn't need to have his parents to worry about at the moment.

He'd been forced out of Crane, Hayes and Benton while he was still unconscious. The vindictive bastards had sacked Jacqui as well. She might have been mad at him if he hadn't been shot.

As it was, she was his only visitor aside from the police. She gave him the heads-up on Curtis while everybody else believed he was still too ill to comprehend, tentatively, in case the news had an adverse effect on the equally tentative grip he seemed to have on life.

The information had, however, had the opposite effect and

he'd rallied. Perhaps it was the healing impact of fury, but he improved. Slowly his condition moved from critical to serious to stable, and he began to ask questions.

The police were allowed to question him when he was no longer critical, which they did multiple times. Gus was surprised they didn't arrest him, but he supposed it was not like he could go anywhere. They probably wanted to save the time that would start running when the arrest was made for when he could physically leave.

Jacob Curtis's allegations were put to him. Gus was well enough to realize that Curtis could not possibly sustain an action for an unreported, unwitnessed attack, twelve years after the fact and in a different criminal jurisdiction. Not unless Theo testified against him, which he knew she would not. He presumed the Kansas PD's interest in Curtis was to establish some pattern of violence that fit their current theory that he'd murdered Dan Murdoch because of the writer's relationship with Theo. His alibi for that day was not foolproof.

They questioned him extensively on the whereabouts of Theo, his relationship with her, what he allowed her to do. Because of the medication, perhaps, it took him a little while to understand the line of their inquiries.

"Theo is not afraid of me, George," he said, laughing bitterly when it dawned. "I was not keeping her prisoner, and she does not have some kind of weird Stockholm Syndrome. She's my kid sister. Her mistake was to get involved with a man who clearly had some serious and dangerous enemies."

"If that's the case, Gus, where is she? Murdoch is dead, and you need her. What would keep her away, unless she still has cause to be scared?"

"Of course, she's scared. There's a murderer on the loose, and the only thing the police can seem to do about it is to shoot me!"

"And Jacob Curtis?"

"Is a liar. Put him on the stand if you want—I'll rip him to fuckin' shreds."

For some weeks Gus assumed that Theo was with Mac Etheridge, as both seemed to have disappeared, and so he did not panic. Mac knew what he was doing. That they'd chosen to become fugitives was probably not ideal, but it would all be sorted out when the real killer was caught. In the meantime, he rested easy knowing she was safe.

It was only when it came out that Mac Etheridge's disappearance had been orchestrated by Homeland Security and that he had been, since the night of the shooting, held in a high-security facility, that Gus understood that his sister was really missing.

When George Mendes came to see him again, he was on his feet, using a walker. It had taken him twenty minutes to get upright, and so he was reluctant when Mendes asked him to sit down.

"Look, Gus, I really think you should sit down."

"Don't I have to be standing when you arrest me?"

"Gus, please."

There was something in Mendes's tone that scared Gus. And so he refused.

Mendes sighed. He glanced at Jacqui, who had also caught the gravity in the detective's manner and moved to stand beside Gus.

Mendes held out a piece of paper. A copy of a letter in Theodosia Benton's handwriting. Jacqui took it and held it for Gus. He read it quickly. He was a little relieved that she'd been found, though he showed none of that, responding hotly from the first. "What the hell did you do to her?" he demanded. "You've coerced her into confessing everything but the bloody Kennedy assassination. Have you had her all this time? There isn't a court in the country that won't throw this out!"

"We don't have her, Gus."

"Of course, you do... How else would you get her to write this trumped-up confession?"

"This arrived by mail." Mendes looked at him. "Gus, we haven't seen her since the day after you were shot, and we can't find her."

"What do you mean?" Gus's knuckles were white on the walker.

"Read the letter again, Gus. It's written by someone who was distraught, very troubled, and remorseful. Three murders—you on death's door... Do you think she might try to hurt herself?"

"No."

"She talks about feeling numb, like she's not here. Our psychologist believes she could be thinking about harming herself."

Fleetingly, Gus remembered Theo telling him she felt numb, like it was not happening to her. "No."

"Look, Gus, I'm sorry, I really am. I believe her when she says you didn't know, but we are really worried about her state of mind. For her sake, do you have any idea where she might—"

"Might what? Off herself? No, I don't, because Theo wouldn't. And she wouldn't...didn't kill anybody."

"She came to visit you just before she absconded." It was a statement not a question.

"Or was abducted," Gus said slowly.

"What did she say?"

"Not much—she cried mostly."

"She gave you a book?"

Gus nodded. Theo had slipped a copy of Jack Chase's *Airborne* under his pillow. "I gave it to her years ago… She uses it as a kind of good luck charm. I guess she figured I needed it more."

"People intent on doing themselves harm often give away their most precious possessions," Mendes pointed out. "If you were about to be charged for a capital crime for which she was responsible, she may well have been that desperate." Mendes moved closer so that Gus could not avoid his gaze. "It explains how the knife and keys ended up at your house. Come on, man, I know she's your kid sister, but sometimes we know the least about the people closest to us… Sometimes we don't want to see—"

"No. Go to hell, George!"

"If you help us find her, I think I can convince the district attorney to drop all the charges against you. And you could be saving her life."

"For fuck's sake, only an idiot would think for a moment that this confession isn't a complete fantasy… Theo's a writer—" Something started to beep again. It startled Gus as much as Mendes.

"Now look what you've done!" Jacqui snarled at Mendes. "It's not enough that your people shoot him, you've got to try and finish the job!"

All sorts of alarms were going off now. Doctor and nurses converged upon the room.

Mendes backed off… "We can talk later."

The detective and Jacqui Steven were pushed out of the room to make way for a crash cart.

CHAPTER 30

Jacqui put the coffee on the on the table beside the bed. She pushed the hair back off Gus's forehead. "How are you feeling?"

"Confused."

"That's probably the painkillers."

"My doctors are confused too, and they're not on anything, as far as I know."

"Why are they confused?" Jacqui's smile was innocent.

"Well, the machines seem to think my heart stopped, and yet I remained standing."

"They malfunction sometimes, I suppose."

"Jac—"

She wrinkled her nose. "I may have accidentally disconnected a couple of wires for a while."

"Why?"

"I wanted to make sure you didn't talk yourself out of a pass because you lost your temper."

He shook his head.

She took his hand and held it in both of hers. "Gus—"

"Theo didn't kill anyone, Jac."

Jacqui's voice was metered. "I agree."

"Then—"

"Theo may have decided to run while she still could." Jacqui sat down on the bed, knowing Gus was going to resist this. "Maybe she's scared, or exhausted. Maybe it got to be too much and she could see no other way. That confession was her trying to help you."

"And any prosecutor worth their salt is going to see that. Theo isn't an idiot—whatever she's doing, she must know it isn't going to work."

Jacqui shrugged. "I don't know, Gus. The decision to arrest you was based on the knife and the keys they found at your house, and now Theo has said she hid them there."

"She was living at Mac's when Mary Cowell was killed."

"Which is why it makes sense she would hide them somewhere else. She had a key to your place." Jacqui pressed on, though she could see Gus was tiring, and in pain. "That letter is going to give you reasonable doubt—you heard Mendes. Whatever he says, they've already given up on you being their man." She hesitated. "Gus, a couple of days before you were shot, Theo asked me about what was happening at the firm." Jacqui gathered her courage and told him about the day she met Theo for coffee, and the conversation they'd had.

"You told her that? Dammit, Jac! What were you thinking?"

"I didn't want to lie to her. I didn't think she'd—"

"She hasn't—"

"Of course, she hasn't…but Gus, whatever she has or has not done, she wrote that confession to protect you."

Gus closed his eyes. "She thinks I did it," he said quietly. "She thinks I killed Murdoch and Mary Cowell."

Jacqui grabbed his hand, startled by the pain in his voice. "That's not what I meant at all. Why would she think you were capable of killing anyone?"

Gus gasped as physical pain broke through his endurance with the memory of what he'd done, what Theo had seen him do. And a new thought tortured him. Was Theo afraid of him? Was that why she'd run?

───

Nancy Etheridge had decorated her son's house for his return. Welcome-home banners, balloons, and a table laden with everything he would not have eaten in prison. When he walked in the door, she led the cheering and the applause.

He was subdued, she thought. Happy enough to see them but not as excited as she expected. He greeted them all warmly, and he didn't protest the fuss, but he and the boy Benton were noticeably quiet. To do with Gus's sister, no doubt. The girl was still causing trouble. The mood was catching, and Caleb became surly.

Still, Nancy was determined that they all should celebrate. Gus at least was downing his fair share of champagne, however morosely. She filled the silences with chatter, calling on her sons and husband for affirmation from time to time. "Your sister couldn't come, what with the new baby and all—you do know you've got a new niece, don't you, Cormac? She sends her love, in any case."

Mac nodded. "I'll go see her soon."

"Perhaps you should come back to the Ponderosa for a while, son."

"Thanks, Mom, but I've got work to do," he said, glancing at Gus.

Mac had been detained for the months that Gus Benton had been in the hospital and then some, though he hadn't technically served any time. All the charges brought against him had been dropped, one by one, despite his family's attempts to demonstrate that all the Etheridges were mad and dangerous. The time that he'd spent in custody counted for nothing, not even against a sentence, which he supposed was a good thing.

Gus and Jacqui Steven had worked relentlessly to secure his freedom, but it had taken five and a half months in total. And in that time, not one word, not one sign of Theodosia Benton, aside from the written confession, which was being treated with the gravity of a dying declaration.

The media frenzy had died down somewhat, at least for now. Bernadette had kept everything going in his absence, but there were some things that needed his personal attention.

"Mac, can I talk to you?" Caleb asked quietly as their mother carried on the conversation by herself, pointing out the benefits of home and family in times of need.

"Yeah, come out to the backyard," Mac said, suddenly struck with an overwhelming need to get away from his mother's determined cheerfulness.

Somehow they managed to step outside without the rest of the Etheridges following.

He sat on a bench under the shade of the old elm tree that dominated the garden. It was the height of summer, and hot. He'd missed half the winter and all of the spring. "What gives, Caleb?" He knew, of course, but he wanted to give Caleb a chance to tell him. He wanted to make Caleb tell him.

Caleb paced for a while and then turned and blurted, "I told

Mary Cowell that Theodosia Benton was living in your house. I gave her the address."

The line of Mac's jaw was hard. "Yeah, I know."

"How?"

"One of the FBI agents told me. They were trying to shake my belief in the loyalty of my family."

"Did they?"

Mac didn't answer.

"How did they know?" Caleb pressed nervously.

"They checked Mary Cowell's emails, you idiot! They found yours telling her where Theo was."

Caleb was near tears now. "I got her killed, didn't I?"

Mac shook his head. "What the hell were you thinking, Caleb? Theo was under my protection, and you revealed her whereabouts. How am I supposed to ever trust you again?"

"I thought she was dangerous, Mac. You wouldn't listen. I was trying to protect you."

"That's right!" Mac said angrily. "Your idiotic zombie theory! For fuck's sake, Caleb, you might have got us all killed!"

"Mac, you've got to listen...there's evidence..."

"Evidence of what?"

"Dan Murdoch was Primus. He uncovered the Frankenstein Project...they're experimenting on people, Mac, and Primus was afraid they'd come for the children..."

"You're twenty-three, Caleb. Grow up! Life is not some stupid video game—you're not saving the world!" His gaze was cold and furious and unwavering.

"But we are...at least we're trying to. You have to listen, Mac. There's a book. They killed Primus for it... I thought Theo had killed Primus for them... I was afraid for you."

"Who is *them*?" Mac wasn't sure he wanted to know, but he asked anyway.

"The Minotaur…that's what Primus called them." Caleb brightened at what he thought was a sign of interest. "They're an alliance of corporate giants who think they can cure death."

For a few seconds Mac said nothing. Caleb's explanations only made him angrier. "This is stupid," he said finally. "Completely and utterly stupid, but even if it weren't, I trusted you, Caleb. Despite everything, I counted on you. Since when do you betray family?"

Caleb wiped his face. He knew what he knew, but Mac was right. He had broken faith with his family. For the past six months he'd lived in terror of them finding out. Suddenly, he was a child again, appealing to his big brother. "Are you going to tell?"

"I've already told Gus. You're lucky he's in no condition to beat the hell out of you, because I don't think I'd stop him. But I won't tell the others, and neither will he, but you have to show us everything you've been posting on whatever dark web sites you've been accessing. I want to know why the hell this thing blew up the way it did!"

CHAPTER 31

Mac Etheridge lent Gus Benton his shoulder for the spiral stair-case that led up to the tower. Gus was able to walk on crutches now, but stairs were tough physically. Everything else was tough in other ways.

But still, they were at least free men now.

Mac's return had been a grind of rebuilding bridges and net-works, reassuring old clients, and reestablishing his reputation. And readjusting after months of incarceration and interrogation.

Still, he'd had a job to return to, something on which to anchor his life; Gus Benton's career had been destroyed by what had happened. He'd been forced out of his own firm, and in the months that followed his release from the hospital, it became clear that he was not going to be welcomed into another. His house had been burned down by Mary Cowell's grieving father in a drama that had brought the media down upon him again. It had been one thing after another, but though it seemed that Theo had transferred her payout from their grandfather's trust to Gus around the time she disappeared, he steadfastly refused to touch it.

"Whoa!" Mac grabbed Gus as one crutch slipped and clattered down the stairs. Gus swore.

Mac pulled Gus's arm over his shoulder. "Do you want to stop?"

"No... It'll be just as bloody hard going down."

They limped up the last steps and Mac eased Gus into a chair. "You all right?"

"Dandy."

Mac's housekeeper followed them up with a tray of coffee and sandwiches, and the crutch, which she had retrieved from the bottom of the staircase. Gus exhaled, mildly mortified by the ease with which the middle-aged woman managed the stairs. She poured the coffee and left them to it.

Mac was aware that Gus Benton had of late given up coffee and tea for something harder, self-medicating pain of all sorts with bourbon and gin, but he wanted him completely sober for this conversation. He needed to know exactly what had happened if he was going to help Gus, if they were ever going to find Theo.

"Okay, Mac," Gus said, "what was so confidential that we couldn't talk at a bar?"

"Do you want to tell me why you stabbed Jacob Curtis?"

Gus's eyes hardened and flashed. "Not really."

"Do it anyway."

For a moment Gus resisted, and then he sighed. "Jacob Curtis was part of the community in which we lived when we were in Tassie. A place called Harmony. We grew our own food, made our own clothes, were home-schooled and had very little to do with the outside world."

"Curtis says you stabbed him because he was spending time with Theo…that you were pathologically jealous of anyone who even spoke to your little sister."

Gus responded with a string of profanity. If he'd been able, he might have left.

Mac waited. This was something he needed to know.

Eventually, Gus continued, his voice strained and brittle, his eyes fixed on his hands, clenched into fists. "I wasn't jealous."

"What happened, Gus?"

Frustrated, Gus recounted, and in the process, relived. "We're in Harmony and Curtis arrives. Not sure where he's come from—people would come and go all the time. Anyway, he takes a shine to Theo…makes her stuff—skipping ropes, little carved animals, even a billy cart. Theo thinks he's wonderful. Follows him around like a puppy."

There was sweat beading on Gus's brow. Mac didn't interrupt.

"Curtis makes Theo a fishing rod and wants to teach her how to fish." Gus flinched. "The river isn't far, and Theo is so damn excited. He offers to take me too. I think my parents assumed I'd go. But I'm fifteen—I reckon I'm too bloody old to be *taken* fishing, so I find a last-minute excuse." Gus's knuckles were white. He stopped talking.

"And?" Mac prompted.

Gus started twice to speak. It was only on the third attempt that he got it out. "My mother finally notices I haven't gone, tells me off, and sends me to drop some sandwiches out to them, and I…I find him on top of her. He was about thirty then. She was ten. He has one hand over her mouth and the other…" Gus shook his head.

Mac's swallowed, speechless. He'd suspected something—but not this. This was worse than anything he'd imagined.

"There's a fight. I grab his fishing knife and stab the bastard." Gus right arm jerked, his muscles repeating the memory.

"Fuck." Mac rubbed the back of his neck. "What happened?"

"There's a lot of blood. It's spurting. Theo is hysterical… For a while I think I've killed him…but, somehow, I haven't. There are a couple of doctors at Harmony—they save him. And once he's out of danger, Curtis is expelled from the community…me too."

"Nobody called the police?"

"No…it's not the kind of community that trusts the police. And my mother is afraid that I'll be charged, and Theo will be taken away. The others are convinced that the government will use the incident as an excuse to take all the children into care. So nothing is said. Curtis can't go to the police without what he did to Theo coming out, and I can't stay because of what I did. The ancients send me to live with my grandfather over here, just in case the police ever get wind of what happened." Gus shrugged. "He sends me to an analyst, and I haven't stabbed anyone since."

"And Theo?"

"She stays. She survives. Once she starts boarding school, it's easier to keep in touch—she has access to computers and phones." Gus grimaced. "We've never really talked about it. I don't want to bring it up in case she just wants to forget, and she doesn't raise it either." He stopped. "My parents love us, Mac—they do their best. This was just a bad decision."

"I'm in no position to judge anybody's parents, Gus."

"Men like that don't stop," Gus said quietly. "God knows how many—"

"He was arrested and charged yesterday… That's why we needed to talk about this."

"Charged? With what?"

"Indecent assault, rape... It seems he was identified by the scar he was so happy to display on air when he was telling the world how you stabbed him."

Gus looked sick. "If we'd said something twelve years ago—"

"Doesn't sound like you made that decision, Gus. It's not down to you."

Gus shook his head. "God, I need a drink."

Mac pushed a cup of coffee toward him. "Look Gus, I want you to come work with me."

Gus sat up. "I don't need charity, mate. Just a drink."

"It's not charity," Mac said evenly. "I need help. For one thing, I have to get all my assets back from the government—"

"I have to find Theo."

"We can look for Theo," Mac said. "I haven't forgotten her, Gus, and I won't. But you're not going to be able to help her if you're sleeping on park benches."

"Things aren't that bad, Mac," Gus lied, knowing full well his medical debts alone would bankrupt a small country. He'd lost his insurance with his firm, and his chances of getting another job were slim.

"They're not far off, pal. For both of us. I promise you; this is not altruistic. I need your help."

"I'm fine, Mac."

"For chrissake, Gus—" The exchange became heated for a while, but Mac persisted, wearing down Gus's denial, and eventually, because he had no other choice, Gus accepted the job Mac Etheridge offered him.

It proved over time to be a profitable marriage of skills. Gus issued the necessary writs, actions, and challenges to break the government's stranglehold on Mac Etheridge's assets and dealings;

he anticipated new legal obstacles and devised ways around them. His role hybridized beyond legal matters. And when they were not "on a case," as Gus insisted on calling it, and sometimes when they were, he and Mac looked for Theo.

Mac systematically interviewed every person who might have known Dan Murdoch in Lawrence, showing them a photograph of Mary Cowell and the postmortem photograph of Burt Winslow in the hope of finding some connection between the victims that they had missed. Finally, one of Dan Murdoch's neighbors tentatively identified Burt Winslow as the man who clipped the writer's hedges, but from there the trail went dead. It was as if Burt Winslow had existed only to tend Murdoch's garden. He had no discernible address, no family, no history.

Gus trawled through the posts by and about Primus, whom Caleb insisted was Dan Murdoch. He wasn't entirely convinced that was true, although it did give him an insight into why so many people had descended upon Lawrence in December. But even if Dan Murdoch had been some crazy conspiracy theorist, even if he was behind this nonsense about minotaurs and monsters, it was nothing to do with Theo. Primus's promise that there would be a manifesto published caught his attention.

"I reckon Murdoch was just running a teaser campaign of sorts for his new book," he told Mac. "It's actually quite clever. He's directing his paranoid nutcase followers to make his book a bestseller."

"That only works if they knew who he was," Mac observed.

"That's true," Gus conceded. "Perhaps he intended to reveal himself before the book was released."

"Theo said Murdoch's manuscript was missing," Mac recalled. "Assuming he had one in the first place, of course. For all we know he was still blocked and just telling his agent what she wanted to hear."

Gus frowned. "If we assume your brother is right, and Murdoch was this bloke Primus, and that the manuscript did exist, then perhaps it had something to do with the reason he was killed. And maybe whoever killed him couldn't find the manuscript either, and maybe they think Theo has it."

Mac opened his phone and found the pictures he'd taken of the envelope Winslow had delivered. He showed Gus. "Maybe Murdoch did send it to Theo, Winslow intercepted it and wanted to sell it to Theo. That's why he gave her the letter…some sort of proof of life. He may have assumed she'd know the manuscript had been in the package and be willing to pay for its return."

"But why?" Gus shook his head. "Surely, it would be more sensible to try to sell it to Murdoch's agents. They'd be able to do something with it…and they're more likely to have money."

Mac shrugged. "Day Delos was trying to sign Theo too, remember. Perhaps Winslow was trying to approach them through Theo…but someone killed him first."

"So where's the manuscript?"

"We need to find it," Mac decided. "It could lead us to Theo."

That, of course, was easier said than done. Burt Winslow was dead and his existence elusive. And they were not the only ones looking for the missing manuscript, the manifesto promised by Primus to thousands of people determined to defend themselves against a project to raise the dead. Dan Murdoch's agents maintained security at his house to keep treasure hunters at bay.

The police had had no better luck, and with no further murders taking place, deprioritized the search for Theodosia Benton.

The popular wisdom was that Theo had died by her own

hand...somewhere remote and lonely, where her body would not be found until the Lawrence murders were all very cold cases. A woman from Topeka and a bunch of teenagers from Wichita with a Ouija board had claimed to have been in touch with her spirit. Tourists sighted her walking about the Stull Cemetery. But the urban myths as well as a very real police manhunt came to nothing.

When Gus was fit enough to survive the flight, he and Mac flew to Tasmania, in case Theo had fled home. As soon as they got to Hobart, Gus called every person he could think of who she might have gone to for help, who might have given her refuge. The list was not extensive, truncated by the fact that he had left the island so many years before.

The following day they rented a Nissan X-Trail and drove up the east coast in search of the property near St Helens, where the Bentons had once lived. Phones were forbidden in the community that remained, and so there was no other way to speak with them. Gus didn't say a great deal in the hours it took to get there. His eyes remained fixed on the passing landscape, the mountains that met beaches strewn with red algae, the startling beauty of Wineglass Bay, the towns nestled into the hillscape, forests, the occasional sighting of a wallaby. Mac let him be. This, going back, was a lot to ask, but they had to check.

Mac stopped at a pub in St Helens to ask directions—an old establishment unburdened by modernization.

The publican pulled two beers and set the glasses before them. "You're lookin' for the ferals? That Harmony mob?"

"Yes," Gus replied.

"Whadaya want with them? It's a cult, you know. All sorts of strange goings-on." His eyes narrowed. "You're not planning on joinin', are you?" He laughed. "You look a little clean to be ferals—but you wouldn't be the first—what they call you now... millennials—you wouldn't be the first millennials to join that Sodom and Gomorrah."

"We're not joining," Mac replied.

"Well if you're hoping to get someone out, I'd prepare for disappointment. We've seen scores of fathers and mothers, husbands and wives go out to Harmony to rescue their loved ones." The publican shook his head sadly. "Once they got you..."

"We have to try," Mac said ambiguously.

The publican gave them directions. They were basic and scrawled on the back of a napkin but probably more precise than Gus's vague memories of how to get there. Mac didn't want to take the chance that they'd get lost this close to dark.

The property was located well off the tarred road, via a country lane that was barely more than a bush track. The afternoon was mellowing into sunset when they came upon it. A hand-painted sign on the gate read "Harmony." The track led from it to a cluster of yurts surrounded by vegetable gardens, pens of goats, and freeranging chickens on what might once have been a conventional farm. Barefooted, wild-haired children played in the dirt.

"The river's over there," Gus said quietly, pointing to a line of trees.

Mac watched him, knowing he was reliving that day twelve years before. Mac found it hard enough to think about—he could only imagine what it was doing to Gus. "Why don't you wait here? I could go see if those kids have parents somewhere."

Gus shook his head. "They're more likely to talk to me." He beckoned one of the children. They all ran over, curious, talkative, guilelessly cheeky. Gus asked them where their elders were.

"You're an outsider." The little girl who stood at the head of the children folded her arms and regarded them fiercely.

"Yes," Gus said calmly, "but I lived here once. Is the swinging tree still standing…the one with the rope that can take you out to the middle of the river?"

The girl nodded and the children burst into a babel of stories about their adventures on the rope swing, and for a while Gus discussed swinging techniques with them. "Have there been any other outsiders come to Harmony that you can remember?"

"There's always people coming. Athol says we'll be our own country soon."

"Where exactly are your elders now?"

The girl pointed toward a rise. "They're in the potato paddock. There's a round moon tonight…but you can't go in the machine. Come on, we'll show you."

And so they followed the children, who chattered and sang as they walked. Beyond the rise they could see adults working with mattocks in a cleared field. A young woman noticed them then and downed tools to walk over and demand the nature of their business.

When Gus explained that he had lived in the community once, she became less hostile. She shooed away the children and invited Gus and Mac to follow her to meet "the others." They might have asked her about Theo then, but they wanted to see who else was there, look for themselves for any sign of Theo.

The furrowed field was awkward for Gus, who still relied heavily on a cane, but eventually they made their way over to a larger group of men and women who were planting potatoes.

They were greeted with a chorus of "Welcome to Harmony, friend!"

"Augustus Stormboy Benton! Crikey!" An older man—snow-white hair, graying beard, and protruding front teeth that made him lisp a little—walked toward them arms outstretched. "It's you, isn't it?"

Gus nodded. "Athol."

"I never thought I'd see you back here, Augustus."

"It's Gus now. Neither did I." His eyes remained fixed on the line of trees behind which was the river.

"Aug…Gus's folks helped found this place," Athol said for the benefit of the others. "They were good people—keepers of light." He turned to a woman with long cornrowed hair. "You remember Gus, Maura. He stabbed that Jacob Curtis with a five-inch fishing knife."

CHAPTER 32

Some of the people gathered around drew back, alarmed and angry, as Athol described the knife and the resultant wound in somewhat unnecessary detail. There was a recitational quality to it. Mac wondered if the old man was suffering from the beginnings of some kind of dementia. Maura nodded calmly as he spoke, as did others—older men and women who it appeared had been there. Gus listened in silence.

"Not that I blame you, of course," Athol declared. "Curtis was scum. A dark force, a corrupter. Someone needed to stab the mongrel."

Gus's face was unreadable.

"That was one helluva day," Athol said shaking his head. "Blood everywhere...Curtis screaming like a stuck pig. We made a pact to keep what happened to ourselves...for Augustus's sake... and the little girl's. Had John the Lighthealer sew the depraved bastard up... It was bloody hairy for a while, but Curtis survived. And of course, he wasn't going to tell."

Again, Gus said nothing.

Mac glanced uncomfortably at the potato planters, many of whom were clearly surprised by Athol's declarations. It seemed a very public way to keep a pact of secrecy.

"How is Theodosia?" Maura asked gently.

"She's fine," Gus snapped.

"When was the last time you saw Theo?" Mac asked cautiously.

"Oh, years ago now," Maura replied frowning. "Paul and Beth sent her to boarding school on the mainland when she was twelve or so, and then they left too. It was understandable after what happened, I suppose. Theodosia became so withdrawn and she missed her brother so terribly...would cry for him. Paul and Beth tried, but Harmony was destroyed for them. We let them go with our blessings."

"It wasn't that!" Athol folded his arms churlishly. "Paul and Beth had showbiz in their blood! We weren't enough of an audience for Tassie's answer to Sonny and Cher. With the kids out of the way, it was their big chance!"

"So, Theo hasn't been back here?" Mac asked as Gus bristled.

Athol looked sharply at Gus. "Doesn't he know—what happened here? Why you stabbed that lowlife?"

"Yes, I do," Mac interjected firmly, lest Athol feel the need to go into detail.

"Then you'd have to know this is the last place Theodosia would want to revisit." Athol became agitated. "We failed her. We let a monster live among us, and he stole her light."

Maura grabbed his hand. "Athol, we didn't know."

"We tended his wounds," Athol spat. "We saved his life."

"What else could we do?"

"We should have let him bleed to death!" The old man was shaking now.

Mac placed his hand on Gus's shoulder. "We should go."

Gus nodded. He handed Athol a card. "If she does come back here, would you call me somehow? You can reverse the charges."

"We have no need of phones, Augustus. You know that."

Gus reached inside his jacket and extracted a mobile phone complete with charger. One of Mac's burners. "My number is already programmed into this. All you have to do is call. If Theo turns up, for fuck's sake, call! You owe us that."

———

"They seem to have no idea about what happened in Lawrence," Mac observed as they pulled away from Harmony. The Australian connection to the Lawrence murders had been splashed across Australian papers.

"They wouldn't. They don't use phones or computers; they don't even buy the paper. They'd only know if someone told them, and they don't really encourage talk of the outside world and its troubles in the community."

"Geez..."

"Don't get me wrong, Mac. We were like pigs in mud here before Jacob Curtis... It was a kind of idyllic Little-House-on-the-Prairie existence. A little boring, but aside from that, we weren't unhappy."

"Do you think Theo would come back here?"

"No."

"Do you think they would call if she did?"

Gus thought about that. He sighed. "I don't know. They'd probably do what Theo wanted."

Mac frowned. "What if they use that phone to call the police instead?"

"That, I'm pretty sure they wouldn't do." He rubbed his shoulder. "It's not the way Harmony handles things."

They talked a bit after that. About Harmony, Gus's exile to the U.S., life, and reformation under the rule of his grandfather.

"Mum and Dad kept telling me Theo was fine, that she'd forgotten what happened... I wanted to believe it, I guess." Gus shrugged. "I came back when she graduated from that school they packed her off to, and she seemed fine. A little shy, a little dreamy, but fine...happy. Looking forward to university and law school." He laughed. "Poor bloody kid—all those rich princesses in high-end formal gowns, and Theo in some hideous frock Mum had made and dyed with onion skin and rhubarb."

"And she never mentioned what had happened at Harmony?" Mac asked.

"Not then. I take her back to New York with me for the summer—buy her some decent clothes, take her to a couple of shows. She was fun. A normal, slightly naïve eighteen-year-old. An old soul in some ways, innocent in others." Gus paused. "I remember feeling relieved. We only have one fight, just before she returns to Australia." He shook his head as he remembered. "We're out one night, and some loser hits on her. I tell him to take a hike. Theo's furious."

"She liked him?"

"No—I think she just wanted to tell him to buzz off herself. She said I was treating her like a child, like she was damaged. It was the closest we ever came to talking about Jacob Curtis. I knew then that she hadn't forgotten anything, and that maybe she's right. That she might just be stronger and more resilient than I think...than I was. So when she comes to Lawrence, I am so determined not to be overprotective, not to treat like she's a child…" He paused to curse. "I should have paid more attention to her relationship with Murdoch… I should have known—"

"How could you have known, Gus? And, to be fair, he didn't hurt her in any way…"

"He was old."

"I'm sure nothing that happened was because he was old, Gus, and I think Theo did love him—you don't get to choose for other people."

"Yes, that's a stupid bloody rule."

Mac smiled. "For what it's worth, I thought your sister was…" He faltered. "We'll find her, Gus."

"God, I hope so, mate. I'm not sure I can live with having failed her twice."

Mac broached the subject then, tentatively, because Harmony had already been too much. "We should probably track down your parents before we head back."

Gus face darkened. He groaned. "Yes, I suppose we should. God…I told them I would look after her. What am I going to tell them now?"

Mac kept his eyes on the road. "I don't know, Gus. Maybe just that we haven't given up."

CHAPTER 33

Gus located Paul and Beth Benton in the fishing village of Strahan on the west coast. According to a small notice on the Tourism Tasmania website, the Bentons were the headline act at the local hotel.

Mac and Gus headed out from Hobart early, driving through the rolling hills of the Huon Valley to the wild and rugged west coast of Tasmania. Gus seemed to know most of the little towns on the way, pointing out the venues at which his parents had performed, funny stories, mostly about tough crowds and local trivia. Mac could sense he was nervous.

A former port, Strahan was built between two picturesque coves in Long Bay, which itself formed part of Macquarie Harbour. The road into town wound through bushland so the water came as a surprise—a picture postcard town on the water. Mac and Gus arrived at the hotel while the Bentons were still onstage, performing a set they'd dedicated to Theo—a very large hirsute man sang folk songs and played guitar alongside a petite backup vocalist with a tambourine and a still discernible Boston lilt. Mac and Gus took a table and watched unobtrusively for a while.

When Paul Benton finally noticed them, he finished his song and announced that the show was over. Gus stood to greet his parents, both of whom were crying before they reached him. Mac went to the bar to give them time.

Gus came to get him about an hour later. "Come on, they'd like to meet you."

And so they sat and shared a meal of chicken parmigiana and chips. Despite appearances, it seemed that Paul and Beth had also been searching for Theo, certain that she would come home to Tasmania. But they had found nothing. Mac assured them that he and Gus would not stop looking for her. Every now and then, Paul Benton would embrace his son, enveloping him and holding on.

"For God's sake, Dad, I'm trying to eat!" Gus muttered on the fourth occasion, but otherwise he didn't resist.

"We did the wrong thing, didn't we?" Beth said suddenly and quietly. "When we let him go. We should have called the police."

"This has nothing to do with that, Mum," Gus replied absolutely.

"Are you sure?" she said, looking into his eyes as if she was afraid what she might find there.

Then Mac understood. Paul and Beth Benton were not entirely sure that Gus hadn't killed Dan Murdoch.

Gus's smile was forced. He said nothing.

"Curtis turned up in Lawrence just after you were shot," Mac said. "Perhaps that's why—"

"Are you saying he took Theo?" Beth said, clutching for her husband's hand.

"No, he's been arrested," Mac said quickly. "What I mean is, perhaps that's why Theo left. With Gus in the hospital and me behind bars, she might have thought it safer to disappear for a while."

Beth regarded him sharply. "Then where is she? You said this man has been arrested—why hasn't she come back?"

Gus intervened. "If we knew where she was, Mum, we'd just go get her."

"Dammit, Gus, why did you let her stay?" Beth turned on him angrily. "She would have been safe here!"

Gus's eyes hardened. "Safe?" he said bitterly. "Like she was in Harmony?"

"Bethy." Paul reached for his wife.

"Is she dead, Gus?" Beth demanded. "Is your sister dead?"

Mac stepped in as Gus was starting to look a little battered. "There's no evidence that Theo's dead, Mrs. Benton. We're not going give up."

Beth stared at him. Her upper lip trembled. "Good."

Beth Benton calmed a little then. She took Gus's hand and held it tightly. Perhaps it was an apology of sorts—Mac couldn't tell. They finished dinner and sat at the table together until closing time.

"You're not going to try and drive back tonight?" Paul objected as Mac felt his pockets for the car keys.

"We're flying home tomorrow," Gus said.

"This is your home," Beth said. "Even now."

Gus didn't argue. "We're flying back to Kansas tomorrow."

"Darling, you look exhausted," Beth said placing her hand on his cheek. "You can't drive—"

"Actually, I'm not allowed to drive yet," Gus said, grabbing his walking stick from where he'd hung it on the back of the chair. "Mac's doing all the driving."

"Perhaps you should stay here for bit," Paul suggested. "In Tassie, I mean, not here in the pub. Let your mum and I look after you."

"I've got to get back to work, Dad." He stood slowly, using both the table and the stick for support till he felt steady. "And Theo's not here... We've got to keep looking."

CHAPTER 34

The book was a runaway international bestseller, propelling the name of its Chilean author into general recognition. Translation rights became the subject of bidding wars, and the novel became available in over forty languages. Film and television deals had been signed before it was released, and despite its popularity among ordinary readers, the book had been nominated for a slew of literary awards, credited with creating a new genre of fiction.

Even so, *Afterlife* had been on the market for about six months before Mac Etheridge came across it.

He'd bought it because his mother had so roundly condemned its subject matter. Nancy Etheridge considered the book blasphemous, a dangerous promotion of devil worship and easy virtue to young and susceptible minds. She had written letters, called for boycotts, and rallied her fellow Christians to demand the book be banned. Mac hadn't seen her quite this worked up since he'd been released from prison.

Sometime during the second year after the shooting, Gus

Benton seemed to accept that he wasn't going to find his sister, though he would never believe she'd killed anybody. Instead, he became convinced that Theo had fallen victim to whomever had killed Dan Murdoch, Burt Winslow, and Mary Cowell. He grieved for her. He missed her. And for a while he was consumed with thoughts of avenging her and clearing her name. But the killings had stopped. Mendes presented that fact alone as proof positive that Theodosia Benton had been the perpetrator, and try as they did, Gus and Mac had found no more likely suspect.

They talked less about what had happened these days, less about Theo. A mutual belief in her innocence was unsaid now, an unspoken alliance, a silent grief. Gus had been her big brother, Mac the man who'd kissed her on the night it all went to hell. Dual demons of guilt and regret had been subdued, even if they were not defeated.

And so, Mac had not been looking for Theodosia Benton when he opened *Afterlife*.

He began reading it on a flight between New York and Kansas City, expecting nothing more than a tale of Satan worship and easy virtue, the occasional line he could quote to torment his mother. He found a story of grief and separation and fear written from the perspective of those who had died. It was extraordinary and just familiar enough to unsettle him. And then the thread. Unmistakable even in the darkness. "Perhaps the dead are afraid to live as much as we are afraid to die." They were her words, her exact words. When he reached Kansas City, he picked up his car and drove directly to the apartment that Gus rented on Tennessee Street.

He pulled up in front of the building and hesitated, questioned the kindness of bringing this book to Gus's attention. Gus was only just emerging from the wreckage. Mac shook his head. As much as he still thought of Theo, as much as he wondered about what they might have had, she was not his sister. He had no right to keep this from Gus. It wouldn't bring Theo back, but pursuing this might be one last thing they could do for her.

When he knocked, nobody answered the door. It was still light and so Mac elected to wait, taking a seat on the steps and opening the book once again. This was Theo's plot. He'd seen it spread out on the kitchen table, pages taped together...scribbled in her hand with arrows and stars and little pictographs. There were variations, but the essential plot was the same. And those had been her words. He could hear her speaking them.

He became so engrossed in the book that Gus's arrival caught him by surprise.

"Mac? I thought you were in New York." Gus had been out running with Horse. He passed Mac the two pizza boxes in his arms, as he retrieved his keys. Papa Keno's was not as convenient to the apartment as it had been to his house, but he picked up the pies nonetheless and ran the last half mile of his route carrying them.

"Just got back." Mac stood. "Do you have a minute?"

"Sure. Stay for some pizza. There's should be enough." He glanced at the novel in Mac's hand. "Isn't that the book your mum's all worked up about?"

"Yes. It's what I came to talk to you about."

"We're forming a book club?" Gus opened the door and stood back as Horse charged in. "We've completely given up, then?"

Mac laughed as he followed him in. "Just this book."

Gus begged off to shower, which he did in five minutes. He opened the pizza boxes and sandwiched a slice of Hawaiian to a slice of pepperoni. "So, what's the story?"

"The story is the point." Mac handed him the book. "This book has sold over half a million copies in this country alone."

"So?"

"It's Theo's story."

"What?" Gus looked at the book in his hand. So...another bloody unauthorized biography. There'd already been a few: *Killer Plot, The Tasmanian Devil, The Ripper's Daughter.* Poorly researched, sensationalist rubbish. When the first one came out, he'd been livid and devastated, determined to have the publication pulped. He'd failed. And after the third book, he'd learned to ignore it.

"What could this one possibly say that the others haven't?"

Mac shook his head. "Not about her...*her* book."

"Oh." Gus bit his lip. "Are you saying this is about Canberra?"

"Not that one. The next one. She plotted it out on your kitchen table... You must have seen it."

"Yes." Gus's brow furrowed as he struggled to remember the details. "Something about ghosts."

Mac nodded. He told Gus about the idea Theo had explained to him, what they had discussed, the characters, the themes, what she'd hoped to say in that second manuscript. The brightness of her eyes, the exhilaration in her voice. The way she rocked onto her toes when she got really excited.

Gus listened silently until Mac had finished. The realization was sudden and acute. "Were you in love with my sister, mate?" he asked quietly.

Mac didn't flinch. "Maybe. Probably. But that's not the point. This book is her story."

Gus exhaled. "Didn't someone once say that every novel is a variation of the same story?"

"Yes. I expect it was some jerk who'd only read one book."

Gus frowned, turning the volume over in his hands. He and Theo had never had a chance to talk about this book. But she had said she was writing a ghost story, and Mac was not likely to get worked up about nothing. "So what are you saying?"

"The police took Theo's notes and journals. Did they return them to you?"

"Yes, but they were all lost in the fire."

"So you can't be sure they returned everything? And even if they did, it doesn't mean her notebook couldn't have been copied when it was at the station."

"By whom? The police? You think someone in the Lawrence Police Department stole Theo's manuscript and—what?" He turned to the back cover. "Gave it to a Chilean writer who doesn't speak English?"

"How do you know P. S. Altamirano doesn't speak English?"

"Because this book is a translation."

"That doesn't mean the author doesn't speak English...just that he or she likes to write in Spanish. And what better way to hide the fact that you stole the original idea?" Mac walked into the kitchen to boil water for the tea Gus had gotten him used to drinking with pizza.

"Actually, give it back for a second," he said, returning suddenly. He flicked through the pages he had first read only hours earlier and found the reference. "Look at this."

Gus read. In the passage, the deceased protagonist was haunted by a surfer and his dog. The dog was called El Caballo. He looked at Mac blankly. It did sound like the kind of odd thing Theo would write, but he presumed she hadn't been the only writer with a quirky style.

"Gus, *el caballo* is Spanish for *the horse*."

Gus glanced at his dog, remembering how much Theo had loved the hound, how she babied Horse until he was spoiled rotten. When he'd finally returned home from the hospital, there'd been a large package waiting for him: a customized surfboard. At first it had given him hope, but investigations revealed that it had been ordered months before and delivered for Christmas. He stared at the passage for a while. "Let me read it," he said in the end.

Mac nodded. "I'll make some coffee."

"You're going to sit here and watch me read?"

"Yes."

Gus let it go. He read. Like a lawyer at first, quickly, identifying points of interest, allocating pages into evidence for and against it being Theo's story. And then more slowly, savoring sentences. There was a darkness to the novel that didn't sound like Theo, but there were also references, characterizations that he recognized from their childhood. And then a devout matriarch who was preparing to survive all things, to cheat death.

"Angelica sounds like your mother," he murmured.

Mac agreed. Despite making his book her current hobby horse, his mother had not noticed her own inclusion in its pages.

It was the early hours of the morning when Gus closed the book. Mac was still there, waiting. "Okay, I see what you're saying, Mac. But I'm not sure what you think this means."

"Theo made very detailed notes about this book. They were taken from your house after the brick was thrown through the window, and then my place when I was arrested. They were supposedly returned to you and then lost in the fire. The only way they could have ended up with this Altamirano guy is if the original or whatever copies the Kansas PD made, were passed on."

There was a fury building in Mac's eyes. "After everything they did to her, Gus, we can't let them steal her book too."

Gus rubbed his face. Mac was right. This was one cut too many. "How would we prove this was Theo's story, Mac?"

"Copies of her notes are probably in a police file somewhere. I'll find them."

Gus didn't ask how. If anybody could hack the Kansas PD, it was probably Mac Etheridge, but as much as Gus's legal career was over, he was still an officer of the court. There were some things he was more comfortable not knowing.

There was a thought he didn't want to voice or acknowledge. It was ludicrous—Theo would never have walked away and casually restarted her life in Chile. Not while he was in the hospital and Mac in prison. She wouldn't have done that. The idea was stupid.

CHAPTER 35

Has anyone read "Afterlife"? It's a book about ghosts but I think there're
messages in it. Could it be the manifesto Primus promised us before they
killed him?

    WKWWK

    Flagman

Just ordered it.

    Frodo 14

It's on special on Amazon.

    Lostboy

            —⁓—

Gus had closed all his own social media accounts three years
before, after Theo had first disappeared, when he'd become the
target in her stead for the anger of bereaved fans and keyboard
vigilantes. So, he felt a little absurd trying to stalk P. S. Altamirano

online. And to no avail. The writer had no official pages or accounts, nor any personal accounts either. It was unusual for a writer. There was a website...slick, designed, managed by the media company. He found numerous threads discussing the book and some that debated whether Altamirano was male or female, and countless articles on the phenomenal success of the mysterious writer, including one from *Publishers Weekly* featuring a statement from an agent justifying the fact that there were no photographs of the author.

> *"We knew from the first reading that we had a superstar in the making. We made the decision then to preserve as much privacy for P.S. as possible. It is not easy to be in the public eye, and we were well aware that the book would attract a lot of attention. We represent writers not books, so we are interested in ensuring the long-term viability of our clients' lives."*

It was unusual, but Gus could see the sense in it. The public's interest in the lives of writers had increased with the accessibly afforded by social media and the web in general, but that very accessibility was dangerous. Online friendship was a fickle thing. Loose comments, failed jokes, or simple flares of temper could unleash a contagion of outrage and condemnation. It was no longer enough to write a good book; authors had to be photogenic, witty saints as well.

But maybe there was another reason for the inaccessibility of P. S. Altamirano, the complete lack of any information beyond a basic, publicist-produced bio. God, what if there was another reason?

Gus was torn between wanting to believe Theo was alive,

and not wanting to believe that she would do this—to him, to Mac, to everybody who had mourned her. He understood that she'd been scared. He would have helped her run, if that's what she wanted to do, but if she'd just left… He cursed. There was a memory buried in a pethidine haze: Theo apologizing, begging him not to hate her. She'd been terrified. And she'd left that book…the novel he'd had Jack Chase sign for her when she was a kid. Why had she left that?

Mac seemed intent on avenging what he thought was the theft of Theo's manuscript…or the notes for her manuscript. Gus shook his head. He'd suspected that his sister had feelings for Mac, but he'd only recently worked out that Mac returned them. Even after three years.

If not for that realization, Gus might have kept the nagging idea that P. S. Altamirano was Theo, or working with Theo, to himself. It seemed disloyal to suggest, and his instinct was still to defend her even against his own accusation. But he had realized. And Mac Etheridge had stood by him through disaster, grief, and despair. He had to trust him with this.

When Gus Benton arrived on his doorstep the next morning with a laptop and an idea that wouldn't leave him be, Mac listened. He had, after all, started this by showing Gus the book. "You think Theo just took off while you were in the hospital and left you to deal with the fallout?" Mac was skeptical. "I can't see it, Gus. She wouldn't have done that to you. I was with her when she found out you'd been shot—she wasn't thinking of anyone else but you."

"Maybe she thought that confessing was the only way to save me. Mendes was still intent on charging me with Mary Cowell's murder." Gus pulled up the article from *Publishers Weekly*, and then turned his laptop screen to face Mac. "There is this."

Mac saw it immediately. "Day Delos and Associates Management. Isn't that—"

"The mob Theo was talking to? Yes."

"And they were Dan Murdoch's agents too." Mac frowned. "What was her name…the woman Theo was talking to?"

"Cole, I think. Valerie or Victoria or something."

Mac studied the screen thoughtfully. "That is an interesting coincidence."

"More than interesting," Gus insisted.

"Perhaps." Mac punched in a quick search on Day Delos and Associates as he told Gus what he'd found. "The Kansas PD doesn't have a copy of Theo's notes."

Gus bristled. "That's not possible. The case isn't closed."

"Apparently, they were lost."

"All the evidence or just the notes?"

"Just the notes…which means there is no evidence that *Afterlife* is Theo's story."

"That's not true—there's you and me."

"I don't know that we'd make credible witnesses."

Gus shook it off. "Look, I don't think it matters…it isn't theft. This is Theo."

Mac did not contradict him. "You know, that night, when you were shot and I was arrested, Theo was also picked up for questioning."

"That must have been when they talked her into confessing."

"That's the thing." Mac handed Gus a flash drive. "Have a look at the transcript of interview."

Gus was accustomed by now to Mac keeping information he'd

acquired through unconventional channels on easily disposable devices in case his computers and files were ever seized again. Gus opened the file. It was only two pages long. "That's it?"

"Yes…it seems the interview was cut short on compassionate grounds—to allow Theo to see you before you died, I expect."

"Who is this guy Alexander Wilson? Did you retain him?"

"Nope—no idea who he is or who called him." Mac used Gus's laptop to pull up the files they obtained years ago when they were looking for Theo. "She came into the hospital at four in the morning, six hours after she'd left the police station. By that time you'd come out of surgery. According to this, she sat with you for three hours until you were taken back into the OR to stop postoperative internal bleeding."

Gus nodded. "I remember. I must have regained consciousness at some point."

"What exactly did she say?"

"That she was sorry, that she loved me." He grimaced. "If you want to terrify someone in hospital, tell them that you love them. I thought I was dying."

Mac smiled. "You were. But do you think there was more to it? Could Theo have been saying goodbye for some other reason?"

"She looked terrified…not generally my-brother-has-been-shot-and-my-friends-arrested terrified. She looked what the law would call *in fear of an immediate and present danger*. Though," Gus conceded, "I'm not sure how clearly I was thinking at the time."

"I'm inclined to trust your instincts, all things considered."

"And she left that book," Gus added. "A young adult novel by Jack Chase. I sent it to her when she was fourteen or close enough to. It was a good luck charm or something equally daft."

"I presume the police still have that."

Gus nodded. "So where does this leave us?"

Mac stared at the screen. "I think we find this guy Alexander Wilson, and then we talk to Day Delos and Associates."

The offices of Wilson Freeman were in New York, where they occupied two floors in the upper part of the skyline. Getting an interview with Alexander Wilson had proved difficult. In the end, Bernadette had set it up through one of Mac's companies.

"What exactly does Bolt Hole Pty Ltd do?" Gus asked as the cab pulled up in front of the appropriate skyscraper. As involved as he was in the legal management of Mac's assets, it wasn't necessary for him to be familiar with what exactly each company did. Mac Etheridge's holdings were quite vast and diversified.

"We build and install underground bunkers."

"For the military?"

"Them, too, but mostly for preppers. They're basically hideouts for doomsday theorists."

"Surely there can't be much of a market for—"

"You'd be surprised. "

"What kind of people—"

Mac laughed. "Most are pretty regular…just taking a hobby too far."

"Do you—"

"Hell, no." He grinned. "But in the event of an apocalypse, I do know where they all are."

They took the elevator to the ninety-eighth floor and stepped out into the dimly lit, conservatively furnished reception area. Mac spoke to the receptionist, who ushered them into a vast corner office and announced their arrival to its inhabitant.

Alexander Wilson looked to be in his early forties, but his face did bear signs of cosmetic and surgical intervention, so he could well have been much older. Mac introduced Gus as his corporate legal advisor. Wilson shook hands with both men, asked about their flight—the usual introductory small talk, after which he suggested that since it was nearly midday, perhaps they should go to lunch. There was a place he knew that served the best quail in New York.

Mac declined, saying they had another appointment for lunch. "Before we discuss what Wilson Freeman could do for Bolt Hole, Mr. Benton and I have a couple of questions…"

Wilson opened his arms. "Of course. Anything."

"Three years ago," Mac began, "you represented a young woman called Theodosia Benton who had been taken in for questioning by the Kansas PD."

Wilson looked startled now. He glanced at Gus, making the connection.

"Can I ask you, Mr. Wilson, who retained you to represent Theodosia Benton?" Mac asked.

"I'm afraid that's confidential."

"We're not asking you to reveal any communications between you and your client, Mr. Wilson," Gus said, "merely his or her identity."

"And as you well know, Mr. Benton, that too is privileged."

Mac tried a different approach. "Bolt Hole's head office is in Lawrence—"

"Yes, I did wonder why—"

"I live there." Mac's tone made it clear that the location was not negotiable. "As such I want any firm dealing with our business to be conveniently located. Do you have offices in Lawrence?"

Wilson looked a little confused. "No, I'm afraid we don't… Rarely is immediate personal appearance required—. Of course if we were to secure a significant client in Lawrence, there is a definite possibility that we would establish—"

"You appeared for Theodosia Benton pretty quickly after she was brought in."

"On that occasion, I was already in Lawrence."

"Why?"

Wilson adjusted the knot of his tie. "Again, Mr. Etheridge, that's confidential."

"Are you aware, sir," Gus said coldly, "that Theodosia Benton disappeared shortly after you extracted her from questioning?"

"I'm sorry to hear that, Mr. Benton. She did seem mentally fragile, but I am a lawyer, not a psychiatrist. Am I to assume you are the brother she was so keen to visit in the hospital? I'm glad to see you've made a full recovery." Wilson stood. "Gentlemen, it appears to me that you are more interested in Wilson Freeman's past clients than in joining our register. If that is the case, I'm afraid we have no more to say to each other."

Mac met his eye and then he stood. Gus followed suit. "Thank you for your time, Mr. Wilson."

CHAPTER 36

In Afterlife the dead are afraid of the living. It's a message.

   Patriot Warrior

It's fiction you moron.

   SpaceMonkey 1343

Mac waited until the bartender had left to serve the next customer before he spoke. He kept his voice low. "According to the transcript of the interview, Wilson arrived an hour after Theo and I were picked up."

Gus nodded. "It's a two-and-a-half-hour flight between New York and Lawrence."

"Which means he was retained to represent Theo well before she was picked up."

Gus tapped the table as he thought. "He did say he was in Lawrence. Could he have been retained there and sent straight out?"

"It's possible, I suppose…but what was he doing there? I doubt he vacations in Lawrence."

"Another client?"

"Who was important enough for a partner to fly out to Lawrence but whom he abandoned to represent Theo at police questioning?" Mac shook his head. "I think it was more likely that he was there for Theo."

"Which means?"

"I'm not sure." Mac typed a message into his phone. "I'll get Bernie to find out what she can about Wilson Freeman and its clients."

Gus stared at his drink. "You know, this all started with that bloke Murdoch. Maybe the key to this is finding out more about him."

"Unfortunately, it seems he's always been a bit 'private' in terms of public profile." Mac opened his laptop and pulled up the information they'd managed to gather on Dan Murdoch over the years. Date and place of birth, education, habits, friends. "You know, all the stuff until his second book was published seems very neat, contrived. If he wasn't an internationally acclaimed bestselling author, I'd say he was in witness protection. He's been a fairly big deal bookwise for six or seven years, give or take, and yet there is not one clear photograph of him."

"Theo said they were hiding his image on purpose because of some over-earnest fans." Gus stared at the artistic, shadowy publicity shots on the screen. He squinted. "I'm not even sure these are of the same bloke." He cursed. "Why the hell didn't I go over to eyeball the joker when Theo—"

"Because she was twenty-two, not fourteen," Mac replied. "Anyway, wasn't she trying to set up a meet-the-family type dinner when he died?"

Gus winced as he remembered. He'd been worried that Murdoch was so much older than Theo. It seemed a trivial thing in light of what had ensued. "What makes you think he was not in witness protection?"

"If you're in the program, trying to become famous is usually prohibited. It kind of defeats the purpose of disappearing."

"Fair enough," Gus said quietly. "Unless, of course, you became famous as someone else." He met Mac's eyes, his own fixed on a flickering light at the end of the tunnel. "Could this be what we're looking at, Mac? Theo disappears and then her story comes out under another name...one that cannot be connected to hers."

"Theo didn't turn state's evidence, Gus."

"She confessed. Maybe that's what they wanted from her."

"Come on, man, you're an attorney. You know that's not how it works."

"What if whoever really killed Murdoch, and the others, also sent Wilson, and helped Theo disappear and create a new identity in exchange for her confessing?"

"Perhaps if the President was a suspect...but there were no other suspects aside from you and me."

Gus groaned. Mac was right. They were probably the only people who gained anything from the fact that Theo confessed.

"Forget the confession for a moment," Mac suggested. "We know that Altamirano's book is the story Theo plotted on your kitchen table. And though we can't be certain, the writing itself does sound like Theo."

Gus nodded. All this was true.

"We have no evidence, aside from the fact that you haven't heard from her, that she's dead, and she had not actually started writing this story when she left."

"Then, she could have written *Afterlife…*" Gus caught himself wanting to believe it, desperately. Did Mac wish it too? Were they both just wishing? "Are we finding Theo in this book because we want to, Mac?"

Mac's lips twitched upwards. "I don't know about you, Gus, but this isn't the first book I've read in the last four years. And I've never recognized anything before." He shrugged. "I assume if it was wishful thinking, it would have happened years ago when we…you missed her most."

Gus swirled the whisky in his glass. He didn't drink so much anymore. There was a time when he was drinking to numb all kinds of pain and fury, when he was still using a walking stick, and his house and career were ashes.

Mac had taken him out to the Ponderosa for a while. Nancy Etheridge would not allow alcohol in the house, and Mac was convinced that being forced to survive his family without the help of the occasional stiff drink was better than any twelve-step program. To be honest, Nancy had been kind, and the Etheridges' insane convictions about imminent Armageddons and right-wing conspiracies had been distracting. They taught him to preserve food and filter water from puddles. It was a bit like living with the Boy Scouts. And he had begun to get his head together. "So we try to find P. S. Altamirano?"

Mac agreed. "Yes. Though I don't know how we're going to find her…or him…not unless we go door to door in Lemur."

"There might be a way to smoke Altamirano out," Gus sad thoughtfully.

Mac's brow rose, expectantly rather than skeptically.

Gus smiled now. "At the risk of sounding like a lawyer, why don't we sue the bastard?"

Gus Benton initiated an action against P. S. Altamirano, his or her agents, and all the publishers of *Afterlife* for breach of copyright. He drafted the statement of claim on the basis that the defendants had stolen and used his sister's ideas and notes without permission, acknowledgment, or fair compensation. The claim was ambit and bold, brilliantly drafted to imply that the claimant had evidence without actually making an untrue statement. Gus knew full well that they would probably fail in court, but that was not the purpose of filing the action. He made an appointment to see Jacqui Steven, telling himself it was because it had been a while since he'd practiced law, and he would only have one chance at this.

Two years ago now, Jacqui had taken a job with a small firm in Kansas City months after she'd been fired by Crane, Hayes and Benton, now just Crane and Hayes. Gus had stayed away from her, determined that she, at least, should have the chance to rebuild a career.

And so when he called by, she closed her office door and shouted at him for a good ten minutes. Indeed she might have hit him if the walls of her office had not been glass and assaulting clients frowned upon. He let her go on. Standing in front of her, there seemed no good reason for having allowed her to drift from his life.

"I'm sorry, Jac," he said in the end. "I thought...I just didn't want you to... Hell, I was an idiot."

She glared at him. "Was?"

He smiled. "Okay, I am an idiot. I'm not sure what I was thinking, but it was never that I didn't want you. I've missed you."

Her arms remained folded across her chest. "You look well. No walking stick."

He jumped and clicked his heels, wincing as he landed. "Good as new...nearly."

"What do you want, Gus?"

"Two things...neither dependent on you agreeing to the other."

"What?" Jacqui demanded, irritated that he was so disarming.

He handed her the documents. "I was hoping you'd check these over for me."

Jacqui took the file back to her desk and ran her eye over the pages. "You're suing P. S. Altamirano?"

"Just trying to get her attention." Gus told her everything, aware as he voiced it that he sounded delusional.

Jacqui's face softened, her eyes sympathetic and concerned.

He countered preemptively, in case she decided to call security or a doctor or both. "Look, Jac, I know this sounds absurd, wishful...but it's not just me. Mac agrees."

Jacqui rolled her eyes. "Mac fell in love with Theo the day he met her." She looked back at the file. "You have Theo's notes?"

Gus shook his head. "Not really. They were lost when Cowell burned my house down. But Mac saw them."

"You're sailing pretty close to the edge here, Gus. You could get yourself disbarred."

"I couldn't get a job as a lawyer now, anyway. And didn't you hear? I'm a private eye now."

Despite herself, Jacqui smiled. "I think I know where you could find copies of Theo's notes... They may be admissible since the originals have been destroyed."

"Theo made copies?"

"After the first time the police seized everything, I advised Theo to take photographs of all her notes with her phone and send the images to herself." Jacqui didn't take her eyes off his face. "I created an account for her on my private server as an added backup. They could be there."

"Don't you know?"

"No." She broke the gaze and moved behind the desk to her computer and typed. "To be honest, I forgot about it till just now, and it was never intended for me to monitor what Theo was doing…only so she had somewhere to send and back up her files. Here you go." Jacqui turned the screen around. About ten emails with attached files. She opened the first—an image of two pages of a notebook, written in Theo's hand with the characteristic pictographs she used when plotting.

Gus stared. "My God, that's it!"

He transferred the emails onto a flash drive, as Jacqui continued to read the documents he'd prepared.

"Gus, are you sure you want to do this?" she asked, frowning. "You're suing one of the biggest publishers in the country— actually the world. They'll come after you with rotating shifts of lawyers. And even with the notes, I'm not sure you can win."

"I'm not planning on actually fighting this, Jac. Just hoping the response might help us find P. S. Altamirano."

"Because you think she's Theo?"

"Or knows where Theo is…or what happened to her."

"If you're right, it doesn't seem to me that Theo wants you to know where she is."

"I don't care."

"I'm not going to talk you out of this?"

"I'm afraid not."

Jacqui sighed. "Then I'd better help you make sure these documents are in order." She folded her arms again. "What's the second thing?"

"Oh." Gus hesitated, suddenly nervous. However, much he'd been trying to protect her, he'd obviously hurt Jacqui Steven. "I was hoping...what I mean to say is...will let me take you to dinner, Jac?"

CHAPTER 37

Theodosia Benton ran her hand over the cover of *Afterlife*. Her book. Her message in a bottle. The thread she'd laid as she walked into the Labyrinth.

It had been over seven months since its release, and in that time, she had watched a writer's dream unfold. It was as they'd promised—an international bestseller, critically acclaimed and widely loved. Her thirty pieces of silver.

She looked down at the city of Dallas below her. The suite was the hotel's best. There was security in the hallway, and cameras—ostensibly for her protection. But she knew the truth now. The only way out would be to climb over the railing of her high-rise balcony and jump.

She was only in the U.S. for a week and five days. It had been hard won with years of compliance, a new book set in Dallas so that she could make her case for a research trip. Not Lawrence but close enough.

Veronica would call for her in exactly fifteen minutes, to take her to the locations she'd insisted she needed to visit in person before she could write them with any sense of place.

Idly, recklessly, she wondered what would happen if she just called Gus. Or Mac—Gus had changed his number several times in the wake of Mary Cowell's death, and Theo didn't know it anymore. She knew at least he'd survived, and the charges had been dropped in light of her confession. For that she'd bartered her freedom, walked voluntarily into a gilded cage from which she would perform for the rest of her life like a bejeweled mechanical bird with no name. Day Delos and Associates had promised that they could have the charges dropped, but only if there was someone else to take the blame.

It hadn't been a difficult decision then. Gus was being charged because of her, he had been shot because of her. Mac, too, was being dragged into the vortex of it all. And the only reason she had not been arrested was that Day Delos and Associates had sent Alexander Wilson. Somehow, she had become the focus of Dan Murdoch's vigilante fans, and it had become clear to Theo that it was only a matter of time until they killed her or Gus or Mac. She would certainly never be allowed to move on, to live, to write. Her only option was to run and hide. Or so she thought three years ago when she'd allowed Alexander Wilson and Veronica Cole to take control of her life.

But now she wondered.

Theo shook her head. It was a conspiracy theory worthy of the Etheridges, and she was embarrassed that it had even occurred to her. She had ultimately agreed to it all.

She looked again at *Afterlife*. Could Mac have read it by now? His mother was leading the charge to have it banned. Nancy Etheridge had even built a website dedicated to the cause. It had been seven months, but she knew it might be seven years, or never. There were a million books, why would he pick up hers? But if he did… It was not the same as talking to them again, but she liked the idea that they would hear her.

Theo wanted them to know she was still here. A ghost, unable to be a part of their world anymore, but she was here.

———

The day Gus Benton filed his claim was uneventful. He and Mac worked on other cases without any acknowledgment between them of the proverbial elephant, trying to keep their minds else-where. He sent Jacqui Steven flowers and worked late. He ate dinner in his apartment and called his parents.

His mother told him she'd felt Theo's presence in the sunrise that day. That his father was carving a memorial out of Huon pine, which they would leave in the forest to be a home to birds. He did not tell them about the book; he would not add to the agony of their grief with the acrid pain of faint hope. If he ever had good news, he would tell them; otherwise he would bear it himself.

The first call came at eight o'clock the next morning. It was Alexander Wilson of Wilson Freeman. The attorney was outraged at what he saw as a fanciful and vexatious claim designed to defame and slander the good name of P. S. Altamirano.

"Am I to understand you represent the writer?"

"Wilson Freeman has been retained to represent P.S. Altamirano in this matter."

"I'll drop the suit if I can speak to her directly."

"Don't be fucking ridiculous!" Wilson exploded. "Look, you jumped-up little lapdog, if you think I'm going let you extort my client with some fabricated claim, you are out of your fucking mind! I'll have this thrown out before you can open your filthy lying mouth!"

Gus replied calmly. He played his trump card. "Maybe. But I will be speaking to *Good Morning America* tomorrow. I expect the media is very interested in my suit… Heck, I could probably sell the movie rights."

Another explosion of profanity.

Gus's response was unwavering, he sounded almost bored. "I want to talk to your client directly. Arrange that, and I'll back off."

The deluge began then. Lawyers representing the various publishing houses who had been joined in the action, and then Veronica Cole.

"Mr. Benton, I think there has been some misunderstanding…"

"Not at all, Ms. Cole. You seem to have sold my sister's book to a number of publishers."

"Mr. Benton, whatever similarity you may imagine exists between *Afterlife* and—"

"I'm not imagining anything, Ms. Cole. *Afterlife* is Theodosia's book, at least in conception."

Veronica Cole tried to reason with him. She claimed to understand. Perhaps if Day Delos and Associates was to sell the book Theodosia Benton did submit to them—*Underneath*—then he would get the resolution he was obviously seeking through this suit.

"I want to speak to P. S. Altamirano—"

"He doesn't speak English."

"And yet he did not seem to have had a problem reading Theo's notes. Look, Ms. Cole"—Gus made his last offer—"I want to know how Altamirano got my sister's plot, her ideas, even her bloody characters. Honestly, I hope he tells me she gave them to him because I don't want to believe that Day Delos and Associates stole the one thing she truly owned."

There was a flint to Veronica's tone now. "You should understand, Mr. Benton, that we will countersue."

"You have twenty-four hours, and then I'm going to start calling reporters."

"That really wouldn't be a good idea, Mr. Benton."

⁓

Theo opened the phone she'd stolen. An old lady who'd used the restroom at the same time as she had had left her bag open as she fussed with makeup. Theo hoped she'd still be looking for it, and didn't have any of those disabling apps downloaded to protect it. It wasn't password or fingerprint protected.

She dialed Mac's number, whispering, "Please answer, please answer…"

"Etheridge."

"Mac…it's Theo."

A beat. "Theo…where are you?"

"Mac, you've got to tell Gus to stop. He doesn't understand."

"Theo…where are you? Wherever you are—"

"Mac, please. Tell Gus to stop."

⁓

Mac Etheridge rang Gus as he climbed into the Mercedes. The line was busy. He redialed with no luck until he pulled up outside Gus's apartment. He parked next to a black Buick on the street in front of the building. As he approached the stairs, he began to run.

Horse barking madly, sounds of a scuffle behind the open crack of Gus's door.

Mac charged the door into the middle of a fray. There was blood on the floorboards. Two intruders. A blood-covered knife embedded in a surfboard on the floor. Gus's sleeve was soaked crimson, and Horse had cornered one of the men. The other had a gun.

Mac used the surprise of his own entry, swinging before the gunman had time to aim. The weapon was knocked loose, and the two grappled desperately to retrieve it. Mac reached it first, but there were hands around his throat as the other tried to choke the advantage from him. And at those close quarters Mac recognized a face, but he had no breath to express surprise. He twisted in an attempt to break free, unwilling to risk using the gun in the confined melee. Gus pulled the man off as Mac gasped for air, but with one arm he could not hold him. The second man seemed to have finally realized that Horse was all snarl and no bite. He fell upon Gus, with blow after blow.

From the floor, Mac pointed the gun. "Stand down or I'll shoot."

Hesitation.

"Believe me, I can shoot you both before you get the knife out of that board," Mac said without even appearing to glance at the man who'd moved to the surfboard. The gun was rock steady in his hands, the grip that of someone who knew how to handle a weapon.

The man in front of him stepped back.

"Who the hell are you?" Gus demanded, straightening painfully. He moved away from the intruders. If Mac was forced to shoot, he was keen to be well clear.

A blast of sound. Unexpected, undefinable. Just noise.

Mac was jolted only briefly, but the break was enough. The surfboard was flung from behind him, collecting him on the shoulder and momentarily deflecting his aim. He recovered quickly but not quickly enough. Mac might have been able to shoot the second man as both assailants bolted through the open door, but he didn't. He went after them as far as the door, but a screech of tires ended any thought of a chase.

Mac closed the door and locked it, then turned off the television, which had been turned on at maximum volume. When he could be heard, his voice was hoarse. "Are you all right, Gus?"

Gus nodded as he pulled back his sleeve to inspect the gash on his forearm. "Yeah...though my surfboard may no longer float...and I think the bastards took my remote control. We should call the police."

"Maybe." Mac rummaged in Gus's tiny, disheveled kitchen for some kind of first aid kit.

"Under the sink," Gus said. "Why maybe?"

Mac told him about the call.

Gus sat down. "She's alive? Are you sure it was her?"

"Yes. But she sounded frightened, Gus." He took gauze and bandages from the kit. "Do you have any alcohol?"

"There's some Copperhead in the fridge."

Mac grimaced. "You can't clean a wound with pale ale...you can barely drink it. Hold your arm under the tap."

"Where is she?" Gus asked as he rinsed off the blood.

"I don't know." Mac packed the cut with gauze and bound it tightly. "It probably needs to be stitched."

Gus flexed his hand. "This is good enough... Theo said I should stop—are you sure?"

"She seemed scared." Mac looked around the apartment, the pool of blood on the floor in which Horse was showing a mildly revolting interest. "I guess this is why."

Gus swore. "We have to find her, Mac."

Mac rubbed the back of his neck. "She's turned off the phone she used to call me. Bernie is watching for the moment it's turned on again. Gus…the guy with the gun was Robbie Shaw."

"Who's Robbie Shaw?"

"He was a writer—ex-army, wrote military adventure novels. Sam would read vast tracts of his books to me, which is why I remember the picture on the back cover. Shaw was identified as one of the idiots involved in the attack on the Capitol building back in 2021—it ended his career. Publishers and agents couldn't drop him fast enough."

"And so he became a burglar?" Gus asked, confused.

Mac shook his head slowly. "He died. Drowned."

Gus tensed. "Like Theo died?"

"Yes." Mac frowned. "Is your computer okay?"

"Yes—it's on the bed in the bedroom."

Mac fetched the laptop, and Gus opened it and logged in.

"Search for writers who have died or disappeared in the past fifteen years."

Several sites came up.

Mac looked over Gus's shoulder. "Let's just see the images."

Gus scrolled. They found a picture of Robbie Shaw pretty quickly. And then another they recognized. "Wasn't this the guy Horse had cornered?"

Gus pulled up the details of the image. "John Wells…had a couple of best sellers about twenty years ago…charged with statutory rape…believed to have fled the country to avoid prosecution."

Then Gus cursed suddenly as a thought occurred. He typed in "Jack Chase." A number of images came up. Gus groaned. How could he have not recognized the man earlier?

"What?" Mac demanded.

"This is Dan Murdoch."

Mac stared at the image of a man in his forties, clean-cut, posed beside a Saint Bernard. "Are you sure?"

"He was about twenty years older with a beard and was dead when I saw him…but this is him. I'm certain of it. Maybe that's what Theo was trying to tell me when she left his book in my hospital room…" Gus was furious with himself. "I could have stopped all this… God, Mac, I met Jack Chase, got his book signed for Theo… If I'd recognized him—"

"If you'd spontaneously recognized him after meeting him once for a few minutes ten years before, you would have been some kind of freak." Mac began to pace. "So, we're surrounded by fallen writers… What the hell is going on?"

"That woman, Cole—the agent from Day Delos and Associates called me today," Gus said. "She warned me against going public. Day Delos were Murdoch's agents, are Altamirano's agents, and were talking to Theo."

"How much do you want to bet they had something to do with Shaw and Wells too?"

And then Mac Etheridge's phone rang.

CHAPTER 38

Mac answered on speaker, in case it was Theo, hoping it was Theo. Maybe Gus's voice would be enough to convince her to tell them where she was.

"Mac, it's Bernie."

Gus turned away disappointed.

"What's up, Bernie?"

"The phone number you gave me was turned on again, so I called it."

Gus's head and attention snapped back.

"It was an old lady. I told her I was returning a call to someone from that number. She said it must have been from one of the girls behind the desk at the Mayhew to whom the phone was handed in. She expected they misdialed when they were trying open her phone."

"The Mayhew? Is that a hotel?"

"Yes. It's in Dallas. Shall I get you and Gus on the next flight?"

"No—I've got a better idea."

"Do you want me to book you rooms at the Mayhew then?"

"No—there isn't time to do this quietly." Mac thought quickly. "Ring the police. Tell Mendes that Theo is at the Mayhew. He'll get the Dallas police involved."

Gus stopped, regarding Mac incredulously. "What are you doing? He'll arrest her."

"They've failed to kill you, Gus. They may just decide to kill Theo instead."

"God, you're right." Gus grabbed his jacket.

"We're taking Horse," Mac said as he dialed again. "Zeke—would you call Patsy and tell her I'm calling in that favor. We need to get to Dallas… We'll be at her place in about thirty minutes."

Mac slipped the firearm he had wrested from Shaw into the inside breast pocket of his jacket. "They might be waiting for us outside."

Gus nodded. He'd been surprised when he first learned that Mac didn't carry a gun as a matter of course, given the way he was raised. The rest of the Etheridges were walking arsenals. Still, in this situation, borrowing a gun didn't seem like such a bad idea. "Who is Patsy, and how is she going to get us to Dallas?"

"Patsy McKenny, a constitutional lawyer—she's prepping for some kind of government collapse." Mac unlocked the door.

"Really?"

Mac shrugged. "She'd know, I suppose." He scanned the street in front of the apartment building to check it was clear. "Patsy has a helicopter."

⌇⌇

Theo dragged the table into position and climbed onto it. Even so, she couldn't quite reach the fire alarm on the high ceiling, but

it was close enough. Aerosol deodorant in one hand, a lighter—
which she also stolen from the old lady's bag—in the other. A
little bit of coordination, and she had a flame thrower. She worked
quickly, strangely calm. Bedlam was her only chance. Day Delos
would be watching her every move in light of Gus's lawsuit. All
the trust she'd built, the plans she'd carefully put in place were
undone. She had to go now before they shipped her off to God
only knew where. "Dammit, Gus! Why now?" Still, it wasn't his
fault. She'd handed in that manuscript, allowed it to be published,
and sent it out as a message, though she wasn't really sure what it
said. What did she expect Gus would do? She should have known
it would be something.

Theo took a deep breath, held it, and flicked open the lighter
and pressed the nozzle. Carried on propellant, the flame surged
and licked the sensor. Two seconds and the alarms went off. Theo
kept pressing, to make sure the alarm would be well and truly
tripped. That done, she climbed down. She grabbed the backpack
she had prepared from what she could find in the suite and acquire
without suspicion—aerosols, packing tape, cash she'd collected in
small amounts over months, water. She was wearing three layers of
clothing. Her hair was tucked under a knitted cap.

She cracked open the door. Guests were spilling out into the
hallway, making for the fire escape. Theo slipped out into the
stream of people and followed the only slightly panicked flow to
the stairwell. Theo stopped at top of the stairs to tie her shoelace
and then stepped back into the line behind a woman with an over-
stuffed tote bag under her arm. The anxious guests barely noticed,
let alone protested her movements in and out of the line.

Theo stumbled, falling onto the woman in front of her, and
in the process slipping her phone into the tote bag. Given to her

by Day Delos and Associates, the cell phone had a tracking device. She'd silenced the ring, so its new bearer wouldn't be alerted to its presence in her bag. And then Theo stopped to tie her shoelace again and quietly slipped back into the hotel at the next floor.

Mac cursed as he glanced into the rearview mirror. The Buick. It was close on their tail. He pressed the accelerator and called Zeke again, giving his brother their exact location.

"Zeke—we're going to be coming in hot. A black Buick."

"Roger that, Mac. We'll take care of them. Caleb's been itching to put the tank through its paces."

"Thanks, Zeke."

"Tell me he was kidding about the tank?" Gus asked tentatively.

"Probably not."

"They're not going kill them, are they?"

"They did just try to kill you."

"Mac…"

"No…they won't. Not intentionally, anyway." He glanced again at the rearview mirror and put his foot down as he hooked the Mercedes into the turnoff. "If the bastards catch up, they'll try to force us off the road, and then their good health will be the least of our concerns."

Gus looked over his shoulder. The Buick had its headlights on high beam. They were gaining. Horse licked his face from the back seat. He put his arm back to settle his dog. Horse was an old dog now… Knife fights and car chases were probably a bit much to expect him to endure.

The Buick tried to get abreast of them. The Mercedes jolted as its back bumper was struck. Mac turned hard to compensate and keep the car from careering. The Buick tried to push them off the road again, but somehow Mac coaxed out another burst of speed.

The road they were on was unlit—the way out to the Ponderosa. Mac knew the road, could anticipate each wind and sweep, and so he was able to gradually stretch the distance between them and the Buick. Gus spotted the vehicles on the side of the road in the Mercedes headlights. Not tanks but modified pickups with armor plating and floodlights fitted to roll bars.

As the Mercedes passed, they screamed onto the road and the floodlights came on. In the rearview mirror they could now see the Buick fishtailing off the road.

Mac slapped the steering wheel triumphantly. "Yes!"

Gus flinched as gunshots cracked behind them. "Should we—"

"Caleb and Sam have been practicing defending this road since they were kids. They'll be all right." Mac said confidently. "Patsy's place is a couple of properties down the road."

"Should I ask why she owes you a favor?"

"Probably not."

The property into which they were admitted through a series of monitored gates was not unlike the Ponderosa. Mac slowed the car down to ensure they didn't hit crossing livestock—goats mainly. The surrounds were heavily wooded and the house almost invisible until you were nearly upon it. Mac drove past the house, to what appeared to be an old tennis court, in the middle of which, under floodlights, was a helicopter.

"The ultimate bug-out vehicle," Mac said. "Patsy has bunkers all over the country and a property in New Zealand. She's a lot more high-tech and organized than normal preppers."

"Normal preppers?"

Mac grinned. "Run-of-the-mill preppers."

Patsy, a woman in her fifties, wore diamond earrings with her army fatigues. Zeke Etheridge was with her as they approached the helicopter. She flung her arms around Mac and kissed him on the mouth and then made huge fuss of Horse, kissing him similarly.

Gus braced himself, but she merely shook his hand, vigorously. "Gus, is it? Welcome. Any friend of the Etheridge boys is a buddy of mine!" She looked down at his hand in hers. "You do know you're bleeding, don't you? Mac, did you realize your friend was bleeding?"

Neither of them had. There was blood all over Gus's hand, and now Patsy's.

"Damn!" Gus checked his pockets for a handkerchief with which to clean himself up. The blood must have soaked through the bandages. "I'll fix it on the way…we haven't time—"

"We'll have to make time. I'm not having you bleed all over Bessie's upholstery."

"Here, let me have a look," Zeke said, grabbing a first aid kit from the helicopter. "Mac—you help Pat take out some of her food supplies so there's room for the two of you."

Once Gus had removed his jacket, Zeke inspected the wound and cursed at Mac for what was apparently a "lame-ass job" of bandaging it. He sprayed Gus's forearm with antiseptic and stitched it—all in the space of about five minutes without once asking how he sustained the injury or why they needed to fly to Dallas.

Gus tried not to look at what Zeke was doing to his arm in case he disgraced himself by fainting. Instead, he watched Mac and Patsy remove boxes packed with preserves and pickles from the helicopter. It was surreal—like the bloody County Women's

Association was going to war. He half expected one of them to disembark a plate of scones.

Mac took a call from Sam and Caleb. It seemed they had managed to "take the enemy" alive and were holding them at the Ponderosa. "Do me a favor, Caleb," Mac said checking his watch. "Wait a few hours before you call the police. I'll call you from Dallas. Just hold them."

"You can trust us, Mac," Caleb replied. "You can trust me."

"What—" Gus began.

"The police will allow them to make a phone call. I'm a bit concerned about who they'll call."

"All done," Zeke announced. "I'll take the stitches out in a few days. If you're not back by then, just snip the knots off the ends and pull them out yourself."

"Thanks, Zeke." Gus held up his arm to have a closer look at Dr. Etheridge's handiwork.

"I'll send you my bill—you'd better get going. Patsy's got to be back to get her kids ready for school." He unbuckled his shoulder holster and handed it and its contents to Mac. "I assume you've stepped out undressed again... You might need this." He looked back at Gus. "What about the Aussie?"

"I don't know how to shoot a gun," Gus said, alarmed. He looked at Mac. "Unless you want to be accidentally shot again—"

"Oh, I don't think Mac's actually ever pulled a trigger either," Zeke said sadly. "Not since Mom shot him, anyway... PTSD I expect. Still, you don't want the enemy or the ladies to think you don't have the equipment, even if you can't use it."

"For God's sake, Zeke, shut up!" Mac growled. He handed Gus the gun he'd wrestled from Shaw. "It's not loaded anymore, but just so you look the part."

"You boys want to keep chatting or are we going?" Patsy climbed into the cockpit. "Saddle up."

The helicopter's interior had been customized in the same glam-camouflage style in which Patsy was attired. Mac sat beside Patsy; Gus climbed into the back beside a water purifier and a steel lockbox.

And then they were in the air, Zeke and Horse and the floodlit tennis court receding as Bessie climbed into the night sky. The rhythm of the blades in rotation had a rocking effect. Gus wasn't sure if he'd fallen asleep—he must have—because it seemed like minutes before they were landing again in what seemed to be a paddock.

"Where are we?"

"Just out of Tulsa," Patsy said taking off her helmet. "Sit tight and we'll be refueled and then landing in Dallas in a jiffy."

CHAPTER 39

Theo flattened herself against the wall so that she did not block the flow of foot traffic out of the hotel. She felt a bit guilty when she saw how frightened some people were, but she resisted the impulse to comfort them, to say she was sure it was a false alarm, which, of course, she knew it was.

She needed to find a place to hide—she wasn't sure for how long, but she knew that they would come for her, cancel her research trip, and she would never escape. Day Delos had turned her into a ghost, and they needed her to remain a ghost.

Theo had once let herself believe she could replace everything with her writing, that the life she'd been offered would compensate for the one she'd had. But it wasn't enough. She missed her family; she missed Gus; she worried about him. The months he'd been in the hospital had been more agonizing from afar. The agency had kept her informed; she had sat by the phone monitored by Day Delos through every surgery, cried through every setback, and celebrated when he'd finally been discharged. She'd even seen his physio and rehabilitation reports. But she hadn't been allowed to be there, to sneak pizza into the hospital, to do his washing, to cheer him up or help him fight. Day Delos and Associates had sent their lawyers to work behind the scenes to ensure Gus had never been charged and to free Mac. They had made sure Gus's insurance company had covered the fire, though he'd missed a payment or two when he was in hospital. She owed them a great deal. They'd given her a new life, a publishing contract, a place to hide. And all she had to do was write...and continue to hide.

But Gus's lawsuit had changed everything.

The murder of Mary Cowell had never been officially solved; the case had been abandoned more than closed. Theo's confession had simply stopped the prosecution of Gus Benton. There had been no real evidence to corroborate her confession and it had not fully exonerated him.

That knowledge had rendered her unable to argue with whatever Day Delos decided. Gus's freedom was dependent on the agency's goodwill. Now that he had decided to sue them, they would no longer protect him, and a little part of her was afraid that they would take more proactive action than simply removing their benevolence.

Sometime in the past year, Theo had begun to wonder about the knife and the key found at Gus's house. She had not for a single heartbeat believed that Gus had had anything to do with Mary Cowell's murder, and so someone must have planted that evidence. Alexander Wilson and Day Delos and Associates had appeared at just the right time to save her, but she wondered if perhaps that was a time of their own making. Had they exploited the death of Mary Cowell to recruit Theo on their terms? Was that what Dan Murdoch had meant when he said Day Delos was not the right agency for her? Had he signed on those terms...and if so, why?

There had been something in Veronica's voice when she told her about the lawsuit. A suspicion. She had urged Theo not to worry, assured her that they would persuade Gus to move on, to leave her alone, but she would have to return to Europe.

Theo had kept calm. Feigned fury at Gus and puzzlement that he had guessed that *Afterlife* was hers. Of course, she had to leave the U.S., she told Veronica. The sooner the better. Damn Gus— just when her writing was really making its mark...why couldn't he just let her go? She worked herself up and then excused herself to use the ladies' room to pull herself together. In the stall she'd rung Mac with her stolen phone. She'd returned, composed, and apologetic, her eyes tear-washed. Perhaps she'd fooled Veronica... she wasn't sure.

Veronica had tried to comfort her. Big brothers were difficult, she'd said. Perhaps Theo had unintentionally included some turn of phrase in *Afterlife* that he'd recognized. But she was not to worry. They would take care of this.

And so, in the fifteen minutes she was given to pack, Theo had set off the alarm, knowing it would disable the elevators going up, that the tracking device on her phone would show her making her way down the fire escape to where Veronica was waiting for her. Hopefully, they were still looking for her in the foyer or at the marshalling points outside the hotel.

Theo wasn't entirely sure what to do now. At some point, the intentionally tripped alarm would be discovered and the evacuation of the hotel called off. She would have to find a place to hide until she could figure out a way to get past Veronica and whoever she'd called to bring her fugitive writer into line.

Patsy landed the helicopter on a private pad atop a high-rise apartment block. She pointed out the metropolis that was the Mayhew complex.

Gus cursed. "That's huge. How are we ever going to find her?"

"I don't know that you'll even get in," Patsy said, studying the hotel building through binoculars. "It looks like the entire Dallas PD is surrounding the building. Were you expecting some kind of siege?"

Gus glanced at Mac. God, how were they going to undo this now?

Mac exhaled. "We'd better go talk to them."

"I can wait for three hours." Patsy checked her watch. "If you're not back by then, you're on your own."

"Thanks, Pat," Mac said, embracing her. "If we're not back, don't wait. We'll be all right."

She placed her acrylic-nailed hands on either side of his face and pecked him on the lips. "You be careful—this place is full of cowboys."

They made their way down to the ground floor and hailed a cab to take them to the police cordon on the street outside the Mayhew.

"How are we going to play this?" Gus murmured as they tried to push their way toward the tape.

"We try and speak to whoever's in charge."

"Won't he or she be a bit busy dealing with the murderer we told them is loose in the hotel?"

"You, pal, are the murderer's beloved brother, and I'm the last person she called." Mac waved to grab the attention of the policeman guarding the barrier. He introduced himself and Gus to the officer. "We thought we might be able to help."

The officer motioned them to step under the tape and took them to the detective in charge.

Detective Maguire was irritated. He had arrived on some courtesy mission to check the hotel for a fugitive supposedly staying at the hotel under the name of Altamirano, only to find that the place was being evacuated because someone had burned toast in one of the suites. It was bedlam. Some people had already been let out of the building when they arrived. The remainder were being held in the foyer and the attached shopping district. Both areas were perfectly comfortable but not when you were prevented from leaving. Altamirano was not in her room and scorching on the ceiling indicated she may well have tripped the alarm herself…which meant the whole fucking hotel had to be thoroughly searched before they could allow people back up to their rooms, even if it was more than likely that Altamirano, or Benton as she apparently was, had simply walked out with everybody else and disappeared into the city. The photo provided by the Kansas PD was four years old, and there were literally thousands of people, most of them idiots, demanding to speak to whomever was in charge.

And now Benton's family had arrived with some insane story about a frame-up and a rogue agency worthy of Grisham. He was in the middle of telling them what they could do with their theory when reports of gunfire on the second floor came through.

Panic spread like contagion, and the people still within the foyer rushed the doors. There was nothing to do but let them out. And then a phone call made from within the hotel on one of the room phones. A woman. She said her name was Theodosia Benton.

Maguire asked her to hand herself in.

She begged for help. Someone was trying to kill her. And then she dropped the phone.

Maguire waved for someone to get the family out of his way as he barked orders at his men in the hotel.

Mac and Gus retreated without being asked, slipping into the crowd charging out of the hotel and using the confusion to slip in. They moved quickly to the farthest set of fire stairs, which had been wedged open to accommodate all the people who had descended through it. When the policeman who had been stationed outside it to ensure that no one tried to go up, moved away to break up a fight between two hysterical guests, they took the opportunity to bolt up the steps.

"The shots were on the second floor," Mac said.

"We'll start there," Gus agreed. "But, mate, this place is huge."

"Where the hell are the police?" Mac said quietly as they stepped out into the hall of the second floor. It seemed deserted. "Shouldn't they be up here trying to figure out who's shooting?"

"I'm more worried about who they're shooting at." Gus tried each door, looking into the rooms for his sister. "Theo…"

"This'll take us hours," Mac said, frustrated. He pulled the phone out of his pocket and dialed. "Patsy…we're in the hotel. I need you to tap into the police frequency and text me anything you find out…where the police are, where they think Theo might be."

Patsy messaged back almost immediately.

Mac read the text. "Apparently Theo phoned from inside the hotel to say she's planted a bomb—that's why they called the police back."

"For the love of—" Gus erupted. "That's just absurd! Did she just pop along to ACME and ask for a bomb so she could blow up the Road Runner?"

Mac slipped the phone back into his pocket. "Either Theo made that call under duress, or someone else calling themselves Theodosia Benton made the call."

"But why?"

"It gives them a bit of time before the police charge in, I suppose."
Gus cursed.

"It might mean they need to find her," Mac said, bracing Gus's
shoulder. "We'll have to find her first." He looked back at the fire
stairs. "Shots were fired on this floor—look for bullet damage. It
might give us some idea where she was."

They moved down the hall looking for any sign—bullet holes,
damage, blood. Gus spotted the door of room 253 about halfway
down the corridor, partially splintered.

He signaled Mac and steeled himself for what they might find,
before he walked in. The room had obviously been turned over.
"Maybe she wasn't here."

"The doors have been electronically unlocked," Mac said, inspect-
ing the door. "So this could only have been bolted from the inside."

Gus checked the en suite, noticing then a door on the other
side of the large bathroom. He walked through and opened it into
a second room with twin beds rather than a king. "Mac, this is a
connected room...for a family."

Mac followed him through and out the door of the second
room. "So, if she came out here, whoever's chasing her is in the
other room... Where does she go?"

"The fire stairs," Gus said. "I'd try and make it to the fire stairs."

"God...we're back to not even knowing what floor she's on."
Mac slammed his fist against the wall. His phone rang. It was Patsy.

"Mac, sweetie, I'm just watching the coverage of the siege.
A woman has just come out onto a balcony on the twenty-third
floor. They think she's going to jump."

"Right," Mac said, moving already for the fire escape. "Patsy,
get through to the police. Tell them where we are and tell them
that there is no bomb."

CHAPTER 40

They ran the twenty-one flights of stairs to the twenty-third floor, pausing for only seconds to catch what breath they could. They were too desperate to be silent, to be careful. That was their mistake. Gus had for so long refused to believe his sister had taken her own life. Had some malevolent god contrived to make him watch it this time? Well, to hell with that! He pulled open the fire door.

There was a gun to Gus's head before Mac could even reach for his own. Two men—both armed. One wore a bellhop's uniform. Neither was familiar.

"On your knees."

They were frisked and disarmed.

"They're not cops."

Bellhop dragged them to their feet while his partner covered. He swore. "We'd better find out what she wants us to do. Fuck! This job has gone to fuck."

Gus and Mac were marched with hands on their collars and

muzzles against the bases of their neck to the suite at the end of the hallway.

They stopped outside the door, ajar due to the deactivation of the electronic locks. From within, a woman's voice was clear, though it wasn't raised. The voice was not Theo's.

"There's no other way. Jump, and we'll be able to explain this all away. There's no link between Theodosia Benton and Day Delos. Make us shoot you, and we'll have to take care of your brother too—"

"Theo, no!" Gus shouted despite the gun at his head. They slammed him into the wall.

———

Theo stared in horror and confusion as her brother and Mac Etheridge were dragged into the room. What were they doing here? Why were they in this nightmare?

She tried to run to them, to embrace them, to tell them she was sorry.

"Get back now!" Jock's gun and gaze were trained on her, regardless of what else was happening in the room. Jock with his suspenders and ponytail, who'd sat at the bar as she and Dan wrote, who'd pointed Mary Cowell in her direction.

She backed up against the balcony rail. She knew there were snipers in the buildings around them.

Veronica Cole glanced coldly at the two men held at gunpoint. If their presence concerned her, she gave no sign of it.

Theo noticed the glance and new dread surged. She now knew what Veronica was capable of doing, of directing, of living with.

"I'll jump," Theo said. "Just let them go."

"I'm afraid that option's off the table, Theo." She looked both men up and down, contemplating, plotting the next chapter. She turned to Bellhop. "Were they armed?"

He produced both guns.

"Excellent." She shook her head. "I hope you clowns know what you've done. We've done everything to protect Theo and you! Invested fucking millions! And now we have no choice but to clean up and move on."

Bellhop aimed at Gus.

"No," Veronica said. "Let's tie this up now. It must look like Gus Benton shot his sister... She ruined his life, after all. Then he and Mr. Etheridge, who arrives too late to stop him from killing Theo, manage to shoot each other." Her head tilted to one side as she considered the sequence. "Yes, we can sell that. We'll get James or Lee to write it into the Minotaur storyline.

Mac replied with equal calm. "Except that Shaw and Wells are tied up in my brothers' barn...if they haven't been handed to the police already."

Gus kept his eyes on Theo. She was thinner than when he'd last seen her, and less girlish, but it was definitely her. "We've already told the detective in charge what we suspect about Day Delos and Associates, Ms. Cole. He didn't believe us then, but once Shaw and Wells are taken in, the police will know everything, whatever you do to us. Your only chance is to go now while they still think there may be a bomb in the building."

Veronica Cole was unmoved. "You will find that Alexander Wilson already has the abduction of Mr. Shaw and Mr. Wells by Mr. Etheridge's criminal relatives in hand, Mr. Benton."

She held out one of the confiscated guns to Jock. "Take care of Theodosia Benton. I am sorry, Theo, you are a real talent, and I tried to save you, but you won't cooperate."

Jock lowered his own gun to take the one that Mac had given Gus. Gus moved before the man realized it was unloaded, hoping, praying, that Mac would be able to handle Bellhop and the other man. He threw himself at Jock, grabbing hold of the ponytail as he dragged him down.

Simultaneously, Mac charged Bellhop. Someone got off a shot, and for a moment no one was quite sure where the bullet had gone. And then a searing pain, which started at a point in Mac's side, seemed to spread with the blood. Even so, he could twist away from the dying grip of Bellhop into whose chest the bullet had finally lodged.

Theo ran in off the balcony. "Mac!" she screamed as the third man took aim again, while Gus struggled with Jock.

Already bent double, Mac bowled into the shooter and the shot went wild, ricocheting off the faux marble fittings and shattering the chandelier, which sprayed splinters of glass across the room. Gus swore as a larger shard embedded in his upper back and, as he weakened, Jock threw him off. Then Jock moved for the gun that had fallen from his grip when Gus had brought him down. Theo scrambled into the path, kicking the weapon out of his reach onto the balcony. Furious, he struck her on the back with a force that almost rendered her senseless before he turned to retrieve the gun. The sniper shot him as he picked it up.

Now Mac and Gus surged against the last man, who had begun to panic as his comrades fell away. He tried to run, but he opened the door to armed police. And it was over. Only then did they notice that Veronica Cole was gone.

CHAPTER 41

Despite having declared that beyond three hours, they were on their own, Patsy McKenny stayed to apply her legal skills on their behalf. Jacqui Steven arrived the next day.

It was established that there was no bomb, and that the phone call claiming there was had not been made by Theodosia Benton.

Jock's body was identified as that of Nenad Dojic, who had written historical epics until he'd been accused of committing war crimes in his youth. Bellhop had been dishonorably discharged from the army and had a manuscript under consideration by Day Delos and Associates. The third man, Joe Meagher, who survived the battle on the twenty-third floor, seemed to be no one in particular, until the police searched his apartment and found his mother decomposing in the bathtub and a manuscript on his computer.

Theodosia Benton was arrested, but in light of new information, those charges were eventually dropped. Under interrogation she explained that she had made a false confession thinking it would be the only way to help her brother, to save him from what she had been led to believe was an orchestrated campaign by a deranged group of fans looking to punish her for her relationship with Dan Murdoch. It seemed ridiculous as she said it, but at the time nothing else had made sense and she had trusted Veronica Cole. She described how Day Delos and Associates had smuggled her out of the country, moving her from one remote location to the next. How her first manuscript had been discarded just in case anyone recognized it.

The detectives had listened impassively. Maguire might have dismissed it as a self-serving fantasy if Mac and Gus had not brought him their suspicions before it all unfolded, if the young man with the moldering mother had not broken down when the detective had threatened to simply delete his manuscript, and confessed his own relationship to Day Delos and Associates.

Joe Meagher insisted he'd not killed anyone, aside from his mother. He claimed that Nenad Dojic, otherwise known as Jock, had killed both Burt Winslow and Mary Cowell. Winslow because he'd been Dan Murdoch's gardener and had stolen the manuscript that his employer had asked him to post to Theo Benton with his letter. Day Delos and Associates had purchased the manuscript back from Winslow, who might have gotten away with the extortion if he had not, in a fit of sentimentality, passed on the love letter that had been with it. Gus's house was by then being watched by the agency, and when Winslow was seen talking to Theo, it was decided that he was too great a risk and action was taken immediately. According to Meagher, Mary had been eliminated simply because she had continued to dig into the story they'd initially fed her in order to put pressure on Theo and give her a reason to run from the life she had into the arms of Day Delos and Associates Management.

Meagher claimed to be uncertain who exactly had "done Murdoch." Day Delos and Associates, after all, represented a lot of fugitive writers, many of whom had come by their status because they knew how to kill.

"Just how many writers are beholden to Day Delos and Associates?" Maguire demanded.

A shrug. "All of them maybe. Day Delos and Associates deals in secrets and ghosts—you'll never find them all."

Alexander Wilson had, as Veronica promised, appeared when Wells and Shaw were turned in by the Etheridges. He was promptly arrested for conspiring to pervert the course of justice. The FBI became involved and eventually claimed jurisdiction over it all.

Theo and Gus were treated for relatively minor injuries and questioned extensively before they were allowed to talk to each other. The bullet that had passed through Mac Etheridge to kill the man dressed as a bellhop, had torn through the flesh and muscles in his side but managed to avoid any vital organs. Once the bleeding was brought under control, the police were allowed into his hospital room to interrogate him.

The Etheridges arrived in Dallas, which served to complicate matters somewhat. They were convinced that the machinations of Day Delos and Associates were not the only conspiracy at play. Sam Etheridge publicly demanded proof that Theodosia Benton was not in fact a doppelganger of some sort planted by an enemy of America. Caleb was more concerned that Theo had actually risen from the dead. Zeke Etheridge examined Mac himself to verify that the shooting had indeed taken place and was not a hoax, an elaborate ruse designed to induce them to leave the property undefended—to which end at least Nancy had remained on the Ponderosa. Mac's reaction to their efforts on his behalf was, admittedly, less than grateful. But they were at least a distraction as he waited to be allowed to speak to Gus and Theo.

He was arguing with Zeke when Theo appeared at the door to his room.

"Do you have any idea what kind of tracking devices could have been implanted in your body when you were in surgery?"

"For God's sake, Zeke, they'd have discharged me yesterday if you hadn't been such a pain in the ass!"

She knocked tentatively on the frame. For a moment Mac seemed lost for words.

Zeke broke into a grin. "Well, well…"

Mac found his voice. "Theo—"

Theo smiled, suddenly a little shy. "Hello, Zeke. How are you, Mac?"

"Don't just stand there," Zeke boomed. "Come on in! Mac's been going crazy wondering what they were doing to you."

"They had a lot of questions." Theo entered and stepped over toward the bed.

Mac sat up. "Okay, Zeke, I'll see you later." His eyes did not leave Theo's face.

"But—"

"Get out, Zeke."

Zeke Etheridge laughed. "Yeah, all right, I'm going." He shook Theo's hand before he left. "Welcome home, Theo. Nice speakin' atcha."

"Gus…?" Mac began when his brother had finally gone.

"He's okay. We're both okay." She took his hand. "What about you? I…we've been so worried about you, but they wouldn't let us—"

"I'm fine. The bullet didn't hit anything important."

"I'm so sorry, Mac. You must rue the day you ever met the Bentons. If you had any sense, you'd refuse to have anything to do with us ever again."

He laughed, squeezing her hand as he did so. "As I said, I'm fine."

"I owe you an explanation."

"You don't owe me anything, Theo."

She sat on the edge of the bed and told him everything nevertheless, beginning with the night that Gus had been shot. The strategies used to render her emotionally and actually dependent on Day Delos and Associates—the isolation in countries where she could not speak the language, the monitoring of all her movements and communications—all under the pretext of keeping her and Gus safe. She told him about the nature of Day Delos and Associates, the compromised writers it represented and remade— fugitives from public condemnation, personal vengeance, and the law—each client living under the fear of exposure and enslaved by Day Delos and Associates in the process. The way in which those writers were used in the fabrication of narratives aimed at sowing distrust, inciting action, or merely providing distraction, so that the agency might sell such services to those who might profit from a timely scandal involving their competitors, or require some scandal to supplant their own misdeeds from the media attention, or even seek a revolution to seize power that wasn't theirs. Day Delos controlled storytellers who wove narratives that ultimately controlled those who for whatever reason wanted to believe.

"And Murdoch?"

"Dan used to be Jack Chase until Jack was accused of an

inappropriate relationship with an underage girl," she said, confirming what Mac and Gus had suspected. A shadow flitted across her eyes, and he saw that the knowledge troubled her, that it colored the way she viewed her own decision to love Dan Murdoch. "It explains what he saw in me, I suppose."

"What he saw in you needs no explanation," Mac said firmly. "But it might explain why Day Delos was so concerned about his relationship with you."

Theo nodded. "They turned him into Dan Murdoch. They feared what he might have told me, and what I might have written based on that."

"But your manuscript had nothing to do with Day Delos."

"No." Theo said wistfully. "But Dan's did. His new manuscript was about the agency, apparently. I don't know what he was thinking…what he was trying to do. He had to know they would…" She exhaled. "When they found out what he intended to do, they killed him for it. Veronica courted my manuscript and me, just in case he had told me something, and because they had a 'vacancy,' I guess."

"When did you find out about Murdoch?" Mac asked gently.

"That he was Jack Chase?" Theo asked. "Alexander Wilson—the lawyer—told me after he secured my release the night Gus was shot." She looked at Mac. That night seemed like yesterday now. She felt like she'd kissed him yesterday. "He left out that they'd killed Dan, of course, but the rest of it—how they'd given him back his career and his life." She looked down at his hand as it held hers. "They said they could do that for me, and when I said I didn't care about writing anymore, they told me it was the only way to save Gus." She shook her head. "I knew, Mac. Every part of me wanted to run, to get as far from Day Delos as possible, but there was Gus, lying in hospital with a guard on the door. And it was all because of me. It seemed the only way to save him was to confess, and have that confession unshakable. That night, that horrible, awful night, it seemed to make sense; it seemed to be the only thing I could do."

"For what it's worth, you did save Gus," Mac said. "They stopped pursuing him the moment your confession came in.

She asked him questions then. What had happened in her absence, to him, to Gus?

He replied honestly and gently, tempering what had transpired with reassurances that they had all survived it. As much as Theo had suspected that Gus had suffered in the wake of those events, she was winded by how utterly his life had been destroyed. At times she wept for him and for Mac, who had spent five and half months in prison, simply because he'd been their friend, and at other times she was overcome with a sense of relief and profound joy that she was here holding Mac's hand. Tentatively, Mac told her about Jacob Curtis—his allegations against Gus, and the charges the exposure unearthed.

Theo pulled back her hand as she realized then that he knew, horrified, and though intellectually she fought against the feelings, mortified and humiliated. She'd buried this memory, refused to think about it, mourned its consequences almost as a separate tragedy. The memory still existed, of course, a distorted thing— moments amplified, others lost—but she had put it away. And now here was Mac...Mac whom she'd thought of so often, who'd been one of the memories she hung on to for sanity and hope, telling her he knew and suddenly she was in dread that Jacob Curtis would take more than he already had.

Mac took her hand again. "He's in prison, Theo. If you don't want to talk about this, I swear I'll never mention it again. But if you do, please don't be afraid."

Another knock on the doorframe and Gus came in. He groaned. "Are you two making gooey-eyes at each other already? That's my kid sister, Etheridge!"

Theo blushed. "Shut up, Gus!"

Mac laughed, and Gus shook his hand. "How are you, mate?"

"Fine. They're only keeping me here because my brothers have made them worry about a genetic predisposition to lunacy."

Gus exhaled. "Gotta tell you, Mac, trying to explain what happened made me feel like I might be flaming crazy." He shook his head. "I'm still not sure Maguire believes us... Who the hell sets up a literary agency like that?"

"I think Day Delos started out as an ordinary agency," Theo said quietly. "Years ago, one or two of their writers were involved in a scandal that should have destroyed their careers. Day Delos and Associates helped them, managed to give them a way to write again. No one ever found out who they really were...and then, as staying clear of controversy became more and more difficult, the agency saw a gap in the market. Eventually, they started dealing exclusively with writers who needed to hide their pasts, or at least believed they did."

Gus looked at her. "How do you—"

"I was one of their most protected writers for three years, Gus. I heard things occasionally, and I had a lot of time to figure things out." Theo exhaled. There was more. "In 2021, when QAnon came to the aid of the outgoing president, Veronica Cole realized that fictional narratives could be used to influence people into all sorts of things, to vicariously control democracy. And so she had her writers create strategic conspiracy theories and then sold those to people or entities to whom that influence would be valuable. If you needed people to distrust the education system, or the media, or fast food, a Day Delos writer would develop a conspiracy theory that would do it."

Inwardly, Mac cursed. Caleb. Even now, Mac wasn't sure he could get his brother to stop believing. "Do you know who was in charge of Day Delos and Associates, Theo?" he asked.

She shook her head. "Veronica took care of me. She referred to the partners every now and then. I never saw them. As far as I could work out, Day Delos and Associates operated in cells—it's how they maintained secrecy and loyalty. You never knew who you could trust. And it worked. They knew how to make authors into bestsellers and to keep them...even if they moved to other agencies."

"Dan Murdoch—" Gus began.

"Used to be Jack Chase—I know. About him and his new manuscript." She hesitated for just a moment. "He sent it to me...to try to warn me." Theo took a deep breath. "But Day Delos was watching. The manuscript never reached me, and Veronica found out."

"She killed Winslow?"

"No. She sent a man called Nenad Dojic... I knew him as Jock. He seemed to hold up the bar at Benders."

"So you were supposed to spend your life in hiding, pretending to be a Chilean man?" Gus asked hotly.

"Eventually, I would have been given a new name that I could live and write under. But not while there were still people looking for me," Theo replied.

Gus's eyes darkened. "I can't believe you agreed."

"I didn't have any choice, Gus. I'd confessed to murder."

"I can't believe you did that either."

"Gus—" Mac began uneasily. But the argument was unstoppable now.

Theo tried to defend herself. "I thought—"

"That I'd done it—I know."

For a moment Theo was struck silent by the accusation and the edge of real hurt behind it. When she spoke, her voice was hard, angry. "I never for a second thought that, you stupid bloody idiot!" She took a breath to calm herself. "But the police shot you trying to arrest you. They were going to charge you if you survived!" She was shouting at him now. "And it wasn't going to stop, not as long as I was here... I was trying to protect you, to buy a little time. You blew it all up by trying to sue everybody!"

Gus reached out and grabbed her, pulling her into an embrace, though she was furious enough to resist him. "You're right, I'm sorry."

"You're an idiot!"

He smiled ruefully. "I'm an attorney... Well, I *was* an attorney. I don't like confessions in the ordinary course of events. When it's my sister confessing to something she didn't do..."

Theo stopped fighting him. "At the time, I couldn't see any other way."

He looked at her seriously. "They could still charge you with obstructing justice."

Theo continued to glare at him. "I have a good lawyer."

Theo and Gus waited until Mac was discharged from the hospital before they all returned to Lawrence. The Etheridges were unhappy that their theories of the crime were dismissed so out of hand, but consoled themselves with the idea that at least Mac had finally pulled a trigger and taken out not one, but two enemies. Mac gave up trying to convince them that he hadn't fired a shot.

Of course, the saga was an international news sensation. Writer after writer officially declared that they had no association with Day Delos and Associates, as the firm's clients were investigated. Some of the world's most successful authors were revealed to be fugitives, arrested, and destocked from shelves for past crimes and indiscretions. Some scandals had become insignificant with the passing of time, and those writers told stories of a life under the control of Day Delos and Associates Management. But others disappeared like the ghosts they'd become, leaving only their words to rattle like chains in the night.

Neither Veronica Cole, nor indeed any of Day Delos and Associates's agents, were apprehended. They vanished, leaving various authorities to try to unravel the convolutions of its operations and networks, the dark extent of its manipulations.

———

Theo leaned her head back against Mac's chest as they watched Gus screw in the sign above the old offices they'd just painted and furnished on New Hampshire Street: STEVEN AND BENTON, ATTORNEYS AT LAW. Jacqui emerged with champagne and glasses to toast Lawrence's newest law firm.

She looked up. "I think it's crooked, Gus."

Gus climbed down and assessed the sign for himself. "You can hardly tell."

"A law firm shouldn't have a crooked sign."

Gus smiled. "I don't know... Could be very good for business."

"Gus..."

"Mate, have I explained the fine Australian tradition of 'good enough'?"

Jacqui rolled her eyes, handed him the champagne, and took the electric drill from his hand. "I'll do it myself...*mate*."

He kissed her. "Is this how it's going to be—you rewriting my advice?"

"Only when it's crooked."

Mac felt Theo shiver suddenly in his arms. "Are you okay?" he whispered, pulling her closer.

She turned and looked up at him. Sometimes it was still hard to believe that she had found her way out, that the fragile, tangled thread that had anchored her to Gus and Mac had held, despite everything. That she was allowed to be this happy…because she was happy. "Someone must have walked over my grave."

He pushed a stray lock of hair away from her face. "You look a little spooked."

"I'm not…well, maybe a little." She tried to explain because she wanted him to understand. "Everything is so perfect right now, I'm terrified of losing it."

"You won't lose it, Theo. It might not always be perfect—in fact it's only a matter of time before my brothers do something stupid—but I won't lose you again."

"I know," Theo said quietly. "But a little part of me wonders if Veronica Cole is hanging out her shingle again, if Day Delos and Associates Management has a new name."

Mac smiled faintly.

Theo pulled away from him, embarrassed. "I know, I'm being idiotic. It's over. There's no point thinking about all this."

"I wouldn't say that." Mac pulled her back. "It's a brilliant premise for a book."

CHAPTER 42

There's a facility in Kansas, undocumented except for the occasional mention in these forums. It's known only as the Labyrinth. I've got a job there now and I've seen the results of the Frankenstein Project with my own eyes. It's not over.

WKWWK
   Flagman

READ ON FOR AN EXCERPT FROM

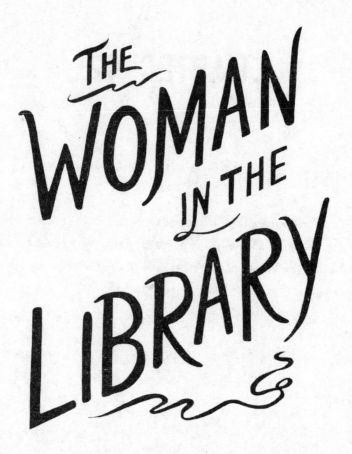

THE WOMAN IN THE LIBRARY

ANOTHER THRILLER BY
USA TODAY BESTSELLING
AUTHOR SULARI GENTILL

CHAPTER 1

Writing in the Boston Public Library had been a mistake. It was too magnificent. One could spend hours just staring at the ceiling in the Reading Room. Very few books have been written with the writer's eyes cast upwards. It judged you, that ceiling, looked down on you in every way. Mocked you with an architectural perfection that couldn't be achieved by simply placing one word after another until a structure took shape. It made you want to start with grand arcs, to build a magnificent framework into which the artistic detail would be written—a thing of vision and symmetry and cohesion. But that, sadly, isn't the way I write.

I am a bricklayer without drawings, laying words into sentences, sentences into paragraphs, allowing my walls to twist and turn on whim. There is no framework, just bricks interlocked to support each other into a story. I have no idea what I'm actually building, or if it will stand.

Perhaps I should be working on a bus. That would be more

consistent with my process such as it is. I'm not totally without direction…there is a route of some sort, but who hops on and who gets off is determined by a balance of habit and timing and random chance. There's always the possibility that the route will be altered at the last minute for weather or accident, some parade or marathon. There's no symmetry, no plan, just the chaotic, unplotted bustle of human life.

Still, ceilings have a wonderful lofty perspective that buses do not. These have gazed down on writers before. Do they see one now? Or just a woman in the library with a blank page before her?

Maybe I should stop looking at the ceiling and write something.

I force my gaze from its elevated angle. Green-shaded lamps cast soft ellipses of light that define boundaries of territory at the communal reading tables. Spread out, by all means, but stay within the light of your own lamp. I sit at the end of one of dozens of tables placed in precise rows within the room. My table is close enough to the centre of the hall that I can see green lamps and heads bent over books in all directions. The young woman next to me has divested her jacket to reveal full-sleeve tattoos on both arms. I've never been inked myself, but I'm fascinated. The story of her life etched on her skin… She's like a walking book. Patterns and portraits and words. Mantras of love and power. I wonder how much of it is fiction. What story would I tell if I had to wear it on my body? The woman is reading Freud. It occurs to me that a psychology student would make an excellent protagonist for a thriller. A student, not an expert. Experts are less relatable, removed from the reader by virtue of their status. I write "psychology student" onto the blank page of my notebook and surround it with a box. And so I hop onto the bus. God knows where it's going—I just grabbed the first one that came along.

Beneath the box I make some notes about her tattoos, being careful not to make it obvious that I am reading her ink.

Across from me sits a young man in a Harvard Law sweatshirt. He cuts a classic figure—broad shoulders, strong jaw, and a cleft chin—like he was drawn as the hero of an old cartoon. He's been staring at the same page of the tome propped before him for at least ten minutes. Perhaps he's committing it to memory...or perhaps he's just trying to keep his eyes down and away from the young woman on my left. I wonder what they are to each other: lovers now estranged, or could it be that he is lovelorn and she indifferent? Or perhaps the other way round—is she stalking him? Watching him over the top of Freud? Might she suspect him of something? He certainly looks tormented... Guilt? He drops his eyes to check his watch—a Rolex, or perhaps a rip-off of the same.

To the left of Heroic Chin is another man, still young but no longer boyish. He wears a sport coat over a collared shirt and jumper. I am more careful about looking at him than I am the others because he is so ludicrously handsome. Dark hair and eyes, strong upswept brows. If he catches my gaze he will assume that is the reason. And it isn't...well, maybe a little. But mostly I am wondering what he might bring to a story.

He's working on a laptop, stopping every now and then to stare at the screen, and then he's off again, typing at speed. Good Lord, could he be a writer?

There are other people in the Reading Room, of course, but they are shadows. Unfocused as yet, while I try to pin a version of these three to my page. I write for a while...scenarios, mainly. How Freud Girl, Heroic Chin, and Handsome Man might be connected. Love triangles, business relationships, childhood friends. Perhaps Handsome Man is a movie star; Heroic Chin, a fan; and

Freud Girl, his faithful bodyguard. I smile as the scenarios become increasingly ridiculous and, as I do, I look up to meet Handsome Man's eyes. He looks startled and embarrassed, and I must, too, because that's how I feel. I open my mouth to explain, to assure him that I'm a writer, not a leering harasser, but of course this is the Reading Room, and one does not conduct a defence while people are trying to read. I do attempt to let him know I'm only interested in him as the physical catalyst for a character I'm creating, but that's too complex to convey in mime. He just ends up looking confused.

Freud Girl laughs softly. Now Heroic Chin looks up too, and the four of us are looking at each other silently, unable to rebuke or apologize or explain, lest we incur the wrath of the Reading Room Police.

And then there is a scream. Ragged and terrified. A beat of silence even after it stops, until we all seem to realise that the Reading Room Rules no longer apply.

"Fuck! What was that?" Heroic Chin murmurs.

"Where did it come from?" Freud Girl stands and looks around.

People begin to pack up their belongings to leave. Two security guards stride in and ask everyone to remain calm and in their seats until the problem can be identified. Some idiot law student starts on about illegal detention and false imprisonment, but, for the most part, people sit down and wait.

"It was probably just a spider," Heroic Chin says. "My roommate sounds just like that whenever he sees a spider."

"That was a woman," Freud Girl points out.

"Or a man who's afraid of spiders…" Heroic Chin looks about as if his arachnophobic friend might be lurking somewhere.

"I apologize if I was staring." Handsome Man addresses me

tentatively. I have enough of an ear for American accents now to tell he's not from Boston. "My editor wants me to include more physical descriptions in my work." He grimaces. "She says all the women in my manuscript are wearing the same thing, so I thought… Heck, that sounds creepy! I'm sorry. I was trying to describe your jacket."

I smile, relieved. He's volunteering to take the bullet. I'll just be gracious. "It's a herringbone tweed, originally a man's sport coat purchased at a vintage store and retailored so the wearer doesn't look ridiculous." I meet his eye. "I do hope you haven't written down that I look ridiculous."

For a moment, he's flustered. "No, I assure you—" And then he seems to realise I'm kidding and laughs. It's a nice laugh. Deep but not loud. "Cain McLeod."

After a second I register that he's introduced himself. I should too. "Winifred Kincaid…people call me Freddie."

"She's a writer too." Freud Girl leans over and glances at my notebook. "She's been making notes on all of us."

Damn!

She grins. "I like Freud Girl…I sound like an intellectual superhero. Better than Tattoo Arms or Nose Ring."

I slam my notebook shut.

"Awesome!" Heroic Chin turns to display his profile. "I hope you described my good side and…" he adds, flashing a smile, "I have dimples."

Handsome Man, apparently also known as Cain McLeod, is clearly amused. "What are the chances? You two should be more careful who you sit next to."

"I'm Marigold Anastas," Freud Girl announces. "For your

acknowledgements. A-N-A-S-T-A-S."

Not to be outdone, Heroic Chin discloses his name is Whit Metters and promises to sue if either Cain McLeod or I forget to mention his dimples.

We're all laughing when the security guards announce that people may leave if they wish.

"Did you find out who screamed?" Cain asks.

The security guard shrugs. "Probably some asshole who thinks he's a comedian."

Whit nods smugly and mouths "spider."

Cain's brow lifts. "It was a convincing scream," he says quietly.

He's right. There was a ring of real mortal terror in the scream. But that's possibly a writer's fancy. Perhaps someone simply needed to expel a bit of stress. "I need to find coffee."

"The Map Room Tea Lounge is the closest," Cain says. "They make a decent coffee."

"Do you need more material?" Marigold asks. With coat sleeves covering the ink which had held my attention, I notice that she has beautiful eyes, jewel green and sparkling in a frame of smoky kohl and mascara.

"Just coffee," I reply for both Cain and myself, because I'm not sure which one of us she was asking.

"Can I come?"

The childlike guilelessness of the question is disarming. "Of course."

"Me too?" Whit now. "I don't want to be alone. There's a spider somewhere."

And so we go to the Map Room to found a friendship, and I have my first coffee with a killer.

Dear Hannah,

Bravo! A sharp and intriguing opening. You have made art out of my complaints. The last line is chilling. An excellent hook. I fear that a publisher will ask you to make it the opening line to ensure you catch the first-page browsers. All I can say is: resist! It is perfect as it is.

That line, though, is as brave as it is brilliant. Bear in mind that you've issued your readers a challenge, declared one of those three (Marigold, Whit, or Cain) will be the killer. They'll watch them closely from now on, read into every passing nuance. It may make it more difficult to distract their attention from clues in the manuscript and keep them guessing. Still, it's kind of delicious—particularly as they each seem so likeable. As I said, brave.

Dare I hope that since your setting is Boston, you'll make a research trip here sometime soon? It would be wonderful to suffer for our art face-to-face over martinis in some bar like real writers! In the meantime, I'd be delighted to assist you with sense of place and so forth. Consider me your scout, your eyes and ears in the U.S.

A couple of points—Americans don't use the term *jumper* (description of Handsome Man). You may want to switch that reference to sweater or pullover. It's also much less common in the U.S. for women to be as heavily inked as women in Australia. I haven't seen any full-sleeve tattoos on women, here. Of course, that doesn't mean Marigold can't have them—perhaps that's why Winifred notices them particularly.

I returned to the Reading Room after I received your email and chapter to check, and I'm afraid there's no explicit rule against talking. It's more a general civility. Easy to fix. Insert a disapproving shushing neighbour or two on the table and the pressure for silence won't be lost. I had lunch in the Map Room, so if you need details, let me know. As an Australian, you'll probably find the coffee appalling out of principle, but since Winifred is American, she is not likely to find it wanting.

Do you need somewhere for Freddie to live? If money is no object, you could put her in Back Bay, right in the BPL neighborhood. Many of the apartments are converted Victorian brownstones, but Freddie would have to be an heiress of some sort to afford one! Is she a struggling hopeful, or an author of international renown? The former would probably live somewhere like Brighton or Alston. Let me know if you'd like me to check some buildings for you.

I received my tenth rejection letter for the opus yesterday. It feels like something which should be marked. Perhaps I shall buy a cake. This one said my writing was elegant but that they felt I was working in the wrong genre... which I suppose is an indirect way of saying they want my protagonist to be a vampire and the climax to involve an alien invasion...and not the kind with which our President seems preoccupied!

I know the repeated rejections are a rite of passage, Hannah, but, honestly, it hurts. I don't know if I'm strong enough for this business. It must be wonderful to be at that stage where you've paid your dues, where you know that whatever you write now, it will at least be seriously considered. This stage just feels like a ritual humiliation.

Yours somewhat despondently,

Leo

READING GROUP GUIDE

1. The author includes snippets from conspiracy theory chat rooms almost immediately in this story and continues their use throughout. What was your first reaction to that part of the storytelling? Did it make you think you were about to read a particular type of novel? What do these passages accomplish in terms of the larger story?

2. Theo's bold decision to abandon her law education and the career path she was expected to follow in favor of pursuing her passion—writing—had some unexpected, some dangerous, and some surprising results. Given what happens to her character throughout the book, do you think she would have been happier if she had stuck with law and the more stable, traditional lifestyle it would have provided? Why or why not? Have you ever chosen to pursue a passion over a more "reliable" profession? What was the outcome?

3. Cormac Etheridge grew up in a family of doomsday preppers, who can come across to some as extreme in their ideologies and behaviors. Often when we encounter people whose views and lifestyles are diametrically opposed to our own, our reaction is to dismiss, poke fun, or become angry when we can't sway them to our way of thinking. While it's easy enough to "unfriend" someone on social media, have you had to "ghost" a close friend or family member over "irreconcilable differences"? Or have you found strategies that allow you to still like and respect—and, when necessary, forgive—them?

4. When Theo meets Dan Murdoch, she is flattered and excited that a bestselling author has taken an interest in her and her writing. Do you think Theo was actually in love with Dan the person, or simply infatuated with Dan the writer and what he might do for her career? Have you ever been in a relationship in which you questioned your own motivations?

5. In this digital age, it's almost impossible to escape one's past and "start fresh" where no one knows you or your history. Day Delos and Associates Management offers new beginnings for talented high-earning authors who have committed crimes or otherwise disgraced themselves in the public's eye. Do you think it's fair that past mistakes should follow the perpetrators forever, influencing the professional opportunities available to them? If you had committed a crime or indiscretion and had atoned or served your time, would you expect to be able to pick up your life where you left off and resume your career? Why or why not?

6. If an agency or publisher offered you representation or publication on the condition that you turn over complete control of your social media to them, would you do it? Why or why not?

7. Mac's youngest brother, Caleb, claims he was acting in Mac's best interest when he leaked Theo's whereabouts to the reporter who then turns up murdered. Do you think he may have had other motivations for his actions? Given the circumstances, would you have done the same?

8. Theo also feels she is acting in her brother's best interest when she confesses to Dan's murder and disappears. Do you think her main motivation was love, or guilt over having blown up Gus's life, both now and a decade earlier? Was her decision selfless or selfish?

A CONVERSATION WITH THE AUTHOR

This is the third standalone mystery you've written that deals with writers and the writing process (following *After She Wrote Him* and *The Woman in the Library*). Did you have specific goals in mind for each book before you started writing? What were they?

Prior to beginning a novel, I'm not sure I have any specific goal beyond writing a good book. I'm not a plotter. I just sit down and start writing. For me, the story unfolds as I write it. I don't really know what will be on the next page, let alone at the end of the book, and I discover what I'm trying to say through the novel as a whole as I write it. A phrase or a piece of dialogue written intuitively will seize me, and I'll realize that this is what this book is really about. Perhaps I do have a goal at the outset, but I'm not consciously aware of it. But at some point in the story, that goal becomes clear or at least clearer. In *After She Wrote Him*, I found myself writing a mystery that spoke about the writer's relationship with her characters. *The Woman in the Library* turned out to be about the relationship between the writer and the reader, and how the real world influences the imagination. *The Mystery Writer* is about the writer's place in society and the power of the story to influence behavior. And, of course, all three are about murder!

Why did you choose Lawrence, Kansas, as the setting for this story?

I was looking for place to which someone might escape. An American friend suggested Lawrence in Kansas and offered me the use of his insights as a Kansan. The town itself seemed to offer the right balance of size and politics and history. I wrote the book, moving about in Larry's memories.

Theo abandons her career path as a lawyer to devote herself to writing, much the same as you did. Are there any other similarities between you and Theo's character and/or experiences (aside from your love of chocolate, of course)?

Theo is much more certain of what she wants than I was. I was a lawyer for fifteen years before I ever thought to write a novel, whilst she abandoned her degree and moved to the other side of the world to pursue her dream. Giving up an established legal career is also probably easier than giving up the possibility of one—you know exactly what you're abandoning, and if the experiment fails, you're still qualified. Theo's move was more all or nothing and much more courageous. In many ways she has the clarity that I wish I'd discovered when I was her age. In terms of similarities, though, we are both Australian, have a similar sense of humor, and we love dogs.

What are you reading now?

I'm rereading *Murder on the Orient Express* by Agatha Christie.

ACKNOWLEDGMENTS

Much of what writers do is solitary. But we do not write alone. *The Mystery Writer* owes its existence to more than the efforts of just *this* mystery writer. Please indulge me while I acknowledge them here.

L. M. Vincent and Don Mayberger, whose generosity with their knowledge and experience of Kansas and Kansans, allowed me to write a story set in Lawrence—to walk into its coffee shops, wander around its streets, and most of all, to regard it with understanding and affection. I so appreciate your help, gentlemen.

My agents, Jill Marr and Andrea Cavallaro, and the amazing team at the Sandra Djikstra Literary Agency, who tell me when a manuscript is ready and then keep me from selling it for six magic beans, thank you. It is so easy to move forward when someone has your back.

My beloved publisher, Sourcebooks, whose belief in my work, and me as a writer, has become the foundation of my career. To my guides and champions, Anna Michels, Diane DiBiase, Beth

Deveny, Mandy Chahal, Dominique Raccah, and all the wonderful, talented people at Sourcebooks, thank you with all of my heart. I love making books with you.

Barbara Peters and Robert Rosenwald, who, several years ago, brought me into Poisoned Pen and who remain a part of my American family. I am so grateful for your advice, your warmth and support, and Robert's cranberry pie!

My husband, Michael, and my boys, Edmund and Atticus, who have lived with a writer for over a decade and complain very little, all things considered; my dear friends Robert Gott, Dan O'Malley, and Leith Henry, whose insight and advice have kept more than my books from going horribly wrong. Jo Butler, in whose company and conversation the idea behind this novel first arose. At the time, I thought I was making a joke. She recognised it as the bones of a story.

Finally, and preemptively, the readers of Lawrence, Kansas, who I hope will tolerate my literary visitation and the fictional liberties I have taken with their beautiful city. Thank you.

ABOUT THE AUTHOR

Sulari Gentill is the author of the multiaward-winning ten-book series, The Rowland Sinclair WWII Mysteries; the Hero Trilogy, based on the myths and epics of the ancient world; and *After She Wrote Him*, for which she won the 2018 Ned Kelly Award. Her most recent release, *The Woman in the Library*, became a *USA Today* bestseller, won the Crime Fiction Lover Award for Best Novel by an Independent Publisher (UK), and was an Edgar Award nominee.

Sulari lives with her husband, Michael, and their boys, Edmund and Atticus, on a small farm in the foothills of the Snowy Mountains of Australia, where she grows truffles, keeps donkeys, and writes about murder and mayhem.

© Edmund Blenkins